THE CITY

Dean Koontz is the author of more than a dozen *New York Times* No.1 bestsellers. His books have sold over 450 million copies worldwide, a figure that increases by more than 17 million copies per year, and his work is published in 38 languages.

He was born and raised in Pennsylvania and lives with his wife Gerda and their dog Anna in Southern California.

By Dean Koontz

DEAN KOONTZ

THE CITY

HARPER

Harper
An imprint of HarperCollins*Publishers*
1 London Bridge Street
London SE1 9GF

www.harpercollins.co.uk

This paperback edition 2015
1

First published in Great Britain by HarperCollins*Publishers* 2014

A catalogue record for this book
is available from the British Library

ISBN: 978-0-00-752030-5

Set in Old Style 7 by Palimpsest Book Production Limited,
Falkirk, Stirlingshire

Printed and bound in Great Britain by
Clays Ltd, St Ives plc

Find out more about HarperCollins and the environment at
www.harpercollins.co.uk/green

This novel is dedicated,
with affection and gratitude,
to Jane Johnson,
who is one continent
and one sea away.

And to Florence Koontz
and Mildred Stefko,
who are one world away.

Hold every moment sacred. Give each clarity and meaning, each the weight of thine awareness, each its true and due fulfillment.

—Thomas Mann, *The Beloved Returns*

Prelude

MALCOLM GIVES ME A TAPE RECORDER.

He says, "You've got to talk your life."

"I'd rather live the now than talk about the was."

Malcolm says, "Not all of it. Just the . . . you know."

"I'm to talk about the you know?"

Malcolm says, "People need to hear it."

"What people?"

Malcolm says, "Everybody. These are sad times."

"I can't change the times."

Malcolm says, "It's a sad world. Lift it a little."

"You want me to leave out all the dark stuff?"

Malcolm says, "No, man. You need the dark stuff."

"Oh, I don't need it. Not me."

Malcolm says, "The dark makes the light stuff brighter."

"So when I'm done talking about the you know—then what?"

Malcolm says, "You make it a book."

"You going to read this book?"

Malcolm says, "Mostly. Parts of it I wouldn't be able to see clear enough to read."

"What if I read those parts to you?"

Malcolm says, "If you're able to see the words, I'd listen."

"By then I'll be able. Talking it the first time is what will kill me."

One

MY NAME IS JONAH ELLINGTON BASIE HINES Eldridge Wilson Hampton Armstrong Kirk. From as young as I can remember, I loved the city. Mine is a story of love reciprocated. It is the story of loss and hope, and of the strangeness that lies just beneath the surface tension of daily life, a strangeness infinite fathoms in depth.

The streets of the city weren't paved with gold, as some immigrants were told before they traveled half the world to come there. Not all the young singers or actors, or authors, became stars soon after leaving their small towns for the bright lights, as perhaps they thought they would. Death dwelt in the metropolis, as it dwelt everywhere, and there were more murders there than in a quiet hamlet, much tragedy, and moments of terror. But the city was as well a place of wonder, of magic dark and light, magic of which in my eventful life I had much experience, including one night when I died and woke and lived again.

Two

WHEN I WAS EIGHT, I WOULD MEET THE WOMAN who claimed she was the city, though she wouldn't make that assertion for two more years. She said that more than anything, cities are people. Sure, you need to have the office buildings and the parks and the nightclubs and the museums and all the rest of it, but in the end it's the people—and the kind of people they are—who make a city great or not. And if a city is great, it has a soul of its own, one spun up from the threads of the millions of souls who have lived there in the past and live there now.

The woman said this city had an especially sensitive soul and that for a long time it had wondered what life must be like for the people who lived in it. The city worried that in spite of all it had to offer its citizens, it might be failing too many of them. The city knew itself better than any person could know himself, knew all of its sights and smells and sounds and textures and secrets, but it didn't know what it felt like to be human and live in those thousands of miles of streets. And so, the woman said, the soul of the city took human form to live among its people, and the form it took was her.

The woman who was the city changed my life and showed me that the world is a more mysterious place than you would imagine if your understanding of it was formed only or even largely by newspapers and magazines and TV—or now the Internet. I need to tell you about her and some terrible things and wonderful things and amazing things that happened, related to her, and how I am still haunted by them.

But I'm getting ahead of myself. I tend to do that. Any life isn't just one story; it's thousands of them. So when I try to tell one of my own, I sometimes go down an alleyway when I should take the main street, or if the story is fourteen blocks long, I sometimes start on block four and have to backtrack to make sense.

Also, I'm not tapping this out on a keyboard, and I tend to ramble when I talk, like now into this recorder. My friend Malcolm says not to call it rambling, to call it oral history. That sounds pretentious, as though I'm as certain as certain can be that I've achieved things that ensure I'll go down in history. Nevertheless, maybe that's the best term. Oral history. As long as you understand it just means I'm sitting here shooting off my mouth. When someone types it out from the tapes, then I'll edit to spare the reader all the you-knows and uhs and dead-end sentences, also to make myself sound smarter than I really am. Anyway, I must talk instead of type, because I have the start of arthritis in my fingers, nothing serious yet, but since I'm a piano man and nothing else, I have to save my knuckles for music.

Malcolm says I must be a closet pessimist, the way I so often say, "Nothing serious yet." If I feel a phantom pain in one leg or the other and Malcolm asks why I keep massaging my calf, I'll say, "Just this weird thing, nothing serious yet." He thinks I'm convinced it's a deep-vein blood clot that'll break loose and blow out my lungs or brain later in the day, though that never crossed my mind. I just say those three words to reassure my friends, those people *I* worry about when they have the flu or a dizzy spell or a pain in the calf, because I'd feel relieved if they reassured *me* by saying, "Nothing serious yet."

The last thing I am is a closet pessimist. I'm an optimist and always have been. Life's given me no reason to expect the worst. As long as I've loved the city, which is as long as I can remember, I have been an optimist.

I was already an optimist when all this happened that

I'm telling you about. Although I'll reverse myself now and then to give you some background, this particular story really starts rolling in 1967, when I was ten, the year the woman said she was the city. By June of that year, I had moved with my mom into Grandpa's house. My mother, whose name was Sylvia, was a singer. Grandpa's name was Teddy Bledsoe, never just Ted, rarely Theodore. Grandpa Teddy was a piano man, my inspiration.

The house was a good place, with four rooms downstairs and four up, one and three-quarter baths. The piano stood in the big front room, and Grandpa played it every day, even though he performed four nights a week at the hotel and did background music three afternoons at the department store, in their fanciest couture department, where a dress might cost as much as he earned in a month at both jobs and a fur coat might be priced as much as a new Chevy. He said he always took pleasure in playing, but when he played at home, it was *only* for pleasure.

"If you're going to keep the music in you, Jonah, you've got to play a little bit every day purely for pleasure. Otherwise, you'll lose the joy of it, and if you lose the joy, you won't sound good to those who know piano—or to yourself."

Outside, behind the house, a concrete patio bordered a small yard, and in the front, a porch overlooked a smaller yard, where this enormous maple tree turned as red as fire in the autumn. And when the leaves fell, they were like enormous glowing embers on the grass. You might say it was a lower-middle-class neighborhood, I guess, although I never thought in such terms back then and still don't. Grandpa Teddy didn't believe in categorizing, in labeling, in dividing people with words, and neither do I.

The world was changing in 1967, though of course it always does. Once the neighborhood was Jewish, and then it went Polish Catholic. Mr. and Mrs. Stein, who had moved from the house but still owned it, rented to my grand-parents in 1963, when I was six, and sold it to them two years later. They were the first black people to live in that neighborhood. He said there were problems at the start, of the kind you might expect, but it never got so bad they wanted to move.

Grandpa attributed their staying power to three things. First, they kept to themselves unless invited. Second, he played piano free for some events at Saint Stanislaus Hall, next to the church where many in the neighborhood attended Mass. Third, my grandma, Anita, was secretary to Monsignor McCarthy.

Grandpa was modest, but I won't be modest on his behalf. He and Grandma didn't have much trouble also because they had about them an air of royalty. She was tall, and he was taller, and they carried themselves with quiet pride. I used to like to watch them, how they walked, how they moved with such grace, how he helped her into her coat and opened doors for her and how she always thanked him. They dressed well, too. Even at home, Grandpa wore suit pants and a white shirt and suspenders, and when he played the piano or sat down for dinner, he always wore a tie. When I was with them, they were as warm and amusing and loving as any grandparents ever, but I was at all times aware, with each of them, that I was in a *Presence.*

In April 1967, my grandma fell dead at work from a cerebral embolism. She was just fifty-two. She was so vibrant, I never imagined that she could die. I don't think anyone else did, either. When she passed away suddenly, those who knew her were grief-stricken but also shocked. They harbored unexpressed anxiety, as if the sun had risen in the west and set in the east, suggesting a potential apocalypse if anyone dared to make reference to that development, as if the world would go on safely turning only if everyone conspired not to remark upon its revolutionary change.

At the time, my mom and I were living in an apartment downtown, a fourth-floor walk-up with two street-facing windows in the living room; in the kitchen and my little bedroom, there were views only of the sooty brick wall of the adjacent building, crowding close. She had a gig singing three nights a week in a blues club and worked the lunch counter at Woolworth's five days, waiting for her big break. I was almost ten and not without some street smarts, but

I must admit that for a time, I thought that she would be equally happy if things broke either way—a gig singing in bigger and better joints or a job as a waitress in a high-end steakhouse, whichever came first.

We went to stay with Grandpa for the funeral and a few days after, so he wouldn't be alone. Until then, I'd never seen him cry. He took off work for a week, and he kept mostly to his bedroom. But I sometimes found him sitting in the window seat at the end of the second-floor hallway, just staring out at the street, or in his armchair in the living room, an unread newspaper folded on the lamp table beside him.

When I tried to talk to him, he would lift me into his lap and say, "Let's just be quiet now, Jonah. We'll have years to talk over everything."

I was small for my age and thin, and he was a big man, but I felt greatly gentled in those moments. The quiet was different from other silences, deep and sweet and peaceful even if sad. A few times, with my head resting against his broad chest, listening to his heart, I fell asleep, though I was past the age for regular naps.

He wept that week only when he played the piano in the front room. He didn't make any sounds in his weeping; I guess he was too dignified for sobbing, but the tears started with the first notes and kept coming as long as he played, whether ten minutes or an hour.

While I'm still giving you background here, I should tell you about his musicianship. He played with good taste and distinction, and he had a tremendous left hand, the best I've ever heard. In the hotel where he worked, there were two dining rooms. One was French and formal and featured a harpist, and the décor either made you feel elegant or made you ill. The second was an Art Deco jewel in shades of blue and silver with lots of glossy-black granite and black lacquer, more of a supper club, where the food was solidly American. Grandpa played the Deco room, providing background piano between seven and nine o'clock, mostly American-standard ballads and some friskier Cole Porter numbers; between nine and midnight, three sidemen joined him, and the combo pumped it up to dance music from the 1930s and '40s. Grandpa Teddy sure could swing the keyboard.

Those days right after his Anita died, he played music I'd never heard before, and to this day I don't know the names of any of those numbers. They made me cry, and I went to other rooms and tried not to listen, but you couldn't *stop* listening because those melodies were so mesmerizing, melancholy but irresistible.

After a week, Grandpa returned to work, and my mom and I went home to the downtown walk-up. Two months later, in June, when my mom's life blew up, we went to live with Grandpa Teddy full-time.

Three

SYLVIA KIRK, MY MOTHER, WAS TWENTY-NINE
when her life blew up, and it wasn't the first time. Back
then, I could see that she was pretty, but I didn't realize
how young she was. Only ten myself, I felt anyone over
twenty must be ancient, I guess, or I just didn't think
about it at all. To have your life blow up four times before
you're thirty would take something out of anyone, and I
think it drained from my mom just enough hope that she
never quite built her confidence back to what it once had
been.

When it happened, school had been out for weeks.
Sunday was the only day that the community center didn't
have summer programs for kids, and I was staying with
Mrs. Lorenzo that late afternoon and evening. Mrs.

Lorenzo, once thin, was now a merry tub of a woman and a fabulous cook. She lived on the second floor and accepted a little money to look after me when there were no other options, primarily when my mom sang at Slinky's, the blues joint, three nights a week. Sunday wasn't one of those three, but Mom had gone to a big-money neighborhood for a celebration dinner, where she was going to sign a contract to sing five nights a week at what she described as "a major venue," a swanky nightclub that no one would ever have called a joint. The club owner, William Murkett, had contacts in the recording industry, too, and there was talk about putting together a three-girl backup group to work with her on some numbers at the club and to cut a demo or two at a studio. It looked like the big break wouldn't be a steakhouse waitress job.

We expected her to come for me after eleven o'clock, but it was only seven when she rang Mrs. Lorenzo's bell. I could tell right off that something must be wrong, and Mrs. Lorenzo could, too. But my mom always said she didn't wash her laundry in public, and she was dead serious about that. When I was little, I didn't understand what she meant, because she did, too, wash her laundry in the communal laundry room in the basement, which had to be as public as you could wash it, except maybe right out in the street. That night, she said a migraine had just about knocked her flat, though I'd never heard of her having one before. She said that she hadn't been able to stay for the dinner with her new boss. While she paid Mrs. Lorenzo, her lips were pressed tight, and there was an intensity, a power, in her eyes, so that I thought she might set anything ablaze just by staring at it too long.

When we got up to our apartment and she closed the door to the public hall, she said, "We're going to pack up all our things, our clothes and things. Daddy's coming for us, and we're going to live with him from now on. Won't you like living with your grandpa?"

His house was nicer than our apartment, and I said so. At ten, I had no control of my tongue, and I also said, "Why're we moving? Is Grandpa too sad to be alone? Do you really have a migraine?"

Instead of answering me, she said, "Come on, honey, I'll help you pack your things, make sure nothing's left behind."

I had my own bright-green pressboard suitcase that pretty much held all my clothes, though we needed to use a plastic department-store shopping bag for the overflow.

As we were packing, she said, "Don't be half a man when you grow up, Jonah. Be a good man like your grandpa."

"Well, that's who I want to be. Who else would I want to be but like Grandpa?"

Not daring to put it more directly, what I meant was that I had no desire to grow up to be like my father. He walked out on us when I was eight months old, and he came back when I was eight years old, but then he walked out on us again before my ninth birthday. The man didn't have a commitment problem; the word wasn't in his vocabulary. In those days, I worried he might come back again, which would have been a calamity, considering all his problems. Among other things, he wasn't able to love anyone but himself.

Still, Mom had a weak spot for him. If he showed up, she might go with him again, which is why I didn't say what was in my heart.

"You've met Harmon Jessup," she said. "You remember?"

"Sure. He owns Slinky's, where you sing."

"You know I quit there for this other job. But I don't want you thinking your mother's flaky."

"Well, you're not, so how could I think it?"

Folding my T-shirts into the shopping bag, she said, "I want you to know I quit for another reason, too, and a good one. Harmon just kept getting . . . way too close. He wanted more from me than just my singing." She put away the last T-shirt and looked at me. "You know what I mean, Jonah?"

"I think I know."

"I think you do, and I'm sorry you do. Anyway, if he

didn't get what he wanted, I wasn't going to have a job there anymore."

Never in my life, child or man, have I been hotheaded. I think I have more of my mother's genes than my father's, probably because he was too incomplete a person to have enough to give. But that night in my room, I got very angry, very fast, and I said, "I hate Harmon. If I was bigger, I'd go hurt him."

"No, you wouldn't."

"I darn sure would."

"Hush yourself, sweetie."

"I'd shoot him dead."

"Don't say such a thing."

"I'd cut his damn throat and shoot him dead."

She came to me and stood looking down, and I figured she must be deciding on my punishment for talking such trash. The Bledsoes didn't tolerate street talk or jive talk, or trash talk. Grandpa Teddy often said, "In the beginning was the word. Before all else, the word. So we speak as if words matter, because they do." Anyway, my mom stood there, frowning down at me, but then her expression changed and all the hard edges sort of melted from her face. She dropped to her knees and put her arms around me and held me tight.

I felt awkward and embarrassed that I had been talking tough when we both knew that if skinny little me went gunning for Harmon Jessup, he'd blow me off my feet just by laughing in my face. I felt embarrassed for her, too, because she didn't have anyone better than me to watch over her.

She looked me in the eye and said, "What would the sisters think of all this talk about cutting throats and shooting?"

Because Grandma worked in Monsignor McCarthy's office, I was fortunate to be able to attend Saint Scholastica School for a third the usual tuition, and the nuns who ran it were tough ladies. If anyone could teach Harmon a lesson he'd never forget, it was Sister Agnes or Sister Catherine.

I said, "You won't tell them, will you?"

"Well, I really should. And I should tell your grandpa."

Grandpa's father had been a barber, and Grandpa's mother had been a beautician, and they had run their house according to a long set of rules. When their children occasionally decided that those rules were really nothing more than suggestions, my great-grandfather demonstrated a second use for the strap of leather that he used to strop his straight razors. Grandpa Teddy didn't resort to corporal punishment, as his father did, but his look of extreme disappointment stung bad enough.

"I won't tell them," my mother said, "because you're such a good kid. You've built up a lot of credit at the First Bank of Mom."

After she kissed my forehead and got up, we went into her room to continue packing. The apartment came furnished, and it included a bedroom vanity with a three-part mirror. She trusted me to take everything out of the many little drawers and put all of it in this small square carrier that she called a train case, while she packed her clothes in two large suitcases and three shopping bags.

She wasn't finished explaining why we had to move. I realized many years later that she always felt she had to justify herself to me. She never did need to do that, because I always knew her heart, how good it was, and I loved her so much that sometimes it hurt when I'd lie awake at night worrying about her.

Anyway, she said, "Honey, don't you ever get to thinking that one kind of people is better than another kind. Harmon Jessup is rich compared to me, but he's poor compared to William Murkett."

In addition to owning the glitzy nightclub where she'd been offered five nights a week, Murkett had several other enterprises.

"Harmon is black," she continued, "Murkett is white. Harmon had nearly no school. Murkett went to some upper-crust university. Harmon is a dirty old tomcat and proud of it. Murkett, he's married with kids of his own and he's got a good reputation. But under all those differences, there's no difference. They're the same. Each of them is just half a man. Don't you ever be just half a man, Jonah."

"No, ma'am. I won't be."

"You be true to people."

"I will."

"You'll be tempted."

"I won't."

"You will. Everyone is."

"You aren't," I said.

"I was. I am."

She finished packing, and I said, "I guess then you don't have a job, that's why we're going to Grandpa's."

"I've still got Woolworth's, baby."

I knew there were times when she cried, but she never did in front of me. Right then, her eyes were as clear and direct and as certain as Sister Agnes's eyes. In fact, she was a lot like Sister Agnes, except that Sister Agnes couldn't sing a note and my mom was way prettier.

She said, "I've got Woolworth's and a good voice and time. And I've got you. I've got everything I need."

I thought of my father then, how he kept leaving us, how we wouldn't have been in that fix if he'd kept even half his promises, but I couldn't vent. My mom had never dealt out as much punishment as the one time I said that I hated him, and though I didn't think I should be ashamed for having said it, I was ashamed just the same.

The day would come when despising him would be the least of it, when he would flat-out terrify me.

We had no sooner finished packing than the doorbell rang, and it was Grandpa Teddy, come to take us home with him.

Four

THE *FIRST* TIME MY MOTHER'S LIFE FELL APART was when she found out that she was pregnant with me. She'd been accepted into the music program at Oberlin, and she had nearly a full scholarship; but before she could even start her first year, she learned I was on the way. She said she really didn't want to go to Oberlin, that it was her parents' idea, that she wanted to fly on what talent she had, not on a lot of music theory that might stifle her. She wanted instead to work her way from one dinky club to another less dinky and steadily up, up, up, getting *experience.* She claimed I came along just in time to save her from Oberlin, and maybe I believed that when I was a kid.

She'd taken a year off between high school and college,

and her father had used a connection to get her an age exemption and a gig in a piano bar, because she was a piano man, too. In fact, she was good on saxophone, primo on clarinet, and learning guitar fast. When God ladled out talent, He spilled the whole bucket on Sylvia Bledsoe. The bar was also a restaurant, and the cook—not the chef, the cook—was Tilton Kirk. He was twenty-four, six years her senior, and each time she took a break, he was right there with the charm, which, as far as I'm concerned, he got from a different source than the one that gave my mom her talent.

He was a handsome man and articulate, and as sure as he knew his name, he knew that he was going places in this world. All you had to do was say hello, and he'd tell you where he was going: first from cook to chef, and then into a restaurant of his own by thirty, and then two or three restaurants by the time he was forty, however many he wanted. He was a gifted cook, and he gave young Sylvia Bledsoe all kinds of tasty dishes refined to what he called the Kirk style. He gave her me, too, though it turned out that taking care of children wasn't part of the Kirk style.

To be fair, he knew she'd have the baby, that the Bledsoes would not tolerate anything else. He did the right thing, he married her, and after that he pretty reliably did the wrong thing.

I was born on June 15, 1957, which was when the Count

Basie band became the first Negro band ever to perform in the Starlight Room of the Waldorf-Astoria hotel in New York City. *Negro* was the word in those days. On July 6, tennis star Althea Gibson, another Negro, won the All-England title at Wimbledon, also a first. And on August 29, the Civil Rights Act, proposed by President Eisenhower the previous year, was finally voted into law by the congress; soon thereafter, Ike would start using the national guard to desegregate schools. By comparison, my entrance into the world wasn't big news, except to my mom and me.

Trying to ingratiate himself with Sylvia's parents, well aware of Grandpa Teddy's musical heroes, my father chose to name me Jonah Ellington Basie Hines Eldridge Wilson Hampton Armstrong Kirk. Even all these years later, almost everyone has heard of Duke Ellington, Count Basie, Earl "Fatha" Hines, Lionel Hampton, and Louis Armstrong. Time doesn't treat all talent equally, however, and Roy Eldridge is known these days pretty much only to aficionados of big band music. He was one of the greatest trumpeters of all time. Electrifying. He played with Gene Krupa's legendary band through the early war years, when Anita O'Day was changing what everyone thought a girl singer ought to be. The Wilson in my name is for Teddy Wilson, whom Benny Goodman called the greatest musician in dance music of the day. He played with Goodman, then started his own band, which didn't last long, and then he played largely in a sextet. If you can find any of the twenty sides that he recorded with his band, you'll hear a piano man of incomparable elegance.

With all those names to live up to, I sometimes wished I'd been born just Jonah Kirk. But I guess because I was half Bledsoe, anyone who ever admired my grandpa—which was everyone who knew him—would have looked at me with some doubt that I could ever shape myself into a man like him.

The day I was born, Grandpa Teddy and Grandma Anita came to the hospital to see me first through a window in the nursery and then in my mother's arms when I was brought to her room. My father was there, as well, and eager to tell Grandpa my full name. Although I was the center of attention, I have no memory of the moment, maybe because I was already impatient to start piano lessons.

According to my mom, the revelation of my many names didn't go quite like my father intended. Grandpa Teddy stood bedside, nodding in recognition each time Tilton—who was cautious enough to keep the bed between them—revealed a name. But when the final name had been spoken, Grandpa traded glances with Grandma, and then he frowned and stared at the floor as if he noticed something offensive down there that didn't belong in a hospital.

Now, you should know Grandpa had a smile that could melt an ice block and leave the water steaming. And even when he wasn't smiling, his face was so pleasant that the shyest of children often grinned on first sight of him and walked right up to him, a stranger, to say hello to this friendly giant. But when he frowned and when you knew that you might be the reason he frowned, his face made you think of judgment day and of whatever pathetic good deeds you might be able to cite to balance the offenses you had committed. He didn't look furious, didn't even scowl, merely frowned, and at once an uneasy silence fell upon the room. No one feared Grandpa Teddy's anger, because few people if any had ever seen it. If you evoked that frown, what you feared was his disapproval, and when you learned that you had disappointed him, you realized that you *needed* his approval no less than you needed air, water, and food.

Although Grandpa never put it in words for me, one thing I learned from him was that being admired gives you more power than being feared.

Anyway, there in the hospital room, Grandpa Teddy frowned at the floor so long, my father reached out for my mother's hand, and she let him hold it while she cradled me in one arm.

Finally Grandpa looked up, considered his son-in-law, and said quietly, "There were so many big bands, swing bands, scores of them, maybe hundreds, no two alike. So much energy, so much great music. Some people might say it was swing music as much as anything that kept this country in a winning mood during the war. You know, back then I played with a couple of the biggest and best, also with a couple not as big but good. So many memories, so many people, quite a time. I did admire all those names between Jonah and Kirk, I did very much admire them. I loved them. But Benny Goodman, he was as good as any and a stand-up guy. Charlie Barnet, Woody Herman, Harry James, Glenn Miller. Artie Shaw, for Heaven's sake. *The* Artie Shaw. 'Begin the Beguine,' 'Indian Love Call,' 'Back Bay Shuffle.' There are so many names to reckon with from those days, this poor child would need the entire sheet of stationery just for his letterhead."

My mom got the point, but my father didn't. "But, Teddy, sir, all those names—they aren't our kind."

"Well, yes," Grandpa said, "they're not *directly* in the bar and restaurant business, like you are, but their work has put so many people in the mood to celebrate that they've had an impact on your trade. And they most surely are my kind and Sylvia's kind, aren't they, Anita?"

Grandma said, "Oh, yes. They're my kind, too. I love musicians. I married one. I gave birth to one. And, dear, you forgot the Dorsey brothers."

"I didn't forget them," Grandpa said. "My mouth just

went dry from naming all those names. Freddy Martin, too."

"That tenor sax of his, the sweetest tone ever," Grandma said.

"Claude Thornhill."

"The best of the best bands," she declared. "And he was one *funny* man, Claude was."

By then, my father got the message, but he didn't want to hear it. He had a big chip on his shoulder about race, and he probably had good reason, probably a list of good reasons. Nevertheless, for the sake of family harmony, maybe he should at least have added Thornhill and Goodman to my name, but he couldn't bring himself to do that.

He said, "Hey, look at the time. Gotta get to the restaurant." After he kissed my mom and kissed me, he hugged Anita, nodded at Grandpa Teddy, said, "Sir," and skedaddled.

So that was my first family gathering on my first day in the world. A little tense.

The *second* time that my mother's life fell apart was eight months later, when my father walked out on us. He said that he needed to focus on his career. He couldn't sleep with a crying baby in the next room. He claimed to have a potential backer for a restaurant, so he might be able to go from cook to chef in his own place, and even if it would be a hole in the wall, he would be moving up faster than originally planned. He really needed to stay focused, do his work at the restaurant and pursue this new opportunity. He promised he'd be back. He didn't say when. He told her he loved us. It was always surprisingly easy for him to say that. He promised to send money every week. He kept that promise for four weeks. By then, my mom had gotten the job at Woolworth's lunch counter *and* her first singing gig at a dump called the Jazz Cave, so it was a difficult time, but only difficult, nothing serious yet.

Five

I'M NOT GOING TO BE ABLE TO TALK MY LIFE month by month, year by year. Instead, I'll have to use this recorder as if it were a time machine, hop around, back and forth, so maybe you'll see the uncanny way that things connected, which wasn't apparent to me as I came to my future one day at a time.

Here is where I should tell you a little about the woman who kept showing up in my life at key moments. I never once saw her coming. She was just always there like sudden sunshine breaking through clouds. The first time was a day in April 1966, when I tried to hate the piano because I thought I'd never get to be a piano man.

I was nearly nine, and Grandma Anita still had a year to live. The previous December, my father had come back to stay with us again in the walk-up. Mom never divorced him. She considered it, even though she knew—and believed—that marriage was a sacrament. But she claimed that when she sang in places like the Jazz Cave and Brass Tacks and Slinky's, she could more successfully discourage come-ons from customers and employees if she could honestly say, "I've got a husband, a baby boy, and Jesus. So as handsome as you are, I'm sure you can see I have no need of another man in my life." According to Mom, just husband or child or Jesus alone wouldn't have kept the most determined suitors at bay; with them, she needed the three-punch.

In the nearly eight years he'd been gone, Tilton Kirk hadn't found a backer, hadn't opened his own place, but he *had* left the restaurant where he worked as a cook to take the chef position in a somewhat higher-class joint. He was earning less because every year the owner compensated him also with five percent of the stock in the business, so that once he had accumulated thirty-five percent, he could buy the other sixty-five at an already agreed-upon price, using his stock to swing the bank loan.

With him at home again, my mom was more happy than not, but I was all kinds of miserable. The man really didn't know how to be a dad. Sometimes he was a hard-nosed disciplinarian dealing out a lot more punishment than I deserved. At other times he'd want to be my best pal ever, hang out together, except that he didn't know what kind of hanging out kids think is cool. Strolling the aisles of a restaurant-supply store, obsessing over different kinds of potato peelers and pâté molds, just doesn't thrill a child. Neither does sitting on a barstool sipping a Coke while your old man drinks beer and swaps nagging-wife jokes with a stranger.

The worst was that by then I wanted to take piano lessons, and my father refused to let it happen. I had noodled the keyboard at Grandpa Teddy's house, and I understood the layout on a gut level, the way Jackie Robinson could read a ball in flight. But Tilton said I was too little yet, my hands too small, and when my mom disagreed and said I was big enough, Tilton said we couldn't afford the lessons yet. Soon but not yet, which meant never.

Grandpa offered to drive me over to his place and back a few times a week and give me lessons himself. But my father said, "It's too far to run a little kid back and forth all the time, Syl. And we don't have a piano here for him to practice between lessons. We'll get a house soon, and then he can have a piano, and it'll all make sense. Anyway, honey, you know I'm not your old man's favorite human being. It breaks my heart how maybe he'll poison the boy's mind against me. I know Teddy wouldn't do it on purpose, Syl, he's not a mean man, but he'll be poisoning without even knowing it. Soon we'll rent a house, soon, and then it'll make sense."

So I was sitting on the stoop in front of our building, such a sullen look on my face that most passersby glanced at me and at once away, as though I, only eight, might try to stomp them in a fit of mean. It was an unseasonably warm day for April, the air so still and humid that a feather, cast off by a bird in flight, sank like a stone in water to the pavement in front of me. As sudden as it was brief, a wind came along, lifted the feather, spun dust and litter out of the gutter, and whirled all of it up the steps and over me. I sneezed and spat away the feather that stuck to my lips.

As I wiped at my eyes, I heard a woman say, "Hey, Ducks, how's the world treating you?"

My mom had a couple of friends who were professional dancers in musicals that were always being talked about by people who loved the theater, and though this woman didn't look like any of them, she did look like a dancer. Tall and slim and leggy, with smooth mahogany skin, she came up the steps so easy, with so little movement, you'd have thought she must be on an escalator. She wore a primrose-pink lightweight suit, a white blouse, and a pink pillbox hat with a fan of gray feathers along one side, as though dressed for lunch in some place where the waiters wore tuxedos.

In spite of her fine outfit and air of elegance, she sat beside me on the stoop. "Ducks, it's rude not to answer when spoken to, and you look like a young man who'd rather poke himself in the eye than be rude."

"The world stinks," I declared.

"Certain things in the world stink, Ducks, but not the whole world. In fact, most of it smells wonderfully sweet. You yourself smell a little like limes and salt, which reminds me of a margarita, which isn't a bad thing. Do you like my perfume? It's French and expensive."

The sweet-rose fragrance was subtle. "It's all right, I guess."

"Well, Ducks, if you don't like it, I'll go straight home this minute and take the bottle off my dresser and throw it out a window and let the alley reek until the next rain."

"My name isn't Ducks."

"I'd be stunned if it was, Ducks. Parents saddle their children with things like Hortense and Percival, but I've never known one to name them after waterfowl."

"What's your name?" I asked.

"What do you think it is, Ducks?"

"Don't you know your own name?"

"I just sometimes wonder what name I look like, so I ask."

She was pretty. Even an eight-year-old boy knows a pretty girl when he sees her, and beauty lifts the heart no matter what your age. Her perfume smelled all right, too.

I said, "Well, I saw this movie on TV about these guys chasing after a treasure down in the Caribbean. This was way back when there were pirates. What they all wanted was this special pearl, see. Three things made it really, really special. It was large, like as big as a plum. And it wasn't white or cream-colored or pink, like other pearls. It was black, pure shiny black, but it still had depth like the best pearls all do, so you could see into it, and it was very beautiful. So maybe I think the name you look like is Pearl."

She cocked her head and sort of smirked at me. "Young man, if you are already this smooth with the ladies, won't a one of us be safe when you're all grown up. I *am* Pearl. There's no other name I'd want to be. You call me Pearl, Jonah."

Only hours later would I realize that I'd never told her my name.

"You said there were three special things about this pearl in the movie. Its size and its color and . . . ?"

"Oh, yeah. Well, they said whoever possessed it could never die. It was the secret to immortality."

"Black, beautiful, and magical. I *love* being Pearl."

Two years would pass before she told me that she was the soul of the city made flesh.

"So there you sit, Jonah, as gloomy as if you're still in the belly of the whale, when in fact it's a fine spring day. You aren't being digested by stomach acid, and you don't need a candle to find your way back up the gullet. Don't waste a fine spring day, Jonah. There's not as many of them in a lifetime as you think there will be. What's dropped your heart into your shoes?"

Maybe she was easy to talk to because she talked so easy. Next thing I knew, I heard myself say, "I want to be a piano man, but it won't ever happen."

"If you want to be a piano man, why aren't you at a piano right this minute, pounding the keys?"

"I don't have one."

"That community center you go to when your folks are working and Donata isn't available—they have a piano."

Donata was the first name of Mrs. Lorenzo, my some-times babysitter, so I figured Miss Pearl knew her and was coming to visit.

"I never saw any piano at the community center."

"Why, sure there is. For a while this man was in charge down there, he didn't have an ear for piano, it was all just noise to him. He didn't like loud birds, either, or a certain shade of blue, or the number nine, or Christmas. He put the Christmas tree up on December twenty-fourth and took it down the morning of the twenty-sixth, and the only decoration he'd allow on it was a Santa Claus doll hung by the neck where a star or angel should have been at the top of the tree. He took the nine out of the address above the front door and just left a space between the eight and the four, repainted all the blue rooms, moved the piano down to the basement. Some say he killed and ate Petey, the parrot that used to be in a cage in the card room. But he's gone now. He didn't last long. He was run down by a city bus when he jaywalked, but in a short time he did a lot of damage to the center. They can bring the piano up in the freight elevator."

Loud and belching fumes, a bus went by, and I wondered if it might be the one that ran down the parrot-eater.

When the street grew quieter, I said, "They won't bring up the piano for a kid like me. Anyway, it's no good without a teacher."

"There'll be a teacher. You go in there tomorrow morning, soon after they open, and see for yourself. Well, this glorious day is slipping away, and I am all dressed up with someplace to go, so I better get there."

She rose from the stoop and went down the stairs, her high heels making no more noise than a pair of slippers.

I called after her: "I thought you came to visit Mrs. Lorenzo."

Looking back, Miss Pearl said, "I came to visit you, Ducks."

She walked away, and I went down to the sidewalk to

watch her. With those slim hips and long legs, so tall in all that pink, she resembled a bird herself—not a parrot, an elegant flamingo. I waited for her to glance over her shoulder, and I meant to wave, but she never looked back. She turned left at the corner and was gone.

I raised my hands to my face and sniffed them and detected the faint scent of the lemons that earlier I had helped my mom squeeze for lemonade. I'd been sitting in the sun, and the film of sweat on my arms tasted of salt when I licked, but I couldn't smell salt.

In the years to come, I would encounter Miss Pearl on several occasions. Now that I'm fifty-seven and looking back, I can see that my life would have been far different—and shorter—if she hadn't taken an interest in me.

The next morning at the community center, the piano was in the Abigail Louise Thomas Room, which had been named after someone who'd done some good deed for the center back before I was even a gleam in Tilton's eye. The Steinway was polished and tuned, even prettier than the woman in pink.

One of the center staff, Mrs. Mary O'Toole, was playing Hoagy Carmichael's "Stardust," and just then it was the loveliest melody I'd ever heard. She was a nice lady with lively blue eyes, freckles that she said had come all the way from Dublin to decorate her face, and a pageboy cap of red hair shot through with white that an unskilled friend chopped for her, as she disdained beauty parlors. She smiled at me and nodded to the bench, and I sat beside her.

When she finished the piece, she sighed and said, "Isn't this a hoot, Jonah? Someone took away the spavined old piano in the basement and gave us this brand-spanking-new one and did it all on the sly. I can't imagine how."

"Isn't it the same piano?"

"Oh, it couldn't be. The lid was warped on that old one, the felt on the hammers moth-eaten, some of the strings broken, others missing. The sostenuto pedal was frozen. It was a fabulous mess. Some awfully clever philanthropist has been at work. I only wish I knew who to thank."

I didn't tell her about Miss Pearl. I meant to explain, and I started to speak. Then I thought, if I mentioned the name, it would be a spell-breaker. Come the next day, the Steinway would be back in the basement, as broken down as before, and Mrs. O'Toole would have no memory of playing "Stardust" in the Abigail Louise Thomas Room.

That day I started formal lessons.

Six

THAT SAME NIGHT, AS I LAY SLEEPING IN MY SMALL room, someone sat on the edge of the bed, and the mattress sagged, and the box springs creaked, and I came half awake, wondering why my mother would visit me at that hour. Before I could fully sit up in the dark, a hand gently pressed me down, and a familiar voice said softly, "Go to sleep, Ducks. Go to sleep now. I have a name for you, a name and a face and a dream. The name is Lucas Drackman and the face is his."

Strange as the moment was, I nevertheless settled to my pillow and closed my eyes and drifted down through fathoms of sleep. Out of the depths floated a young man's face, eerily up-lit and starkly shadowed. He was maybe sixteen, seventeen. Hair disarranged, forehead beetling over

deep-set eyes open wide and wild in character, hawkish
nose, a ripe and almost girlish mouth, blunt chin, pale skin
glazed with sweat . . . Never before and only once again
in all my life was a face in a dream so vivid and detailed.
Lucas had an air of urgency and anger, but at first there
was no nightmare quality to the moment. As a full scene
formed around him, I saw his features were revealed by
the backwash from a flashlight held low and forward.
Lucas took necklaces and brooches and bracelets and rings
from a jewelry box, diamonds and pearls, and dropped
them into a cloth sack that might have been a pillowcase.
In one of those fluid transitions common to dreams, he was
no longer at a jewelry box, but in a walk-in closet, stripping currency and a credit card from a wallet that had
been left there on a shelf. The Diner's Club card had been
issued to ROBERT W DRACKMAN. Then Lucas was bedside,
playing the flashlight beam over the body of a man who
apparently had been shot to death in his sleep. Still, I was
not afraid. Instead, a deep sadness overcame me. To the
dead man, Lucas said, "Hey there, *Bob*. What's it like in
Hell, *Bob*? You think now maybe sending me away to a
freakin' military academy was really stupid, *Bob*? You
ignorant, self-righteous son of a bitch." The flashlight beam
found a forty-something woman who must have been
awakened by the first rounds that Lucas fired. His mother.
She could be no one else, for the possibility of Lucas's face

could be seen in hers. She'd thrown aside the covers and sat up, whereupon she had been shot once in the chest and once in the throat. She'd fallen back against the headboard, blue eyes wide but blind now, mouth hanging open, though she'd probably never had a chance to scream. Lucas called her a vile name, a single word that I have never used and won't repeat here. A hallway. He walked away, and I did not follow. The light dwindled with him, dwindled and faded, and then a desolate darkness prevailed, and a sadness so keen that tears filled my eyes. She who had conjured a piano into the Abigail Louise Thomas Room spoke again: "Remember him, Ducks. Remember his face and his hateful words. Keep the dream to yourself, don't tell others who might question or even mock it and lead you to doubt, but always remember it."

I think I was awake when she spoke those words, but I can't swear to that. I might have been asleep through all of it, might have dreamed everything, including her entrance into my room, her weight on the edge of the bed, the mattress sagging, the springs creaking. In the darkness, I felt a hand on my brow, such a tender touch. She whispered, "Sleep, you lovely child," and either I continued sleeping or fell asleep once more.

When I woke with dawn light at my window, I felt that the dream hadn't been just a fantasy, that it had shown me true things, murders that already had been committed somewhere, at some point in the past. Lying there as the morning brightened, I wondered and doubted and then banished doubt only to embrace it again. But for all of my wondering, I couldn't answer even one of the many questions with which the experience had left me.

At last, getting out of bed, for a moment I smelled a certain sweetness of roses, identical to Miss Pearl's perfume, which she had been wearing when she sat beside me on the stoop. But after three breaths, that, too, faded beyond detection, as though I must have imagined it.

Seven

THE NEXT BIT OF MY STORY IS PART HEARSAY, BUT I'm sure this is how it went down. My mother would fib to help a child hold on to his innocence, as you'll see, but I never knew her to tell a serious lie.

I was just over a week away from my ninth birthday, and Grandma Anita had ten months to live. I'd begun piano lessons thanks to Miss Pearl, and my father had been back with us about six months when he messed up bigtime. We were still in that fourth-floor walk-up, and he wasn't bringing home much money because he was getting part of his salary in stock.

Mrs. Lorenzo lived on the second floor, but Mr. Lorenzo hadn't yet died, and Mrs. Lorenzo was thin and "as pretty as Anna Maria Alberghetti." Anna Maria was a greatly gifted singer and a misused actress in films and eventually a Broadway star, petite and very beautiful. She won a Tony for *Carnival!* and played Maria in *West Side Story*. Although Anna Maria wasn't as well known as other performers of Italian descent, anytime my mother meant to convey how lovely some Italian woman was, she compared her to Anna Maria Alberghetti. If she thought a man with Italian looks was especially attractive, she always said he was as handsome as Marcello Mastroianni. Anna Maria, yes, but I never understood the Mastroianni business. Anyway, Mr. Lorenzo didn't want his wife to work, wanted her to raise children, but it turned out he couldn't father any. So Mrs. Lorenzo ran a sort of unlicensed day care out of their apartment, looking after three little kids at a time, and on occasion me, too, as I've said.

When it happened, noonish on the first Tuesday in June, I was at Saint Scholastica, on the last day of the school year, being educated by nuns but dreaming of becoming a piano man.

My mom had left for Woolworth's lunch counter at 10:30. When she got there, she discovered there had been a small kitchen fire during the breakfast shift. They were shutting down for two days, until repairs could be completed. She came home four hours early.

Because my father worked late nights at the restaurant, he slept from 3:00 A.M. until 11:00. She expected to find him still asleep or at breakfast. But he had showered and gone. She made the bed, and as she was changing from her waitress uniform, she heard Miss Delvane rehearsing her rodeo act up in Apartment 5-B.

Miss Delvane—blond, attractive, a free spirit—had lived above us for three years. She earned a living as a freelance writer of magazine articles and was working on a novel. Sometimes, from her apartment would arise a rhythmic knocking, maybe a little bit like horses' hooves, gradually escalating in a crescendo, as well as voices muffled and wordless but urgent. On previous occasions, when I wondered about it, my mom said Miss Delvane was practicing her rodeo act. According to my mother, Miss Delvane's first novel was going to be set in the rodeo, and because she planned eventually to ride in the rodeo as research, she kept a mechanical horse in her apartment to practice. I was five years old when Miss Delvane moved in and only eight when my mom came home from Woolworth's early, and although I had doubts that a rodeo act was the *full* explanation, I accepted the basic premise. When I asked about the low groans, my mom always said it was a recording of a bull, because you had to lasso bulls or even wrestle them if you were in a rodeo, and Miss Delvane played the record to put her in the mood when she rode her mechanical horse. I had more questions than a quiz show, but I never asked Miss Delvane one of them, because Mom said the poor woman was embarrassed about how long it was taking her to get her rodeo act together.

Miss Delvane lived above us from mid-1963 through 1966, and though people in those days had a considerable interest in sex, the country hadn't yet become one gigantic porn theater. Parents could protect you and allow you to have a childhood, and even if you might have vague suspicions of forbidden secrets, you couldn't switch on a computer and go to a thousand websites to learn that . . . Well, that Bambi hadn't been *wished* into existence by his mother, and neither had you.

So there was my mom, changing out of her uniform, listening to the rodeo act overhead, and it seemed to her that the groans and the trumpetings of the recorded bull were familiar. During the more than seven years when Tilton hadn't lived with us, Mom had seen him from time to time, and she had stayed married to him, and when he wanted to come back, she'd taken him. Now she didn't want to believe that it had been a mistake to let him through the door again. She told herself that all men sounded the same when playing the bull, when their cries of pleasure were filtered through an apartment ceiling. She told herself that it might even be Miss Delvane, whose voice had considerable range and could lower all the way to husky. By then, however, life had dealt Sylvia Bledsoe Kirk numerous jokers in a game where they weren't wild cards, where they counted for nothing, and she knew this joker because he had ruined her hand before.

She threw his clothes and toiletries into his two suitcases and carried them out of the apartment. The building had front and back staircases, the second narrower and grubbier than the first. My mom knew that, by his nature, Tilton would be prone to slipping out the back, even though he had no reason to think he'd be seen descending from the fifth instead of the fourth floor or that the significance of that extra story would be obvious to anyone.

That day, Mom had decided that Tilton wasn't just a skirt-chaser and a pathological liar and a narcissist and a self-deluded fool as regarded his career. He was all those things because he was a coward who couldn't look at life head-on and face it and make a right way through it, regardless of the obstacles. He had to lie to himself about life, pretend it was less hard than it really was, and then press forward by one slippery means or another, all the while deluding himself into believing that he was conquering the world. My mother would never have called herself a hero, although of course she was, but she knew she wasn't a coward, never had been and never would be, and she couldn't stand to live with one.

She set the suitcases on the cracked and edge-curled linoleum on the back-stairs landing between the fifth and fourth floors, and she sat a couple of steps lower, with her back to them. She had to wait for a while, and with every minute that passed, she had less sympathy for the devil. Eventually she heard a door close somewhere above and a man slow-whistling "You've Lost That Lovin' Feelin'," which had been a hit for the Righteous Brothers back in February.

Tilton was crazy about the tune and whistled it that afternoon without any sense of irony, although later he might have realized it wasn't the perfect track for that particular scene in the music score for the movie of his life.

He opened the stairwell door and started down and stopped whistling when he recognized his suitcases. The man was an excuse machine, and I imagine at least three marginally believable and a dozen preposterous excuses flew through his mind before he continued to the landing. Of course, when he discovered my mom sitting a few steps down on the next flight, he stopped again and stood there, not sure what to do. He had always been quick with words and especially with justifications, but not that day. He was apparently unnerved by the way she sat in silence, her back turned to him. If she'd made accusations or started crying, he might have dared a lie, pretended he was innocent, but she merely sat there ready to bear witness to his departure. Maybe he thought she had a knife and would stab him in the back when he squeezed past her, encumbered by the suitcases. For whatever reason, Tilton picked up the two bags and, instead of continuing down with them, he returned to the fifth floor.

Sylvia got up from the step and followed. At the fifth-floor landing, when my father glanced back and saw her coming slowly after him, he grew alarmed and stumbled over the threshold, knocking the luggage against the jamb and the door, against his legs, like those old-time movie guys, Laurel and Hardy, trying to maneuver a jumbo packing crate through an opening too small for it. As he hurried along the hallway, my mom followed, saying nothing, not closing on him but not losing ground, either. At the head of the front stairs, he lost his grip on one of the bags, and it tumbled down the steps, and he almost fell after it in his eagerness to retrieve it and get out of there. Expressionless, never taking her eyes off her errant husband, Sylvia followed flight by flight, and Tilton's hands were apparently so slick with sweat that the suitcases kept getting away from him, thudding against the walls. Because he couldn't resist glancing back in anticipation of the nonexistent but expected knife, he misstepped a few times and careened from wall to wall as if the bags he carried were filled with bottles of whiskey that he'd spent the past few hours sampling.

At the landing between the third and second floors, pursued and pursuer encountered Mr. Yoshioka, a polite and shy man, an impeccably dressed tailor of great skill. He lived alone in an apartment on the fifth floor, and everyone believed that this gentle man had some dark or tragic secret, that perhaps he'd lost his family in Hiroshima. When Mr. Yoshioka saw my father ricocheting downward with reckless disregard for the geometry of a staircase and for the law of gravity, when then he saw my stone-faced mother in unhurried but implacable pursuit, he said, "Thank you very much," and turned and plunged two steps at a time to the ground floor, to wait in the foyer with his back against the mailboxes, hoping that he had removed himself from the trajectory of whatever violence was about to be committed.

Tilton exploded through the front door, as though the building itself had come alive and ejected him. One of the abused suitcases fell open on the stoop, and he frantically stuffed clothing back into it. My mom watched through the window in the door until he repacked and departed. Then she said, "Lovin' feelin', my ass," and turned and was surprised to see poor Mr. Yoshioka still there with his back against the mailboxes.

He smiled and nodded and said, "I should like to ascend now."

She said, "I'm so sorry, Mr. Yoshioka."

"The sorrow is all mine," he said, and then he went up the stairs two at a time.

The event as I have just described it was the version that my mom told me years later. After school that day, I walked to the community center to practice piano. When I got home, all she said was, "Your father's no longer living here. He went upstairs to help Miss Delvane with her rodeo act, and I wasn't having any of that."

Too young to sift the true meaning of her words, I found the idea of a mechanical horse more fascinating than ever and hoped I might one day see it. My mother's *Reader's Digest* condensation of my father's leaving didn't satisfy my curiosity. I had many questions, but I refrained from asking them. Truth is, I was so happy that I would never again have to sit in a barroom listening to nagging-wife stories, I couldn't conceal my delight.

Right then I told Mom the secret I couldn't have revealed when Tilton lived with us, that I had been taking piano lessons from Mrs. O'Toole for more than two months. She hugged me and got teary and apologized, and I didn't understand what she was apologizing for. She said it didn't matter if I understood, all that mattered was that she would never again allow anyone or anything to get between me and a piano or between me and any other dream I might have.

"Hey, sweetheart, let's toast our freedom with some Co-Cola."

We sat at the kitchen table and toasted with Coca-Cola

and with slices of chocolate cake *before* dinner, and all
these years later, I can relive that moment vividly in my
mind. She had moved on from Brass Tacks to Slinky's by
then; but that wasn't a night when she performed, so I
had her all to myself. We talked about all kinds of things,
including the Beatles, who'd hit number one on the U.S.
charts just two years earlier with "I Want to Hold Your
Hand" and "She Loves You" and four others. Four more
chart-topping songs followed in '65. Already in 1966, they'd
had another tune reach number one. My mom liked the
Beatles, but she said jazz was her thing, especially swing,
and she talked about the big-band singers from Grandpa
Teddy's day. She knew all their work and could imitate a
lot of them, and it was as if we had them right there in
our kitchen. She showed me a book about that time, with
pictures of those girls. Kay Davis and Maria Ellington,
who sang with the Duke. Billie Holiday with Basie. They
were all pretty and some of them beautiful. Sarah Vaughan,
Helen Forrest, Doris Day, Harriet Clark, Lena Horne,
Martha Tilton, Peggy Lee. Maybe the most beautiful of
them all was Dale Evans when she was in her twenties,
the same one who later married Roy Rogers, who had a
real horse, but even the young Dale Evans wasn't as pretty
as Sylvia Bledsoe Kirk. And my mom could do Ella. She
could scat so you thought for sure it was Ella and your
eyes were deceiving you. We made Campbell's tomato soup

and grilled-cheese sandwiches, and we played 500 rummy. Years later, I realized that was the third time when my mother's life fell apart, but in the moment, I didn't see it that way. When I went to bed, I thought that had been the best day of my life to date.

The next day was better—magical, one of those days that my friend Malcolm calls a butter-side-up day. Trouble was coming, sure, but it's always coming, and meanwhile it's best to live with a smile.

Eight

A BUTTER-SIDE-UP DAY . . .

Let's take a little detour here called Malcolm Pomerantz. He's a first-rate musician. He blows the tenor sax. He's something of a genius who, even at fifty-nine, can still play an entire tone scale.

He's crazy, too, but mostly harmless. He's so superstitious, he'd rather break his back than break a mirror. And though he's not so much of an obsessive-compulsive that he needs to spend a few hours a week on a shrink's couch, he has routines that would make you crazy if you didn't love him.

For one thing, he has to wash his hands five times—not four, not six—just before he joins the band onstage. And after his nimble fingers are clean enough to play, he won't touch anything with his bare hands except his saxophone because, if he does, he'll have to wash them five times again. The cleanliness of his hands doesn't concern him when he practices, only when he performs. If he wasn't such a superb musician and likable guy, he wouldn't have a career.

Malcolm reads the newspaper every day but Tuesday. He will not buy a Tuesday newspaper, nor will he borrow one. He won't watch TV news or listen to a radio on Tuesdays. He believes that if he dares to take in the news on any Tuesday, his heart will turn to dust.

He won't eat mushrooms either raw or cooked, not in any sauce, even though he loves mushrooms. He won't eat any rounded cookie that reminds him of a mushroom cap. In a market, he avoids that end of the produce section where the mushrooms are offered for sale. And if the market is new to him, he avoids the produce section altogether, out of fear that he'll have a sudden fungal encounter.

As for the butter-side-up day: Each morning, he makes one extra slice of toast with breakfast, lays it on his kitchen table, and in a contrived-casual way, he knocks it to the floor. If it lands butter side up, he eats it with pleasure, confident that the day will be good from end to end. If it lands butter side down, however, Malcolm throws the toast away, wipes up the butter, and goes about his day with heightened awareness of potential danger.

On the first night of every full moon, Malcolm makes his way to the nearest Catholic church, puts seventeen dollars in the poor box, and lights seventeen votive candles. He claims not to know why, that it's just a compulsion like the others with which he's afflicted. I am inclined to think that he really doesn't know the reason, that the seventeen candles are a way of keeping his pain at bay, and that if he allowed himself to understand his motivation, the pain could no longer be relieved. For most of us, the wounds that life inflicts are slowly healed, and we're left only with scars, but maybe Malcolm is too sensitive to let the wounds fully close; maybe his obsessive-compulsive little rituals are like bandages that keep his unhealed wounds clean and staunch the bleeding.

Although I can't explain all of Malcolm's quirks, I know why never mushrooms and why always full-moon candles and why never the news on Tuesday. We have been friends since I was ten. Back then, he was not as he is now. His sweet kind of craziness evolved over the years. Malcolm is white, and I am black. We aren't brothers bonded by blood, but we're as close as brothers, bonded by the same devastating losses. I respect his ways, odd as they are, of dealing with his enduring pain, and I will never explain to him the meaning of his rituals, because that might deny him the relief he gets from them.

On one terrible day, each of us lost someone whom he

loved as much as life itself. And some years later, again on the same day, we once more lost someone beloved, and yet again after that. I'm still an optimist, but Malcolm is not. Sometimes I worry about what might happen to him if I were to die first, because I suspect that his eccentricities will metastasize, and in spite of his talent, he will not be able to go on working. The work is his salvation, because every song he plays, he plays for those whom he loved and lost.

Nine

BECAUSE WOOLWORTH'S WAS STILL CLEANING UP from the kitchen fire, my mother didn't have to work the lunch shift. She wanted to come with me to the community center, to hear what I'd learned of the piano, which I worried wouldn't be impressive to someone who could sing like Ella. You should have seen her that day. She dressed as though it must be an *occasion,* as if she were accompanying me to some concert hall where two thousand people were waiting to hear me play. She wore a yellow dress with a pleated skirt and with black piping at the cuffs and collar, a black belt, and black high-heeled shoes. We walked the block and a half, and she was so gorgeous that people turned to look at her, men and women alike, as if a goddess had come down to Earth to walk this skinny boy someplace special for some reason too amazing to imagine.

Mrs. O'Toole was there, and I introduced them, and it turned out they had something in common: Grandpa Teddy. Mary O'Toole said, "My first husband played tenor sax with Shep Fields in '41. Shep's band was heavy with saxes—one bass, one baritone, six tenors, and four altos— and Teddy Bledsoe was the piano man part of that year, before moving on to Goodman." Mary looked at me in a new way when she knew I was Teddy Bledsoe's grandson. She said, "Bless you, child, now it makes perfect sense how you could come along so fast on the ivories."

I had progressed quickly through the lessons, but what had excited Mrs. O'Toole was that recently I'd gotten to the place where I could listen to a piece of music and sit down and play it right away, insofar as my arms could reach and my fingers could spread. I had an eidetic memory for music, which is the equivalent of reading a novel once and being able to recite it word for word. If I was alone at the keyboard, I was able to play just about anything, regardless of the complexity or tempo, not a fraction as well as Grandpa Teddy could have played it, but still so you'd recognize the tune. I needed to have the bench to myself because I had developed this butt-slide technique, polishing the bench with the seat of my pants, slipping left, right, left as required without bumping my elbows or disturbing my finger placement, so I had good reach for a kid my age and size.

My mom stood listening to me play, and I didn't dare look at her. I didn't want her to make nice and pretend I was better than I truly was, but I didn't want to see her trying to keep from wincing, either. The second thing I played was a favorite of hers, an old Anita O'Day hit, "And Her Tears Flowed Like Wine." I was but three bars into it when Mom started to sing. Oh, man. Community center acoustics don't measure up, but maybe that was still what those lyrics sounded like at the Paramount Theater or the Hotel Pennsylvania, back when O'Day was with Stan Kenton and was better than the band, before I was born.

I became aware that people were crowding into the Abigail Louise Thomas Room, drawn by my mom's singing. I was so proud of her and embarrassed that she had no one more accomplished than me to accompany her. We were rolling toward the end, and she was better than great, her tone and her phrasing, and just then, among the little crowd, I saw Miss Pearl.

She wore the same pink outfit with the feathered hat that she had been wearing almost three months earlier when she sat on the stoop with me and called me Ducks. She wiggled her fingers at me, and I smiled.

I couldn't wait to introduce Miss Pearl to Mrs. O'Toole,

so that our benefactor could be thanked for the piano. I figured the shiny-as-new Steinway had been there too long suddenly to be dilapidated and in the basement again, with nobody to remember that it had been restored or replaced, which was the fear that had kept me from mentioning Miss Pearl on the first day I'd seen the piano glossy and black and beautiful. There you have the magical thinking of an eight-year-old boy: that when the miraculous happens, it soon can be undone by the whim of God, but if it isn't undone in a day or a week or a month, then it becomes permanent, and even God doesn't have the power to take it away.

The truth is, to this day I still pretty much operate under that assumption. If chaos plagues the world—and it does—and if there's any benign power that wants the world to survive, then stability will be encouraged and rewarded. Maybe not all the time. But most of the time.

Anyway, we came to the end of "And Her Tears Flowed Like Wine," when I stupidly added a concluding flourish that wasn't part of the number. Fortunately, the crowd of community-center staff and patrons knew the song was over when my mom hit the last word, and they broke into applause that saved me from the embarrassment of them having heard the unnecessary flourish. A lot of the people who came there to play cards and socialize were older than Grandpa Teddy, and they knew the old tunes so well that they might have sung along if they hadn't wanted to hear Sylvia Bledsoe solo. They called for more, and I looked at Mom, and she nodded.

The community center had some old records, and only a couple of days before, I'd heard "It All Begins and Ends with You," sung by Mildred Bailey backed by the Red Norvo band. Without thinking to ask if my mom knew it, I ham-handed my way into it, and she sang along so beautifully that I sounded way better than I was. When I noticed that some of the gray-haired ladies had tears in their eyes, I understood for the first time why music matters so much, how it reminds us of who we are and where we came from, of all the good times and the sadness, too.

When we finished, everyone wanted to talk to us. I didn't have much to say except "Thank you," and they really had more interest in Mom than in me. They wanted to know where she performed. When she told them Slinky's, many hadn't heard of the place, and those who had heard of it looked disappointed for her.

While they gathered around my mom, I went looking for Miss Pearl, but I couldn't find her anywhere. I asked several people if they'd seen this tall woman in a pink suit and feathered hat, but no one remembered her.

From the center, my mother and I walked to the nearest park, which was her idea. It wasn't much of a park, some trees and benches and a bronze statue of some former mayor or someone who would have been embarrassed to have his image in a park that had gone as crummy as that one, except that he was probably dead. There had been a plaque under the statue, telling who the bronze man had been, but vandals had cut it off the granite base. There were bare patches in the grass, and the trees weren't properly trimmed, and the trash baskets overflowed. My mom remembered a vendor's shack where you could buy newspapers and snacks and packets of little crackers to throw down for the pigeons, but it wasn't there anymore, and what pigeons still hung around looked too red-eyed and kind of strange.

"What the heck," she said. "Why not."

"Why not what?"

"Why not make a day of it? Just you and me on a date."

"What would we do?"

"Anything we want. Starting with a better park."

We walked out to the main avenue, and we stood by the curb, looking for a taxi. She hailed a couple, and finally one stopped, and a man named Albert Solomon Gluck drove us to a better park, to Riverside Commons. In those days, there weren't Plexiglas shields between the front and back seats, because no one yet imagined a time when drivers would be in danger from some of their passengers. Mr. Gluck entertained us with imitations of Jackie Gleason and Fred Flintstone and Ernest Borgnine, who were all big on TV back then, and he said he could do Lucille Ball, too, but he made her sound just like Ernest Borgnine, which really made me laugh. He wanted to be in show business, and one joke after another flew from him. I had my mom write down his name, so when he became famous, I would remember meeting him. Years later, I had reason to track him down, and though he didn't become famous, I'll never forget the first or the second time we met.

At Riverside Commons, he pulled to the curb and, before Mom could pay him, he said, "Wait, wait," and got out of the taxi and came around to the rear curbside door and made a production out of opening it for us and presenting the park with a sweep of his hand, as if he had prepared it just for us. He was a portly man with bushy eyebrows and a rubbery face made for comedy, and everything about him suggested fun, except that I noticed his fingernails were bitten to the quick.

When we were on the sidewalk and Mom paid him, he took the fare but refused the tip. "Sometimes the quality of the passengers *is* the gratuity. But here's something I want you and your boy to have." From a pocket he took a pendant on a chain. When my mom tried to refuse it, he said, "If you don't take it, I'm going to yell 'Help, police' until they come running, and I'll make the most outrageous charges, and by the time we resolve the matter down at police headquarters, it'll be too late to have your day in the park."

Sylvia laughed, shook her head, and said, "But I can't accept—"

"It was given to me by a passenger six months ago, and she told me she wanted me to give it to someone, and I asked who, and she said I would know when I met the person, but now it turns out to be two people, you and your boy. It's luck on a chain. It's good luck. And if you don't take it, then it's *bad* luck for me. Good luck for you, bad luck for me. What—you want to ruin my life? Were my jokes that terrible? Have a heart, lady, give me a break, take it, take it, before I scream for the city's finest."

There was no refusing him. After he drove away, we found a bench and sat there to examine the pendant. It had been fashioned from two pieces of Lucite glued together and shaped into a heart roughly the size of a silver dollar. Within the heart was a small white feather. It must have been glued there, but such an excellent job had been made of it that the feather looked fluffy, as though it would flutter inside the heart if you blew on the Lucite. A small silver eyehook, screwed into the top of the heart, received a silver chain.

"It must be really valuable," I said.

"Well, sweetie, it's not Tiffany. But it is pretty, isn't it?"

"Why did he give it to you?"

"I don't really know. He seemed to be a nice man."

"I think he likes you," I said.

"Actually, Jonah, I believe he gave it to me to give to you."

With something like awe, I took the pendant from her when she held it out to me. "You really think so?"

"I'm sure of it."

When I held the chain and allowed the dangling heart to turn back and forth, the polished Lucite looked almost liquid in the sunlight, as if the feather floated in a great drop of water that cohered magically to the eyehook. Or in a tear.

"What bird do you think it's from?" I asked. "A pigeon?"

"Oh, I expect it's from something more grand than a pigeon. Don't you think it must be from some kind of songbird, one with a particularly sweet voice? I do. That's what I think."

"Then it must be," I said. "But what'll I do with it? It's a heart, it's like a girl's jewelry."

"And you can't be seen wearing a girl's jewelry—is that it?"

"I already get teased about being skinny."

"You're not skinny. You're lean." She elbowed me in the side. "You're a lean, mean music machine."

She always made me feel like more and better than I knew myself to be. I thought then that lifting a child's spirits was something every mother did effortlessly. But as the years passed, I saw the world more clearly and knew how fortunate I was to have been brought to life by the grace of Sylvia Bledsoe.

There on the park bench, I said, "Mr. Gluck said it'll bring good luck."

"Never hurts to have some."

"He didn't say you could make a wish on it."

"That's easy luck, Jonah. Easy luck always turns bad. You want the kind of luck you have to earn."

"Maybe it'll be okay if I carry it in my pocket—you know, instead of wearing it."

"I'm sure that's fine. Or keep it in a nightstand drawer. The important thing is to keep it safe. When someone gives you a special gift, never treat it lightly. If you treat it like a treasure, then it'll be one."

When, years later, I learned who had given it to the cabbie and what it meant, the pendant would indeed prove to be a treasure.

Ten

WITH THE PENDANT IN MY POCKET, IT SEEMED that the cloud-free summer sky blazed bluer than ever. The day was warm, and this part of the city looked cleaner than the part that we'd come from. As noon approached, the trunk shadows shrank toward the trees, and the web of branch shadows spread equally in all directions as if spooled out by spiders. The sun spangled the big pond, and through the quivers of light, we watched scores of fat koi that swam there from spring through autumn before being moved to indoor aquariums. Mom bought a twenty-five-cent bag of bread cubes, and the fish ventured right up to us, fins wimpling, mouths working, and we fed them.

I felt the most unexpected tenderness toward those koi, because they were so beautiful and colorful and, I don't know, like music made flesh. My mom kept pointing to this one and that one—how red, how orange, how yellow, how golden—and suddenly I couldn't talk about them because my throat grew tight. I knew if I talked about them, my voice would tremble, and I might even tear up. I wondered what was wrong with me. They were just fish. Maybe I was turning sissy, but at least I fed the last of the bread to them without embarrassing myself.

Almost half a century later, I feel that same tenderness toward nearly everything that swims and flies and walks on all fours, and I'm not embarrassed. Creation moves and astonishes if you let it. When I realize how unlikely it is that anything at all should live on this world spun together from dust and hot gases, that creatures of almost infinite variety should at night look up at the stars, I know that it's all more fragile than it appears, and I think maybe the only thing that keeps the Earth alive and turning is our love for it.

That day in the park, after the koi, we walked the paths through the groves of trees and through the picnic grounds and around the baseball field. There weren't as many people as I expected, probably because it was a workday. But when we started to talk about lunch, two guys, maybe sixteen or seventeen, fell in behind us, walking close to us, moving faster if we moved faster, slowing when we did. They were talking about girls they dated the night before, how hot the girls were and things they did to them. They wanted my mother to hear. I didn't know all the words they used, didn't understand everything they were bragging about having done, but I knew they were being rotten. That kind of thing didn't happen often back then. It just didn't. People wouldn't tolerate it. People weren't so afraid in those days. I threw the two trash talkers a couple of mean looks, and my mother said, "No, Jonah," and kept walking toward the Kellogg Parkway exit from the Commons. But the braggarts talked filthier and started to comment on my mother's shapeliness.

Finally she stopped and turned to them, one hand in her purse, and said, "Back off."

One of them was a white kid, the other a mulatto, which was a word we used back then, meaning half black, half white. They were cocky and grinning, hoping to terrify her a little if nothing else.

The white one raised his eyebrows. "Back off? This here's a public park, sugar. Ain't it a public park, bro?"

His friend said, "It's damn sure public. Man, the front view's even more righteous than her ass."

My mom raised her purse, her hand buried in it, and said, "You have a death wish?"

The white guy's grin went from Cheshire to shark. "Sugar, there ain't hardly any legal guns in this city, so what you've got in that purse is just a tampon."

She stared at him as if he were a cockroach with pretensions, standing upright and talking, but a cockroach nonetheless. "Listen, shithead, do I look like some schoolteacher who cares what the law says? *Look at me.* You think I'm some hotel maid or dime-store clerk? Is that really what I look like to you, asshole? What I've got is a drop gun, no history to it. I kill you both, throw down the piece, and when the jackboots show up, I tell 'em *you* pulled the heat, it was robbery, but you fumbled, dropped it, I snatched it, thought you might have another one, so I used it. Either you walk away or we do it now, I don't care which."

All the wicked fun had gone out of their grins. They looked now as if they were wincing in pain, though there was cold fury in their eyes. I didn't know how it might go, even in bright sunshine with other strollers in view, but my fear was exceeded by an exhilarating amazement. Sylvia's performance had been so convincing that she almost seemed to be someone other than my mom, who never used bad language and who was as likely to be carrying a gun as I was likely to have earned a black belt in karate.

The two creeps salvaged their pride by insulting her— "Bitch" and "Skank" and worse—but they backed off and turned away. We stood watching them until we were certain they wouldn't come back.

My mother said, "Just because you heard me use a couple of nasty words doesn't mean you ever can."

I was speechless, but for different reasons from the one that had rendered me silent by the koi pond.

"Jonah? Did you hear me?"

"Yes, ma'am."

"Then tell me what I said."

"Not to use nasty words."

"Do you understand why I used them?"

"You faked out those guys."

"I did, didn't I?"

"You faked them out big-time."

She smiled and took her hand out of her purse and zippered the purse shut and said, "How do you feel about lunch?"

"I'd like some."

Surrounding Riverside Commons were fancy homes, but we had to walk only ten minutes or so to some shops and other businesses.

We had gone about a block when I asked, "What's a tampon? That guy said you didn't have a gun, all you had was a tampon."

"It's nothing, just a kind of sponge."

"You mean like the one on the kitchen-sink drainboard?"

"Not exactly like that."

"Like the ones they use at the car wash over on Seventh Street?"

"No, not that big."

"Why would he think you had a sponge in your purse?"

"Well, because I do. Women do."

"Why do you carry a sponge in your purse?"

"I like to be prepared."

"Prepared for what? You mean like if you spill something?"

"That's right."

"Have you ever needed it?"

"Sometimes."

"You're a very neat person," I said. "I try to be neat, too."

We were passing a bus stop, and she said she needed to sit down on the bench, and when she sat there, she started laughing so that tears came to her eyes.

Sitting beside her, looking around but seeing nothing hilarious, I said, "What's so funny?"

She shook her head and took a Kleenex from her purse and blotted her eyes. She tried to stop laughing but couldn't, and finally she said, "I was just thinking about those two idiot delinquents."

"They weren't funny, Mom. They were scary."

"They were scary," she agreed. "But silly, too, in a way. Maybe I'm just laughing with relief, neither of us hurt."

"Boy, you sure faked them out."

She said, "And you kept your cool."

When she finished blotting her eyes and blowing her

nose, she tossed the Kleenex in a waste can beside the bench.

I said, "Are you sometimes able to fool idiots like them because the tampon sponge is shaped like a gun?"

That started her laughing again. I decided she had a case of the giggles, like when something strikes you a lot funnier than it really is but then for some reason *everything* seems funny until finally the giggles go away, sort of like hiccups.

Between giggles she said, "Honey . . . tampon isn't . . . a nasty word. But you . . . shouldn't use it anyway."

"I shouldn't? Why?"

"It's not a word . . . little boys . . . should use."

"How old do I have to be to use it?"

"Twenty-five," she said, and just the number made her laugh harder.

"Okay, but is it still all right to say *sponge*?"

And there she went again.

Soon some people came along who were waiting for the bus, and we got up and let them have the bench and continued toward the shops. Walking seemed to cure my mom, and I was glad for that. I'd worried that the two delinquents might show up, because I was certain Mom wouldn't fake them out again if she was unable to stop giggling.

We couldn't afford to dine out often, and when we did

dine out, we always went to the lunch counter in Woolworth's, because as an employee Sylvia got a discount. That day, however, we went to a real restaurant, which she said was French, and I was relieved when it turned out they spoke English. The place had a holding bar with a scalloped canopy and a big mirror at the back, a black-and-white checkerboard floor, black tables and chairs with white tablecloths, and black booths with black-vinyl cushions and white cloths. The salt and pepper shakers were heavy and looked like crystal, and I was afraid to use them because if I broke one it would probably cost a fortune.

They had a few items for kids, including a cheeseburger, so of course I ordered that with fries and Coca-Cola. My mom had a green salad with sliced chicken breast on top and a glass of Chardonnay, and then we had what I called the best pudding in the history of the world and what Mom called crème brûlée.

We were waiting for that dessert when I leaned across the table and whispered, "How can we afford this?"

She whispered, "We can't. We aren't paying."

Clutching the edge of the table, I said, "What'll they do to us when they find out?"

"We're not paying, your father is."

Alarmed, I said, "He's not coming back?"

"You know that quart mayonnaise jar he puts his pocket

change in every night? When I packed his things for him, I didn't pack that."

"Maybe he'll come back for it."

"He won't," she said with conviction.

"But isn't it wrong to take his money?"

"No, it's his security deposit."

"His what?"

"Landlords make you put down a security deposit, some hard cash, when you move in, so if you damage the apartment before you move out, they already have the money to cover it and don't have to chase you for it. Your father never paid his share of rent since he moved back in, and he did some damage yesterday. He sure did some damage. So I kept his jar of change as a security deposit, and now he's buying us a fancy good-bye lunch."

Years would pass before I had crème brûlée again and could learn if it really was the best pudding in history or if it just tasted so good because of the circumstances. Nothing could have been better, after all, than the gift of an expensive good-bye lunch from my father without him there to ruin it.

That afternoon, we saw a funny movie starring Peter Sellers, and that evening I spent with Mr. and Mrs. Lorenzo, where I fell asleep on their sofa with Mr. Gluck's pendant held tightly in my right hand. Sometimes I half woke and thought I could feel the feather fluttering softly. When my mother came home after midnight, following a four-hour set at Slinky's, Mr. Lorenzo carried me up to our apartment, and I was so sleepy that Mom tucked me in bed in my underwear rather than make me get into pajamas. She wanted to put the pendant safely in a nightstand drawer, but I held fast to it.

I dreamed of a great white bird as big as an airplane, and I rode on its back with no fear of falling, the world sparkling below, forests and fields and mountains and valleys and seas where ships sailed, and then the city, our city. People looked up and they pointed and waved, and I waved back at them, and it was only when the bird began to sing that I realized it wasn't as big as an airplane anymore and wasn't in fact a bird anymore, but was instead my mother dressed all in flowing white silk, with wings more beautiful than those of a swan. Carried safely upon her back, I could feel her heart beating, her pure heart beating so steady and strong.

Eleven

THE FOLLOWING SUNDAY, JUNE 12, GRANDPA AND Grandma drove downtown in their 1946 black Cadillac Series 62 Club Coupe, which they'd bought nineteen years earlier and which Grandpa had maintained in as-new condition. It was a big boat of a car yet sleek, with enormous bullet-shaped fenders front and back and fastback rooflines. Cadillac never made a car as cool thereafter, especially not when they went finny. Teddy and Anita took us to their place for an early celebration of my birthday, which turned out to be memorable.

They were amazed by my eidetic memory for music, which matured in me only as I had learned the piano from Mrs. O'Toole. On his piano in the front room, Grandpa Teddy played a number he was sure that I couldn't have heard before, "Deep in a Dream," written by Will Hudson and Eddie DeLange, who had a band together for a few years in the 1930s. He played it superbly, and when he finished, I played it with my limited skills and strained reach, but though I could hear the difference between us, I was thrilled to be able to follow him at all. He tested me with a couple of other pieces, and then we sat to play together. He took the left hand of the board plus the pedals, and I took the right, which was a trick but one that worked, and we ran through a tune I already had heard often, Hudson and DeLange's "Moonglow," and didn't make one mistake in tempo or chords or melody, sweet and smooth to the end.

We might have sat there for hours, but what I think happened is that I was preening too much, and nobody wanted to indulge me if healthy pride in accomplishment might be souring into conceit. My grandparents had taught my mother—and she had taught me—that when you did anything you should do it well, not for praise but for the personal satisfaction of striving to be the best. I was young and only now discovering my talent, and I was exhilarated and prideful and probably getting obnoxious.

Grandpa Teddy abruptly stood up from the piano and said, "Enough. It's my day off. Jonah and I are going for a little walk before lunch."

The day was warm but not suffocating. The street

maples, which would be scarlet by October, were green now, and a faint breeze trembled the leaves, so that on the sidewalk, patterns of light and shadow quivered like dark fish schooling in sun-spangled water, reminding me of the koi in Riverside Commons.

Grandpa Teddy towered over me, and he had a deep voice that made me sound like a chipmunk. He was as stately in his bearing as a grand ocean liner, while I was a bouncing little boat with a buzzing outboard motor, but he always made me feel that I belonged with him, that there was nowhere else he would rather be. We talked about all kinds of things as we walked, but the purpose of that stroll was what Grandpa Teddy had to say about my father.

"Your mother gave you a new apartment key."

"Yes, sir. She did." I took it from a pants pocket and dangled it, sunlight winking off the bright brass.

"Do you know why the locks were changed?"

"Tilton."

"You shouldn't call your father by his first name. Say, 'My father.'"

"Well, but it doesn't feel that way."

"What way doesn't it feel?"

"I mean, it doesn't feel like he's my father."

"But he is, and you owe him some respect."

"You feel more like my father."

"That's sweet, Jonah. And I give thanks every day that you're in my life."

"Me, too. I mean, that you're my grandfather."

"Your father isn't the easiest man to keep your equilibrium with. You know equilibrium?"

"Yes, sir. Like balance."

"It isn't easy to keep your balance with him, but you always have to walk a line of respect because he's your father."

As we progressed, we passed people sitting on their porches, and they all called out to Grandpa Teddy, and he called back to them and waved. Sometimes drivers of passing cars tooted their horns or passengers shouted his name, and he waved to them, and we met a few people walking their dogs or just out for some fresh air, and they had to talk with him and he with them. In spite of all that, he kept coming back to the subject at hand.

"You have to walk a line of respect, Jonah, but you also have to be cautious. What I'm going to say to you isn't meant to make you think any less of your father. I would feel terrible if it did. But I would feel even worse if I didn't say this—and then had reason to regret holding my tongue."

I understood that whatever he told me would be something I must take as seriously as anything that I heard in church. That's what it felt like—as if Grandpa was churching me not on the meaning of a psalm or the story of Bethlehem, but on the subject of my father.

"Your mother is a wonderful woman, Jonah."

"She's perfect."

"She just about is. None of us is absolutely perfect in this world, but she's but a breath away from it. She and I were once miles apart in our estimation of your father, but now it's an inch or two. But it's an important inch or two."

He stopped and looked up into a tree for a long moment, and I looked up, too, but I couldn't see what interested him. There wasn't a squirrel up there or any bird, or anything.

When we started walking again, he said, "I hope this is the right way to say it. Your mother's current assessment of your father is that he's basically a good man, means well, wants to do what's right, but he's damaged by some bad things that happened to him as a child, and he's weak. I agree with the weak part. There's no way to know if what he says happened to him as a boy actually happened. But even if it did, bad things happen to all of us, and that doesn't mean we can hurt others just because we ourselves have been hurt. Are you with me so far?"

"Yes, sir. I think so."

"Your father's going to divorce your mother."

I almost broke into a dance. "Good. That's good."

"No, son. Divorce is never good. It's sad. Sometimes it might be necessary, but never good."

"Well, if you say so."

"I do. And these days it's no-fault. If there's no property to split—and there isn't—and if he doesn't want custody of you or even visitation rights—which he doesn't—then it's not even necessary for your mother to agree."

"She should agree."

"It'll happen just the same. Anyway, when marriages fall apart, some people sometimes get bitter, they get very angry."

"Not my mom."

"No, not her. But sometimes people can get so angry, they do foolish things. Sometimes the fight in court is about the children, one of them trying to punish the other by taking away the children."

Alarmed, I halted. "But you said he doesn't want me. And if he does, he can't have me. I won't go. Never."

Grandpa Teddy put a hand on my shoulder. "Don't worry, son. No judge in this city would take you away from a woman like Sylvia and give you to your father."

"Really? You're sure?"

"I'm sure. And he *says* he doesn't want you, but he's a man who says all kinds of things he doesn't entirely mean. Sometimes people do reckless things, Jonah, they don't want to leave it to a court, they take matters into their own hands."

"Could he do that? How would he do that?"

We had walked almost to Saint Stanislaus, and Grandpa said, "Let's rest a bit on the church steps there."

We sat side by side on the steps, and he took a pack of Juicy Fruit gum from a pocket and offered me a stick, but I was too scared to want any. Maybe he was a little scared, too, because he didn't want any chewing gum, either, and he returned the pack to his pocket.

"Let's say you're walking home from the community center one day, and your father pulls to the curb in a car and wants to take you somewhere. What should you do?"

"Where would he want to take me?"

"Let's say it was somewhere you'd like to go, maybe to a movie or for a milk shake."

"He wouldn't take me anywhere like that. He never did before."

"Well, maybe he wants to make things right with you, apologize for things he's done by taking you out for some fun."

"Would he? I don't think he would."

"He might. He might even have a present for you, wrapped and on the passenger seat. You'd just have to get in the car and unwrap it while you go to the movie or for that milk shake."

The air was warm and the steps were warm from the sun, but I was cold. "I've got to walk the line you talked about, give him respect."

"So what should you do?"

"Well . . . I'd have to ask Mom, was it all right to go with him."

"But your mother isn't there."

"Then he'd have to come back later, after I talked to her, but even if Mom said it was all right, I wouldn't want to go."

Three crows landed on the sidewalk and hopped along, pecking at grains of rice from a wedding the day before, each of them studying us warily with glistening black eyes.

We watched them for a while, and then I said, "Would Tilton . . . would my father ever hurt me?"

"I don't believe he would, Jonah. There's an emptiness in him, a hollow place where there shouldn't be, but I don't think he'd hurt a child. It's your mother he might hurt by taking you away from her."

"I won't let that happen. I just won't."

"That's why I wanted us to talk, so you wouldn't let it happen."

I thought about the two trash-talking delinquents in Riverside Commons a few days earlier. "Boy, it's always something, isn't it?"

"That's life. Always something, more good than bad, but always interesting if you're paying attention."

He offered me the gum again, and I took a stick, and so did he. He took the paper and foil from me, and he folded them with his paper and foil, and he put them in his shirt pocket.

After we chewed the Juicy Fruit for a minute or two and watched the crows at the rice, I thought of Mr. Gluck's pendant and took it from my pocket and showed it to Grandpa.

"Isn't that a marvelous piece of work." He took the pendant and dangled it in the sunlight and asked where I'd gotten it. When I told him, he said, "Son, that is a classic story of the city if I ever heard one. Just classic. You've got a lasting conversation piece."

"What kind of feather do you think it is, Grandpa?"

He gently twisted the chain between his fingers, so that the Lucite heart turned back and forth. "I'm no expert on feathers, but there's one thing I can say with complete confidence."

"What's that?"

"It's not an ordinary feather. It's extraordinary. Otherwise no one would've gone to the trouble of sealing it in Lucite and shaping the Lucite into a heart." He frowned at the pendant for a moment, then smiled. "I feel comfortable saying it's not a bit of juju."

"What's juju?"

"A religion in West Africa, full of charms and curses and lots of gods, good ones and bad ones. In the Caribbean, they mix it up with some Catholic bits and call it voodoo."

"I saw this old voodoo movie on TV. It scared me, so I had to turn it off."

"Nothing to be scared about, because none of it's true."

"In the movie, the voodoo wasn't on some island somewhere, it was right in the city."

"Don't give it a thought, Jonah. This piece the taxi driver gave you, it's too well meant to be anything dark and dangerous. Whatever feather this might be, you should figure it was so important to someone that they preserved it. You should keep good care of it."

"I will, Grandpa."

Returning the pendant to me, he said, "I know you will."

We got up, and the crows squawked into flight, and we walked back to the house, where lunch would soon be ready.

"The little talk we had about your father is just between you and me, Jonah."

"Sure. We don't want to worry Mom."

"You're a good boy."

"Well, I don't know."

"I do. And if you stay humble about it and remember talent is a gift you didn't earn, then you're going to be a great piano man. If that's what you want to be."

"It's *all* I want to be."

Under the maples, the black-and-white patterns of leaf shadow and sunlight didn't remind me of schooling fish in bright water, as before. They sort of looked like piano keys, not all lined up in the usual order but instead intersecting at crazy angles and shimmering with that kind of music that makes the air sparkle, what Malcolm calls banish-the-devil music.

Twelve

DURING HIS OFF-THE-RAILS PERIOD, WHEN Malcolm was twenty-two, he lost his way in grief. He began secretly using drugs. He withdrew into himself and went away and didn't tell anyone where he was going. Later, I learned that he had left the city, which was a mistake for a young man so suited to its streets. He had enough money for a year, and he rented a cabin by a lake upstate.

He smoked pot and did a little cocaine and sat on the porch to stare at the lake for hours at a time. He drank, too, whiskey and beer, and ate mostly junk food. He read books about revolutionary politics and suicide. He read novels, as well, but only those full of violence and vengeance and existential despair, and he sometimes was surprised to rise out of a kind of stupor, bitterly cursing the day he was born and the life in which he found himself.

One night, he woke past one o'clock in the morning, at once aware that he had been talking in his sleep, angry and cursing. A moment later, he realized that he wasn't alone. Although faint, a foul odor filled him with revulsion, and he heard the floorboards creak as something moved restlessly back and forth.

He had fallen asleep half drunk and had left the bedside lamp set low. When he rolled off his side and sat up, he saw a shadowy form on the farther side of the room, a thing that, to this day, he will not more fully describe than to say that it had yellow eyes, that it wasn't any child of Nature, and that it was no hallucination.

Although Malcolm is superstitious, neurotic in a charming sort of way, and undeniably eccentric, he recounts this incident with such solemnity, with such disquiet, that I've never doubted the truth of it. And I can't hope to convey it as chillingly as he does.

Anyway, he knew that his visitor was demonic and that he had drawn it to him by the acidic quality of his anger and by his deep despair. He realized that he was in grave danger, that death might be the least he had to fear. He threw back the covers and got out of bed in his underwear, and before he realized what he was doing, he went to a nearby armchair and picked up his saxophone, where he had left it earlier. He says that his sister spoke to him, though she was not there with him, spoke in his mind. He can't recall her exact words. All he remembers is that she urged him to play songs that lifted the heart and to play them with all the passion he could summon—music that made the air sparkle.

With the unwanted visitor circling him, Malcolm played for two hours, at first a lot of doo-wop but then also many numbers written long before the rock 'n' roll period. Isham Jones tunes like "It Had to Be You" and "Swinging Down the Lane." Loesser and Carmichael's "Heart and Soul." Watson and Monroe's "Racing with the Moon." Marks and Simons's "All of Me." Glenn Miller's "In the Mood." He looked only indirectly at the yellow-eyed presence, afraid that a direct look would encourage it, and after an hour of music, it slowly began to fade. By the end of the second hour, it had been dispelled, but Malcolm continued to play, played passionately and to exhaustion, until his lips were sore and his jaws ached, until he was dripping perspiration and his nose was running nonstop and his vision was blurred by sweat and tears.

Banish-the-devil music. If only it had worked as well on my father—and those with whom he eventually became associated—as it did on that yellow-eyed fiend in the lakeside cabin.

Thirteen

WE HEARD THE SIREN, BUT THERE WERE ALWAYS
sirens in the city, police zooming this way and that, weaving
through traffic in their cruisers, more sirens every year—so
my mom said—as if something was going wrong with the
country just when so many things had been going right.
The worst thing to do when you hear a siren is to go
see what it's about, because the next thing you know,
part of what it's about might be you.

It was Monday evening, eight days after the talk I had
with Grandpa Teddy. My mom didn't work Monday nights,
and we were playing checkers at the kitchen table when
the siren swelled loud and then wound down somewhere
in our block. We stayed at the game, talking about just
everything, so I don't know how long it was until the knock

came at our door, maybe twenty minutes. We had forgotten the siren by then. There was a bell, but this caller rapped so lightly we wouldn't have heard it if our apartment hadn't been so small. We went into the living room, and the rapping came again, hesitant and timid, and Mom looked through the fish-eye lens and said, "It's Donata."

Mrs. Lorenzo stood at our threshold, as pretty as Anna Maria Alberghetti and as pale as Wonder Bread, her hair disarranged, face glistening even though the evening was mild for late June. Body rigid, hands fisted and arms crossed over her breasts, she stood as though she had turned to stone the moment she'd finished knocking. Her face, her eyes were those of a woman lost, struck senseless and uncomprehending by some shock. She spoke as though bewildered, "I don't know where to go."

"What's wrong, Donata, what's happened?"

"I don't know where to go. There's nowhere for me to go."

My mother took her by one arm and said, "Honey, you're like ice." The glaze on the woman was sweat, but cold sweat.

Mom drew her into the apartment, and in a voice colored less by grief than by bewilderment, Mrs. Lorenzo said, "Tony is dead, he stood up from dinner, stood up and got this terrible look and fell down, fell dead in the kitchen." When my mother put her arms around Mrs. Lorenzo, the woman sagged against her, but her voice remained as before. "They're taking him now, they say, taking him for an autopsy, I don't know where. He was only thirty-six, so they have to . . . they have to . . . they have to cut him open and find was it a heart attack or what. There's nowhere I can go, he was all I had, and I don't know where to go."

Maybe she hadn't cried until then, maybe the shock and terror had numbed her, but now the tears came in great wrenching sobs, pent up but released in a flood. She was racked by the kind of grief that is part horror, when the mourner suddenly knows death to be not just a profound loss but also an abomination, and the wretched sounds that came from her made me tremble and raised in me a feeling of absolute helplessness and uselessness unlike anything I'd felt before.

As usual, my mother coped. She brought Mrs. Lorenzo into our kitchen and settled her in a chair at the table and pushed aside the checkerboard. She insisted that Mrs. Lorenzo had to drink something warm, and she set about making tea, all the while commiserating not in a phony way but with the right words that I could never have found and with tears of her own.

Mrs. Lorenzo was gentle and kind, and I couldn't stand watching her coming apart like that or the thought of her widowed so young. I went to a living-room window and looked out and saw the ambulance still at the curb in the crimson twilight.

I had to get out of the apartment. I don't entirely know why, but I felt that, were I to stay there, I'd start crying, too, and not just for Mrs. Lorenzo or Mr. Lorenzo, but for my father, of all people, because he had that awful emptiness inside himself, and for myself, too, because my father couldn't ever be a father. Grandma Anita was still alive, and I'd never known anyone who died. Mr. Lorenzo had been a waiter; he often got home late, and he sometimes carried me up to our apartment when I was asleep and my mom returned from work at the club, and now he was dead. I was glad my father moved out, but this was like two deaths close to each other, one the death of a neighbor, the other the death of my father-son dream, which I would have denied having, if you'd asked me, but to which just then I realized I'd still been clinging. I ran out of the apartment and down six flights of stairs to the foyer and outside to the stoop and down more stairs to the sidewalk.

The paramedics were loading the body into the back of the van ambulance. A sheet covered Mr. Lorenzo or maybe he was in a body bag, but I couldn't see him, only the shape of him. Across the street, a crowd of twenty or thirty had gathered, probably people who lived in the apartment houses over there, and they were watching Mr. Lorenzo being taken away. Some kids were over there, too, my age and younger. They chased around and danced and acted silly, as if the flashing beacons of the ambulance were holiday fireworks. Maybe if the death had occurred on the other side of the street, I'd be watching from here with different kids, acting as foolish. Maybe the difference between horror and holiday was just the width of an ordinary street.

At nine I knew about death, of course, but not as an intimate truth, rather as something that happened out there in the world, in other families, nothing for me to worry about for a long time yet. But now people I knew were going away forever. If two could go in just two weeks, three others could go in just three more—Grandpa, Grandma, and my mother—and I would be like Mrs. Lorenzo, alone and with nowhere that I belonged anymore. It was crazy, a little-kid panic, but it grew out of the undeniable realization that we're all so fragile.

I thought that I should do something for Mr. Lorenzo, that if I did something for him, God would see and approve and not take anyone from me until I was much older. I guess if I hadn't been so crazy afraid, I might have gone to church and lit a candle for him and said a few prayers. Instead I thought that I should play the piano for him, one of his favorite songs that he listened to on his stereo.

The community center stayed open until 10:30 on

Monday because it was bingo night. As one paramedic closed the rear doors of the ambulance and the other started the engine, I turned away and headed toward the Abigail Louise Thomas Room.

Perhaps in my peripheral vision, I saw him moving, paralleling me. But as long as I live, I will credit luck and the feather pendant in my pocket, because I was in a distraught emotional state that made it unlikely that I would have picked up on clues glimpsed from the corner of my eye. My father must have been among the crowd across the street, because now he paced me. When he realized that I had seen him, he didn't call out to me or wave, which would have been much less creepy. He only walked faster when I did and broke into a run when I ran.

If I made it to the community center, he might come in after me. No one there knew that my mother had thrown him out or that divorce was imminent. Sylvia didn't wash her dirty laundry in public. They knew me at the center, and they didn't know him, and if I caused enough of an uproar, they would surely call my mom.

But then I saw that he was glancing both ways along the street as he ran, checking on the traffic, looking for an opening, ready to dash across all three lanes at the first opportunity. The center was still more than a block away. His legs were longer than mine. I'd never make it there before he caught me. He wouldn't hurt me. I was his son.

Grandpa Teddy said Tilton wouldn't harm me. Might snatch me and take me away. But wouldn't harm me. To snatch me, he needed a car, surely a car. You didn't absolutely need a car in the city; and Tilton hadn't owned one. Maybe he owned one now, but he would have to drag me to it, and I'd fight all the way, and he wouldn't want that. So maybe he meant to hurt me, after all.

At the corner, one-third of the way to the community center, I turned left, heading for the alleyway behind our building. I glanced over my shoulder and saw Tilton crossing the street, dodging cars as the drivers pounded their horns and brakes squealed. He looked wild. I wouldn't make it into the back street and half a block to the rear entrance of our building before he overtook me.

Twilight slanted through the streets, fiery in the windows and painting emberglow across tenement walls, purple shadows swelling, but night already claimed the narrow alley. Not all the buildings had back entrances; some had switchback fire escapes, and where there was rear access, the security lamps above the doors were often broken. On both sides, Dumpsters rose, hulking shapes in the gloom, some lids up, some down, some stuck halfway. I climbed the side of a Dumpster where the lids were open and dropped inside, landing on slippery piles of plastic garbage bags, in a stink of rotting vegetables and God knew what else.

I knelt with my back pressed to the metal wall, trying to be still, cupping both hands over my nose and mouth, not because of the stench but to soften the sound of my breathing. His shoes slapped loud on the blacktop and on the bricks where the blacktop had worn off, and as he passed me, he was panting louder than I was. He came to a halt about where I figured the back door to our building must have been, and I listened to him muttering in frustration and making small noises for which I couldn't account.

I began to wonder if I had done the right thing by fleeing from him. He was my father, after all, not a good one but my father nonetheless. Maybe I'd misjudged his mood and was mistaken about his intentions.

When he began to curse and when my name proved to be part of it, I stopped worrying that I'd been unfair. He rattled the knob and kicked the door hard. I didn't understand what had foiled him. The superintendent had cut new keys to our apartment; but Tilton still possessed the other key, the one to the back stairs, which unlike the front entrance was kept locked. He became increasingly agitated, cursing explosively, and when he repeatedly kicked a Dumpster—not mine but one nearby—I figured he'd been drinking. The big trash bin gave off hollow drumlike beats that echoed along the alleyway—*boom, boom, boom.* A man shouted from a high window, "Knock it off!" Tilton shouted back at him, cursed him out, and the man said as if he meant it, *"I'm comin' down there, you bastard."* My father hurried away then, but no one came down to look for him. Comparative quiet settled over the alleyway, disturbed only by the muffled sounds of traffic out on the main street and by music and voices from a TV channeled through an open window overhead.

Suspicious, I waited a few minutes. But I couldn't spend the night in the Dumpster, and finally I climbed out. I half expected a shadowy figure to break from cover and rush at me, but if there were rats in the alley, they were genuine rodents, nothing more.

Above the rear door to our building, the lamp protected by a wire cage had not been broken, and by its light I saw the bent key protruding from the deadbolt lock. In his eagerness to nab me before I got back to the apartment, my father evidently had inserted the wrong key, and when it wouldn't turn, he forced it, nearly breaking it off in the lock. I wiggled it, trying to extract it from the keyway. The key was bent not just at the shoulder, but also along the blade, and its serrations were wedged in the pin tumblers. In the morning, the superintendent would need to take the lock apart to remedy the situation. In the meantime, I could return to the building only by the front entrance.

The blush of twilight had faded to maroon, but the streetlamps hadn't yet brightened. Shadows filled doorways. The headlights of passing vehicles flared off the parked cars, revealing or conjuring sinister figures inside them; it was impossible to tell which. I expected my father to throw open a car door and scramble after me or to rise up from between cars, but I made it to our building and pelted up the steps and into the foyer, almost knocking down Mr. Yoshioka.

He said, "Is it true, is the poor man dead? It cannot be true, so young."

For a moment, I thought he was referring to my father, but then I remembered, and I assured him that Mr. Lorenzo had died.

"I am so entirely sorry. He was a nice man. Thank you very much."

I said he was welcome, although I didn't know what he might be thanking me for, and I ascended six flights to the fourth floor. I didn't dare to race up because maybe my father was waiting for me around one turn or another, but neither did I proceed slowly, because maybe he would suddenly appear on the stairs behind me.

Fourteen

WHEN I LET MYSELF INTO THE APARTMENT AND closed the door and engaged both deadbolts, I'd been gone no more than ten minutes. Mrs. Lorenzo still sat at the kitchen table with my mother, and she still wept, though the wrenching sobs had passed for now. Neither of them knew that I'd gone out.

At one of the living-room windows, I peered down at the swarming street as light bloomed in the frosted glass of the lamps, and they seemed to float like aligned and miniature moons in the early dark. Every pedestrian interested me, every driver of every vehicle, and though none of them proved to be my father, I didn't grow bored with sentry duty. If he had come back once, he would come back again, as though a bad-juju penny rattled within the hollow space inside him, a penny with two heads and both of them my face, by its every clink and spin reminding him of me and of how my mother would be devastated if she lost me.

After a while, my mom came to me and put a hand on my shoulder and said, "Are you all right, Jonah?"

That didn't seem to be the best time to tell her about Tilton. Mrs. Lorenzo needed her.

"Yeah, I'm okay. It's awful, though. How's Mrs. Lorenzo?"

"Not good. Tony was an immigrant. He has no family in America. Donata's father died when she was young, and she has no brothers or sisters, and I gather her mother's . . . well, difficult. There's nowhere she can go but back to their apartment, and she can't face that right now. Maybe tomorrow. I've asked her to stay the night with us. She can have your bed, and you can sleep in mine."

I looked out at the street and then at the sofa, to which I pointed. "Can I sleep there?"

"The bed would be more comfortable."

"Well, sleeping with your parents, a parent, whatever, it's for scared little kids, it's little-kid stuff."

"When did it become little-kid stuff?"

I shrugged. "I don't know. A while ago, weeks ago maybe. I mean, I'm *nine*."

Sometimes it seemed that she could look right into

my head and read my thoughts, as if my forehead were glass and my brain a neatly printed scroll. "Are you sure you're all right, sweetie?"

She never lied to me, but I didn't always measure up to her when it came to truth-telling, although this wasn't lying, not really. I intended just to withhold the truth from her for a few hours, until Mrs. Lorenzo gathered the courage to go downstairs to her apartment in the morning.

"See, the sofa is . . . cool. Not kid stuff." I sounded so lame, and I could feel the blush burning in my cheeks, but one of the benefits of dark skin is that a blush can't give you away even to your perhaps psychically gifted mother. "The sofa is like an adventure. You know? The sofa is righteous."

"All right, Mr. Jonah Kirk. You may sleep on the sofa, and I'll lie awake all night worrying about how soon you'll want to drive a car and date grown women and go away to war."

I hugged her. "I'm never going away anywhere."

"You go strip your bed and put on clean sheets for Donata. I've got to dash downstairs and get her pajamas and some other things she needs. She just falls to pieces at the thought of going back there even if I'm with her."

Here at the front of the building, they hadn't heard the ruckus in the alleyway, Tilton kicking the Dumpster and cursing.

"You shouldn't go there alone." When she gave me an odd look, I said, "I mean, not this late."

"Late? It's twenty past nine and it's just downstairs. If this was a work night, sweetie, I'd be coming home alone *hours* later, just me with a pretend gun in my purse."

"Well, but Mr. Lorenzo *died* down there."

Although we were speaking softly, she glanced toward the kitchen and lowered her voice further. "He didn't die of disease or anything, Jonah. And in this family, we believe there's only one ghost this side of Heaven, and it's the holy one."

Having committed myself to withholding the news of my father's return until Mrs. Lorenzo was able to go home, I felt that the manly thing would be to stay the course and not complicate the situation by dumping my fears onto my mom when she still had to help Mrs. Lorenzo get through the shock of being widowed. It made sense at the time. A great many things make sense when you're nine years old that appear senseless years later. As justification, I can only say that during the eventful summer of 1966, I became concerned for the first time about behaving in a manly fashion, no doubt out of fear that if I didn't discipline myself, I might wind up like my father, a perpetual adolescent.

"Now go change those sheets," Mom said, "and I'll be back in a few minutes."

She left the front door ajar, and I ran to it and listened to her going down the stairs. When I heard her cross the first landing, I eased the door shut and, just in case Tilton was out there, locked it to prevent him from coming in behind my back. I hurried into my bedroom and tore the sheets off the bed and carried them to the hall closet where the laundry basket was kept and grabbed the spare set of sheets and raced back to my bedroom and made the bed. I returned to the front door and stood on my toes and barely managed to look through the fish-eye lens—nobody out there—and opened the door and stood on the threshold and waited for my mom.

She seemed to be taking forever. I didn't believe there was a ghost in the Lorenzo apartment. And they had taken away the body, so there couldn't be a zombie like in the voodoo-in-the-city TV movie that I'd had to turn off. But Mrs. Lorenzo, confused and hurting, might have left her door unlocked, and maybe my father had gone in there for God knows what reason, and then my mother had walked in on him. The rest would be total horror movie.

Maybe the manly thing would be to grab a butcher knife from the kitchen and go down to the second floor to check on my mother, but I couldn't imagine what I'd say to Mrs. Lorenzo, who was in the kitchen crying again, when I burst in there and snatched the butcher knife out of the drawer. She might think I'd gone mad and meant to kill her, and that would be one shock too many, and she'd have a stroke, and then they'd haul me off to prison or the nuthatch or wherever they took crazed and dangerous boys.

I heard footsteps ascending. They sounded like the footsteps of one person, and they didn't seem to be those of someone with a gun to her head or a knife to her throat. I stepped inside, eased the door almost shut, as my mother had left it, and hurried to the window.

When Mom came through the door, she had a little travel case in which she had packed Mrs. Lorenzo's things. She closed the door and locked both deadbolts. She said, "You better put on your peejays and brush your teeth, honey. It's getting late."

"Okay, Mom."

"You'll need a blanket for the sofa."

"It's warm enough."

"To protect the upholstery."

"Oh, yeah. Got it."

Minutes later, I was lying on a blanket, on the sofa, in my pajamas, with one of the pillows from my mother's bed. The front windows remained open because we didn't have air-conditioning, and traffic noise rose from the street. I could hear my mom and Mrs. Lorenzo talking in the kitchen, but I couldn't catch enough words to make sense of what they were saying. They were taking a long time, longer than I expected, and I grew anxious about not being able to keep a watch on the street. Later, I would learn that Mom gave Mrs. Lorenzo a few Benadryl and then insisted that they each have a large glass of red wine, which I guess seemed just the right thing to an Italian lady like the widow. When they finally left the kitchen, I pretended to be sleeping, and I pretended all the time that they used the bathroom and dressed for bed. When my mother came to the sofa and whispered good-night and kissed me on the cheek, I lay there with my mouth open, breathing through it, making a soft snoring sound. Before she turned away and switched off the lights and went to her bedroom, she said, "My angel," which made me feel lowly and deceitful and the very spawn of Tilton Kirk, even though I knew that my motives were good and my heart sincere.

Lying there in the dark, with the glow of the city invoking ghostly shapes from the familiar objects in the living room, I waited until I thought Mom and the widow might be asleep before I got off the couch and felt my way to one of the windows. The flow of traffic had diminished, and there were fewer pedestrians, as well. I didn't see my father, but the longer I knelt at the window, with my arms folded on the sill, the more it seemed to me that of the people who walked past or drove by, *every one of them* appeared suspicious. More than suspicious. There had been another old movie I'd watched about two-thirds of before turning it off. Instead of zombies, the bad guys had been

seed-pod people from another world, and they had dupli-
cated real people and had taken their place; you couldn't
tell them from the people they imitated except that they
had no real emotions.

Fifteen

EVENTUALLY I RETURNED TO THE SOFA, TOO exhausted to stand an entire night watch. I dropped into a deep well of sleep and floated there until, after a while, the dream began in a pitch-black place with the sound of rushing water all around, as if I must be aboard a boat on a river in the rain.

I was lying on my left side, in the fetal position, on an uncomfortable surface, clutching something in my right fist, holding it so tightly that my fingers ached. A great fear overcame me, but of what I couldn't say, a blind terror in the blind dark of the dream, and my heart was as loud as a felt hammer on a timpani skin, beat and backbeat all but simultaneous. The object in my hand was a penlight.

Later, I would realize that no previous dream had ever included a fragrance or a flavor, but in this one I tasted blood. My lower lip was swollen, throbbing. When I licked, it stung where split.

I was holding a penlight, for what reason I don't know, as I never had possessed one in real life. Still lying on my side, I cried out, startled, when the beam revealed a face directly in front of mine, less than a foot away, a girl perhaps in her early twenties, dark hair wet with rain and pasted to her face, eyes seeming to swell from their sockets, strangled to death with a man's necktie that still cinched her throat.

Thrusting up from the darkness of the dream into the lesser darkness of our living room, I came off the sofa and onto my feet, breathless for a moment, and then inhaled with a gasp. I shuddered and put a hand to my mouth, expecting my lower lip to be split and bleeding, but it was not. Because my legs were weak, I sat down at once, grateful that I hadn't cried out in my sleep as I had done in the nightmare, hadn't awakened my mother or the widow Lorenzo.

In my mind's eye, I could still see the dead girl as clearly as I had seen her in sleep—and as in the dream about Lucas Drackman, a few months earlier, she wasn't a half-imagined phantom, but instead as vividly detailed as a portrait by Norman Rockwell. Wet hair thick and glistening with rain. Blue eyes shading toward purple, the pupils wide in death. Delicate features, pert nose formed to the perfection of the finest porcelain figurine. Generous mouth. Smooth creamy skin unmarred except for a small beauty mark at the high point of the left cheekbone.

When I'd awakened from the dream of Lucas Drackman, I had known that he murdered his parents sometime in the past, that what I'd seen wasn't prophetic, but instead a done deed. In this case, I suspected that I'd been given a predictive vision while asleep, that a day would come when I would find myself surrounded by the sounds of rushing water, enclosed in darkness with a corpse.

As I sat there on the edge of the sofa, I caught the faint scent of roses and came to my feet. Turning, I saw a woman's silhouette at one of the front windows, backlit by the night glow of the city. She was too tall to be either Mrs. Lorenzo or my mother. She said softly, "Fiona Cassidy," and I knew that she had just given me the name of the dead girl in my dream.

She moved away from the window, vanishing into shadows. When I switched on the lamp beside the sofa, I found myself alone in the living room. If she had really been there, she could not have exited so quickly. Yet I had seen her silhouette, had heard her voice. I had no doubt that she'd been present, although in what sense and to what extent I couldn't say. She wasn't a ghost, but she was something more than I had taken her to be on the day when she had first appeared to me, dressed all in pink and promising a piano.

Sixteen

I SHOULD HAVE TOLD MY MOTHER ABOUT TILTON chasing me into the alleyway, but for the next two days, she occupied herself with Mrs. Lorenzo, helping the widow to arrange the funeral, contacting the life-insurance company regarding Tony's small policy, which would give the widow only a few years of security, and packing the deceased's clothes to take them to the Salvation Army because Mrs. Lorenzo had no heart for the job. At the end of each day, Mom was tired and sad, and I didn't want to burden her with my worries.

By the time we returned to our usual schedule, I was hesitant to tell her what Tilton had done. By delaying, I had to some extent deceived her, which I had never done before, at least not about anything serious. Although my reason for doing so was honorable, I was concerned that she would in the future wonder what else I might be withholding from her, that this would in some way permanently change our relationship.

Of course, I *was* keeping another secret: Miss Pearl, my guide through dreams of terrors both past and pending. The mysterious woman had instructed me to tell no one of Lucas Drackman, and I understood intuitively that the same discretion was required of me regarding Fiona Cassidy. Honoring Miss Pearl's instructions meant being less than entirely forthcoming with my mother, and though that wasn't the same thing as lying, it was not worthy of a well-churched boy. Miss Pearl had given me a piano, yes, but my mother had given me *life*.

I adored my mother and hoped that she would always trust me. And so, having delayed telling her about my father's pursuit of me, I made the further mistake of deciding to remain silent on the subject. Most nine-year-old boys want to be seen as more grown up than they are. Considering that I was now the man in the house, I convinced myself that I alone should deal with Tilton if he came around again, that I *could* deal with him, and that in this troubled time, I needed to spare my mother from unnecessary anxiety.

The nation seemed to be sliding toward one existential crisis or another. Growing casualties in Vietnam spawned street demonstrations against the war, and a seventy-two-year-old woman named Alice Herz had even set fire to herself in protest. The previous year, during Martin Luther King's march from Selma to Montgomery, Alabama, marchers were beaten and trampled by horses ridden by state troopers, and a shocked nation watched it all on television. Malcolm X was assassinated, not by racist whites but by other blacks, probably Black Muslims, and everywhere you looked, there was discontent and anger, envy and loathing. Respect for authority was down, crime was up, and illegal drugs were being peddled as never before. Not in our neighborhood but in another part of the city, there had been race riots, as there had also been in Watts, a Negro section of Los Angeles, in which thirty-four people died and whole blocks were burned to the ground. And this summer was no less violent than the last one. A couple of times, I'd overheard Mom worrying about the future with Grandpa and Grandma, not about her prospects as a singer but about my safety and about the war and about what might be in store for all of us. By comparison, my father seemed to be more of a nuisance than a threat.

The summer wore on, hot and humid and eventful. Search-and-destroy missions in the Mekong Delta of Vietnam led to nightly death tolls reported on the evening news. In July, in Chicago, Richard Speck stabbed and strangled eight student nurses in their dormitory. On the first day of August, an honor student named Charles Whitman climbed to the top of the twenty-seven-story University of Texas tower and with a rifle killed sixteen and wounded thirty, an unprecedented slaughter that alarmed the nation because it felt not like an aberration but like the start of something new.

Mom came home from her job at Woolworth's one afternoon and found that I, having returned early from the community center, sat mesmerized by TV-news film of the war and the raging riots. I was only nine, but I think even before I started to recognize the tumult in the world, I already had an awareness of how unstable life could be, born in part from my father's inconstancy but also from the fact that, in spite of my mother's undeniable talent and drive, her quest for a career as a singer encountered setback after setback. The L.A. fires, the explosions in Vietnam, the gunfire in both places, the dead bodies in streets foreign and domestic, the crimes of Lucas Drackman and the death-to-come of a girl named Fiona Cassidy, Mr. Lorenzo standing up from the dinner table and dropping dead of a heart attack, the two trash-talking thugs who followed Mom and me through the park earlier in the summer, Speck, Whitman: All of it came together like many different winds joining forces and spinning into one tornado, so that, sitting there in front of the television, I suddenly felt that everything I knew and loved might be blown away, leaving me alone and vulnerable to threats beyond counting.

Riveted by the spectacle of destruction on the screen, I said, "Everybody's killing everybody."

Mother stood watching the TV for a moment and then switched it off. She sat beside me on the sofa. "You okay?"

"Yeah. I'm all right."

"You sure?"

"It's just . . . You know. All this stuff."

"Bad news."

"Real bad."

"So don't watch it."

"Yeah, but it's still happening."

"And what can you do about it?"

"What do you mean?"

"The war, the riots, the rest of it."

"I'm just a kid."

"I'm not a kid," she said, "and I can't do anything about it, except sit here and watch it."

"But you turned it off."

"Because there's something else I *can* do something about."

"What?"

"Mrs. Lorenzo's all alone, so I asked her to dinner."

I shrugged. "That's nice."

She turned on the TV but muted the sound. People were looting an electronics store, taking TVs and stereos.

"There's something you need to understand, Jonah. For every person who's stealing and setting fires and turning over police cars, there are three or four others in the same neighborhood who want no part of it, who're more afraid of lawbreakers than they are of the law."

"Doesn't look that way."

"Because the TV only shows you the ones who're doing it. The news isn't *all* the news, Jonah. Not by a long shot. It's just what reporters want to tell you about. Riots come and go, wars come and go, but under the tumult, day after day, century after century, millions of people are doing nice things for one another, making sacrifices, mostly small things, but it's all those little kindnesses that hold civilization together, all those people who live quiet lives and never make the news."

On the silent TV, as the face of an anchorman replaced the riots, I said, "I don't know about that."

"Well, I do."

The anchorman was replaced by a wind-whipped rain-lashed town over which towered a giant funnel cloud that tore a house apart in an instant and sucked the ruins off the face of the Earth.

"When weather's big news," my mother said, "it's a hurricane, a tornado, a tidal wave. Ninety-nine-point-nine percent of the time, Mother Nature isn't destroying things, she's nurturing us, but that's not what gets ratings or sells papers." She switched off the TV again. "What do you want to be, Jonah—news or nice?"

"Nice, I guess."

She smiled and pulled me against her and kissed the top of my head. "Then help me get ready for Mrs. Lorenzo. You can start by setting the table for dinner."

A few minutes later, in the kitchen, as I was putting the plates on the place mats, I said, "Sooner or later, do you think my dad's going to be news?"

She recognized the implication that I thought him incapable of being nice. "Be respectful, Jonah."

I figured she knew the answer as well as I did.

Seventeen

THE FOLLOWING MORNING, AFTER MOM HAD left for Woolworth's, I carried the kitchen trash bag to the alleyway behind the apartment building. The sky had lowered, as smooth and gray as concrete, as if the entire city had been roofed over and enclosed in a structure of fantastical dimensions. The air was still when I stepped outside, but as I tossed away the trash and turned from the Dumpster, a cat's paw of wind came along the center of the littered alley, leaving most debris undisturbed, batting before it only a sphere about the size of a golf ball. It rolled to a stop in front of me, as the breeze died, and I saw that it was an eyeball. Not a real eye, this was one that might have once been sewn to a stuffed toy.

The orb looked up at me from the pavement. I didn't

remember bending down to retrieve it, but the next thing I knew, I held the object in my right hand. It was made of neatly stitched furry fabric and filled with some spongy material, overall beige, though affixed to it was a circle of white felt that bore a small blue disc at its center. Beige threads, with which it had been attached to some plush toy, trailed from it.

Perhaps because of the recent strange events and disturbing dreams, I was disposed to regard the eye as if it were not merely litter, as if it must have some ominous significance. As it gazed at me from the cupped palm of my right hand, I didn't realize that the sounds of the city were diminishing, until suddenly I became aware that a profound silence had fallen over the alleyway. For an instant, I thought that I had gone deaf, but then I heard myself say, "What's happening?" The silence was real, not a failure of perception, as though the metropolis had never been a human habitat, as if it were instead a vast clockwork mechanism that, after centuries of reliable performance, had exhausted the tension of its mainspring.

I glanced toward one end of the alleyway, then toward the other, wondering at the absence of traffic. In the warm August morning, many windows were open in the surrounding apartment buildings, though no voices issued from them, no music, no sounds of activity whatsoever. From the sky: no jet roar, no chatter of police helicopters.

When I turned my attention once more to the faux eye in my hand, I could not dismiss the ludicrous conviction that it could see me. It was inert materials, crafted by human hands, just fabric and thread and a bit of colored plastic, and yet I felt watched—and not just watched but also pondered and analyzed and judged—as if every detail this eye beheld was transmitted to some remote and highly curious entity that, but for me, was the only living creature still afoot in this silent city of stilled pendulums and frozen gears.

As I recount this, at the age of fifty-seven, I remain full of childlike wonder, arising every day to the expectation of mysteries and miracles. When I was nine years old, I wasn't such an unflagging romantic and delighted believer as I have now become, but that boy possessed the capacity for enchantment and awe that made it possible for time and experience to mold him into me.

I swear that when I closed my fist around that fabric eye, I felt it roll from side to side, as though seeking some gap between my clenched fingers that would provide it with at least a narrow view of me. As if my spinal fluid had been replaced with a refrigerant, a chill climbed vertebra to vertebra from the small of my back to the base of my skull.

Moving toward the nearest Dumpster, remembering what Grandpa Teddy had said about juju, I intended to throw the eye into the trash, but before I could fling it away, I realized that the wiser course might be to retain possession of the thing, so that I would always know its whereabouts and could keep it in a container to ensure it remained blind to my activities. If memory serves me well, this bizarre notion came to me less as a thought than as whispered words in the vaguely familiar voice of a woman, a voice hardly louder than a breath in the inexplicable stillness of the city.

Among the debris in the alleyway lay a discarded empty pint of whiskey and the brown-paper bag in which it was now only partially concealed. I left the bottle, replaced it with the eye, and twisted shut the neck of the bag.

Sound quickly returned to the world, faint at first, but within a few seconds rising to the usual level of a metropolis populated by industrious—or at least restless and bustling— citizens. I stood there for a minute, listening, wondering, no longer chilled but mystified and wary.

After using a key to let myself in through the alley entrance of the apartment building, I decided not to use the back stairs, because I half expected to find Tilton waiting for me on the landing where Mom had put his packed suitcases back in June. I imagined that he might have with him a chloroform-soaked rag with which to subdue me and a steamer trunk in which he would take me away forever.

I followed the first-floor hall to the front stairs and, having totally spooked myself, sprinted two flights before discovering a woman who was halfway up the third flight. She was dressed all in black, her long hair black as well. On the handrail, her pale left hand appeared as well formed as the finest porcelain.

She heard me, paused, and looked back. Blue eyes shading to purple. Pert nose formed to perfection. Generous mouth. Small beauty mark at the high point of the left cheekbone. Here stood the dead girl from my dream, still alive, no throttling necktie cinched around her throat. Fiona Cassidy.

In my surprise, I merely gaped at her, holding the twisted neck of the paper bag as if I might offer her the contents, and no doubt I appeared simpleminded. She neither smiled nor frowned, and without a word, she continued climbing the stairs.

I left the stairwell then, hoping she wouldn't suspect that I was especially interested in her. I didn't allow the door to close entirely, but stood in the second-floor hallway, listening to her ascend, and when I thought she had passed the third floor and had continued toward the fourth, I returned to the stairs to follow her as stealthily as possible.

Eighteen

FIONA CASSIDY WENT PAST THE FOURTH FLOOR, on which I lived with my mother, went past the fifth, where Miss Delvane wrote her magazine articles and researched her rodeo novel, where also Mr. Yoshioka led his quiet and perhaps tragic life in Apartment 5-C. She continued to the sixth and highest floor.

Each floor of our building offered three apartments. Two were of the size in which Mom and I lived. The third offered twice as many square feet as those smaller units and was better suited to families with more than a single child, although they were far from spacious. The superintendent, Mr. Reginald Smaller, occupied an apartment on the ground floor, leaving seventeen available for paying tenants.

Because the building offered neither an elevator nor desirable views of the city, fourth-floor units leased for less than those on the first three levels, fifth-floor units for less than fourth, and sixth-floor units for less than fifth. Back in those days, rent subsidies for the poor were a trickle, not yet the flood they would one day become. My mother received no subsidy at all and didn't want one. If the government had covered all or nearly all of the monthly cost, the sixth-floor apartments would have been filled; but when tenants had to pay their own way, they were not quick to shell out good money for the privilege of climbing ten flights of steep stairs and bathing in water that often came out of the tap lukewarm by the time that it was piped from the basement boiler to the top of the building. Consequently, rarely were more than two sixth-floor units rented, and there were periods when all three remained vacant.

Some of our neighbors kept to themselves, but even if they were inclined only to grunt when I said hello and to avoid eye contact, I knew their faces and their names. I was no less inquisitive than I was imaginative. That August, I knew only fourteen apartments were rented, and all three on the highest level were currently for lease.

At each floor, the door to that hallway featured a foot-square window, so that as you approached it, you could see whether someone was about to open it from the other side. When I stood tiptoe, I could see through that pane into the sixth-floor hall, where Fiona Cassidy just then entered 6-C.

Maybe she was considering renting and Mr. Smaller had given her a key so she could tour the unit, but I figured such a maybe was as thin as a human hair. The superintendent always accompanied potential tenants and never let them have a key until he had received the first month's rent with a security deposit.

Mr. Smaller was a jack of all trades, capable of repairing any of the building's systems, but he was an eccentric, a believer in all sorts of conspiracies. He once told me that I should trust no one, "not even God, in fact especially not God, because He wouldn't have given us life and made us a whole world to live it in if He didn't want something big and terrible in return."

Carrying the juju eyeball in a bag, I stepped silently along the hallway to 6-C. The door stood half open.

I knew that I should be cautious, that the wisest thing I could do would be to leave at once, return to our apartment, and engage both locks. I had seen Fiona Cassidy dead, however, if only in a dream, and the woman on the stairs had been no ghost. I felt that I should warn her, although I doubted that she would believe a scrawny boy who, in our first encounter, gaped at her as though he must be a simpleton.

Through the open door, I saw a shabby vestibule with yellowed and peeling wallpaper. Beyond lay an unfurnished room carpeted in cracked linoleum, its ash-gray walls streaked with rusty stains.

The city hadn't fallen silent again; the old building issued its endless settling noises, and the discordant symphony of the busy world outside penetrated its windows. But I couldn't hear any sound particular to the apartment, no footsteps, no closing of a door, no voice.

Although I was not a reckless boy, I crossed the threshold, dismayed by my boldness but compelled as if some powerful spell of mortal curiosity had been cast upon me. The lowering sky must have grown darker even in the short time since I had left the alleyway, because when I proceeded from the vestibule into the living room, the light at the windows wasn't just cheerless but steely with storm threat.

To the right lay a dining area and an open door through which I could see a portion of the kitchen. To the left, shadows as soft as crêpe de Chine swagged a windowless hallway.

With no windows open for ventilation, the air was warm and heavy and stale, woven through with old cooking odors and the reek of cat urine and the sourness of cigarette smoke that had condensed into a thin yellow film on many surfaces.

The linoleum looked as if it must be brittle and would crackle underfoot. Instead it proved to be unpleasantly spongy, as if webbed with mold, and I made hardly a sound as I went to the kitchen door and dared to look beyond. No one.

On the farther side of the living room, the hallway served a bathroom and four small bedrooms without furniture. In one of the latter, I discovered a sleeping bag beside which stood a large canvas satchel.

All of the closet doors had been standing open, perhaps as a less-than-adequate precaution against mildew growing and sporing while the apartment had remained unoccupied. I didn't believe I had overlooked any corner in which Fiona Cassidy could have hidden.

The bottom sash of the single bedroom window had been raised. A feeble influx of air couldn't stir the greasy, threadbare draperies.

Surely the young woman had not bunked here the previous night only to leap to her death in the morning. Nevertheless, with some dread, I ventured to the window and leaned out and peered down into the serviceway. No dead girl sprawled below.

If my dream ever proved in fact to be predictive, her fate was to be murdered, not to leave this world by suicide.

Turning from the window, I expected to find her behind me, but she wasn't waiting there. Heart knocking, mouth dry, wondering again at my uncharacteristic audacity, I returned to the half-open front door and stepped into the sixth-floor hallway without encountering anyone—though I suspected that my intrusion had not gone unnoticed and that there would be a price to pay for having followed the girl across that threshold.

As I reached the stairwell but before I entered it, I heard the door to Apartment 6-C slam shut. I looked back. No one. Either the door had been closed by a draft or . . . Or what? Was I to suppose that Fiona Cassidy had flown, not fallen, out of that open window to elude me and had flown back in after I'd gone? Even my spacious imagination could make no room for that possibility. And there had been no draft.

Nineteen

IN OUR APARTMENT ONCE MORE, I TOOK THE plush-toy eye from the paper bag and put it in the center of my freshly made bed, looking toward the pillows. I walked from one side of the bed to the other and back again, watching the eye, but it didn't turn to follow me.

"Idiot," I said, chastising myself for indulging in such a childish fear.

In the kitchen, I took a pitcher of lime Kool-Aid out of the refrigerator, poured a glassful, and sat at the table.

I thought about going to the community center and putting in four hours at the keyboard. School would start in less than two weeks, and after that my practice time would be limited to at most two hours in the late afternoon. Usually I couldn't wait to get to the piano and see Mrs.

O'Toole, but that day, I felt something big was happening right under my nose, something incredible, like on Christmas Eve when I still believed in Santa. Except that this was not all sparkly and hopeful and fun like Christmas; it was something closer to that old movie about voodoo in the city.

Except that this was for real. I couldn't just switch it off.

On the Formica-topped dinette table, sweat beaded the drinking glass. The droplets of water on the upper part of it were clear, glimmering, like diamonds. The beads on the lower part of the glass, which still contained the lime drink, were as green as emeralds. They were neither diamonds nor emeralds, of course; they were just beads of water, but I couldn't stop staring at them and thinking about jewels, about being rich, about how if I were rich, we wouldn't have any problems. Mom wouldn't have to work at Woolworth's lunch counter. We could *own* a nightclub, and she could sing there as much as she wanted, and we could own a record company, too, and she could be as famous and happy as she deserved to be. We wouldn't have to worry about Tilton trying to snatch me away from her, because we'd have expensive lawyers and bodyguards. We'd live in a big house on a hill somewhere, with lots of land around it and a high fence, and we'd be safe from everyone, everything, even riots and war and young punks who talked dirty to women they didn't know.

After all these years, I vividly remember that sweating glass of Kool-Aid, the anxiety that plagued me, anxiety on the trembling edge of foreboding, too much for a boy of nine to handle, and the false hope of riches that, even if it had been fulfilled, would have solved nothing.

One of the best things about growing up is that, if you can learn from experience, you come to the realization that two things matter more than anything else, truth with a lowercase *t* and Truth with an uppercase *T*. You have to tell the truth, demand the truth from others, recognize lies and refute them; you've got to see the world as it is, not as you want it to be, not as others who wish to dominate you might say it is. Embracing truth frees you from false expectations, fruitless pursuits, disappointment, pointless anger, envy, despair. And the bigger kind of Truth, that life has meaning, is the surest source of happiness, because it allows you to recognize your true value and potential, encourages a humility that brings peace. Most important, the big-*T* Truth makes it possible for you to love others for who they are, always without consideration of what they might do for you, and only from such relationships arise those rare moments of pure joy that shine so bright in memory.

Little more than two months past my ninth birthday, I

was many years short of understanding all of that. In our tenement kitchen, I daydreamed of diamonds and emeralds, wishing away all troubles and threats. When I finished the Kool-Aid, I washed the glass, dried it, put it away. I wiped the condensation from the dinette table. I went into the living room and stared at the TV. I didn't turn it on, which I suppose might have been a small step toward a far-off maturity.

In my bedroom, the fabric eye lay on the mattress, still gazing at the pillows. I'd been foolish to think it might be animated by juju. There was nothing supernatural about it. It was just trash.

I didn't return it to the paper bag, which lay on the floor, where earlier I'd dropped it. But I didn't throw it away. Instead, I hesitated, picked it up, circled the bed, and opened my nightstand drawer, from which I withdrew a metal box with a hinged lid.

The fancy painted box had once contained candy, a Christmas gift from Mr. and Mrs. Lorenzo the previous year. The lid featured a portrait of an Italian maiden dressed in a costume from centuries past. Flowing, gold-trimmed red script declared *La Florentine,* and below that, in a different font, blazed the word *Torrone.* The box had contained a pound and a half of almond nougat candies, a product of Italy, in three flavors—lemon, orange, and vanilla. The candy had been delicious, but of the bonbons and the colorful metal container, the latter seemed to be a greater treasure.

I kept things in the box that I valued or that intrigued me for reasons only a boy my age would understand, some more important than others. There were a dozen items, among them: a cat's-eye marble in vivid shades of gold and blue, a penny flattened by train wheels and now the size of a half dollar, the copy of the lunch check from the restaurant where Mom and I ate the day after she sent Tilton packing, a silver dollar Grandma Anita had given me when I memorized the Our Father, which she said I should spend on the day of my confirmation.

The box didn't contain the heart pendant with feather. I still kept that in a pants pocket, always with me.

I hesitated before adding the plush-toy eye to the trove. In the unlikely event that some dark magic was embodied in it, perhaps it might in some way contaminate the other items.

"Idiot." I dropped the eye in the box, and replaced the lid.

I put the box on the nightstand, rose from the bed, and turned to discover Fiona Cassidy standing in the doorway.

Twenty

I WAS CERTAIN THAT I HAD ENGAGED THE DEADBOLT on the apartment door. A couple of windows were open, but she couldn't have gotten to them either from the sixth floor or from the street.

She didn't say anything. She stared at me, expressionless, her face lovely but robotic, as if what she did next would be decided by the application of certain algorithms and computations run on printed circuit boards. Her blue-purple eyes seemed to be luminous.

I would like to say that I was worried but not afraid, though the truth is that she scared me, the way she materialized like a ghost, the way she just stood there, staring.

Instinctively, I sensed that I shouldn't speak first, that repaying her stare with a stare and silence with silence might unnerve her. But I couldn't restrain myself: "What're you doing here?"

She stepped off the threshold, into the bedroom.

"How'd you get in?"

Not deigning to answer me, she looked around the small room, paying special attention to the poster of Duke Ellington in a tuxedo—he was standing in the Cotton Club sometime in the late 1920s, with the famous murals behind him—to a framed photograph of Grandpa Teddy with Benny Goodman, to a poster of my favorite TV star, Red Skelton, dressed as Freddy the Freeloader because I hadn't found a poster of him as Clem Kadiddlehopper, the character who made me laugh the most.

She closed the door behind her, alarming me, and I said, "You better get out of here."

Returning her attention to me, still expressionless, she finally spoke. "Or what?"

"Huh?"

Her voice was soft and dead-flat. "I better get out of here—or what?"

"You don't belong here."

"Or what?" she insisted.

"You'll be in big trouble."

The lack of inflection in her voice chilled me more than would have any quality of threat. "What're you going to do—scream like a little girl?"

"I don't need to scream."

"Because you're so tough?"

"No. Because my mom will be home in a minute."

"I don't think so."

"Well, she will. You'll see."

"Liar."

"You'll see."

I began to think that her emotionless demeanor was not the truth of her, that under her surface calm was volcanic potential.

"You know what happens to little snoops?" she asked.

"I'm not a snoop."

"Bad things happen to them."

In the ashen day beyond the window, light pulsed, pulsed again, so that the building next door, just six feet away, seemed to leap closer, as if collapsing toward us, and in the aftermath of those flashes, thunder rolled deep in the throat of the sky.

The woman started around the bed, and I thought about jumping onto it and plunging across it, but I knew she'd catch me before I reached the door.

"You don't scare me," I said.

"Then you're stupid. A stupid, lying little snoop."

Backing into the corner, acutely aware of my vulnerability, I said, "I'll bite."

"Then you'll be bitten."

She was maybe five foot seven. I was a lot shorter. I felt like a pygmy, if you want to know.

As she rounded the foot of the bed and as stutters of lightning again broke across the wall beyond the window, I said, "The thing is, I saw you in a dream."

This time when thunder chased the light, it seemed to me that she had brought the storm with her, had called it forth. "How old are you, snoop?"

"What's it to you?"

"Better answer me."

I shrugged. "Going on ten."

"So you just turned nine."

"Not just."

She stopped and stood looking down at me, an arm's length away. "You dream about girls, do you?"

"Just you. Once."

"Awful young for a wet dream."

Surprised, I said, "How'd you know there was water in it? At least the sound of water all around."

Instead of answering me, she said, "Why did you follow me to the sixth floor, liar?"

"Like I said before. I recognized you from the dream. That's the truth."

At last an edge, just a thin one, came into her deadpan voice. "I don't like you, snoop. I'd love to smash your monkey face. Don't tempt me. Don't you ever follow me again."

"I won't. Why would I? You're not that interesting."

"I can turn interesting from one second to the next, snoop, more interesting than you ever want to know. You stay away from the sixth floor."

"I don't need to go up there."

"You don't want to, either, unless you're even dumber than I think. And you don't want to be talking about me to anyone, not to *anyone*. You never saw me. We didn't have this little chat. You get my point, snoop?"

"Yeah. All right. Okay. Whatever. Jeez."

She stared at me for a long moment and then looked at the La Florentine box on the nightstand. "What'd you just put in there?"

"Nothing. Stuff."

"What stuff?"

"My stuff."

"Was it something you took from my satchel or my bedroll?"

"I didn't touch your things. I just looked."

"So you say, liar. Open it."

I picked up the metal box but held it against my chest.

She wanted another staring contest, and I did my part even though her eyes were disturbing, full of wildness.

She said, "What's black on the outside and red on the inside?"

I didn't know what she meant, what she wanted. I shook my head.

From a pocket of her lightweight jacket, she took a folding knife. Switchblade. Seven inches of razor-sharp steel flicked from the yellow handle. "I'm very serious, boy."

I nodded.

"I like to cut. You believe I like to cut?"

"Yes."

"Open the box."

Twenty-one

USING THE BLADE OF THE KNIFE, SHE PROBED through the contents of the box while I held it out to her. "Just crap," she said.

"It's all my stuff."

"What—you're in training to be some junk-crazed pack rat? What did you put in here when I was watching you from the doorway?"

"The eye."

"What eye?"

"I found it in the alley. From a teddy bear or something."

She picked it up between thumb and forefinger. "Why this?"

"I don't know. It's interesting."

"Interesting? Why?"

"I don't know. It just is."

She searched my eyes again, and then she rested the point of the knife on the tip of my nose. "Why?"

I was up against the wall, nowhere to go. Fear of the knife made me speechless.

She slid the blade into my left nostril. "Be very still, snoop. You move too suddenly, you'll cut yourself. Why is this teddy-bear eye so interesting?"

"I thought it maybe had some juju."

"Juju?"

"Yeah. Juju is—"

"I know what it is. Juju eye? You're a real little freak in the making, aren't you?"

She dropped the fabric eye into the box. Sparing my nose, she stirred the contents with the blade once more, but she quickly lost interest. "Put it away."

After I put the box on the nightstand, I couldn't take my eyes off the blade.

For maybe half a minute, she didn't say anything, and neither did I, and finally she put the knife away. "Good thing you were lying about your mama coming home. If she'd walked in and seen me with that knife in my hand, I'd have used it on her and then on you. You love your mama, snoop?"

"Of course."

"Not everyone does. Mine was a selfish bitch."

I turned my attention to the window, to see if rain might be falling yet, though mostly so I wouldn't have to look at her.

"If you love your mama, then you think about what I said. I like to cut. I could make her a new face in half a minute. Look at me, boy."

No rain yet.

"Don't you dis me, boy."

I looked at her.

"You understand me, how it is, how it has to be?"

"Yeah. I understand. No big deal."

She turned away from me, crossed the room, opened the door.

I don't know why I needed to make one more revelation, except that I was a small boy, rattled, and not thinking clearly. "In the nightmare, you were dead, and I was very sorry for you."

On the threshold she turned and regarded me as when she'd first appeared: not with robotic indifference, as it had previously seemed to me, but with the contempt of a machine intelligence that despised weak creatures of flesh and blood.

"What're you trying to do with this seeing-me-in-a-nightmare shit?"

"Nothing. I felt sorry, that's all."

"Am I supposed to be afraid? Is this a threat or something?"

"No. It's just . . . the way it was. In the nightmare, I mean."

"Then maybe you better not dream anymore."

I almost spoke her name, so that she might believe me about the nightmare, but something stopped me, whether instinct or guardian angel, I can't say.

"What? What is it?" she asked, as though she could almost read my mind.

"Nothing."

Her face was simultaneously beautiful and cruel, but as I would learn in time, cruelty was the truth of Fiona Cassidy. She stared at me, and I held her stare because I thought that if I glanced away she would come around the bed again and hurt me. Finally she stepped into the hallway, leaving the door open, and moved out of sight toward the front of the apartment.

At that moment, as though she willed it to add drama to her exit, the sky loosed an entire quiver of lightning bolts, and cataclysmic thunder followed closely, rattling window glass and reverberating through the walls as if the building were a drum, and rain fell in torrents.

I stood there, trembling, mortified, having betrayed the image of myself that I had crafted and cherished. The man of the family. How absurd that seemed now. I was a boy, not a man, and the merest stick figure of a boy.

Grandpa Teddy often said that musical talent was an unearned grace, that I should give thanks for it every day, and that it was my obligation and my honor to make the most of the gift. But right then, I would have traded talent for brawn, youth for age, wishing myself a grown man, thick-necked and broad-chested, a tower of muscle.

Although I intended to give Fiona Cassidy plenty of time to leave the apartment, shame and a need for redemption compelled me to follow her sooner than might have been prudent. I hurried along the hallway to the living room, but she wasn't there. The apartment door was shut, the deadbolt engaged, which suggested that she remained somewhere in our few rooms.

Summer rain slanted under the raised sash of each front window, spattering the sill and spilling into the apartment. I closed one, then the other, and with considerable trepidation, I searched our rooms and closets and even looked under my mother's bed, and then under mine. I was relieved to find myself alone, but I was also mystified. Creepy. Definitely creepy. But nothing serious yet.

Twenty-two

WHEN MR. SMALLER, THE SUPERINTENDENT AND conspiracy theorist, failed to answer his bell, I sought him elsewhere. He might have been in any apartment, attending to repairs of one kind or another, but first I went to the basement, where he could often be found. I used the interior stairs instead of going outside to the alley entrance, and as I descended those steep wooden treads, I heard my quarry talking to himself from somewhere in the labyrinth of mechanical systems that sustained the building.

The footprint of that lower realm was the same as any floor of the apartment building, and yet it seemed larger, cavernous, partly because the pipes and boilers and electrical conduits and big fuse boxes and other equipment created a maze bewildering to one as small as me, and partly because the lighting scheme was decades old and inadequate. Shadows pooled everywhere and hung like funeral bunting along the work aisles. Here also were many unlabeled barrels and large packing crates stenciled with numbers that didn't reveal what they contained, contributing to the basement's air of mystery.

With the muffled tumult of the storm echoing down through vents that led all the way to the roof, with wind-blown rain churning at the narrow and filthy ground-level windows near the ceiling, the basement had become an even more off-putting realm than usual.

On the floor, a spider the size of a quarter scurried out of shadows and along a band of light. I froze at the sight of it. I didn't like spiders, but my aversion to this one was inexplicably strong. The encounter with Fiona Cassidy had spooked me more than any movie about space aliens or voodoo. My nerves were taut. Instead of stamping on the spider, I watched with apprehension as it crossed my path, convinced that every moment of this strange morning was fraught with occult meaning and peril, and I thought, *Worse luck than a black cat.*

When the spider vanished into shadows, I continued to follow the voice of Reginald Smaller as he grumbled to himself. I found him in the downfall of light from a portable work lamp that was hooked to an overhead water pipe, performing routine maintenance on the third of three large boilers, the one that brewed hot water and sent it to radiators throughout the building to heat the apartments. Here in the waning days of summer, when no one needed heat, Mr. Smaller was draining sediment from the bottom of the big tank, an almost syrupy sludge with which he'd filled one bucket and was now filling a second.

A short man with a big middle, he wore as usual a white tank-top undershirt, khakis with an elastic waist, and suspenders as insurance against a failure of the elastic, industrial suspenders that looked as if they had been fashioned from racehorse tack. He once said that he had been raised by a grandmother who was "a mean old cuckoo-bird," and when he was a young boy, if he displeased her, she stripped him down to his underpants and turned him out into the street to be mortified. He insisted there was nothing worse than being pantsless in public, especially if you had bandy legs and lumpy knees that made people point and laugh. In Mr. Smaller's case, I thought it was just as bad to wear a tank top, because his chest and back and arms were covered in wiry, poodle-curly hair, glossy black against his white skin, like the coat of a bear with an advanced case of mange.

When I came upon him that morning, he was on his knees beside the hulking boiler, muttering almost as if he were two people having a vigorous debate, but when he saw me, he smiled and said, "Ain't it but Sammy Davis

Junior himself. Will you sing 'What Kind of Fool Am I' for me, Sammy?"

"You know I don't sing, Mr. Smaller."

"Now, don't go pullin' my chain, Sammy. You sing all the time in Vegas when they pay you the big bucks."

"Maybe I *would* sing if I got the big bucks."

"Soon as I drain this disgustin' muck," he said, indicating the soupy stuff coming out of the boiler hose, "I'll hustle upstairs, get a couple thousand from my cookie jar. That be enough for just one song?"

"Sometimes you're really silly, Mr. Smaller."

"Yeah, I guess you won't never sing no song that cheap. How much they pay you to star in *Ocean's Eleven*?"

"About a hundred million."

He pretended to be impressed. "Why're you still in this dump?"

"Living flashy isn't my style."

"Guess it ain't." The last slop oozed out of the boiler, and he twisted shut the petcock. "Wish you really *was* Sammy Davis. Then you'd know that actor Peter Lawford. I'd sure like to talk to Peter Lawford. He knows somethin' about who really killed the president."

"You mean President Kennedy?"

"Don't mean Abe Lincoln. Lawford, he's married to that Patricia Kennedy. Tell you one thing, it weren't no Lee Harvey Oswald pulled the real trigger. Castro mighta been mixed up in it. If I had your hundred million, I'd bet it all ties back to Roswell in July of '47."

"Who's Roswell?"

"Ain't a who. Roswell is a what, a place. New Mexico. Flyin' saucer crashed there, July of '47. Some dead aliens was recovered, and maybe one alive. Government's been lyin' about it ever since."

"Wow."

Disconnecting the short hose from the boiler drain, Mr. Smaller said, "For sure the April '62 saucer crash near Vegas is part of it, 'cause it just so happens Jack Ruby was in Vegas then." When I asked who Jack Ruby was, Mr. Smaller said, "He killed Lee Harvey Oswald right after Oswald didn't kill Kennedy. Them Bilderberger bastards are mixed up in it, too."

From past conversations, I knew that the Bilderbergers were an international secret society headquartered in Geneva, Switzerland, formed to be the secret government of the world in league with the aliens from other planets who lived among us. Being only nine years old, I didn't know if the Bilderbergers were real or something Mr. Smaller invented. I thought he was a little crazy, but mostly in a nice way, and some of his stories were fun to hear. Because he was so much older than I was, I owed him respect, and I never expressed disbelief.

That morning, however, I'd been spooked by Fiona

Cassidy, who was without a doubt real and who was a more immediate threat than the Bilderbergers out there in Geneva. I hoped it would seem the most natural thing in the world when I changed the subject: "The new lady is pretty."

Getting to his feet, Mr. Smaller said, "All that's goin' wrong these days, war and riots, it's them damn Bilderbergers." He picked up a bucket of sludge in each hand and walked toward the exterior basement door, which was served by a short ramp. "All them tornadoes last year, two hundred dead, that nurse killer in Chicago, them dangerous new skateboard things, and Nat King Cole gone from lung cancer, only forty-five."

Following him, I said, "She has nice eyes, how they're blue and purple at the same time."

"Girls in silly go-go boots, miniskirts, all them weird-fangled new dances, the watusi, the frug. What kind of dance is a frug? Don't nobody fox-trot no more? It's all their plan, the Bilderbergers."

As he put the buckets down and ascended the ramp to unlock the door, I said, "I guess she's renting on the sixth floor."

Disengaging the deadbolt, opening the door, seeming to be surprised by the rain, he said, "Makes no sense in this weather. Sludge can wait. It's just sludge." Closing the door, locking it, turning, he said, "Lung cancer ate up Edward R. Murrow, too, but pardon the hell out of me if

I ain't grievin' over that, 'cause all them big-time newsmen like him ain't nothin' but puppets for the Bilder—"

He cut off in mid-word, cocked his head, and looked at me as if what I'd been saying had gotten to him on a delayed broadcast.

"Who're you talkin' about, Jonah?"

"The pretty lady in Six-C."

When I had seen her sleeping bag and satchel, no furniture or other luggage, I thought maybe she was a squatter, that she might have picked the lock and settled in until someone found her and made her leave. She seemed too good-looking for a squatter, but you never know. When she'd threatened to hurt me if I talked about her to anyone, my suspicion seemed to have been half confirmed.

Now Mr. Smaller proved me wrong. "You think she's pretty?"

"Well, sure, because she is."

"Not to me she ain't. Truly pretty's more than looks. She's got a hard, cold edge can't never be pretty. A piece of work, that one."

I knew what he meant. But now I was puzzled. "Then why did you rent to her?"

Coming down the ramp, he reminded me of a well-meaning troll in a kid's book I'd read. On the part of his head that wasn't bald, the black hair bristled everywhichway, like ragged twists of steel wool.

"Son, I don't do no rentin'. The lease agents work downtown, where corporate bastards get big pay for pickin' their noses." He stopped at the buckets, considered them, decided to leave them where they were. He walked back toward the boilers. "Black-hearted company owns maybe a hundred dumps like this. I'm just a guy gets free rent, piss-poor pay, and all the cockroaches I want in return for keepin' this here place from fallin' down on top of us."

Following him, I said, "What's her name?"

"Eve Adams."

"Are you sure?"

"So I been told. Name could be Frankenstein, for all I care. She ain't no business of mine. Ain't a renter. She gets free rent like me, but only two months, till she scrapes off all the peelin' wallpaper in Six-C, takes up the crumblin' linoleum, paints the walls. She goes place to place doin' the same. Everybody has a way of gettin' by in a hard world."

As he picked up his toolbox from beside the boiler, I said, "She doesn't look like an Eve Adams."

"Is that so? What does an Eve Adams look like?"

"Not like her. She should have a prettier name."

He stared at me for a moment and then put down the toolbox. He settled into a squat, so that we were eye to eye. "Young boys, they get crushes sometimes. Had one on my second-grade teacher. Not just how she looked. The way she was, all she was. Figured she'd wait till I growed up, so then we'd be together forever. Damn, but don't I find out she's married. Broke my stupid heart. Then what happens but she divorces him and marries some other guy. I realize she don't know—or care—how I love her. So then I hated her as best I could, but that hurt me, not her. When you grow up, Jonah, women are gonna break your heart so often, you lose count. You want my best advice? Don't let them start on you so young as you are."

I didn't have a crush on Fiona Cassidy, aka Eve Adams, who in my experience might have been a maniac or even a witch. But for two reasons, I chose not to reveal as much to Mr. Smaller. First, it was nice of him to care about what happened to my heart, and he might be embarrassed if I told him that his tender advice was misdirected. Second, and more important, he must never let the woman know that I had been asking about her. She liked to cut; I didn't like being cut. His assumption that I had a crush on her gave me reason to plead with him not to humiliate me by informing her of my infatuation.

He swore to keep my secret, and I promised to heed his advice. With a handshake we sealed our agreement: two men of the world, generations apart yet nonetheless united by our recognition that romance was perilous and that no other sadness quite equaled the sorrow of unrequited love.

Rising to his full height, Mr. Smaller morphed from

fatherly advice-giver to his more familiar role as paranoid curmudgeon. As peals of thunder rolled through the city and storm light flickered at the high basement windows, he said, "Got work to do, though it don't make no sense to do it if we're gonna nuke the Russians and they're itchin' to nuke us. War here, war there, crime everywhere, yet nobody cares about nothin' but the Beatles and some guy who paints giant soup cans and sells them as art, this movie star, that movie star, blah-blah-blah. The world's a nuthouse. It's insane. It's scary. It's—"

"—those Bilderbergers," I suggested.

"Ain't truer words ever been spoken."

Twenty-three

BECAUSE I DIDN'T FEEL LIKE MAKING MY WAY TO the community center in the rain, I should have gone down to the second floor and rung Mrs. Lorenzo's bell and joined her little day-care group. I wasn't supposed to spend more than a few minutes alone in our apartment when my mother was at work. For a boy my age, I was responsible, and my mother had no reason to worry that I would do something like play with matches and burn down the building. Nevertheless, she was more of a Bledsoe than she was a Kirk, and Bledsoes didn't leave a young child alone for extended periods of time during which he might be tempted to engage in one type of misbehavior or another.

Half a century after the fact, I better understand my potential for mischief than I did back in the day. In spite of all the trouble that found me, I wonder in retrospect why I didn't bring even more calamity down upon myself.

I knew that my mother's rules were not to be subjected to the creative interpretations that wily attorneys brought to the wording of laws that snared their criminal clients. She was a plainspoken woman who said what she meant. But after leaving Mr. Smaller to his grumbling in the basement, I convinced myself that the rule against being alone in our apartment for an extended period of time didn't apply to lingering alone for hours elsewhere in the building, as if Mom would approve of me loitering in concealment for the purpose of spying on one of our neighbors.

I took the back stairs to the sixth floor. Looked through the small window in the door. No one. Imagining myself to be as stealthy as Napoleon Solo, the Man from U.N.C.L.E., which had been a hit on TV the previous year and had fired my imagination even though the stories never made sense to me, I traveled shadow-quiet along the public hallway, Apartment 6-C to my right.

On the left, between Apartments 6-A and 6-B, a door opened to a service closet. The hinges creaked but not loudly. I entered without hesitation and drew the door shut. Fiona Cassidy could be aware of my presence only if she had been standing in her vestibule, keeping watch through the fish-eye lens in her door.

After turning on the service-closet light, I pulled down

on the dangling cord attached to a hinged ceiling trap, which swung toward me and brought with it a ladder that unfolded in sections to provide access to the building's attic.

Doubt afflicted me just then. The woman had threatened me with a knife. Hiding under a bed might be smarter than trying to learn more about her. No, no, no. I'd seen her in a dream and she'd gotten into our apartment through a locked door. She was a threat like no other. I *had* to know who she was.

I took from my pocket the heart pendant with the captured feather, and my confidence returned at the sight of it.

I was a boy who readily believed in magic, even if I didn't understand the source of its power or its purpose. Perhaps I was so easily enchanted because, as a Bledsoe, I had been born to music, imbued with it. Music—good music, great music—is itself magical, its mysterious inspiration entwined with the mystery of all things. When we are transported either by Mozart or Glenn Miller, we find ourselves in the presence of the ineffable, for which all words are so inadequate that to attempt to describe it, even with effusive praise and words of perfect beauty, is to engage in blasphemy.

At the top of the ladder, on the frame that enclosed the trap, a switch brought sour light to bare bulbs in ceramic sockets placed at wide intervals between the overhead beams. Shadows did not flee, but merely retreated and regrouped and stood sentinel.

Clearance in the attic wasn't such that a grown man could stand erect, but a boy like me had plenty of headroom. Water pipes for the sixth-floor units were routed through this space, as were electrical conduits and bathroom vents. Between the floor joists, the primitive insulating materials of previous decades had in recent years been replaced with rolls of pink fiberglass.

I pulled on the top tread, and the segments of the spring-loaded ladder folded up upon themselves with a faint protracted twang. The trap thumped softly as it nestled into its frame.

If I stepped wrong and missed the two-inch-wide edge of a joist, my foot would plunge through the insulation. If it also broke through the plasterboard ceiling, it would dangle in view of anyone below.

Fortunately, here and there, thick sheets of particleboard had been screwed to the joists, providing the equivalent of stepping stones. I carefully made my way north, to the flank of the building occupied by Apartment 6-C. The wide cooktop vent identified the kitchen below, and I settled there to listen.

Even as skinny as I was, I raised a few creaks and crackles from underfoot, though I doubted that those noises would trigger Fiona Cassidy's suspicion. The driving rain upon the roof and the wind battering the walls brought forth numerous complaints from the bones of the ancient building, among which my movements couldn't be separately discerned.

I had awakened sleeping moths, which darted now from lamp to lamp. They hovered, quivering, opening their gray robes to bare their vulnerable bodies to the light they worshipped. Between the floor joists, legions of busy silverfish no doubt lived in the layers of fiberglass insulation, on which they enjoyed dining, but only a few ventured onto the particleboard and skittered through the denim folds of my jeans. I steeled myself not to brush them noisily away.

A hole had been cut in the kitchen ceiling to accommodate the sheet-metal duct that vented smoke and odors from the cooktop all the way to the roof. The hole was more than a quarter of an inch wider on each side than the ductwork, and the gap had not been caulked. Through that narrow space, rather than by way of the duct itself, I might be able to hear activity in the room below.

Having learned patience during the months that Tilton thwarted my desire to take piano lessons, I waited without fidgeting. After about fifteen minutes, I heard muffled voices, and I was surprised when an up-flow of light came through the gap and sheathed the metal ductwork at which I listened.

If they had been looking up just before the kitchen light had been switched on, they might have seen the dim attic lampglow through these same gaps, might have realized that someone lurked above them.

I assumed that the woman's voice was that of Fiona Cassidy, although it was too muffled and distorted by intervening structures for me to identify it with certainty. I thought I caught the words *little shit* and *snoop,* but I could just as easily have imagined them. The woman did most of the talking and seemed to be the dominant one. The man spoke softly—deferentially, I thought—and for all I could tell, he might have been speaking in a foreign language.

After about ten minutes, the man left. A door closed. The woman remained, humming a tune that I didn't recognize. Soon I smelled coffee brewing. Spoon and china clinked as she stirred. She didn't switch the light off when she left the kitchen.

Moving slowly and cautiously from one island of particleboard to the next, I sought Fiona Cassidy. Eventually, through the white noise of the rain on the roof and the wind blustering around the building, I heard her singing "Paint It Black," which had been a hit for the Rolling Stones that summer. As a singer, she was no threat to my mother—or to anyone. Just as my mother never washed her dirty laundry in public, this woman should never sing outside of her apartment—if even there.

Eventually I was driven out of the attic not by her singing but by boredom. Spying on her, I expected to learn some deep and terrible secret. But life isn't as predictable as the movies. In life, deep and terrible secrets are usually revealed not when you're searching for them, but when you least expect them and are unprepared.

And if I'm going to be truthful, I have to admit, after a while, I began to suspect this strange woman knew that I was in the attic, that she was listening to me as I listened to her. When she started singing a painful version of "Hang On Sloopy," I was pretty sure she changed the word to *Snoopy.*

Twenty-four

IN SPITE OF THE RAIN, I WENT TO THE COMMUNITY
center, after all, and spent the afternoon at the piano. The
storm faded as I came home shortly before five o'clock.
The gutters no longer overflowed, and the streets were
washed clean. The windshield wipers on all the cars were
set at slow speed, and as if exhausted by the storm, motorists were not pounding their horns. The city seemed to be
winding down.

In the foyer, I found Mr. Yoshioka wiping his umbrella
dry with a white cloth. He had already taken off his
galoshes and wiped them, as well. He nodded, sort of
bowed a little, and said, "Good afternoon to you, Jonah
Kirk."

"Good afternoon, Mr. Yoshioka."

"Is it very wet enough for you?"

His smile told me that he thought this was an amusing question, and I smiled in return. "It's a good day for ducks."

"Is it?" he said. "Yes, I suppose it must be. Though I have not seen one. Have you?"

"No, sir."

Crouching to wipe up the water that he had tracked into the foyer, he said, "Perhaps even on days for ducks, they stay to the parks that have ponds."

Because the foyer featured a tile floor and because Mr. Smaller mopped it regularly on bad-weather days, I had never thought to clean up after myself like this. In fact, neither had anyone else in the building except Mr. Yoshioka.

He picked up his galoshes and his furled umbrella, half bowed to me again, and said, "Let us hope tomorrow is a day for songbirds."

"Let us hope." I sort of bowed to him and immediately wished I hadn't, afraid that he might think I was mocking him, which I wasn't.

He climbed the stairs toward the fifth floor. Because I was embarrassed to leave a puddle of rainwater on the floor, I didn't move until he was at least four flights ahead of me.

In our apartment, I put the wet umbrella in a pot that stood beside the door for that purpose, and I set my galoshes to dry on a rubber mat beside the pot.

By then I had realized that Mr. Yoshioka lived in 5-C, the apartment directly beneath that in which Fiona Cassidy—aka Eve Adams—was a temporary resident. The possibility that he might be enlisted as an ally in my investigation of the woman began to intrigue me.

My mother had not yet returned from Woolworth's because she'd had some other task after work. She didn't expect to be home until six o'clock, which would leave her little time to change and be off to Slinky's.

The previous day, she had made peanut-butter cookies according to Grandma Anita's recipe. Unlike most cookies of that type, they were not oily or chewy, but crisp and crunchy. After she took them from the oven, as they cooled, she shredded dark chocolate on top, which melted and then solidified into a thin crust.

The cookies were stored in a deep, round tin. Too pleased by my cunning, I put half a dozen of the treats on a paper plate, covered them tightly with Saran Wrap, and carried them up to the fifth floor, to present them to Mr. Yoshioka, less as a neighborly gift than as an inducement to conspiracy. My motives were not *entirely* deplorable. I did in fact like the tailor and felt sorry for him if, as everyone suspected, he had a tragic past.

In our lives, we come to moments of great significance that we fail to recognize, the meaning of which sometimes does not occur to us for many years. Each of us has his agenda and focuses on it, and therefore we are often blind to what is before our eyes.

On the fifth floor, when Mr. Yoshioka answered his doorbell, all I saw was a neighbor, a shy man, who was still dressed for work. He hadn't taken off his suit coat, hadn't loosened his tie.

I held out the plate. "My mom made these. You'll like them."

He appeared to be uncertain, not sure that I meant to give him the cookies. "These are the product of your mother's labor?"

"She baked them. Peanut butter. They're delicious with milk. Or without. You don't have to have milk to eat them. I mean, if maybe you don't like milk or it makes you sick, or something."

"I am making tea."

"They might go with tea. Milk or coffee, absolutely."

Tentatively, he took the plate of cookies. "Would you like to join me for tea, Jonah Kirk?"

"Yeah, that would be great. Thank you."

His dress shoes were on a mat beside the door. He still wore socks, but the shoes had been replaced by white slippers.

"It is not necessary for you to take off your shoes," he said.

"No, I want to. I want to do what you do in your own place."

"I do not keep all traditions of Japan. You should not be worried we will sit on the floor to eat. I do not."

"Neither do we," I said, as he closed the door. "We never did. My people, I mean. Unless maybe back when they were slaves, maybe they weren't given furniture, though I think they were. Not fancy furniture, of course, not from Macy's, just crudely made stuff."

He smiled and nodded. "I assure you also that I do not subscribe to the ancient tradition of *seppuku*." When I stared blankly at him, he said, "That is the polite word for hara-kiri."

I'd seen some old war movies. I knew what hara-kiri was. Suicide by sword. Disembowelment.

"Relax in the living room, Jonah Kirk. I will return with tea."

I wondered if I had gotten myself in trouble and, if so, just what kind of trouble it might be.

Twenty-five

AFTER I REMOVED MY SHOES, I WENT INTO THE
living room in my stocking feet.

First I noticed how clean Mr. Yoshioka kept his apartment. Mom was obsessive about cleaning, but our place
didn't *gleam* like this.

The room seemed immaculate partly because it didn't
contain much; there was no possibility of clutter. The lines
of the slat-back walnut couch were stark, with box cushions
covered in a gold fabric. The matching chairs had black
cushions. Two simple side tables held black-ceramic lamps
with gold shades.

The wood floor had been sanded smooth and finished
in a high gloss. I figured Mr. Yoshioka must have done the

work himself. Mr. Smaller performed only the most necessary repairs, not décor changes.

Large six-panel Japanese screens of pale-gold silk faced each other from opposite walls. On the one to the left, a single tiger was lying at rest, though its eyes were wide and watchful. To the right were two tigers at play, their power and grace so convincingly portrayed that I almost expected them to move upon the silk.

Mr. Yoshioka returned with a lacquered tray on which were two white porcelain plates, one bearing my mother's cookies, the other holding an assortment of inch-square cakes with pastel icing in a variety of colors. There were also smaller plates and cloth napkins.

As he transferred the items on the tray to the coffee table, Mr. Yoshioka said, "You admire the screens."

"They're really cool."

"These are copies of those by the Meiji master Takeuchi Seiho. I commissioned these. Faithful reproductions. But the originals were more powerful. My family once owned them. Then they were lost."

"Wow. How do you lose something so big?" I asked.

"Not easily."

"Where were they lost?"

"California," said Mr. Yoshioka, and he returned to the kitchen with the empty tray.

The only other work of art stood on a pedestal between

two windows that were covered by rice-paper shades the color of weak tea. This was an ivory sculpture of unusual size, about two feet high and two wide and a foot deep: a pretty Japanese lady in an elaborate kimono, carved with great realism.

When Mr. Yoshioka returned, carrying a tray laden with a teapot and two delicate cups, he said, "That is a Meiji original by the unequaled Asahi Gyokuzan. It is dated 1898. In 1901, he unveiled a larger, even more splendid version that was acquired by the emperor."

As Mr. Yoshioka poured tea, I stood transfixed by the ivory carving. It was the most beautiful thing I had ever seen.

"She is a court lady. Her ceremonial kimono has nineteen layers, the folds of each expressed by the sculptor in minute relief."

The statue was so sensuous, I wanted to touch it, but I knew that I shouldn't.

"My family once owned it but then lost it. Years later, I found and purchased it. That was a most happy day. I have poured the tea."

He sat on the sofa, and I took a chair. I sipped the tea, which was hot, almost colorless, nearly tasteless, and some-what bitter.

Watching me, Mr. Yoshioka seemed amused. "I thought you would feel that way," he said, though I hadn't complained. He indicated a miniature porcelain pitcher the size of a man's thumb. "Orange-blossom honey will sweeten it."

I added honey to the cup and was grateful for it. My host took his brew unsweetened.

When I sampled one of the tiny cakes, it was subtly flavored, perhaps with almond extract, and only slightly sweet, but edible.

He tried one of the cookies and was delighted, which didn't surprise me if those little pastel cakes were his idea of a treat. A whole new world must have opened to him when he took his first bite of one of my mother's peanut-butter cookies.

"What is May-gee?" I asked.

"A period of Japanese history. The rule of Emperor Mutsuhito, from 1868 to 1912. *Meiji* means enlightened peace. Are you bored?"

"No, sir. I really like the tigers and the court lady."

"I am not an interesting man," he said. "Sooner or later, I will bore you. Be certain to tell me when I do."

"All right. But I don't think you will."

"I will," he insisted. "The Meiji artists continued to produce in that style long after Mutsuhito's reign ended. My sainted father and precious mother collected Meiji and from the earlier Edo period. They owned hundreds of pieces. Objects of art. I grew up in rooms filled with Meiji magic."

"Hundreds? What happened to them?"

"Lost. All lost except the court lady carved from ivory, which I found."

"Why were your folks always losing things?"

He shrugged. "It was nobody's fault."

"Were they artists?"

"My mother was, of a kind. She worked with thread and needles on elaborate embroidered scenes. My father was a humble tailor. Your mother's cookies go with tea."

"So do these cakes," I said, and took a third, though I didn't really want it. The tea was better with honey, but it wasn't Co-Cola.

"Your mother has great talent."

"You've heard her sing?"

"Yes, at the club where she works."

I couldn't picture him in such a place. "You mean . . . Slinky's?"

"That is correct. I only went there once. They wanted me to order alcoholic beverages. From time to time, as seemed required, I asked for a martini."

"I think martinis are pretty potent."

"Yes, but I do not drink. I paid for the martinis but left them untouched. For some reason, this disturbed the management. I felt that I should not go back again."

Something about the way he spoke, the formality of his sentences and the lack of slang, was familiar to me, as if

I'd known someone else who spoke in this manner, not stilted but with grave restraint.

"Did Mom see you at Slinky's?"

"No. I sat in a corner table, far from the stage. I did not wish to intrude, only to listen. I am boring you."

"No, sir. It's pretty much the opposite of boredom. Where did you and your folks live in California?"

"First in Los Angeles. Later in a place called Manzanar."

"Palm trees and beaches and always warm. I might want to live there when I'm grown up. Why did you leave?"

He was quiet, staring into his tea as though he could read the future in it. Then he said, "I was able to get work here. Work is life and meaning. Sloth is sin and death. At the end of the war, I was eighteen and needed work. I came here from California to work."

"You mean World War Two?"

"Exactly, yes."

I calculated. "You're almost forty, but you don't look old."

Raising his stare from tea to me, he smiled. "Neither do you."

"I didn't mean that the way it sounded."

"It sounded honest. Honest is good."

I was blushing again, but still black, so he couldn't know.

"Now I am boring myself," he said. "I must be boring you."

I thought maybe this worry about boring me was his way of politely putting an end to our visit, and I realized that I hadn't even raised the subject that had inspired me to bring him cookies.

Looking at the ceiling, I said, "It's so quiet here, so peaceful. I hope the new lady in Six-C doesn't ruin your quiet."

"Why should she?"

"Stripping up linoleum, scraping off wallpaper . . ."

"Most likely she will be doing that while I am away at work."

"Yeah, but she looks . . ."

He cocked his head, his black eyes as inquisitive and direct as those of a wary crow. "Yes? Looks? How does she look?"

"Noisy."

He studied me over his raised teacup, as he tilted it and took a sip. Then he said, "You do not mean noisy."

"I don't?"

"You do not."

"Then what do I mean?"

"I await the revelation."

"Nasty," I said. "Maybe a little crazy. She's a little nasty-crazy."

He put down his teacup and leaned forward. "I met this woman on the stairs yesterday. I said good afternoon, but she did not."

"What did she say?"

"She made a suggestion I will not repeat. Nasty—I am sorry to say, yes. Crazy—maybe." He leaned forward even farther. "May I share this with you, Jonah Kirk, and be certain you will never quote me?"

I raised my right hand. "Swear to God."

"The best word to describe her is *dangerous*. I have known dangerous people in my life. Please believe me that I have."

"I believe you, sir."

"If you are intrigued by this Eve Adams, resist your curiosity. She is only trouble. We must hope she will be gone without damage."

For a moment, I considered sharing my experience with the woman, but it seemed that if I told him about her threats, I'd have to tell him also that I had seen her in a dream, strangled and dead. I didn't want him to think that the best word to describe me was *nutcase*.

I allowed myself to say only, "I think maybe she's a witch."

He raised his eyebrows. "How extraordinary. Why do you think this?"

"Sometimes she just . . . appears."

"Appears what?"

"You know, sort of like out of thin air. In places where she couldn't be."

"I myself have not observed this."

Having said too much, I rose to my feet and added only, "It's freaky. Anyway, if you hear anything funny up there . . . I mean anything suspicious . . ."

"I expect to hear many suspicious things, Jonah Kirk. But I will not listen."

"Huh? Won't listen?" I tried to puzzle out his meaning. "Don't you care if she's up to no good?"

"I am concerned. But I want no trouble. I have had enough of trouble, you see. More than enough."

"Well . . . okay, sure, I guess." As he rose from the couch, I said, "Thanks for the little cakes. And the tea. And the honey."

Half bowing, he said, "Thank you, Jonah Kirk, for sharing your mother's delicious cookies. It was most kind of you."

Walking down to Mrs. Lorenzo's apartment, I carried a weight of disappointment. I had hoped Mr. Yoshioka and I might join forces to discover the truth of Fiona Cassidy. He was a small man, perhaps five foot six and slender, but during our visit, I had become convinced—I don't know why—that he was brave, even courageous. Maybe I had been too impressed by the fact that he had tigers on his walls.

Twenty-six

I DON'T RECOLLECT WHAT I EXPECTED TO HAPPEN next. Perhaps memory has failed me after all these years. Or perhaps I didn't anticipate any specific act of evil, but instead lived in the shadow of general apprehension regarding both my father and Fiona Cassidy.

The Labor Day weekend arrived. I would be back in classes at Saint Scholastica School on Tuesday. Saturday, after a long piano session at the community center, I returned to our apartment at 5:20 P.M., after my mother had left early for Slinky's.

In the bathroom, I washed my face and hands at the sink. Then I went to my room, took the chenille spread off the bed, folded it, put it on a shelf in the closet, and then turned down the bedclothes, so that I wouldn't have to do all that later. The day was warm, the room stuffy. I put up the lower sash of the window for ventilation.

In the kitchen, a note was fixed to the refrigerator with a magnet: *Tell Donata when you're home. She'll bring dinner and stay so you can sleep in your own bed. Love you more than anything. Mom.*

A couple of days had passed since I'd had tea with Mr. Yoshioka, and I had not seen Fiona Cassidy again. I considered going up to the attic for a few minutes, to listen for whatever I might hear in 6-C. Just as I decided not to be stupid, the doorbell rang, and through the fish-eye lens, I saw Mr. Yoshioka.

When I opened the door, he said in a whisper, "Good evening, Jonah Kirk. Has the day been gentle with you?"

Taking my cue from him, I also whispered. "Gentle? I guess so. What about you, sir?"

"I have known worse, thank you. I wish to have a word."

Stepping back, I said, "Oh, sure, come in."

"A word alone," he whispered.

"There's no one here but me."

He entered, closed the door, and stood with his back to it, as if to brace it shut against some hostile force. "I am sorry for the intrusion."

"No problem," I assured him. "You want to sit down and have something to drink? I can't make tea, but I can make hot chocolate or maybe open a root beer or something."

"You are very kind, but I can only stay a moment. My apologies."

"What's up?"

"Miss Eve Adams has not been noisy, not at all. However, on two occasions, each lasting an hour, there has been a most disturbing"—he looked pained, as though by the necessary crudeness of his next word—"stink."

"A stink?"

"Yes. Quite strong."

"What kind of stink?"

"A chemical smell. It is like but not precisely the same as trichloroethylene. That is the fluid used by dry cleaners. Being a tailor, I know it well."

"Maybe it's something she's using to take up the old linoleum."

"I do not think so. Not at all. No."

His brow was furrowed, his lips pinched.

I said, "You seem worried."

"It is like trichloroethylene but I believe more volatile."

"Volatile? I know some piano, nothing about chemicals."

"More flammable," he explained. "Possible fire, explosion, catastrophe. I do not mean to be an alarmist."

"Volatile," I said, and I thought the word applied to the woman as well as to whatever chemical Mr. Yoshioka had smelled. "You sure it came from Six-C?"

"Last evening, I went to the sixth floor to smell." His

skin was not dark enough to conceal his blush. I wasn't sure what embarrassed him—maybe that he'd been snooping on a neighbor, maybe that I would think he was an alarmist. "The odor was strongest at her door."

"Did you tell Mr. Smaller?"

"I decided to wait and see if it happened a third time, this evening. But minutes ago, when I came home from work, I found this in my kitchen."

From a pocket, he produced four pieces of a photograph taken with a Polaroid camera. He handed them to me, and I didn't have to fit them together correctly to see they constituted a photo of the six-panel painted-silk screen that featured two tigers.

Mr. Yoshioka said, "The pieces were stacked and then pinned to my cutting board with a knife taken from one of my kitchen drawers." I returned the scissored photo, and his hand shook as he accepted the pieces. "I believe it to be a threat. I am being warned not to come smelling around her door again—or to complain about the stink."

"You think Eve Adams saw you at her door?"

"I do not know what to think."

"How'd she get into your apartment to take a Polaroid?"

"How indeed," he wondered, his hand trembling as he returned the fragments of the picture to a suit-coat pocket.

"Your door was locked?"

"Yes. And like you, I have two deadbolts." He started

to say something more, but then looked around the room, focused on one of the street-view windows, and finally looked down at his right hand, first at the palm, then at the back of it, at his slender wellmanicured fingers, as he continued. "I have come here only to tell you that I intend to stay away from this woman, stay away from the sixth floor, and give her no reason to be angry. I believe you should do the same, for your sake and your mother's."

A voice in memory: *I like to cut. You believe I like to cut?*

"What is it?" he asked.

"I haven't told you everything about this woman."

"Yes, I am aware."

Surprised, I said, "You are? How?"

"What do they call the face of a good poker player?"

"A poker face," I said.

"Yes, I believe that is correct. You do not have one. I have no idea what you have withheld, but I am aware you are withholding."

I hesitated but then said, "She threatened me with a knife."

Although I thought he was shocked, I couldn't tell for sure, because he *did* have a poker face. "Where did this occur?"

"Here in the apartment. Remember how I said she can appear like magic, where she wasn't a moment ago."

"Why would she threaten you with a knife?"

I cleared my throat, wiped my nose on one sleeve even though it didn't need to be wiped, laced my fingers together and cracked my knuckles, and at last said, "Well, see, she left the door open to Six-C, and I kind of like took a tour of the place."

Poker face or not, he couldn't quite conceal the fact that my nosiness struck him as offensive. "Why would you do that?"

I was not ready to tell him that I had seen her strangled and dead in a dream. "I don't know. She's . . . different. I kind of . . . maybe I had a crush on her. A crush at first sight."

His stare was direct, and somehow I met it, and after a moment he said, "That will be good enough for now. We all have things to say that can be said only when the time is right to say them."

Although I considered telling him more, I shrugged and looked at my feet as if they were fascinating, as if I might break into a dance at any moment.

Mr. Yoshioka sighed. "I keep my head down, Jonah Kirk. I do not make a great noise as I pass through the years. I do not allow myself curiosity about women . . . like Miss Eve Adams. Head down. Head down. I do not wish to shine. I prefer shadows, quiet, periods of solitude. I do not wish to be noticed. If one is all but invisible to others, one cannot be envied, inspire anger or suspicion. Near invisibility is a way of life that I recommend."

"You think Eve Adams might really kill you?"

Although his hands hardly trembled now that he'd put away the pieces of the photograph, he remained disquieted—and too embarrassed to look at me. "There are worse things than death. I do not think the threat was to me. It is, as it appears, to the tiger screen. I cannot risk the screen. It is too valuable."

"Valuable? But didn't you say it was just some kind of copy, not the original?"

"It is more valuable than the original."

"How can that be? I mean, if it's not an antique."

Raising his head, he met my eyes. He seemed to want to reveal something of importance, but then he said, "I only came to warn you."

He stepped into the hallway and quietly pulled the door shut between us.

I heard no receding footsteps.

After a beat, through the door, Mr. Yoshioka said, "Jonah Kirk?"

"Yes?"

"Lock the deadbolts."

"All right." I did as he asked.

With one ear to the door, as I listened to the tailor walk away, I thought perhaps his embarrassment arose from his lack of courage, from his determination to keep his head down, to be nearly invisible. That possibility made me sad. And worse than sad.

In those days, when you were, like Mr. Yoshioka, an American of an ethnic group whose former homeland had in the not-too-distant past waged and lost a world war, or if you were of a people who had only recently begun to emerge from a century of segregation following generations of slavery, the heroes in books and movies tended not to be like you. We could believe in the characters John Wayne inhabited and admire the grace and humility with which he played heroic men; we could agree that the honor and integrity and courage that were the essence of his image should be values we, too, embraced, but we couldn't see ourselves as John Wayne or imagine he was us. Sure, there was Sidney Poitier, but in those days he played mostly in self-consciously liberal films, raising awareness of injustice rather than taking down bad guys. Taking down bad guys is fundamentally what you want in your model of a hero. Bill Cosby, on TV in *I Spy,* had the physicality and attitude to make bad guys wish they'd been good, but he mostly did so with humor, wit, and smarts, and you never felt he was at risk, therefore didn't need courage. My generation of blacks had two main sources of heroes—sports stars who broke through race barriers and famous musicians—who neither beat up nor shot down villains as part of their job description. When it came to inspiring ethnic icons of heroism in pop culture, Mr. Yoshioka had fewer men to emulate than I did. Japanese American sports stars were unknown in those days, and the only Japanese singer to make the charts was Kyu Sakamoto, whose "Sukiyaki" went to number one in 1963, even though the lyrics were entirely in Japanese.

Back then, I had a narrow definition of heroism. My conclusion that Mr. Yoshioka lacked courage arose from ignorance, as later I would learn. After you have suffered great losses and known much pain, it is not cowardice to wish to live henceforth with a minimum of suffering. And one form of heroism, about which few if any films will be made, is having the courage to live without bitterness when bitterness is justified, having the strength to persevere even when perseverance seems unlikely to be rewarded, having the resolution to find profound meaning in life when it seems the most meaningless.

Twenty-seven

WHEN I CALLED TO TELL HER THAT I WAS HOME, Mrs. Lorenzo came up to the fourth floor with what she said was a "special secret dessert" on a covered plate. Earlier, she'd left a pan of saltimbocca in our refrigerator, prepared but uncooked, as well as the fixings for two side dishes.

As she made potato croquettes and peas with walnuts, I set the table and told her about my day. There wasn't much to tell, because I left out Fiona Cassidy, aka Eve Adams, and Mr. Yoshioka. I was leading a life more secret than the dessert on the covered plate.

As she cooked, she gave me other small tasks, and I assisted as best I could while she told me all about what the three kids in her little day-care business did and said.

"I'm afraid I can't keep up with them quite like before I got so fat."

Mr. Lorenzo had been dead only a couple of months, but already Mrs. Lorenzo was gaining weight. She wasn't yet fat, however, only a little plump, and I didn't like to hear her dissing herself.

"Mrs. Lorenzo, has anybody ever told you how you look like Anna Maria Alberghetti?"

"You're sweet, Jonah, but that's all behind me now." With one hand, she patted her backside and laughed softly. "All behind me."

Somehow I knew she didn't mean the new pounds, which were distributed evenly over her, and so I said, "Behind you? What is?"

"Caring about how I look. Men. Marriage. Tony was the best of men. Trying to have all that again will only lead to disappointment . . . or worse."

Her resignation made me sad. I couldn't think of any words that might change her mind about the future. The longer I was silent, the more awkward I felt, until I had to escape the kitchen for a few minutes. Maybe when I came back, we'd be able to talk about a new subject as if what had just been said had never been said.

I lied: "I'm going to turn down my bed so I won't have to do it later, open a window and get some fresh air in there."

When I went to my bedroom, the window was up, as I had left it, and the bed was turned down, also as I had left it, but on the smooth cotton blanket, as if keeping watch on the doorway, lay the fabric eyeball with its blue-plastic iris.

In memory, I saw the purple stare and heard the dangerous woman say: *Juju eye? You're a real little freak in the making, aren't you?*

I went to the window. Closed it. Locked it.

When I tore open my closet door, she wasn't hiding in there. She wasn't in my mother's bedroom or closet, either. Or the hall closet. Or the bathroom.

In the living room, I found the front door locked, as I'd left it after Mrs. Lorenzo arrived.

I returned to my bedroom and met the Cyclopean gaze. I plucked the eye off the bed. I retrieved the La Florentine candy tin from my nightstand, opened it, and confirmed that nothing else had been taken from—or added to—my collection. I put the eye in the tin and the tin in the night-stand drawer.

The eye hadn't been there when I came home and turned down the bedclothes. While Mrs. Lorenzo and I were busy in the kitchen, Eve Adams—Fiona Cassidy, whoever, what-ever—had come here to get the creepy thing and position it to gaze at the door.

Sitting on the edge of the bed, I had no difficulty

translating the message. The woman must have known that Mr. Yoshioka had come to tell me about the stink like dry-cleaning fluid and about the cut-up Polaroid of the tiger screen. She was warning me not to conspire against her, to stay away from Mr. Yoshioka, to remember that she liked to cut. She was saying, *You think the fabric eye is juju, boy, but the only thing that's juju around here is me.*

When my tremors subsided, I returned to the kitchen, where Mrs. Lorenzo had finished preparing the side dishes. She was frying the tightly rolled saltimbocca in a mixture of butter and olive oil, and the air was fragrant with the aromas of prosciutto, veal, sage, and pepper.

She wanted water to drink with dinner. For myself, I poured cherry Kool-Aid from a pitcherful that Mom had mixed that morning.

When I sat at the table, I had no appetite. I started picking at the food, certain that my suddenly sour stomach would throw it right back at me if I dared to eat. But it was a testimony to Mrs. Lorenzo's cooking that before long I'd finished what she served to me and was asking for seconds.

The special secret dessert proved to be ricotta cream cake sprinkled with icing sugar and shaved chocolate. It wasn't just special; it was a piece of Heaven.

After dinner, when the dishes were done, we played 500

rummy at the kitchen table. Mrs. Lorenzo wanted to turn on the radio and find some good music, but I pretended that, being an obsessive musician, I couldn't concentrate on cards with music playing. What actually concerned me was that music might mask the sound of Eve Adams coming back with bad intentions.

I went to bed at 9:30, like I was supposed to, though I couldn't sleep. Mrs. Lorenzo was watching TV in the living room, but the sound was low. It wasn't the TV that kept me awake; it was the witch from 6-C, if she was a witch. I got to thinking that maybe I should hope she *was* just a witch; there were worse things, after all.

At 10:20, I got out of bed and went into the living room to see if Mrs. Lorenzo was all right. During less than an hour of insomnia, I'd thought of several ways Eve Adams might have killed her suddenly, quietly, with that switch-blade. I found Mrs. Lorenzo lying on the sofa. She wasn't watching TV, but she wasn't dead, either. Sound asleep, she snored softly.

I went back to bed and assured myself that I was a big baby. Whoever the mystery woman might be, she wasn't a witch any more than she was a vampire or a space alien hatched out of a giant seed pod. She was up to no good in 6-C, and she didn't want any interference. A nine-year-old kid was easy to intimidate. A shy tailor living in the shadow of some tragedy or other was easy to intimidate.

All that she wanted was for us to fear her and stay away from her, and in a couple of months she would be gone.

Nevertheless, at 11:00, I crept along the hallway to the living room again, to see if Mrs. Lorenzo was still sleeping or maybe, this time, slashed and dead. She was neither. Sitting on the sofa, bent forward with her face in her hands, ghostlike in the pale flickery light of the TV, she wept quietly but with such grief that her body shook. Nothing on television had made her cry. She didn't need a sad movie or the horror of the news to bring her to tears.

No matter how crazy the occupant of 6-C might prove to be, I was embarrassed to have all but forgotten how recently Donata Lorenzo's world had turned upside down. Although the dream of Fiona Cassidy strangled with a necktie had disconcerted me when later I saw her alive on the stairs, I was nonetheless responsible for whatever woe I brought down on myself; I was reckless when I followed her and inexcusably bold when I entered her apartment and prowled its rooms uninvited. Mrs. Lorenzo, on the other hand, had done nothing to deserve her widowhood; she'd been an innocent whom Fate had struck with great cruelty.

Before she might look up and discover me watching her from the threshold of the hallway, I returned quietly to my room. My shame dampened my fear, and though I doubted that I would sleep that night, I slept.

Twenty-eight

THE NEXT MORNING, BECAUSE IT WAS GRANDMA Anita's birthday, she and Grandpa Teddy picked up Mom and me in their Cadillac Club Coupe, and we went to 10:00 Mass, and after that we stopped for brunch in a big hotel where I went around and around through the revolving doors three times and would have completed a fourth revolution if Mom hadn't given me the Look, which always brought me immediately to my senses.

I had never been to a brunch before, and this was an all-you-can-eat buffet, which amazed me. I was also astonished by the fresh flowers on every table and the ice sculpture of a swan and the white uniforms and tall white chef's hats worn by the men who carved the roast beef and the turkey.

The posh surroundings and the spectacle seemed to sharpen my appetite. After finishing my first plate, when I wanted to go back for a second, Mom warned me to take only what I was certain I could finish. "All you can eat doesn't mean waste as much as you want."

When I came back with a full plate, they looked dubious. But I finished every bit of it.

Grandpa Teddy said, "Anita, I suspect this grandson of ours is from another planet. He's really as big as a horse with a crocodile's mouth, but he's able to hypnotize us into seeing him as a young boy who might be blown away in a strong wind."

Later we went to a movie starring Jack Lemmon and Walter Matthau. It was pretty funny, though not as funny as the cartoon we saw first.

That whole day was perfect; and it is the nature of the nine-year-old mind to believe that each extreme experience signifies a lasting change in the quality of life henceforth. A bad day raises the expectation of a long chain of grim days through dismal decades, and a day of joy inspires an almost giddy certainty that the years thereafter will be marked by endless blessings. In fact, time teaches us that the musical score of life oscillates between that of *Psycho* and that of *The Sound of Music,* with by far the greatest number of our days lived to the strains of an innocuous and modestly budgeted picture, sometimes a romance, sometimes a light comedy, sometimes a little art film of puzzling purpose and elusive meaning. Yet I've known adults who live forever in that odd conviction of nine-year-olds. Because I am an optimist and always have been, the expectation of continued joy comes more easily to me than pessimism, which was especially true during that period of my childhood.

When we came home on the evening of Grandma Anita's birthday celebration, I gave little or no thought to the woman in Apartment 6-C. Such a day of unalloyed delight must mean that my world had begun to rotate around a warmer sun than before, that the mystery woman and the evil she represented were surely now on a different world from mine, in some far arm of the galaxy, and our orbits would never again intersect. I slept deeply and without dreaming.

On Monday morning, Labor Day, I woke and yawned and stretched and sat up in bed—and saw a Polaroid photo propped against the lamp on my nightstand. It was a picture of me sleeping.

Twenty-nine

SITTING THERE IN BED, THIS IS HOW I INTERPRETED the meaning of the Polaroid: *I can get at you anytime I want, snoop. I can put a shiv through your heart while you're sleeping, boy, and you'll be dead before you can wake up and see me.*

That wasn't the worst that she promised. As the glossy photo rattled softly in my trembling hand, I remembered what she had said when she paid a visit to me in this very room, shortly after I had toured 6-C.

You don't want to be talking about me to anyone, not to anyone. *You never saw me. We didn't have this little chat. You get my point, snoop?* She had threatened to use the knife on my mother. *If you love your mama, then you think about what I said.*

Instead of running to my mother and spilling the whole story, I sat on the edge of my bed and took the La Florentine candy tin from my nightstand. I opened the lid and found the fabric eye staring up at me.

When you keep a secret from those closest to you, even with the best of motives, there is a danger that you will create a smaller life within your main life. The first secret will spin off other secrets that also must be kept, complicated webs of evasion that grow into elaborate architectures of repressed truths and subterfuge, until you discover that you must live two narratives at once. Because deception requires both bold lies and lies of omission, it stains the soul, muddies the conscience, blurs the vision, and puts you at risk of headlong descent into greater darkness.

As a boy, I could not have put any of that into words, but I sensed it all and, even if I sensed it vaguely, was distressed by every step I took further into secrecy. If I showed the Polaroid to my mother, I would have to tell her about the woman in 6-C. Mom would want to know why I'd been so bold and rude as to venture uninvited into the apartment of a stranger. I doubted that I could convince her—or anyone—that previously I had seen the mystery woman in a dream, strangled and dead; therefore, I would be suspected of compounding my error with an outrageous lie. I would raise in her mind the prospect that I might be more like my father than she could bear.

And so I put the Polaroid snapshot in the candy tin with the fabric eye and other items, and I told myself that if I stayed well away from the sixth floor and from its temporary tenant, there would be no more threats. First, however, I turned the hateful eye upside down, so that it was looking at the bottom of the tin instead of at me.

Mom had been up long before me. She'd showered, dressed, and set the dinette table. No sooner had I put away the tin box of treasures—and curses—than she rapped on my door. "Rise and shine. Breakfast in five, sleepyhead."

"Okay. I'm awake. Be right there."

In a solemn mood, not the usual chatterbox, I went to the table in pajamas and slippers. I got through breakfast without arousing her suspicion, largely by pretending to be only half awake, still worn around the edges from all the activity of Grandma Anita's birthday.

I was lucky. Because Sunday had been so busy, my mother hadn't read that newspaper, which must have weighed four pounds. She gave her attention to it as she ate eggs, bacon, and fried potatoes. I borrowed the funnies, which gave me an excuse to keep my head down.

Slinky's didn't feature live music on Mondays, except on certain holidays that ensured a good crowd. Like Labor Day. My mother and Virgil Tibbins, the club's other contracted singer, were to perform that evening. She was the star of the early show, six o'clock until nine, and there was a rehearsal, which meant she would be leaving the apartment by three o'clock.

After I showered and dressed, I hugged Mom and said, "Knock 'em dead tonight."

"I'll be happy just to knock 'em speechless, so there won't be any heckling."

Shocked, I said, "Do they heckle you at Slinky's?"

"Wherever there's enough liquor for enough time, everyone gets heckled, sweetie. But whatever there is tonight, it'll be saved for poor Virgil, since he's the second show."

I reminded her that although the community center was sponsoring a couple of holiday events, the Abigail Louise Thomas Room remained open for me to practice the piano.

"If I'm gone when you get home," she said, "go down to Donata's. She's expecting you."

When I returned at 3:15, I didn't proceed directly to Mrs. Lorenzo's. I didn't feel guilty about going to our apartment instead, because I was trying to figure out how to ensure our safety, which was the primary job of the man of the house, after all. As strange as it might sound, however, I *did* feel terribly guilty about not feeling guilty.

In the kitchen, I opened the drawer nearest the wall phone and took out the directory and looked for a listing for my new friend on the fifth floor. I found one at our street address for YOSHIOKA, GEORGE. The mailboxes in the lobby featured only last names. I don't know why I expected him to have a Japanese first name when presumably he had been born in the United States, but I stared at the listing for maybe a minute, wondering if, unknown to me, there could be a second Yoshioka in the building.

As I was finally about to dial the number, the phone rang, startling me. I stared at it, certain that the caller must be the witch—*She knows I've come home!*—but then embarrassed by my fearful reaction, I snatched up the handset. "Hello?"

"Good afternoon, Jonah Kirk," said Mr. Yoshioka.

"Oh. Hi. I didn't think it was you."

"Who did you think I was?"

"Eve Adams."

"I assure you that I am not her."

"No, sir. I can tell you're not."

"I must first inform you that I most happily consumed the last of your mother's cookies, and it was as entirely delicious as the first. Thank you for them."

"I could bring up some more, if you want."

With evident mortification, he said, "No, no. I am so sorry. I did not phone you to request cookies. If I did so, you would think me unspeakably rude."

"No, sir. I would think you know a good cookie when you taste one, that's all."

My reply seemed to confuse him. He was silent for a moment before he asked, "Are you entirely alone, Jonah Kirk?"

"Yes, sir. Mom's gone to Slinky's and I'm supposed to go down to Mrs. Lorenzo's instead of her coming up here."

"I have something important for you, Jonah Kirk. Very important. May I bring it down momentarily?"

"Sure."

"There are unwholesome forces at work in this building. We must at all times be most discreet. I will not ring your bell. I will not knock. You will be waiting for me. Yes?"

"Yes," I agreed.

"If I encounter wickedness on my way to you, I will retreat to my rooms and phone you to discuss another time to meet."

"Wickedness?" I said.

"Wickedness, Jonah Kirk. Great wickedness."

Thirty

I WAITED AT THE FRONT DOOR OF THE APARTMENT, which I'd unlocked and opened just a crack. Peering through the gap, waiting for my co-conspirator, I was taken by surprise when suddenly he appeared from my left, having come down the back stairs instead of the front, as quiet as a cat.

Mr. Yoshioka smiled at me through the gap, and I let him into the apartment. He was carrying a brown-paper shopping bag with cord handles, which he put down next to the door as I closed it.

"How are you this afternoon, Jonah Kirk?"

"Kind of scared, I guess."

"Scared? Frightened? Of what?"

"Whatever great wickedness you're going to tell me about."

"You already know the great wickedness. It is Miss Eve Adams."

Something about the tailor was different. Although this was a holiday, he still wore a suit and tie, but in spite of all his talk of wickedness, he seemed more relaxed than usual.

"You also said there were 'unwholesome forces at work in this building.'"

"That again is a reference to Miss Eve Adams and to those who are in league with her."

"Who's in league with her?"

"Different people come and go. I hear their footsteps overhead, muffled voices, but I never see them."

"Has she been in your apartment again?"

He looked as solemn as if he were at a funeral. "Yes. She left another photograph."

"Of the second tiger screen, of the court lady carved in ivory?"

"It is not a Polaroid. It is instead a page torn from a book, a photograph of Manzanar."

I remembered from our conversation over tea. "One of the places you lived in California."

"A photograph of the gates to the place where I lived."

"How could she know?"

"I believe that she guessed . . . and was right."

"Then she must be a witch, for sure."

Just then I realized why Mr. Yoshioka looked more relaxed than usual. Although he wore a suit and tie, as always, for the first time he wasn't also wearing a vest. He'd made a concession to the holiday.

Only that morning, I'd been terrified when I realized that Eve Adams had worked her way into our locked apartment during the night and had photographed me in my sleep; but now I was excited to have an outrage to share with Mr. Yoshioka, an outrage that seemed to one-up a picture of some little town in California.

I said, "She left another Polaroid here. Come on. I'll show you."

I led him along the hallway to my bedroom. He stood swaying from side to side on the threshold, looking uncomfortable, and wouldn't enter. I got the candy tin and brought it to him.

He smiled at the painting of the woman on the lid, tapped it with one finger, and said, "La Belle Ferroniere."

In truth, at the time, I didn't quite know what he said, except that it sounded French, which seemed strange coming from someone who was so obviously not French. Anyway, I was eager to show him the picture of me sleeping.

"Did not the flashbulb wake you?" he asked.

"Nothing much can wake me when I really want to sleep."

Frowning, he stopped swaying back and forth on the threshold and shook his head instead. "This is not good. This is very bad. What does your mother say?"

"I haven't shown it to her yet. I wanted to think about it first. I didn't want to worry her."

I took the fabric eye from the box and explained its history, but he couldn't quite understand.

"This is an eye from your stuffed toy?"

"Not from my toy. I don't know whose toy. A wind blew it along the alleyway, blew it but nothing else, until it just stopped at me. I thought it had some juju, you know, so I saved it."

"What is juju?"

"Kind of like voodoo." When I saw the word meant nothing to him, I said, "You know, like in the movies."

"I do not attend the movies."

"Well, there was a voodoo-in-the-city thing on TV not long ago."

"I do not watch television. I have often been told that I should purchase one, but I do not believe I ever will."

"No TV? Gosh, what do you do, then?"

"I work."

"I mean when you're not working."

"I read. I think."

"I read, too. And my mom. We like books."

After puzzling over the fabric eye one more time, he

gave it back to me, and I carefully stored it upside down in the La Florentine container.

As I returned the tin box to the nightstand, Mr. Yoshioka said, "There can be only two logical explanations. Either Miss Eve Adams is a most expert lock-picker or she possesses keys to our apartments."

Mr. Yoshioka was the essence of cool, but his kind of cool was unique to him. His precise way of speaking, without contractions or slang, never dropping the *g* at the end of a word, had appealed to my ear for music from the start of our relationship. Now, as we were engaged in deduction, trying to solve a mystery, though he had no accent, he reminded me just a little bit of that intellectual, supersmart detective Charlie Chan, in those old movies. In 1966, Charlie Chan films were still run on TV. Nobody yet found them racially offensive and worthy of censorship, maybe because Mr. Chan was always the smartest person in every scene. Charlie Chan, of course, was Chinese American, and Mr. Yoshioka was Japanese American. I could tell the difference, though I was just nine, because I had seen Mr. Moto on TV, in a series of funky old films about an intellectual, supersmart Japanese American detective based on a series of short stories and novel-length mysteries by John P. Marquand, who won a Pulitzer Prize for a mainstream novel titled *The Late George Apley*. To tell the truth, Fiona Cassidy, aka Eve Adams, scared me, but there were moments when the fun of playing sidekick to Mr. Yoshioka outweighed my fear of that mystery woman, probably because there never had been a series of movies featuring an intellectual, supersmart Negro detective, which was how I was beginning to see myself.

Closing the nightstand drawer and returning to the doorway in which my visitor stood, I said, "She must be a master lock-picker. Because where would she get keys?"

"Perhaps the building superintendent gave them to her."

"Mr. Smaller? He wouldn't do that. He could lose his job for doing something like that."

"I am told that men do reckless things for pretty women. In fact, I have seen it."

I shook my head. "Mr. Smaller says women break your heart so often you can't count how many times. He says don't let them start. Besides, he doesn't like his bosses downtown, and they sent her here to do the work in Six-C. He says they're all black-hearted company men, they get big pay for just picking their noses. Anyway, since they sent her from downtown, he probably thinks she's a Bilderberger."

Mr. Yoshioka's mouth moved as if he were working the word around his tongue, trying to taste some meaning in it. "What is a . . . what you just said?"

"It's a long story," I replied. "Not important. Mr. Smaller wouldn't have given her the keys, and black-hearted company men probably wouldn't, either. So she must be a fantastic lock-picker. What did you bring in the shopping bag?"

"A device to guarantee your safety in the night."

"What—a shotgun?"

He smiled, but it was a thin and nervous smile. "Let us hope that it does not come to that."

Thirty-one

FROM THE SMALL SHOPPING BAG, MR. YOSHIOKA withdrew a manual drill with a crank handle, a tape measure, a pencil, a hammer, a nail, and a two-piece security-chain lock with screws.

"I have already installed one on my door. Of course this cannot keep Miss Eve Adams out when no one is at home to engage the chain. But it will assure us that she cannot intrude at night when you are sleeping."

He held the jamb plate to the door frame and with the pencil marked the holes where the four screws would go.

"Hey, wait a second. How am I going to explain this to my mom?"

"What is there to explain? Miss Eve Adams is a dangerous and unpredictable person. She—"

"I haven't told my mom about Eve Adams or the knife threat or the Polaroid of me sleeping, none of it."

He blinked at me, as though I had suddenly blurred and he were trying to bring me back into focus. "Why have you not told her about such an important thing?"

"It's complicated."

He regarded me with a look that reminded me of someone else, and for a moment I couldn't think who, but then I realized this was the look with which Sister Agnes regarded me on those rare days when I showed up at Saint Scholastica without my homework complete.

"You do not seem to me to be a boy who would lie to his mother," said Mr. Yoshioka.

"I haven't lied to Mom about Eve Adams. I just haven't mentioned her, that's all."

"I suppose there must be a distinction if we think hard enough."

"I didn't want to worry her. She's got enough on her mind."

Putting down the brass jamb plate and the pencil, picking up the hammer and nail, he said, "I will explain to your mother that I worry about the two of you alone in these times of high crime. Therefore, I installed this security chain as I have in my apartment."

"But, see, the thing is—why just us?"

"Excuse me?"

"Why wouldn't you put one on Mrs. Lorenzo's door and on everyone else's door, why just on ours?"

He smiled and nodded. "Of course, because you are my friend and the others are mere neighbors, many of whom never speak to me, none of whom ever brought me cookies."

"Well, okay, but my mother doesn't know we're friends."

"You brought me cookies, we had tea together, we both recognized that Eve Adams is a dangerous person. We are men of very different experiences yet of like minds. Of course we are friends."

When he said "men," I think I loved him a little then, like the way I loved Grandpa Teddy. Mr. Yoshioka didn't pause before using the word, didn't say it with any calculation, but included me among the grown-up and mature with apparent sincerity.

Embarrassed, I said, "Well, see, I didn't tell Mom how I brought you cookies and then had tea."

At nearly forty, he possessed a face as unlined as mine, most likely because he didn't often squinch it up in dramatic expressions. His gentle smile was always slight, his frown hardly detectable, and to assess his mood, you were left with little to read other than his eyes. Now, smooth-faced, allowing no clue in his eyes, his voice without telltale inflection, he said, "You seem to keep more from your mother than you tell her."

Abashed, I said, "Not really. We share almost everything. We really do. Sometimes she calls me a chatterbox because I'm always sharing so much. It's just that if I tell her about the cookies and the tea, I'll have to tell her about Eve Adams, and I don't want to do that because—"

"Because you do not want to worry her. She has enough on her mind," he finished for me, sort of quoting me.

Suddenly I thought I saw the solution to our dilemma. "You know, maybe instead of the security chain, we should just call the police and tell them Miss Adams is messing with stinky chemicals in Six-C, she might blow us up or something."

Because it is impossible for me to turn pale, I am especially aware when white folks lose what color they have, just as I am quick to notice when they blush. Mr. Yoshioka was a kind of light bronze, but when I suggested calling the police, he went pale in his own way. His skin was still bronze, but a little gray now, as though it were an alloy of bronze and pewter, if there was such a thing.

"No police," he said.

"Sure. That's the way. They could go up there and she'd have to let them in. So if she's up to no good—and we know she is—then the cops would see it and arrest her, and we wouldn't have to worry about her taking revenge on us or anything like that."

He shook his head. His skin was more pewter now than bronze. "No police. Bad idea."

"Why's it a bad idea?"

"Not all police are reliable, Jonah Kirk."

"I know that. We all know that. But this woman—anybody can see she's trouble. Not all cops are corrupt, either. Heck, not even most of them."

"They do not have to be corrupt. Sometimes they see bad things being done, they know it is bad, and many of them are not happy about it, but they allow it to happen."

"Why would they let it happen?"

"Maybe they are afraid. Maybe unsure. Maybe they are concerned about losing their jobs. They have to obey their superiors."

"What superiors?"

"The chief of police, the mayor, the governor, the president. They have many superiors." He put the nail to one of the pencil marks he'd made on the door frame, lightly tapped the head of it with the hammer, pulled the nail loose, and explained, "Starter hole for the drill bit," as though I had asked.

As I watched him make three more starter holes, I said, "Well, this doesn't look good for me. How am I going to explain this to my mother?"

"You could simply not say anything about it. That approach has worked for you before."

I thought there might be a little sarcasm in his voice, but I couldn't be certain. "I'm going to have to say something when she asks who put in the security chain."

"Maybe she will not ask."

"Oh, she'll ask, all right."

"If she does not notice right away, she will not ask right away."

He picked up the manual drill, which already had a bit in its jaws, and began to drill out one of the starter holes.

I didn't have to raise my voice to be heard above the soft clicking of the crank handle turning the bevel gears. "How couldn't she notice? It's bright brass."

"She will assume Mr. Smaller installed it."

"What if she asks him about it?"

He moved the drill bit from the first to the second starter hole and turned the crank. "You worry about too many small details, Jonah Kirk. Save your worrying for big problems. Life will bring you enough of those."

"But, see, I've tried to be the man of the house, and that means not bothering her about stuff I should be able to handle myself. So I didn't bother her about this thing and then that thing and this other thing, until now it's a giant mess, and she's going to be mad at me for hiding things, which she has a right to be."

Mr. Yoshioka stopped cranking the drill, looked at me, and said, "Now, *there* is a problem big enough to worry about."

Thirty-two

THE FUNNY THING WAS, NOTHING THAT HAPPENED next proved to be anything that I worried would happen.

Every night, my mother locked the apartment door, sometimes early in the evening and sometimes well after the witching hour on a singing night, after she first fetched me from Mrs. Lorenzo's. She routinely engaged both deadbolts and the security chain without saying a word about the new addition. The fifth or sixth night following Mr. Yoshioka's installation of the chain, at half past one in the morning, she seemed to realize for the first time that it hadn't always been there.

"When did this happen?" she asked, holding the chain and slide bolt in one hand, jingling it slightly.

Half asleep, I might have inadvertently made a revelation

that would have untangled the entire ball of deception. To my discredit, however, even semiconscious, I was guileful enough to mumble, "Don't know. It's been there a while."

She frowned at it, shook her head, and said, "I just realized I've been using it for . . . days, I guess. Huh. Didn't think the landlord would spend a buck to improve anything in this place." Then she slid the bolt into the doorplate and walked me back to my room to tuck me into bed.

Never again did she mention the security chain.

I already thought Mr. Yoshioka was a cool guy in his own sort of buttoned-up way. Now I decided he was a genius, too.

Mother never asked Mr. Smaller about the chain. Later I realized that she pretty much always steered clear of him, most likely because when Tilton lived with us, he sometimes took a six-pack of beer to the superintendent and hung out with him. My father liked to hear Mr. Smaller's wild conspiracy theories, which later he would repeat to my mother and me, making them sound even crazier, mocking Mr. Smaller. Often Tilton's accounts of those theories were funny, but he was so mean in the way he portrayed the superintendent that I couldn't bring myself to laugh. I figured Mom didn't ask Mr. Smaller about the chain because she didn't want him to ask her how Tilton was faring these days; Sylvia Kirk, soon to be Bledsoe again, didn't believe in saying bad things about anyone, but she didn't have a good word for the man who kept abandoning her.

One day in early October, about a week before the legal papers were to be signed to dissolve the marriage, my mother went to the restaurant where Tilton was working for a modest salary plus five percent per year of the business, which eventually he would own. She had no phone number for him, communicated only through his attorney, who was handling the divorce, and wanted to talk face-to-face one more time about the wisdom of what they were doing.

She discovered that he had been fired from that job seven months earlier, long before he had walked out on us. He had never been more than a salaried employee. Worse, his salary had been substantially higher than what he pretended when he lived with us and relied on my mother to pay the rent.

The weak spot she had for him in her heart finally healed that day, much to my relief.

As for Eve Adams, aka Fiona Cassidy, she never bothered either me or Mr. Yoshioka again that summer and early autumn. Periodically, disturbing chemical smells came from 6-C, though never for more than an hour at a time, and my friend the tailor reported them to no one but me. Not long after my mother discovered the truth about Tilton, Eve Adams moved out of 6-C.

We only learned she had gone when, a week later, a crew of workmen set about stripping off the wallpaper, taking up the rotten linoleum, and painting that apartment. In the months she had lived there, she had addressed none of the tasks that she supposedly had been brought in to complete.

When I discovered this, I tracked down Mr. Smaller, who was working again in the spider-infested basement, and I asked about the pretty lady with the purple-blue eyes. I played the crush-stricken boy, bereft that he might never again see that goddess.

Mr. Smaller wasn't dealing with boiler sludge this time. He was filling a glass jug with some kind of smelly lubricant that poured from a tap in one of the unlabeled barrels.

He sported the usual elastic-waist khakis with racehorse-tack suspenders, but not the tank-top undershirt that completed his summer uniform. Instead, in recognition of the cooler weather, he wore a gray sweatshirt with black letters, GET OFF MY CLOUD, which had been the title of a number-one hit by the Rolling Stones almost a year earlier. The faces of the Stones were arrayed across the sweatshirt. This seemed a most unlikely garment for Mr. Smaller. He must have been fifty, not of the demographic that wore garb purchased at rock concerts. Because he never seemed to be concerned whatsoever about his appearance, I supposed that he wore whatever second-hand clothes he found at thrift shops. That GET OFF MY CLOUD sweatshirt had perhaps been thrown out by someone who no longer got a thrill from being a fan of Mick Jagger and the boys, and Mr. Smaller had bought it most likely not because he was an admirer of the Stones, but because the size and the price were right.

"She never done nothin' in Six-C, and I never checked on her to see was she doin' what she was gettin' free rent for. Them pennypinchin' suits downtown send some hippie skank up here so she'll do a cheap job and make their sacred bottom line look good, then they got no right expectin' me to supervise her on top of all my other damn work. I'm happy she stiffed 'em, they ain't deserved nothin' better, but I'm even more happy she's outta here. She's a weirdo, got a screw loose. We'll see that freak on the news one day, and it ain't gonna be 'cause she won herself some Nobel Prize. Son, I done warned you not to go moonin' around her. You're lucky she ain't cut out your heart, dried it, and smoked it to get high."

This was a Friday, after school, when ordinarily I would be in the Abigail Louise Thomas Room, being encouraged by Mrs. Mary O'Toole to move from American standards and current pop to classical music, not as an ultimate destination, just to see if Mozart stirred me as much as did Duke Ellington and Claude Thornhill and Fats Domino. Before I got home from Saint Scholastica's, Mom had left for a meeting with a talent manager, after which she would catch a cab to Slinky's. I had come home to freshen up before going to the community center, but when I'd found the work crew from 6-C taking a cigarette break on the front stoop, my plans had changed.

After racing up to the sixth floor to verify that Eve Adams was gone, and after plunging down to the basement to see Mr. Smaller and confirm that the woman was never coming back, I went next to our apartment. Inside, I engaged both deadbolts behind me but neglected to fix the security chain to the doorplate.

Excited, almost giddy with relief, I went directly to my bedroom and opened the nightstand drawer and took out the La Florentine candy tin. I intended to take scissors to the Polaroid of me sleeping and throw the pieces in the Dumpster in the alleyway.

Thus far I had kept the photograph because it seemed to be proof that Eve Adams had threatened me. I couldn't have taken a snapshot of myself in sleep, especially considering that we didn't own a Polaroid camera. If someday events unfolded in such a way that Mother learned part of what I had been withholding from her and I was required to explain myself, or if Eve Adams, under one name or another, became aggressive toward me again and I needed at last to ask for help, my Polaroid and the one of Mr. Yoshioka's tiger screen—and to a lesser extent the photo of Manzanar torn from a book—would serve as proof, if thin, that she had threatened us.

Now that she had left our building, where obviously she would never again be welcome, the photo would not be needed as proof of anything. But it could serve as *evidence*, evidence that I had kept secret from my mother events of considerable significance. Although she would never invade my privacy, if by some chance she saw the Polaroid, she would wonder who had taken it, why, and when. I could imagine no satisfactory explanation—except the truth. Whatever she might decide was proper punishment for deception, nothing could be worse than her disappointment in me and the sorrow in her eyes. But with Eve Adams gone, I had no need of proof against her and no desire to keep evidence that would convict me of being less of a good son than I wished to be.

In retrospect, as a man of fifty-seven, it's difficult to reconstruct the reasoning of my nine-year-old self, because at that age the brain is literally still forming; the power of reason is not as strong as the power of fantasy. Yet if I remember correctly, when I took the lid off the La Florentine box, my mood was akin to that of a prisoner freed, for the architecture of deceptions and evasions I'd built seemed to be dissolving like a structure in a dream, freeing me from the prospect of one day being shamed before my mother.

Of the familiar items in my eccentric collection—two were missing. The photograph of me sleeping. The fabric eye. I had not looked in the box for more than a week. I knew instantly that Eve Adams had been in the apartment during the day, one day or another, when the security chain was not engaged, that she—no one else—had taken the items. I couldn't imagine why she wanted the fabric eye.

One thing had been added to the collection: a strip of glossy paper clipped from a magazine, two inches by six or seven inches, cut from what must have been a full-page photo of a woman's face, perhaps a glamour shot: the eyes and eyebrows and the bridge of her nose. The subject of the photo must have had blue eyes, but with a purple art pencil, they had been colored to approximately match the shade of Eve Adams's eyes.

I rubbed one of those eyes, and some of the soft purple color came off on my finger.

With the Polaroid, she had taken the evidence of my deception but also the proof of her interest in me. I assumed that the eyes clipped from a magazine meant, *I won't forget you, snoop. I know where to find you, and if you ever speak of me to anyone, I'll have great fun cutting you to pieces.*

Maybe she would start with my eyes.

At that moment, I realized how foolish I had been to think that she was out of my life forever. I had seen her in a dream before I'd seen her for real, which must mean the dream was true, prophetic. So her name indeed was Fiona Cassidy, not Eve Adams, and she would not be out of my life until sometime after I switched on a penlight and found myself in a staring match with her fixed, dead eyes.

Thirty-three

WHAT I DID NEXT MAY SEEM RIDICULOUS AND perhaps amusing, but I can assure you that nothing about it struck me as funny at the time.

I sat there on the edge of my bed, the strip of paper stretched between the thumbs and forefingers of my hands, staring at the eyes clipped from a magazine photo. Those eyes weren't hers, weren't real, and yet I felt that Fiona Cassidy could see me clearly through them, no matter where she might be at the moment, that they were juju for sure. She wasn't just strange, not merely mentally disturbed. I had wanted to believe that she was a master lock-picker; but now I felt *dead certain* that she could conjure herself through doors and walls, that she possessed some occult power of which I had thus far seen only the simplest manifestations.

My first intention was to tear the eyeful strip into tiny pieces and flush them down the toilet. But the next thing I knew, I was in the kitchen, opening a cabinet door under the sink. Among the items stored there was a can with a tightly fitted lid, in which my mother kept a box of six-inch-long matches that she used to reignite the pilot light on the gas oven when occasionally it went out. From a drawer near the cooktop, I withdrew a pair of chef's tongs.

In the bathroom, I held the strip of paper with the tongs and burned it over the open toilet. Curls of ashes fell into the water, and when no paper was left, I flushed them away.

I left the noisy bathroom-ventilation fan running, put away the tongs and matches, and returned with a can of air freshener, which I sprayed liberally throughout the bathroom. By the time my mother came home from performing at Slinky's, there would be no slightest scent of smoke to suggest that I'd been playing with fire.

In my bedroom once more, as I approached the open candy tin, I panicked and became certain that another item had been missing from my collection, its absence previously unnoticed: the Lucite heart containing the small white feather. For the past few weeks, I hadn't been carrying the pendant with me, as I had faithfully done when it was new and still seemed to glow with imminent magic. A sudden flare of intuition filled me with the conviction that in some way I could not understand, the pendant provided ultimate protection, that if the woman had taken possession of it, then I would be defenseless—and doomed.

I shuddered with relief when I found it in the metal box, and I put it, chain and all, in a pocket of my jeans.

By then I had worked myself into a sweat of dread, so that it wasn't surprising I became obsessed with the missing fabric eye. I had saved it because, considering the eerie way it had rolled along the alley to me in a breeze that affected nothing else, I'd thought it might have some juju in it. When I'd told Fiona Cassidy as much, while she held the tip of her switchblade in my left nostril, she'd regarded me with contempt and declared, *You're a real little freak in the making, aren't you?* Now I wondered if her mockery had been misdirection, if in fact she saw some power in the fabric eye and had taken it to use against me and my mother.

There have been times during my life when I have wished to be a boy again, not to have the energy and perfect health of youth, but to know once more the innocence and the delight in even the smallest of things that we often fail to feel full strength as the years drift by. What is easy to forget, however, until you apply yourself to the task of memory, is that childhood is a time of fear, as well; some of those fears are reasonable, others irrational and inspired by a sense of powerlessness in a world where often power over others seems to be what drives so very many of our fellow human beings. In the swoon of childhood, the possibility of werewolves is as real as the schoolyard shooter, the idea of vampires as credible as the idea of a terrorist attack, a neighbor possessing paranormal talents as believable as a psychopath.

After putting away the La Florentine box, I searched my bedroom for the fabric eye, which the woman might have concealed somewhere: under the bed, atop the chest of drawers, behind the radiator, in the folds of the draperies, behind the valance above the window, where it would enjoy at least a narrow view of a portion of the room . . . When I found nothing, I sorted through the contents of drawers and inspected every niche in the closet, because after all, when I went to bed and turned off the lights, it might roll out of concealment to watch over me. Undoubtedly, such an eye would have perfect night vision. Again, I found nothing.

In the hallway, I stood at the threshold of my mother's bedroom, convinced of the necessity to search it as thoroughly as I had combed through my room. Fortunately, a sense of propriety restrained me from rushing madly into her boudoir.

At just that moment of recaptured sanity, the telephone rang, and I hurried into the kitchen to answer it.

"Jonah," said Mrs. Lorenzo, "you were supposed to come

down here as soon as you got back from the community center. Supper's going to be ready soon."

I failed to tell her that I had not gone to the center after I'd learned the woman in 6-C moved out. I don't know if that qualified as a lie of omission, but at least I was deceiving a neighbor rather than my mother. "I'm on my way now, Mrs. Lorenzo."

Reluctantly, I left the apartment, locked the door, and went down to spend the evening with the widow.

Not an ordinary Friday. But nothing serious yet.

Thirty-four

SATURDAY MORNING. BREAKFAST OUT WITH MY mother. A neighborhood diner on Forestall Street. Pancakes with pineapple and coconut sauce. A rare treat. Great fun. Going places with my mother was always fun. *She* was always fun.

But I couldn't stop thinking about the purple-eyed witch.

Mom and I took a bus to the planetarium. I loved that place. Planets and stars and galaxies. A new show about meteors, asteroids, comets. It was good. It was interesting. It was interminable.

Then the Museum of Natural History. What a great place. The huge skeleton of a real brontosaurus. The convincing life-size model of a *T. Rex*. Always before, the *T. Rex* spooked me. It didn't spook me that day.

Lunch at Woolworth's. A grilled-cheese sandwich and coleslaw. Mom couldn't believe I didn't want dessert. She assured me that we could afford it. But I said, "No, thanks, I'm stuffed." The truth is, I wanted it. But I didn't want to take the time to eat it.

We rode a bus back to our neighborhood, all the way down to the community center. For twenty minutes, Mom sat beside me on the bench and listened to me play piano in the Abigail Louise Thomas Room. Then she had to go home, change, and head off to Slinky's.

She said, "You're the man, Jonah. Duke Ellington's got nothing on you," and she kissed my cheek.

She thought I'd spend another couple of hours at the keyboard; and on any other Saturday, I would have. But I had other intentions. Besides, I was too nervous to practice effectively. Nevertheless, I needed to remain at the community center for half an hour to avoid encountering my mother when I returned home. I passed the time by playing the melody of "Magenta Haze," one of Duke's symphonic pieces, a slow and easy drift from first note to last, which I had to translate from the soprano saxophone solo that was the heart of it.

I needed feedback about what to make of the witch's final visit to my bedroom the previous day. The only other person with unnerving experience of her dark side was Mr. Yoshioka.

When I rang his doorbell on the fifth floor, having brought six of my mother's chocolate-chip cookies on a paper plate, I didn't know if he would be home. He worked long hours, sometimes on Saturdays, too. But when he opened the door, he seemed to be expecting me.

"Will this be a celebration, Jonah Kirk?"

"A little bit, yeah, I guess."

He accepted the cookies, and I took off my shoes. Minutes later, we were sitting in his living room with tea, cookies, and those odd little cakes that I pretended to like more than I really did.

I told him everything about Eve Adams that I'd so far withheld, including that her real name was evidently Fiona Cassidy and that I had first seen her in a dream. I didn't mention Miss Pearl, who had brought me that dream as surely as she'd brought me a piano, because she was a mystery in herself, and one mystery layered on another seemed sure to confuse us at a time when I desperately wanted some clarity.

Although Mr. Yoshioka had been understanding in the past and treated me with the same seriousness that he would bring to any conversation with an adult, I was prepared for his expression of disbelief when I spoke of a prophetic dream. Instead, he listened without expression and, when I finished, he nodded and sipped his tea and closed his eyes as if to consider what I had revealed.

His silence somewhat unsettled me, so that I said, "It's true, sir. She was in the dream, the two of us in some tight space, with the sounds of rushing water all around."

He opened his eyes and said, "There is no need to insist. I do believe you. When I was fifteen, I dreamed that my mother and sister perished in a fire. Seven days later, they did indeed burn to death. Their screams were at first very shrill, sharp with pain and terror. But soon they became like the haunting cries of certain nocturnal birds, as if they were beyond pain but not beyond sorrow, as if they were sorrowing over their untimely departure from this world as their souls were borne away on wings and into silence."

As on my previous visit, my host had provided a tiny pitcher of orange-blossom honey, with which I had sweetened the tea that he took straight. His revelation was so horrible that I could not think what to say, and I picked up my cup and took a sip to buy a little time to process what he had just told me. Although the tea had been sweet a minute ago, it was bitter now, and I put down the cup.

"When did it happen?" I asked.

"On September fourteenth, 1942, but I do not wish to talk about it further. I brought it up only to explain why I accept the truth of your dream without reservation. Over the years, Jonah Kirk, I have come to believe that we who have suffered greatly may from time to time be given the grace of foretelling, so that we may act to spare ourselves from further torment."

"But in spite of your dream, your mother and sister . . . they died seven days later."

"Because of my failure to believe in that grace, because of my anger and my bitterness and my denial."

Usually, the condition of his heart could be read, if at all, only in his eyes, for he wasn't given to dramatic facial expressions. Now, however, for a moment, his face became a portrait of desolation.

"Because of my failure," he repeated.

I liked him too much to bear easily his self-condemnation, and a kind of grief overcame me. Although I was curious, I knew better than to ask him to tell me more about that mortal fire twenty-four years earlier.

Apprehension led me to speak. "You said . . . you said foretelling is sometimes a gift for people who've suffered greatly. But I dreamed of Fiona Cassidy . . . and I haven't suffered greatly."

He said, "Then in time, you will."

Thirty-five

THAT NIGHT I DREAMED OF MOONLIT WOODS through which a creature unseen stalked me, of a moon-washed shore along a dark coast where black waves tumbled to the sand and where I felt drawn into the water even though I knew that beneath the turbulent surface swam something more ominous than mere sharks, of a moon-dappled plain where massive slabs of rock thrust skyward like pieces of the shattered vaults of fallen castles and where some presence whispered to me from among the ruins, enticing me into byways where not even the faintest blush of moonlight revealed the way.

Fright woke me. I sat up in bed, listening to the near-total darkness, but nothing in it rustled or creaked, or whispered. After a minute, I stood my pillow on end against the headboard and leaned back, waiting for my heart to stop knocking like a horse's hooves on cobblestones. In a while, I could hear the distant traffic noises of the city at night trembling against the window glass.

My dream of fluidly shifting locations and unspecified monsters was too vague to be prophetic. All of it had been just the phantasms of the sleeping mind, and I knew that if ever I were stalked by an enemy of murderous intention or enticed into a moonless dark where Death waited, the fatal moment would not occur in any of the eerie landscapes from which I had awakened.

I harked back to my conversation with Mr. Yoshioka after he had said that in time I would suffer greatly.

Why would she take those things from the candy tin—the picture of me sleeping, the stuffed-toy eye?

In part to unsettle you, to say to you that by her possession of them, she will remain aware of you.

In part? Why else?

Since our previous tea, in which you raised the subject of juju, I have researched the issue—juju in Africa and the variation that in the New World is called voodoo. If this woman truly believes in black magic, she might keep the photograph of you for use as an effigy.

A what?

Like a voodoo doll. An effigy. A representation of you.

She might believe that if she sticks pins in it, she can torment you long-distance.

That's bad.

Do not worry, Jonah Kirk. There is nothing true about juju or voodoo. Neither works. It is all nonsense.

That's what my grandpa says.

Then you should listen to him and not worry.

Okay, but why did she take the stuffed-toy eye?

I do not have a theory. This Eve Adams, this Fiona Cassidy, is perhaps a psychopath, in which case we have no hope of understanding her motives or her mind.

That's not very comforting, sir.

No, Jonah Kirk, it is not.

Our little get-together to mark the woman's departure had taken on a decidedly solemn note for a celebration. When we found ourselves sharing dour silences more than conversation, I decided it was time to leave. As I opened the door, Mr. Yoshioka handed me a plain white business card that featured only his name, and centered under it a single word in italics, *tailor,* and under that a telephone number.

That is my work number. If I am not at home, you can call me there in an emergency.

What emergency?

Any emergency, Jonah Kirk.

Maybe there won't be one.
Maybe there will not.
But I kinda think there might be.
I think so as well.

Thirty-six

1966 HAD BEEN A YEAR OF GROWING TUMULT. Escalating war in Vietnam. All those murdered student nurses in Chicago. The Austin tower sniper shooting down—and down upon—people as though he were a mad god on a high throne.

Race riots had rocked Atlanta and Chicago, and our city, too. In the civil-rights arena, sober men like Roy Wilkins and Martin Luther King and Ralph Abernathy advised change by peaceable means, while Stokely Carmichael found threats effective, and more radical groups like the Black Panthers advocated violence. As you might assume, Grandpa Teddy's sympathies were entirely with the advocates of nonviolence, as were Grandma Anita's and Sylvia's.

Anti-war protests were growing. In our city, on October 18, bombs went off during the night in two military-recruiting offices. No one was killed or injured. Police released an artist's rendering of a suspect based on eyewitness accounts of a man seen lurking in the vicinity of one of the targets. I'd never seen him before . . . and yet something about him was familiar and intriguing. In fact, after my mother dropped the newspaper in the trash, I quietly retrieved it and clipped out the police artist's portrait and put it in my La Florentine box.

I didn't know what to make of all the social chaos, and I tried to heed my mother's advice, which was essentially to live from the inside out, not from the outside in. The news wasn't *all* the news, she'd said, and what held the world together was the way all those people who never made the news were inclined to live their lives.

Whatever else might be happening, the music that year was so fine. Percy Sledge. The Mamas and the Papas. Simon and Garfunkel. Motown—the Four Tops, the Supremes, the Miracles. The Beatles' album *Revolver.* Bob Dylan's *Blonde on Blonde. Pet Sounds* by the Beach Boys. Jim McGuinn's shimmering guitar on the Byrds' "Eight Miles High."

October gave way to November, and with the approach of winter, the country calmed down somewhat—though not for long. The divorce papers came, signed by my absent father, approved by a court, and although marriage was a sacrament to Sylvia, we were living in a time when fewer and fewer people agreed with her. We enjoyed a wonderful Thanksgiving at my grandparents' house, and they invited friends who had no families of their own.

On Christmas Eve, my mother and I and Teddy and Anita went to Mass together. The shadowy church was lit only by an overhead light trained on the altar and by the flames of hundreds of flickering candles in glass cups set all around the nave. If you squinted, the columns and vaults seemed to melt away, all the grandness of the architecture receded, and the space became intimate, almost as if you were cast back many centuries to a humble place where a miracle had occurred, where the radiance issued not from candles but from the air itself, back to a less hectic era before the invention of clocks, to a night of peace from which a renewed world would then begin to date itself.

Four days later, on the evening of December 28, after reading in bed for an hour, before turning off the light, I took the tin box from my nightstand. In the weeks immediately after the destruction of the two recruiting offices, I had occasionally studied the pencil portrait of the suspected bomber, not sure why it fascinated me, but my interest had waned, and I hadn't looked at the drawing for perhaps a month. This time, the moment I turned the clipping faceup in the lamplight, I realized that the description given by the witness to the police artist had resulted in a woefully inaccurate portrait of Lucas Drackman.

Before I had dreamed of Fiona Cassidy, I had dreamed of Lucas Drackman, on the night of the day that I had gone to the community center, discovered the promised piano, and had begun formal lessons with Mrs. O'Toole. When, in sleep, I first saw him, he was a teenager who had already killed his parents in their bed and was busy stealing what cash and jewelry and credit cards he could find. In memory, I could still hear him as he stood beside the bloody bed, speaking to his dead father: *Hey there,* Bob. *What's it like in Hell,* Bob? *You think now maybe sending me away to a freakin' military academy was really stupid, Bob? You ignorant, self-righteous son of a bitch.*

Either the witness had given an inadequate description or the artist had not successfully translated the description to paper. Lucas Drackman's deep-set eyes had not been captured, nor the true bone structure and shape of his face. Although the nose appeared hawkish, like the murderer's, it was too narrow, too pointed. The feature most accurately portrayed was his ripe and almost girlish mouth, which in life contrasted even more dramatically with his otherwise ascetic face than it did in the drawing.

Thirty-seven

THE NEXT DAY, DECEMBER 29, WAS A THURSDAY, and of course I was still on school holiday. Mom didn't have to sing that night; Slinky's had closed to be lavishly decorated for the huge business it would do on the last two nights of the year. She had a five-hour shift at Woolworth's; and then she would come home to spend the evening with me. Because she couldn't be there on New Year's Eve or on the eve before, she wanted that night's dinner to be our celebration. She gave me money to get takeout from The Royal, the nearby diner on Forestall Street, where on some of our most special days together we had breakfast. They made the best chili in the world—a sign in their window announced that fact—and cheese bread so good that I sometimes dreamed about it. I was tasked with buying chili (which Mom would serve over buttered noodles), cheese bread, and whatever I wanted for dessert.

The day was cold but not bitter. I wore my zip-up quilted jacket, which was somewhat too big for me, because even though I was skinny and a bit short for my age, I grew too fast to get much use out of clothes if everything was bought to fit perfectly. Coats were more expensive than jeans and shirts, so I always had to wear them somewhat large to start and then gradually grow into them. I wore my new toboggan hat, too, which was striped red and white and topped with a red pom-pom that—in retrospect I am amazed to reveal—I thought was the essence of cool.

Although it was smack between breakfast and lunch rushes when I got to The Royal, the place was busy, as always. A few tables were available, so that the only people standing were those at the takeout window near the front.

I got in line to place my order, not at all impatient because I delighted in the atmosphere of the diner. Such a mélange of aromas. Hamburger patties on the griddle, bubbling with melted cheese. Bacon. Butter-scrambled eggs with ham. Mere bread becoming toast. All of those smells and more were threaded through with cigarette smoke; if you did not live through those times, you will need some imagination to understand how reliably people tolerated one another's habits and foibles in those days.

Clink of flatware, clatter of dishes, waitresses calling out orders in diner lingo, a ceaselessly rising and falling and rising tide of conversation among the customers: It was music of a kind, at the same time soothing and invigorating, such a *human* place and time, when no one texted at the table or had an Internet to surf while they ate or carried a cell phone the ring of which could never be ignored.

Waiting in line, I enjoyed looking around, seeing the different kinds of people, wondering who they were, what lives they returned to when they left The Royal—and it was then that I saw Tilton, my father. Against the farther wall, a row of booths extended the length of the diner. He sat in one toward the back, in animated conversation with someone across the table from him, gesturing with a fork.

I almost didn't recognize him because he'd grown a beard. He wore a black turtleneck and some kind of silver medallion on a silver chain.

Because the booths had high backs, I couldn't see the companion with whom Tilton so vigorously conversed. I wondered if it might be Miss Delvane, the writer and would-be rodeo novelist. I was curious, of course, but I was more spooked than anything.

If Tilton glanced in my direction and spotted me, nothing good could follow. Not yet having placed my takeout order, I turned at once away from him and hurried to the door, praying that nothing I wore would identify me to him. The quilted jacket was identical to a million others. Although my striped toboggan cap was a beacon on my head, my mother had given it to me for Christmas, less than a week earlier, and my father had never seen it.

Outside, leaving the congenial world of The Royal, slapped in the face by a gust of cold wind, I initially intended to run, to get out of the immediate neighborhood and beyond Tilton's reach. But I'd gone not ten feet when intuition took hold of me as surely as a hand gripping my arm, brought me to a stop, and told me that I needed to know with whom my father was having a late breakfast or early lunch, that the identity of his companion must be of crucial importance.

After all these years, I occasionally wonder how my life would have been different if in that fateful moment I had followed my first impulse and had run. But I suppose that what we call intuition is just one of the many ways that the still small voice in our souls speaks to us, if we will listen, and that inner companion wants only what is best for us. If I had run, no doubt what might have happened to me would have been far worse than what did happen, my losses even greater than they have been, my story darker than the one I've lived. And yet I wonder.

Thirty-eight

DIRECTLY ACROSS FORESTALL STREET FROM THE
Royal stood a shoe-repair shop on the ground level of a
century-old four-story brick building, the upper floors of
which might have offered either offices for businesses with
uncertain prospects or apartments even cheaper than our
own. Beside that structure lay an empty plot of ground,
where another building had been torn down in the name
of progress; but progress evidently had gone elsewhere. A
decrepit chain-link fence surrounded the lot; years earlier
the gate had been broken down and never replaced. In
warmer weather, neighborhood kids gathered there to play
kickball and other games.

When I came out of the diner, traffic was light, and I
crossed the street in mid-block. The bright sun painted the

pavement with the black shadows of bare-limbed trees, and in the fitful winter wind, those silhouettes twitched underfoot like the many tangled legs of agitated spiders.

I went through the gap in the fence where the gate had once been and stood behind the chain-link, watching the diner. Around me, the ground was mostly barren, hard-packed dirt with here and there a few bristles of withered weeds, empty soda-pop cans, and scraps of paper litter.

Overhead, the winter-stripped limbs of the trees scratched at one another and rattled when a gust of the inconstant wind passed through them. The last birds hardy enough to perch in those leafless bowers cast themselves, with much flapping of wings and shrieking, into a rush of wind and let it carry them to roosts in the more sheltered eaves of nearby buildings.

When my father came out of the diner, he was not in the company of Miss Delvane. Instead, the man with him was a few inches past six feet, with long dirty-blond hair that the wind tossed. They huddled for a moment, sharing a last word, and then my father walked west toward the avenue. His tall companion stood at the curb until a cluster of cars passed, and then he crossed the street as if he had business at the shoe-repair shop.

Having crossed, however, he turned east toward me, and I found a soda can to kick along the fence, hoping to pass for a bored kid with nothing more interesting to do than to haunt a vacant lot and hope others like me might come along for a game of kickball. I noisily booted the can eastward, then turned and kicked it toward the west, looking up at him as he approached along the farther side of the chain-link.

Although his short hair was now long, although he had a poorly groomed mustache when once he had been clean-shaven, although he was perhaps twenty-five instead of seventeen, as he had been when I had seen him in a dream, I recognized him at once. Lucas Drackman. Murderer of his parents. Bomber of military-recruitment offices. He so little resembled the police artist's portrait that he was in no danger whatsoever of being identified by it.

In memory, I heard the voice of Miss Pearl, who had seemed to be in my bedroom, sitting on the edge of my bed, on the night that I dreamed of this killer: *Go to sleep, Ducks. Go to sleep now. I have a name for you, a name and a face and a dream. The name is Lucas Drackman and the face is his.*

His dragon-smoke breath pluming from his open mouth, he met my eyes through the fence, and for a moment I couldn't look away from him, for I felt that I was staring into the eyes not of a man but of a demon. Perhaps in that moment, he sensed that my interest was not that of someone to whom he was a stranger, because when I moved again and sent the can tumbling, he came to a halt. I kept going, kicking that tortured scrap of aluminum to the west end of the property, turned, and started back, pretending that I didn't realize he was waiting for me.

As I approached him, he said, "Hey, kid."

Trying to look pissed-off at the world rather than frightened, I dared to look at him.

He studied me for a moment and then said, "What's with you?"

I did what I thought a juvenile delinquent in the making might have done. I flipped him my middle finger and turned away and booted the can hard toward the center of the vacant lot. I gave that can hell for a while, kicking it this way and that half a dozen times, and when at last I looked toward the fence, Lucas Drackman had gone.

Thirty-nine

AT HOME, AFTER PUTTING THE CHEESE BREAD IN the oven, which served as our breadbox, the chili and cupcakes in the refrigerator, I took Mr. Yoshioka's business card from my wallet and went to the telephone.

The card provided no company name, but a woman answered the phone with, "Metropolitan Suits. May I help you?"

Although she must have thought it peculiar that a young boy would be ringing them up, she didn't hesitate to give me their address when I asked for it.

I felt the need to consult with Mr. Yoshioka at once, but what I had to tell him could be conveyed convincingly only face-to-face. The address I'd been given was in the city's Garment District, two short blocks and four long blocks from our apartment, farther than I had permission to roam alone. I regret to say that I hesitated not at all to be disobedient, but instead set out at once.

At the street number that I'd written on the card, I found a large, plain single-story building, impressive only for its size. The street was almost clogged with big trucks making deliveries and picking up shipments at an array of businesses. A marshaling yard on the north side of Metropolitan Suits, adjacent to the company's loading docks, seemed to be the busiest place of all.

The front door brought me into a reception area. To the right, a counter separated the public space from four desks where women sat typing, working adding machines, and answering phones. The center of the room was open, and to the left were eight chairs, all empty, and a coffee table on which glossy magazines were fanned like a hand of cards.

One of the women got up from her desk, a nice older lady with curly gray hair, and came to the counter and smiled and asked if she could help me.

"I need to see Mr. George T. Yoshioka, please. I'm sorry to bother him on the job, I don't want to get him fired or anything, but it's very important, it's an emergency."

"And your name?" she asked.

"Jonah Ellington Basie Hines—" I checked myself. "Jonah Kirk, ma'am. I'm Mr. Yoshioka's neighbor. He's fifth floor, see, and my mom and me are on the fourth."

Indicating the chairs around the table of magazines, she said, "Have a seat, Jonah, and I'll let Mr. Yoshioka know you're here."

I was too nervous to sit. I stood in the center of the room, shifting from foot to foot, taking off my gloves and stuffing them in my jacket pockets.

When the lady returned to her desk and picked up the phone, I could hear her voice, soft and low, but I couldn't make out a word.

The many trucks in the marshaling yard suggested the company must be successful, but you wouldn't know it from the condition of the reception lounge. Painted concrete floor. Cheap wood paneling. An acoustic-tile ceiling. The chairs looked like army surplus.

At the counter again, the gray-haired lady said, "Mr. Yoshioka will join you in a minute." She seemed to realize that in my highly agitated state, I couldn't bear to sit down. Pointing to an inner door directly opposite the outer one, she said, "He'll be coming through there."

She didn't invite me to open that door, but I opened it anyway, without thinking. Beyond lay an immense, well-lighted chamber with a complex truss ceiling, the thick tie beams of which were supported by rows of tall steel poles. A couple of hundred people toiled in what appeared to be long-practiced rhythms. At the nearer end, men worked in pairs at wide tables, with great bolts of material that could be drawn as needed from enormous spools suspended from the beams overhead. They chalked the material to match patterns they placed upon it and then, with large and wickedly sharp shears, cut quickly and precisely to the chalk line. Farther back, still more men sat at smaller tables, operating industrial sewing machines; each was attended by a younger man ever on his feet, supplying his superior with pre-cut pieces of material, lining fabric, and other items just when needed. These younger men were the only employees on the floor who didn't wear suits and ties, though the older men worked in their shirtsleeves, their suit coats draped on nearby chairs. To a boy's eye, that farther end of the vast room had a macabre quality, for throughout stood tailors' dummies, mannequins of various sizes, all of them headless. In the back wall were three widely separated pairs of doors leading to other realms of the Metropolitan maze.

The sewing machines stuttered ceaselessly in their stitching, and the place smelled of wool. Warm air came in through wall vents near the floor, and exhaust fans pulled it toward fewer but larger vents in the exposed ductwork that snaked through the truss system overhead. In the ascending currents, I saw fabric dust rotating as it rose, like galaxies of tiny suns and planets and moons.

Some might say these were tedious jobs involving mind-numbing repetitive motions, but to a boy like me, the great room and all in it were astonishing, wondrous. The men who labored there seemed too engaged in their work to be bored, and the confidence and speed with which they performed their tasks struck me as wizardly.

Mr. Yoshioka appeared in one of the aisles, in his shirt-sleeves but pulling on his suit jacket as he approached. He smiled and gave me a half bow and said, "What a pleasant surprise to see you, Jonah Kirk."

"I'm so sorry to bother you at work, sir, but something really bad has happened, and I don't know—"

He interrupted me. "Perhaps it would be wise to wait until we can discuss this without raising our voices."

To the left of the door hung a time clock and next to it a file board with hundreds of slots containing envelope-size cards arranged alphabetically. Mr. Yoshioka took his from near the end of the array, inserted it in the clock, and put it away after it had been stamped with the time.

In the reception lounge, we sat in the two chairs farthest from the four women busy at their desks. We didn't whisper, but we spoke softly.

"You know when I finally told you everything, how I'd seen Eve Adams dead in a dream, and her name was really Fiona Cassidy?"

Mr. Yoshioka nodded. "This was after you brought me a plate of your mother's superb chocolate-chip cookies, for which I remain most grateful."

"I thought you wouldn't believe me about the dream, but you did. I'll never forget how you believed me. It was like a huge relief."

He smiled at me and waited.

With some embarrassment, I said, "Well, I didn't really tell you everything. I mean, I told you everything about Fiona Cassidy, but she isn't the only dream."

"And now you will tell me everything."

"Yes. I have to. It's all tied together somehow."

"Perhaps it is a good sign that you have not brought me cookies this time."

"Sir?"

"When you bring me cookies and tell me everything, it turns out that the everything was not everything. Perhaps the cookies are your way of apologizing in advance for not telling me everything."

I progressed from embarrassment to mortification. "I'm sorry. I really am. It's just that . . . I don't know. It's all so weird, so big and so weird, and I'm just a kid no matter what I tell myself about being the man of the house. I'm just a kid."

Mr. Yoshioka's eyes twinkled, like you read about the eyes of good and magical creatures twinkling in fairy tales. "Yes, you are still a child. That is why I have, as I have heard it said, 'cut you some slack.' Now you will tell me the rest of everything?"

"I had another dream. This was even before the one about Fiona Cassidy dead."

I told him about Lucas Drackman, seeing him with his murdered parents in a dream, and then seeing him with my father earlier this same morning.

Mr. Yoshioka listened attentively, and when I finished, he sat with his eyes closed, which by now I knew meant that he was puzzling through the ramifications of what I'd told him. When his silence made me nervous and I started to speak, he anticipated that I had nothing more to say that wasn't babble, and he put one forefinger to his lips to suggest the wisdom of silence.

When he opened his eyes, he said, "You dreamed of Lucas Drackman—and now Lucas Drackman knows your father. Therefore, it is logical to assume that, because you also dreamed of Fiona Cassidy, she might also know your father or will come to know him in the near future."

"That's what I'm thinking, but if—"

Forefinger to lips again. "It is likewise logical to suppose that if both Lucas Drackman and Fiona Cassidy know your father, they might know each other."

I nodded, although until he put it into words, I hadn't reached that conclusion.

"If you are correct that the police artist's portrait of the bombing suspect in the newspaper is a badly rendered likeness of Lucas Drackman, one might conclude that he is destroying recruitment offices with explosives concocted by Eve Adams, aka Fiona Cassidy, when she was using odorous and volatile chemicals in Apartment Six-C."

I said, "Holy mother of God," and at once mentally accused myself of profanity and made the sign of the cross and said, "But that would mean, could mean, might mean that my father, Tilton . . ."

Mr. Yoshioka finished the thought that I couldn't quite speak aloud. "Your father might know Lucas Drackman in some other context than bombing recruitment offices, but the possibility is real that the three of them are part of a conspiracy—the Bilderbergers written small."

Forty

AT THE DESKS BEHIND THE COUNTER AT THE farther end of the room, the four women remained busy and, as far as I could tell, were not curious about my visit with Mr. Yoshioka.

We had been talking softly, but now I whispered. "Is Tilton a mad bomber?"

"As I said, he may know Lucas Drackman in another context and have no idea that the man is a criminal. And if your father is indeed involved in a conspiracy, he is not necessarily mad—if I am correct that by *mad* you mean insane."

"I guess I didn't. Tilton's not insane. He's . . . troubled. We've got to tell the police."

Judging by his expression—a compression of his lips

and sudden little crow's feet at the corners of his eyes—Mr. Yoshioka was no more enthusiastic about going to the authorities than he had been when he had installed security chains to keep Fiona Cassidy out of our apartments. "We cannot tell the police merely that your father is 'troubled.' Of crimes, we have no evidence, Jonah Kirk. You saw your father with someone you *think* might be the bombing suspect. That is even less than hearsay and of no interest to the police."

"But for sure this Drackman guy killed his parents. Shot them in bed while they were sleeping. He's already wanted."

"For sure? How do you know?"

"Well, good grief, I saw it in the dream. Oh, okay. I guess . . . not evidence. So what can we do?"

He tugged on one cuff of his white shirt and then on the other, so that a precise half inch was displayed beyond his coat sleeves. He brushed a few all-but-invisible specks of lint off his pants. He adjusted his necktie.

"If perhaps we were to telephone an anonymous tip to the police, regarding your father, what address would we give them?"

"Since Mom threw him out, we don't know where he lives."

"A telephone number?"

"We don't have one for him."

"Where does he work?"

"As far as we know, he doesn't. He's not big on work. All we have is the name of some lawyer that handled the divorce for him."

"That does not help us. The lawyer-client privilege will keep him silent."

"So what can we do?" I asked again. "What about an anonymous tip to the cops about Drackman?"

"We do not know where he lives, either, and we do not know under what name he may be living."

"We're dead."

"Never say die." With one finger, he traced the crease in his pants along his thigh to his knee, first the left leg and then the right. "I need some time to think about this. It is quite complex."

"Yeah, sure. My head hurts, thinking about it."

"Now that it has come to this, do you think that you will tell your mother everything?"

If I could have gone pale, the thought of telling my mother everything would have bleached me white. "Oh, man, no. I mean, where would I start? What would she think of me? How could she trust me again?"

"The truth heals all, even when it's revealed late, Jonah Kirk, if it is revealed in its entirety and with apologies." I reminded him that I hadn't actually lied to my mother, that I had only withheld certain things, and he said, "Well,

I would never counsel you to continue to withhold information from her . . . But in all honesty, I must say, for the time being, it might be best not to tell her. If she believed you and if she went to the police, she would likely achieve nothing except to alert your father and his associates. And then I believe that both of you might be in grave danger. For the moment, at least, you are not."

He got to his feet, and so did I, and he half bowed to me, and I returned the bow. He held out a hand, and I shook it.

I said, "I'm really sorry I had to come and dump all this on you."

"You should not be sorry. I am not. Give me a few days to work on this. Meanwhile, as detectives say in novels, you should lie low."

He headed toward the door that opened to the work floor, and I started toward the front entrance, but then he called to me. We met in the center of the reception area.

He said, "There must be some missing link in this story."

"You don't mean like half man, half monkey."

"No, I do not. I mean some connection shared by your father, Fiona Cassidy, and Lucas Drackman. I suggest that for the time being you should avoid Mr. Reginald Smaller."

As I was about to defend Mr. Smaller, I remembered how Tilton sometimes took a six-pack to the superintendent, supposedly to loosen his tongue and pump him for ridiculous conspiracy theories with which later to regale Mom and me.

"I find it conceivable," said Mr. Yoshioka, "that the black-hearted company men he talks about had no idea that Miss Cassidy was living rent-free in Apartment Six-C."

I was disappointed. "I wanted to think he was a good guy."

"He might in fact be a good guy. But I would not stake my life on it."

Mr. Yoshioka returned to work, and after the door fell shut behind him, I went to the counter and thanked the nice lady who had called him off the factory floor for me. "I hope he doesn't get in trouble for taking a break."

She had a lovely smile, and I was pleased to see it because I didn't think she'd smile if I'd gotten the tailor in trouble. "Don't worry, Jonah. Mr. Yoshioka is highly regarded around here."

"He's highly regarded by me, too," I said. As I spoke, a funny thing happened, the words turning thick in my throat, almost as if I were going to get all choked up. And the nice lady blurred a little, too.

Outside, the wind blew cold and the sun shone bright. On that bustling street, among those many big trucks and busy people, with the city all around for miles and miles, I felt terribly small, and worse than small. Suddenly I felt alone.

Forty-one

I HIKED FOUR LONG BLOCKS AND TWO SHORT blocks from Metropolitan Suits to our apartment building. Then I walked two more long blocks to the nearest library.

This branch wasn't as large as the central library that stood across from the Museum of Natural History, and it featured a plain limestone floor instead of different colors of marble laid in fancy patterns. But it housed a lot of books.

Although I knew how to use the card catalog, I didn't know under what subject to search. With the librarian's help, in five minutes I settled at a table in the reading room with four books, three that included limited information about Manzanar and one that was devoted entirely to the subject.

Manzanar, which in Spanish meant "apple orchard," had been a farm town 225 miles north of Los Angeles, in Owens Valley, founded in 1910 but abandoned before 1930, after Los Angeles purchased more than 6,000 acres of the valley for the water rights.

After the bombing of Pearl Harbor on December 7, 1941, fear of homeland sabotage swept the country, and in early 1942, President Roosevelt signed Executive Order Number 9066, forcing nearly 120,000 Japanese Americans in western states to ten relocation centers in isolated areas. Whether he had the constitutional authority to do so is argued to this day.

Even before 9066, accounts in all American branches of Japanese banks were frozen. Most who were forced into ten internment camps by the War Relocation Authority lost their homes or sold them at a loss, and their businesses were either sold for a fraction of true value or closed without remuneration.

Even Japanese orphans residing in institutions run by nuns and by the Salvation Army were transported to Manzanar, where a camp orphanage was established for them. Caucasian foster parents caring for Japanese and half-Japanese babies were forced to surrender those children to the War Relocation Authority.

Manzanar, like the other ten camps, was self-sufficient. It had its own hospital, post office, a few churches, schools, playgrounds, football fields, baseball diamonds, tennis courts . . .

The barracks apartments were small, sixteen by twenty feet, providing no privacy, which was especially stressful to the women. The government contractor used inferior materials; the workmanship was poor. Summer temperatures topped 100 degrees. Winters were cold and snowy. The internees did their best to improve accommodations, but comfort was not easily achieved. The barbed-wire fences and eight guard towers surrounding the 540 acres of the main camp made it impossible to imagine that this was ordinary life.

The internees beautified their surroundings with rose gardens and rock gardens, with ponds and streams and a waterfall. When a nursery wholesaler donated a thousand cherry and wisteria trees, internees created a park of considerable grace.

Eventually they were offered the opportunity to sign loyalty oaths, swearing allegiance to the United States and agreeing to serve in the U.S. military if called. Those who did so could leave the camp if they could find sponsors either for jobs or schools in the East or Midwest. Nearly two hundred from Manzanar eventually served in the armed forces, and one of them, Sadao Munemori, received a posthumous Medal of Honor.

No one was physically brutalized in any of the camps,

and they were paid for the work they did, if not well. Two of those interned at Manzanar died of gunshots during a protest of their incarceration, but there were no other deaths by violence among the ten thousand.

In the fourth book, the one that concerned only Manzanar, I found the tailor's surname in the index and paged to a passage about the deaths of Mr. Yoshioka's mother and sister.

Each of the thirty-six residential blocks in the camp had its own mess hall and attached kitchen. Kiku Yoshioka and her daughter, Mariko, were members of the culinary staff for their block. A leak from a propane tank had led to an explosion and a flash fire fueled by cooking oil spilling from shrapnel-pierced containers. They were the only two unable to escape. Mariko was seventeen, two years older than her brother, and her mother thirty-eight.

Omi Yoshioka and his son, George, had been eating lunch in the adjacent mess hall when the explosion rocked the building. Kitchen staff burst through the connecting doors, chased by billows of fire. Even before Omi and George could determine that Kiku and Mariko were not among those who escaped the flames, they heard familiar voices screaming and entreating God. They tried to enter the kitchen, but the heat proved too great, and suddenly there were, as well, masses of blinding smoke. Disoriented, they themselves had to be rescued from the mess hall.

The book contained three signatures of photographs, and in the second group, I found the official black-and-white internment-camp photos of Kiku and Mariko. Kiku appeared solemn and beautiful. The daughter smiled shyly and was even lovelier than her mother.

A tragic past, as long suspected. But not distant relatives lost in the momentous, ever-echoing man-made thunder of Hiroshima, not just two souls among many thousands atomized as a terrible consequence of Japan's war crimes and its refusal to surrender. This was a loss more intimate, random, haunting, impossible to rationalize by resort to history or to the necessary brutalities of war.

I sat in the silence of the library for a long while, staring at those faces.

A public Xerox machine required a nickel to make a copy.

I folded the copy twice and put it in a jacket pocket.

I left the four volumes on the book-return counter.

The librarian asked me if I had found everything that I'd been looking for, and I said yes, but I didn't say that I wished with all my heart that I'd found nothing.

Not a single cloud threatened the December sun, and all the way home, I walked in crisp, cold light.

Forty-two

MRS. LORENZO CAME TO OUR APARTMENT ON NEW
Year's eve. My mother would be very late getting home from
Slinky's, and she didn't want to wake me at 3:30 or 4:00 in
the morning to bring me upstairs from the widow's place.

I was allowed to stay up to watch the New Year's celebra-
tions on TV, Guy Lombardo and his Royal Canadians at
the Waldorf Astoria or whatever, but music wasn't everything to me. Although only in fourth grade, I read at a
seventh-grade level, and to celebrate, I preferred a novel
to watching people be silly on TV. Two days earlier, I had
checked out Robert Heinlein's *Podkayne of Mars* from the
library, and it was extremely cool. I went to bed with the
book, a glass of Coca-Cola, and a bowl of pretzels.

I finished the Coke, the pretzels, and three-quarters of

the novel before falling asleep shortly after midnight. When I woke at 8:40 in the morning, I found a note from my mother on the nightstand: *Sweetie, going to bed almost four ayem. Will sleep till noon. Then you and me and a fancy hotel for a late lunch!*

In the kitchen, I quietly made toast and built two open-face sandwiches of thickly spread peanut butter and sliced banana. I washed them down with a glass of regular milk and then with a glass of chocolate. I figured if I ate this aggressively every day for a month, I'd still gain only an ounce. I'd given up daydreaming over those Charles Atlas bodybuilding ads in magazines. I conceded the portly end of the piano business to Fats Domino; maybe I would call myself Skinny Kirk. Better yet, Skinny Bledsoe.

I let myself out of the apartment, intending to loiter on the fifth floor to listen for activity in Mr. Yoshioka's apartment. I had heard nothing from him since I'd gone to Metropolitan Suits on Thursday morning, three days earlier. I was anxious to know if he had learned anything or had any ideas about what we should do next.

As I locked the deadbolts, I noticed a three-by-five envelope propped against the baseboard to the left of the door. There was no return address and no indication for whom the contents were intended. I opened it and withdrew a note card on which four words were neatly printed: INFORMATION HAS BEEN OBTAINED.

On the fifth floor, when Mr. Yoshioka opened the door, I smelled coffee brewing. "Happy new year, Jonah Kirk."

"Happy new year, sir. I'm thinking of calling myself Skinny Bledsoe."

As he closed the door, locked the deadbolts, and engaged the security chain, he said, "Is that how you wish to be addressed?"

"Not yet. I'll probably have to be eighteen to get my name legally changed."

"Then I will restrain myself until you have done the deed. We will convene in the kitchen." He led me there. "Would you care for anything to drink?"

"I smell coffee. I thought you drank tea."

"I do drink tea. And coffee. I drink as well water, orange juice, the occasional soft drink, and numerous other beverages."

"But not martinis."

"No. I merely buy martinis and leave them untouched to perplex the managers of nightclubs. Would you like the usual tea and honey?"

"I'm allowed coffee now and then."

"How do you prefer it—cream, sugar, both?"

"Black like me."

"I am impressed."

We sat at the kitchen table with mugs of black coffee. The brew was strong but flavorful.

Mr. Yoshioka said, "Mr. Yabu Tamazaki, who calls himself Robert and even Bobby but never Bob, has worked for seventeen years at the *Daily News*. He is an acquaintance of mine and a reliable person. At my request, he spent some time in their morgue, looking into the Drackman murders."

"Morgue? They keep dead people at the *Daily News*?"

"The morgue is the name they give to the file room in which they preserve back issues of the newspaper."

"Cool."

"Because Mr. and Mrs. Drackman were wealthy and prominent in the Chicago arts community, their murder became nationwide news. Even our rather self-involved city was fascinated by the story. They were murdered in a suburb of Chicago on the night of October seventh, 1958, a little more than eight years ago. The coroner estimated the time of death at between one and three o'clock in the morning. The crime was never solved."

I shook my head. "Their son, Lucas Drackman, he killed them. Like I told you, I saw it in the dream."

"When he was a sophomore in high school, this Lucas Drackman's parents sent him to a private military academy located a few miles south of Mattoon, Illinois."

"What kind of name is Mattoon?"

"I did not ask Bobby Tamazaki to research the origin of the name Mattoon."

"Yeah. Okay. I guess it doesn't matter."

Mr. Yoshioka didn't consult any notes, having committed the entire report to memory. "Young Lucas Drackman remained at the academy during summers and came home only on a few selected holidays. On the night that his parents were murdered, he was a senior at the academy, which is one hundred and ninety miles from the Drackman residence—a drive that police estimate would have taken three and a half hours, seven hours round-trip."

"Maybe he didn't obey the speed limits."

"Lucas Drackman had no access to a vehicle."

"Maybe he stole one."

"At ten o'clock, when bed check was conducted, Lucas Drackman was in his room."

"Maybe it was a dummy of him, like in one of those prison-break movies."

Mr. Yoshioka gestured with his right hand, as if chasing away an annoying fly, though the fly was me with all my maybes. "He spoke to the dorm master at bed check, face-to-face. Thereafter, he would have had to pass through security to leave the dormitory, and he did not. What is more, Lucas Drackman reported to breakfast, in uniform, at seven-thirty in the morning."

"Well, so, that's still nine and a half hours," I protested. "Time enough."

"He lived with two roommates. Both of them told the

police that the three remained up far past the turn-in hour.
They played cards by flashlight until almost one o'clock
in the morning. That would leave only a meager six and
a half hours to complete a seven-hour drive and two
murders."

"Maybe the roommates lied. People lie, you know. They
lie all the time, even to protect a murderer."

After sipping his coffee and savoring it, Mr. Yoshioka
said, "I wonder how a nine-year-old boy can have become
such a suspicious soul so young."

"I'm almost as close to ten as to nine."

I gazed down into my mug. A distorted reflection of
part of my face floated on the coffee, a gargoyle peering
up at me, as though the full truth of myself could not be
seen in an ordinary mirror but only indirectly, as in the
undulating surface of the coffee.

Spooked, I said, "When you told me you believed me
about the dream, I thought you really did."

He smiled. "I did believe you, Jonah Kirk. For reasons
that I explained. And I still do believe your dream showed
you the truth."

"You do?"

A moment before he spoke, I saw that, in his way, he
had been teasing me. "One of the two roommates was a
young man named Felix Cassidy."

Forty-three

FELIX CASSIDY. FIONA CASSIDY.

"How can you be sure they're related?" I asked.

"Mr. Yabu Tamazaki is a most thorough man. He did some research beyond what he was able to find in the *Daily News* morgue. Felix and Fiona Cassidy are twins. Not identical twins, of course, fraternal twins. Interestingly, like Lucas Drackman, they are now orphans."

Until this point, I'd had the impression that Mr. Yoshioka, though allowing himself no expression, was on the verge of a smile, as if it pleased him to watch my reaction to his revelations. But now, although his face remained placid, I sensed that his mood had become solemn, darker.

"Like Lucas Drackman, Felix Cassidy was seventeen then and is twenty-five now. Two years later, when Mr.

Cassidy and his sister were nineteen, their parents, who lived in Indianapolis and who were also people of means, died in their sleep of carbon-monoxide poisoning caused by a furnace malfunction."

He watched me, waiting for a response. Considering that he had called me a suspicious soul, I figured he expected me to be skeptical of the circumstances of those deaths. "It was murder."

"Curiously, police were initially reluctant to conclude that these were accidental deaths. They took more than a year to reach that conclusion. Perhaps you should be a detective."

"I'll stick with the piano. Bad guys hardly ever shoot at a piano man."

"I am pleased that you are not just a particularly suspicious young man but also prudent." He got up to fetch the coffeepot. "May I refresh yours, Jonah Kirk?"

"I was already kind of nervous even without coffee."

"Do not expect that I will offer you a martini instead."

I hesitated. "Thank you, yes, I'll take a little more."

When he returned to his chair, he said, "Felix and Fiona inherited everything, but they would not seem to have been under suspicion. At the time of the deaths, he was in New York City, and she was in San Francisco. Their alibis were ironclad."

"Where was Lucas Drackman?"

"That would have been interesting to determine. But two years had passed since the Drackman murders. The Cassidy deaths were not in the same state. No one would have thought to make a connection. But that is not the end of it."

"The end of what?"

"Perhaps, by virtue of the time we have spent together, you have inspired me to become no less suspicious than you. And now, because of me, poor Mr. Yabu Tamazaki at the *Daily News* has become no less consumed by suspicion than the two of us. He may never be the same. Do you recall that Lucas Drackman had two roommates at the academy?"

"Yes."

"The second was Aaron Kolshak. His family lived in Milwaukee, Wisconsin. Did you know Wisconsin is called America's Dairyland?"

"No, sir."

"Did you know that Milwaukee is called the Machine Shop of America because of its industrial capacity?"

"I didn't know that, either."

"I imagine it must be stressful to be a citizen of Milwaukee, Wisconsin, and have to do your part every day to ensure that the state and city live up to those honorable titles. Mr. Aaron Kolshak's father died when Aaron was eleven, perhaps from the stress. The boy became something of a delinquent, and his mother sent him off to the academy in Mattoon, Illinois, when he was thirteen."

"I guess the family was wealthy, huh?"

"As usual, your suspicion serves you well. Mr. Kolshak had been a most successful real estate developer, and his widow proved to be equally adept at the family business."

When he paused to savor his coffee and left me sitting in an expectant silence, I began to suspect that Mr. Yoshioka had once aspired to be a storyteller of some kind, perhaps a novelist, before fate had made of him a tailor.

He resumed: "Mrs. Renata Kolshak, the widow, greatly enjoyed vacationing on cruise ships. I assume, Jonah Kirk, that you have never vacationed on a cruise ship."

"No, sir."

"Neither have I. A year after Mr. and Mrs. Cassidy suffocated in their sleep, Mrs. Kolshak was aboard a Caribbean cruise when she went missing and was eventually determined to have fallen overboard and drowned. Lost at sea. No body ever found."

"Holy Jeez," I said and accused myself of profanity and quickly made the sign of the cross and said, "Jeez," again, and had to do it all a second time. "I bet no one thought to ask where Lucas Drackman was."

"If he was aboard the same vessel, sampling the delights of the Caribbean, he most likely was wise enough to travel under a false identity. But poor Mr. Yabu Tamazaki of the

Daily News has become so curious that he is looking into that."

My host was intent on my reaction, but I gave him some of his own medicine and savored my coffee for a minute. Finally I said, "So in return for Cassidy and Kolshak giving Lucas an ironclad alibi on the night he murdered his parents, he must've made a pact with them to murder theirs, you know, after enough time passed not to raise suspicion."

"We can spin up all kinds of theories, but under the law, the suspect is always presumed innocent until proven guilty."

I remembered Manzanar and said, "Maybe not always. Shouldn't we go to the police?"

"Ah, but which police? None of these crimes was committed in this city or state. Police here have no jurisdiction. Two murders occurred in Illinois, two more in Indiana, and Mrs. Kolshak was out of the country when she was perhaps thrown overboard."

"Maybe it's an FBI thing."

"Maybe it is indeed. But I believe that it would be most unwise to approach the authorities until it can be proved that Mr. Lucas Drackman was on that cruise ship with Mrs. Kolshak or in Indianapolis around the time that Mr. and Mrs. Cassidy died."

"Why wouldn't it be wise? The police, FBI, all those guys know how to prove things."

"Inevitably, Lucas Drackman would be alerted that he was being investigated for some reason. He is not likely to think it is about all those killings, because that is behind him. Criminals think only in the short term. They live in the now, not in the past or future, which is why they always think crime pays, for in the now they are still free."

I looked in my coffee mug again. Then I pushed it aside. "Do you know Mr. Moto?"

"I am sorry to say that I have never made his acquaintance. Who might he be?"

"Never mind."

He folded both hands around his coffee mug, as if to warm them. "The danger is that if Mr. Drackman were to be alerted, he might put two and two together."

"What two and two?"

"Miss Fiona Cassidy believes that you were suspicious of her. She warned you off. Now you turn up across the street from The Royal when Drackman is leaving there with your father."

"He didn't know it was me."

"If he describes you to Miss Cassidy, she will confirm that it was you."

"He won't remember anything but my red-and-white toboggan cap. All little black kids probably look alike to him."

"But if they do not all look alike to him, then once he

has been put on alert by an investigation, he might come looking for you."

I recalled Drackman in the dream, his eyes wide and wild, his tongue ceaselessly licking his full lips, and I thought of him on the farther side of the chain-link fence, his breath smoking from his mouth as if, should he wish, he could breathe fire.

"If we don't report him to the cops or the FBI, how would we ever prove that he was on the cruise ship or in Indianapolis?"

"We must wait for Mr. Tamazaki of the *Daily News* and hope that in his obsession he can find proof."

"I hope he's quick about it."

"Be prepared that he might find nothing."

That was unthinkable. "Anyway, what're Drackman and my father doing together? What are they up to? That's pretty darn scary."

"If you and your mother were to be killed," Mr. Yoshioka said, "would your father inherit millions?"

"How could he inherit millions? We don't have anything. Anyway, he divorced my mom."

"Exactly. Whatever your father and Lucas Drackman are involved in, it surely has nothing to do with you. We can afford to let poor Yabu Tamazaki take his time with his investigation. But you should never again wear that toboggan cap."

Forty-four

ASSUMING THAT MR. YOSHIOKA HAD TOLD ME everything, I pushed my chair back from the table and got to my feet.

I wanted to ask him about Manzanar. I had at least a hundred questions. But I didn't know how to broach the subject.

"One more thing, Jonah Kirk. Another acquaintance of mine, Mr. Toshi Katsumata, who calls himself Thomas or Tom but never Tommy, has worked for nineteen years in city hall, as head clerk of municipal-court records. The final divorce papers that your mother received gave your father's address as 106 Marbury Street, which is actually the address of his rather less than reputable attorney, because he wished to keep his true residence from you and your mother. However, while the court allows your father that privacy, it must have his real address in the case file. Poor Mr. Katsumata has a sterling record and is a man of honor, so I am certain that it pained him to violate the privacy assured by the court and provide me with your father's true address. Nevertheless, he is also a man of his word, and he values friendship."

This development baffled me. "Why would I want Tilton's address? I *don't* want it. I never want to see him again. He's never been a father to me."

"I had made that assumption some time ago," said Mr. Yoshioka. "But considering that you saw your father with the dangerous Mr. Drackman last week, I thought it essential that we know his address. He lives on the north side, quite far from here, a distance that I am certain you would not be allowed to travel on your own. But I will keep the address in case we should ever need it." He got up from his chair. "There is yet one more thing you should know— well, two."

He carried his coffee mug to the sink and stood with his back to me as he rinsed it.

When he shut off the water, he gazed out of the window above the sink as he said, "I must apologize if the first of these two things I have to tell you will in any way cause you pain or embarrass you, but it is information you must have."

"What is it?"

He hesitated, and just then snow flurries blew down through the day and danced along the window glass. He said, "'*Shiraume ni / Akaru yo bakari to / Narinikeri.*'"

I figured he must know that I didn't understand Japanese, even though the nuns at Saint Scholastica expected us to learn everything. But when only silence followed those words, I said, "Mr. Yoshioka?"

"A haiku, a poem by Buson. It means, 'Of late the nights / Are dawning / Plum-blossom white.' It seems to fit the moment. Petals of plum blossoms are white like snow, and night is soon coming."

"It sounds kind of sad."

"Every snow is beautiful and joyful . . . and sad, because every snow will melt."

Lyrics are poetry; therefore, poetry is part of music, but just then I was less a piano man than I was a confused and frightened boy. Impatient, I said, "What two things do you have to tell me?"

"Sharing the apartment with your father is the magazine writer and would-be novelist, Miss Delvane."

It wasn't the prospect of my embarrassment that made him turn his back to me while making this revelation; it was his embarrassment on my and my mother's behalf.

"But Miss Delvane lives here on the fifth floor."

"No longer. She moved out on Thursday. I would not

feel the need to tell you this, Jonah, but it has become necessary because of what I was told by Mr. Nakama Otani, who calls himself Nick or Nicholas but never Nickie. When I learned on Friday morning where your father now lives and with whom, I asked poor Mr. Otani to see if he could conspire to cross her path and, as they say, chat her up. He is very good at chatting people up. He managed to encounter Miss Delvane at a nightclub last night, New Year's Eve, before your father joined her there. He learned much useless information about cowboys and rodeos and about the stingy nature of magazine editors. But he also learned that the man she lives with was recently divorced, that his one child is in the custody of his ex-wife . . . and that he talks constantly about one day getting his son back."

"He gave me up without a fight. He didn't want me. He didn't want me and I sure as hell don't want to live with him ever. Miss Delvane must be lying or probably he's just telling her that because it makes him sound better."

As snow slanted to the glass in thicker skeins, Mr. Yoshioka turned from the window to face me. "You may be right, Jonah. Most likely you are. But as long as your father is out there, you should be . . . watchful, cautious."

"I am. I already am."

"I want you to know that I am so sorry for telling you."

"No, sir. You should have told me. It's okay. Thank you."

"A boy your age should not have to deal with such things."

"I'm not my age," I told him.

"Indeed you are not your age." He smiled, but maybe less with amusement than with melancholy.

Distressed but not because of Miss Delvane, I followed him to the front door.

As he slipped loose the security chain and opened the deadbolts, he said, *"'Kogarashi ya / Ato de me o fuke / Kawayanagi.'"*

"Haiku," I said. "Is that the word?"

"That is the word. The poet Senryu." He translated: "'Bitter winds of winter / But later, river willow, / Open up your buds.'"

"That's a pretty poem."

"I agree. I will be in touch when I know more, Jonah."

For whatever reason, he had stopped always calling me Jonah Kirk. It was just Jonah now. I didn't know what that meant, but I liked it.

"Happy new year, Mr. Yoshioka."

"Happy new year, Jonah."

He bowed to me, and I bowed to him, and he opened the door, and I stepped into the fifth-floor hallway. As I headed toward the front stairs, he closed the door, and suddenly I thought that I would never see him again, not alive at least, that all the talk of murder had somehow made a target of him, not a target specifically for Drackman or Fiona Cassidy, but for fate.

Shaken, I halted and looked back toward his apartment. The fear was baseless, and yet it continued to grip me.

This was voodoo thinking. But all children are prone to voodoo thinking because they're essentially powerless and because they lack so much knowledge of how the world works; therefore, they're quick to imagine mysterious and sinister forces pulling strings behind the scenes, magic and monsters.

In my case, having had prophetic dreams and having had a piano conjured for me by Miss Pearl, I knew that the world was a many-layered mystery. Everyone told me voodoo was nonsense, and I didn't really believe in pin-stuck effigies and effective curses, but I did believe a devil walked the world, ceaselessly harvesting.

I went through the door at the end of the hall, started down the stairs, and had to sit before I reached the first landing, because my legs felt rubbery. I trembled as if I weren't in a warm building but instead were sitting in the falling snow, on a stone stoop as cold as ice. Five—maybe ten—minutes passed before the tremors stopped and my legs no longer felt weak.

I'm not sure I understood at the time why that episode occurred. Decades later I realize that, as a child, I was fond of some nuns and kids at Saint Scholastica and had much affection for Mrs. Lorenzo and Mrs. O'Toole, but I loved wholeheartedly only my mother, Grandma Anita, and Grandpa Teddy. And though I never thought about it this way in those days—it wasn't a thing a child would ever contemplate—that was the largest universe of love I could at the time imagine. But the universe was expanding. I feared for Mr. Yoshioka because he was becoming a surrogate father to me. The better that I knew him, the more I loved him—and the more I feared losing him.

Forty-five

JANUARY OF 1967 BROUGHT TRAGEDY WHEN THREE astronauts—Virgil Grissom, Edward White, and Roger Chaffee—died in a flash fire in their *Apollo* capsule during a simulated countdown at Cape Canaveral. The horror of their deaths set the tone for the year to come.

Later there would be the famous Summer of Love, thousands flocking to Haight-Ashbury in San Francisco to form communes, bliss out at free concerts by acid-rock bands, and make love instead of war. They called it Hippie Haven and meant to start a new and better world, but by the end of summer, crime was soaring in Haight-Ashbury. Hospital ERs were overwhelmed with people hallucinating and psychotic from bad LSD trips, while addiction to hard drugs and deadly overdoses had become epidemic. The music darkened from Scott McKenzie singing about wearing flowers in your hair to the Doors' celebration of psychosis in "The End," a throbbing carnival organ evoking menace and madness. Buffalo Springfield proved prescient in "For What It's Worth," in which their music and voices stirred in the listener a deep uneasiness as they sang about violence in the streets: "There's something happening here . . . There's a man with a gun over there."

That same summer, the worst race riots in the country's history broke out in Detroit. Thirty-eight died and entire sections of that city were reduced to smoking ruins. Meanwhile, the war in Vietnam escalated.

Much to my surprise, months passed without my father abruptly looming out of the shadows. I didn't see Fiona Cassidy again or Lucas Drackman, but I knew they had not gone away forever. Considering the weirdness of the previous couple of years, the sudden ordinariness of my daily life seemed like a setup, false calm meant to encourage me to let my guard down. And after a while, the quiet became tedious, because I guess a person can become as addicted to danger and to weirdness as much as to dope of any kind.

Mr. Yabu Tamazaki of the *Daily News* had nothing more to tell us about the whereabouts of Drackman when the Cassidys and Mrs. Kolshak were killed. I had mistakenly believed that he must be a reporter, but he was instead the curator of the newspaper morgue. In his great enthusiasm for the case, he began to mistake himself for a reporter, and when discovered investigating those murders, he was asked to explain himself and, in the absence of an explanation, was told in no uncertain terms to focus solely on the job for which he was paid.

I learned this one snowy day when I came out of the community center after a piano session and found Mr. Yoshioka walking home, looking rather dashing in a well-cut topcoat, neck scarf, and fedora.

"Mr. Tamazaki does have a degree in journalism," Mr. Yoshioka explained. "In this city, however, most reporters have traditionally been of other ethnic backgrounds, mostly Irish. The Irish are very good at journalism because they are very good also at politics, and politics and journalism are twined. Mr. Tamazaki has no more interest in politics than he has in hara-kiri, which is to say none at all."

"Now what are we going to do?" I wondered.

"Mr. Tamazaki will continue to research the case more quietly, entirely on his own time. And there is also Mr. Nakama Otani, who is interested in the case as a sideline to his primary work."

"He's the one who found where my father is living, with Miss Delvane on the north side. He calls himself Nick or Nicholas but never Nickie."

"That is correct."

"He's good at chatting people up."

"No one is better."

"Who's he chatting up now?"

"We will leave that entirely to Mr. Otani. Because he is doing the chatting, he alone must choose those to whom he wishes to chat."

"What does he do besides chat? Is he a reporter?"

"Mr. Otani does many things well, though he is a humble man who, if you praised him, would deny his competence and plead that he is only lucky."

Whenever it came to revealing anything about Nakama Otani, Mr. Yoshioka became secretive and often responded to my questions with answers that seemed to be answers only if you didn't think too hard about them.

We were passing under bare-limbed maples through which snow streamed, and though my subject wasn't snow, I took the opportunity to reveal my recently gained erudition. "'The sleet falls / As if coming through the bottom / Of loneliness.'"

"Naitō Jōsō," said Mr. Yoshioka. "A poet of the seventeenth century. He was once a samurai, and then he became a priest. A man of many disciplines."

"Sorry I can't say it in Japanese."

He obliged: "'*Sabishisa no / Soko nukete furu / Mizore kana.*'"

He looked so pleased that I had memorized even one haiku, and his smile was the widest I had ever seen on him, but he didn't inquire what had inspired my interest. Because haiku were important to him, almost sacred, maybe he thought that to ask such a question would be too personal. More likely, he knew that my respect for him was the source of my interest in that poetry, and he would have been embarrassed to hear me say as much.

And so the months passed with me suspended in a peculiar state. I felt that I was walking a ledge, yes, but each time I looked down, the ledge was only two feet off the ground. Maintaining a high degree of wariness and the suspicion for which I was known—at least to Mr. Yoshioka—proved difficult when none of the bad guys came sneaking around.

We kept waiting for more bombs to explode, like those that had trashed the military-recruitment centers. Surely if Fiona Cassidy was a skilled bomb-maker, she'd had plenty of time in 6-C to build more than two. But nothing exploded.

When the calamity occurred on Wednesday, April 19, 1967, it was nothing that I'd been anticipating.

At Saint Scholastica's, all the students in the fourth grade were gathered in the music room during the sixth period, practicing the choral piece we would sing as our part in the annual spring recital. The head of the music department, Mr. Hern, was a civilian, not a priest. He knew music, but he wasn't much of a disciplinarian. Some of us boys were horsing around, singing "banana" though the word was *hosanna,* that sort of thing, when Sister Agnes entered in a rustle of habit, and went directly to the piano, where Mr. Hern was playing well the song that we were doing our best to sabotage. He took his hands off the keys the moment that he saw her, and she whispered something to him, and all of the kids stood on the tiered chorus platform in respectful silence because Sister Agnes *was* a dedicated and effective disciplinarian.

When she asked me to come with her, I frantically tried to think what I'd done that warranted her attention. I was sure it couldn't be that she'd been walking by the music room and heard me sing "banana," but as far as I could recall, I hadn't committed any other offense that day.

She walked with me to her office, one hand on my shoulder all the way, which was unusual, as if she thought I might try to escape. When I glanced at her surreptitiously, I saw tears standing in her eyes. I thought that the punishment soon to be administered must be so dire, even this no-nonsense nun had pity for me.

Ushered ahead of Sister Agnes, entering her office, I startled when I saw my mother waiting there, standing at a window with a view of sycamores in early leaf. She turned when she heard us, and her face glistened with tears.

I ran to her, and she knelt to take me in her arms, and I asked what I had done. She said, "Nothing, sweetie, not you, you've done nothing. It's your grandma. We don't have her anymore, Jonah. We don't have her. She passed away a little while ago, and she's with God now."

Ten months earlier, when Tony Lorenzo died, I had thought I knew what Mrs. Lorenzo must be feeling; but now I realized that I had not understood her pain at all. Surely it was as sharp as mine, and mine was excruciating, of such intensity that for a moment I couldn't breathe. And then I thought, *Grandpa Teddy,* and I didn't believe that I could bear to see him racked by grief.

Because Grandma Anita worked for Monsignor McCarthy and because she had done so much good for others in her life, the viewing before the funeral Mass was at the cathedral. So many flowers flanked and backdropped the casket. Among the usual roses and chrysanthemums stood a singular arrangement, not the largest but the most striking, consisting of white peonies with purple-tipped petals combined with purple orchids. I knew from whom they must have come. I took the condolence card from the arrangement and pocketed it. I read it much later, when I was alone in bed at Grandpa's house and unable to sleep. The name of the sender was not included on the card, but it didn't need to be. The neatly hand-printed message identified him, and I read it many times before sleep claimed me.

Dawn breaks
And blossoms open
Gates of paradise.

As I explained near the beginning of this story, we stayed with Grandpa Teddy for a week, and then we returned to our downtown walk-up.

I no longer allowed myself to be impatient for some word from Mr. Yabu Tamazaki of the *Daily News* or from the chatting-up expert, Mr. Nakama Otani. In a low-grade fever of superstition, I felt that my previous impatience, my desire for action, might have in part brought upon us the drama that I didn't want, Grandma Anita's death.

Sure, juju was probably nonsense, but if by some one-in-a-million chance it was *not* nonsense, then somewhere there was a photograph of me sleeping and a fabric eye that perhaps could watch me even from a great distance, and both were in the possession of a woman with purple-blue eyes and a bloody mind and the darkest of dark hearts, who would use those magical items if she knew how.

Nothing more of importance happened until June, when Mom quit her job at Slinky's where Harmon Jessup, the owner, wanted more from her than she would ever give him, and accepted the better job at the first-class nightclub owned by William Murkett. Of course Murkett proved to be a dirty old tomcat, too, and Mother had to walk away from that job even before her first performance.

The night we moved out of the downtown walk-up, as Grandpa Teddy was loading our suitcases and shopping bags into his Cadillac and as my mother paid a visit to Mrs. Lorenzo, I raced up to the fifth floor to tell Mr. Yoshioka what was happening and to provide him with my grandfather's phone number and address. I rang his bell repeatedly, but he didn't answer.

If you want the truth, I felt a little heartsick about not being able to see him before we left. But I would be able to call him at his work number in the morning or at his home number the following evening. We wouldn't be in the same neighborhood anymore, not close enough to have tea whenever we felt like it, but I was certain that we would see each other from time to time and that he would keep me informed about the investigation, such as it was. We shared secrets, after all, and secrets can bind people together as surely as does love. We shared an adversary, as well, one who had threatened both of us, and we had a mutual interest in bringing her to justice, regardless of whether she might be a wicked juju priestess or a scheming Bilderberger, or merely someone who liked to cut and who had conspired in the murder of her parents.

Our first few days at Grandpa Teddy's house were quiet. But the uneasy peace of recent months would soon end.

Forty-six

ON MONDAY, JULY 3, WHEN I MET MALCOLM
Pomerantz, I was ten years and half a month old, and he
was twelve years and two months old. I was a short, black
piano man; he was a tall, white saxophonist. I had a quick-
ness and, if I say so myself, a certain grace of movement,
but Malcolm proceeded always at a measured pace, stoop-
shouldered, almost shambling. On the surface, we were so
radically different that we would never find ourselves in
the same police lineup of suspects.

I was home alone that day. Because Grandpa lived in
a low-crime neighborhood and because I had recently
reached an age expressed in double digits, my mother had
reluctantly conceded that I could stay by myself during
the day. Until she found another singing gig, she had only

the waitressing at Woolworth's, and she felt too pinched to pay for a sitter. In truth, she couldn't have been as bad off as she evidently felt, considering that Grandpa Teddy wouldn't take a dime from her for rent or food. Although he claimed that having us there, no longer being alone, was worth a fortune to him, and although we were more at home than we had been in the fourth-floor walk-up, it galled my mother to be dependent.

In return for her concession, she provided a list of rules that I swore to obey, the first of which was that I would never, never, never, under any circumstances, open the door to a stranger, not even if he wore a police uniform, not even if he dressed like a priest. On those hot summer days, lacking air-conditioning, we needed to keep a number of windows open to cross-ventilate the house, and although the screens snapped into place from the inside, any of them could be cut or wrenched loose from outside in no time at all. Consequently, if some despicable criminal tried to enter the house by a window, I must at once begin screaming as loud as I could for help; I must race to the second floor, lock myself in the master bedroom, remove a window screen, climb out onto the front-porch roof, and continue screaming until neighbors came into the street to see what had me so terrified.

I had no nearby community center to go to, and right there in the first-floor front room stood a fine piano. I had every intention of playing that grand instrument during the day, and Mom knew that I would; but apparently it didn't occur to her that when I was pounding the ivories, I wouldn't be likely to hear a burglar cutting a window screen at the back of the house. If it *did* occur to her, no doubt she assured herself that no sneak thief was likely to break into a place where he could hear someone rocking a piano.

I was doing just that, rocking through Fats Domino's "I'm Gonna Be a Wheel Someday," when Malcolm Pomerantz rang the doorbell. He had to ring it like five or six times before I came to a couple of quiet bars that allowed me to hear it.

Not having forgotten Fiona Cassidy or Lucas Drackman, or my philandering father with his new beard, I approached the door most cautiously and peered through one of the sidelights. On the porch stood an unlikely figure, a gawky boy with a prominent Adam's apple, slumped shoulders, and arms that seemed half again as long as they ought to be. He dressed like an adult in highly polished black wing tips, gray dress pants, and a short-sleeved white shirt with thin blue vertical lines. I hate to say it, but being dressed like an adult did not mean that he had style, because he didn't. His pants were cinched a couple of inches above his navel, revealing white socks in the black brogues and making his torso look as abbreviated as that of a dwarf.

Even on a warm summer day, the spread collar of his white shirt was buttoned all the way to the neck.

The only interesting thing about him was the saxophone he held.

Suddenly aware of me at the sidelight, he stepped away from the door and faced me through the glass. "Good afternoon," he said.

"It isn't noon yet," I replied. "Anyway, I'm not allowed to open the door to strangers."

Long, pale face. Sad hound-dog eyes made large by the thick lenses of his black-rimmed glasses. Hair lightly oiled and combed straight back from his forehead. In spite of the saxophone, I thought he'd probably grow up to be an undertaker.

He said, "I'm not a stranger. I'm Malcolm Pomerantz, and I live across the street."

"You're a stranger to me."

"I heard the piano and thought Mr. Bledsoe must be home."

"I'm not Mr. Bledsoe."

"If you hadn't told me, I would have been entirely fooled. The resemblance is uncanny."

I liked how quick he came back with that, but I wasn't going to be easy. "You're a wise guy, huh?"

"I've been known to be. I guess you're Jonah."

"Maybe I am."

"Maybe? You have amnesia? Listen, sometimes Mr. Bledsoe lets me jam with him."

"How do I know that? He never mentioned you to me."

"And here I thought he talked about me incessantly. Who's got you thinking this neighborhood is Hell's Kitchen?"

"My mom's a worrier."

"Sure, I'm not just a twelve-year-old geek saxophonist. I'm really a thirty-year-old crazed killer and master of disguise. You were totally rockin' that Domino."

"Thanks. He's the greatest."

"You know any other stuff?"

"No. I play 'I'm Gonna Be a Wheel Someday' over and over till I drive everybody insane. If I ever heard it, I pretty much know it."

"I'm just needling you. I know all about your musical memory, if that's what it's called. Your granddad thinks you're the end-all and be-all."

That revelation filled me with pride, but then I remembered what Grandpa Teddy said about talent being an unearned grace, and I said, "Well, I'm not."

"Never thought you were, pilgrim. I'm just telling you what your granddad said."

"Why'd you call me pilgrim?"

"That was my John Wayne imitation."

"Better stick with music."

"Hey, you know who Sy Oliver was?"

"He wrote and arranged some great stuff back when, like for Tommy Dorsey. Four-beat swing, two-beat pop."

"'Easy Does It' and 'Swing High.'"

I said, "'Swingin' on Nothin'.' You know it?"

"Let me in, and instead of stabbing you like four thousand times, I'll play it with you."

"What if you stink at it?" I asked.

"After you hear me, if you think it stinks, then I'll beat you to death with this axe."

"What axe?"

"You yanking my chain? It's slang for saxophone."

"We don't use much slang in our family."

I let him in, and he didn't stab me four thousand times, or even once, and I didn't give him any reason to beat me to death with his saxophone.

Forty-seven

I CONSIDER IT TO HAVE BEEN A SMALL MIRACLE that Malcolm and I, two musical prodigies, lived across the street from each other that summer, and that each of us needed a friend. To other kids, I was a figure of fun because I was on the short side and was as skinny as a pretzel stick, and also because my father didn't live at home. Back then, the vast majority of black families, of *all* families, were still two-parent households, and single mothers—whether divorced or never married—were subjects for gossips. Most kids made fun of Malcolm, too, because he was, well, Malcolm. Mismatched as we seemed to be at first glance, we built the friendship of a lifetime, and in fact I think we were fast friends by the time he left that day, about four hours after he had rung the doorbell.

Sometimes, when he's in a funk, Malcolm says that maybe if we had never met, we wouldn't have suffered through our most difficult losses, because we wouldn't have been in the wrong place at the wrong time, but I never see it that way. Friendship is a great good thing, and the happiness that we got from our friendship did not tempt fate to spring a trap door under our feet. There is no fate, only free will, and we were just in the way of other people's free will when they decided to do the Devil's work. People are doing the Devil's work everywhere you go; there's no avoiding it unless you go live on a mountaintop somewhere, a hundred miles from everyone.

Anyway, Monday was not a night that Grandpa Teddy played at the hotel. After he finished his set in the couture department of the big fancy store in Midtown, he would pick up Sylvia at Woolworth's and they would come home together. I expected them around five o'clock.

After Malcolm left, I turned on the TV and discovered that the regular programming had been interrupted by breaking news. Later in the year, the anti-war protests would grow in number, and there would be a march on the Pentagon that ended in violence and arrests. Though our city was seldom thought to be on the cutting edge of societal evolution, for some reason we had a couple of the larger and more tempestuous demonstrations that summer, as if the various anti-war organizations had decided to practice here before going on to more prominent venues in the autumn.

The demonstration that day was at City College. An angry crowd of three or four thousand were challenging the college regarding its ROTC program, and phalanxes of police in riot gear were trying to prevent them from surging into the building that they most wanted to seize. The race riots in Detroit had ended just the day before, and the news anchor kept teasing that story while covering the current one, from time to time repeating what Jerome Cavanaugh, Detroit's mayor, had said regarding the aftermath: "It looks like Berlin in 1945."

Although my mother had told me that the news is never all the news, only what they want to show you, I found myself riveted to the chaos on the TV screen, and I didn't move even when they went to a commercial break. In those days, cigarette companies could still advertise on television, but lawyers couldn't; some changes are for the better, and others are not.

Seconds after the station came back from the commercials to City College in turmoil, I saw Mr. Reginald Smaller. Most of those in the crowd were of college age, but among those who were older, our former building superintendent stood out like—not to be cruel—a gorilla among gazelles. He wore a colorful bandana that obscured his steel-wool every-which-way hair, but he was still a short man with a big middle, and he wore a tank top that revealed a dismaying amount of hirsute skin. That pelt alone conclusively identified him. Of all those in the shot, he appeared to be angriest, shouting at the police with such force that spittle sprayed, pumping one fist in the air, his face twisted and grotesque with rage.

I rose from the armchair and went to my knees directly in front of the screen, mesmerized by the spectacle and by this revelation of Mr. Smaller's activist side, but perhaps fascinated most of all because this was the first time that I had ever seen someone I knew on television. Just then I saw a *second* person I knew. She wore jeans and a halter top and a cute straw hat with a ribbon that seemed out of place at that event. Unlike those around her, she didn't shout or gesture, and she didn't carry a sign, but instead clicked pictures with a small camera and observed everyone else as though taking copious mental notes. Maybe Miss Delvane was gathering material for a magazine article or for a novel to follow the one about the rodeo.

Right then I knew beyond doubt that if the camera shifted to the left, I would see my father with her, resplendent in his new beard. Tilton didn't believe in much of anything except Tilton, and it made no sense that he would be risking a police baton to the face that might permanently diminish the pleasure he took in a mirror.

But he was there. I could feel it. Maybe he was there only because of Miss Delvane. She was hot, and I don't mean because it was a summer day. Although only ten, I recognized hot when I saw it.

The camera panned left, and suddenly there he was, dear old dad, wearing a black T-shirt instead of the black turtleneck that he'd been wearing more than six months ago when I'd seen him in The Royal. He still sported a well-shaped beard. His previously close-cropped hair had grown into a modest Afro. Also as in the diner, he wore a large silver medallion on a chain around his neck. Back on December 29, I hadn't been able to discern the nature of his jewelry; on the TV, it was clearly a peace sign.

The sight of Tilton in this context was so beyond expectation that I was both astonished and amazed, both my heart and mind quite overwhelmed. Like Miss Delvane, he displayed none of the righteous fury of the demonstrators among whom he moved. He seemed even to be somewhat bemused by their passion, and there was a certain wariness about him, his gaze continuously shifting here and there . . .

I surprised myself when I said aloud, *"What are they up to?"*

Intuitively, based on my experience of my father, I knew that neither he nor Miss Delvane, nor Mr. Smaller, for that matter, was at the City College demonstration because they thought the war was immoral and hoped to end it. Something else must be afoot.

Although I expected next to glimpse Lucas Drackman and Fiona Cassidy, the news went to Detroit to dwell lovingly on the charred and still smoking ruins left behind by the recently ended riots. When I heard car doors slam and stood up and, through a window, saw Grandpa's Cadillac at the curb in front of the house, I shut off the television.

When he and Mom came through the front door and called out to me, I called back to them from the kitchen, where I was busy setting the dinette table for dinner.

They had stopped at the supermarket to buy fresh-ground sirloin and other items. For dinner we enjoyed a tomato-and-cucumber salad, hamburger steaks, baked beans, and potatoes that Grandpa sliced thin and fried in a big iron skillet with butter and slivers of a green pepper.

At the table, as we ate, we shared the events of the day with one another. Two and a half months after Grandma Anita's passing, my grandfather was able to smile again and on occasion even laugh, though there remained in him a sorrow that was obvious when he thought you weren't looking and was evident to a lesser degree when you were.

I told them about Malcolm Pomerantz, how he had to work hard to convince me that he wasn't a murderous stranger, how we had a lot of fun playing together, even if piano and sax made an odd duet. I didn't mention my father on television, because I knew myself well enough to realize that if I talked about him, I might chatter on and tell them about Miss Delvane. I didn't want to hurt my mother, and even though she had given up on Tilton, she might be wounded if she learned that Miss Delvane was with him.

Forty-eight

LATER, I WAS LYING IN BED WITH A COPY OF ROBERT Heinlein's The Star Beast, which I'd started the evening before. The story was hilarious. The previous night, I'd giggled frequently while reading. But now I couldn't get Tilton-on-TV out of my head, and scenes that should have made me laugh out loud could raise no more than a smile.

My door was ajar, and Mom appeared at the threshold. "Hey, big guy, you have a minute?"

"Well, I was about to get dressed and go bar-hopping, then take a jet to Paris for breakfast."

"What time's your flight?" she asked as she came into the room.

"It's a private jet. I can leave anytime I want."

"You've been saving your lunch money, huh?"

"And investing it wisely."

She sat on the edge of the bed. "Are you happy here, sweetie?"

"In Grandpa's house? Sure. It's better than an apartment. It's so quiet here."

"Your room's bigger."

"A piano right in the living room. And no cockroaches."

"It's nice having the second bathroom, even if it does just have a shower without a tub."

Putting the book aside, I said, "I miss Grandma, though."

"I'll miss her till the day I die, sweetie. But she left a lot of love in this house. I feel it all around."

She picked up my left hand and kissed each finger. She always did things like that. I'll never forget the gentle things she did, not ever.

"You like Malcolm, do you?"

"Yeah. He's cool."

"I'm glad you found a friend so soon. Which reminds me, someone came by to eat at the lunch counter today and gave me a message for you. She said you were the sweetest, most courteous boy, and I was so proud of you."

"Who?" I asked.

"I never saw her before, but she said she lived in our building for a short while. Said she met you in the foyer and on the stairs a few times. Eve Adams. Do you remember her?"

If ever I suspected I might be a better actor than musician, that was the moment. "Miss Adams, yeah. Pretty lady with kind of purple eyes. That was way last summer."

"You never mentioned her."

"I just saw her a couple times, coming and going, you know."

"She said she's a photographer."

"I didn't know for sure what she was."

"She said to tell you she still has the photo of you and it's one of her favorites."

I frowned as if trying to remember. "Yeah, she asked to take my picture once, out on the stoop. I don't know why."

"She said you're very handsome and photogenic. She's obviously got the good eye of a first-rate photographer."

I pretended to be embarrassed by the compliment. "Yeah, I'm a regular Rock Hudson." I *was* mortified, but only because I was in a box labeled HE LIES TO HIS MOTHER; and maybe I would never be able to get out of it.

She kissed me on the forehead. "I didn't mean to interrupt your book. I know you love Heinlein."

"He's okay. You're not an interruption."

Getting up from the bed, she said, "I love you, Jonah."

"I love you, too."

"Remember to say your prayers."

"I will."

Leaving, as she pulled shut the door, she said, "Sleep tight, Mr. Hudson."

I felt lower than dirt.

After that, I had no interest in *The Star Beast*.

I said my prayers and turned out the light, but I didn't expect to sleep well.

In my mind, I kept hearing Fiona Cassidy from almost a year earlier: *If you love your mama, then you think about what I said. I like to cut. I could make her a new face in half a minute.*

In the dark, something kept tickling in my left nostril, but nothing was there. Not a tickle, really. A sensory memory of the cold point of the switchblade with which she'd threatened me.

Whatever Fiona Cassidy and Lucas Drackman and Mr. Smaller and my father and Miss Delvane might be planning, if indeed they were scheming together, they must be getting close to executing the plan. The purple-eyed witch had gone to Woolworth's not primarily for lunch but to deliver a compliment that she wanted my mother to pass along to me, a compliment that was actually a threat, to be sure that I hadn't forgotten the consequences of not keeping my mouth shut.

Forty-nine

THIS NEXT BIT IS BASED ON HEARSAY. BECAUSE the source was Mr. Yoshioka, however, I'm certain it is reliable.

At the same time that my mother was telling me about Eve Adams having lunch at Woolworth's, Mr. Yabu Tamazaki of the *Daily News* was sitting at the kitchen table in his apartment, in another part of the city, poring over the passenger manifest of the cruise ship on which, in October 1961, Mrs. Renata Kolshak had booked what turned out to be her death voyage.

Because he was continuing his investigation against the wishes of his superiors at the newspaper, Mr. Tamazaki had proceeded slowly and with caution. He had been delayed, as well, by avenues of inquiry that had proved to be dead-ends. After considerable patient effort, he had found a contact inside the cruise-ship company, Mrs. Rebecca Tremaine, formerly Rebecca Arikawa.

In 1942, at the age of twelve, Rebecca was removed from a foster home and sent to Children's Village, the camp orphanage at Manzanar. The following year, she was raped by a nineteen-year-old internee who was a member of a gang. The rapist was transferred to the more secure camp at Tule Lake, where he stood trial. Late in 1944, at the age of fourteen, Rebecca was returned to her foster parents, Sarah and Louis Walton, who began the process of adoption. With the help of a loving family, she overcame the trauma of rape and eventually married.

On the advice of its attorneys, the cruise line kept passenger manifests of every voyage for ten years. Although that list of names and addresses was proprietary information—a source of likely future customers—Rebecca was persuaded that Mr. Tamazaki, a man of honor, had no intention of harming her employer in any way.

The passenger manifest contained 1,136 names. Mr. Tamazaki did not expect to find Lucas Drackman on it, and indeed he didn't. He was looking for a suspicious name—comparable to Eve Adams—or any suggestion of falsity in an address, or the initials L.D., because both criminals of limited intelligence and those who were smart but cocksure often used aliases with that connection to their real names.

Because Renata Kolshak had booked early, she was passenger number fifty. As he proceeded through the manifest, Mr. Tamazaki marked a few lines with a red pencil, for later reconsideration, but when he reached passenger number 943, he was all but certain that he had found his man. The name Douglas T. Atherton struck him as being familiar, but he couldn't say why. The passenger's home address was also of interest: Charleston, Illinois, which turned out to be about twelve miles east of Mattoon, where Lucas Drackman had attended and graduated from a private military academy.

A quick check of the case file confirmed that the provost of the military school at that time had been Douglas T. Atherton.

The hour was not so late that a phone call would be ill advised. Daring to identify himself as "with the *Daily News,*" Mr. Tamazaki asked to speak to the provost and was told that he should call back during school hours. He took the further risk of saying that he had an important question to ask, that it involved a capital crime, and that he needed only two minutes of Mr. Atherton's time, whereupon he was transferred to the line at the provost's on-campus house.

"I assure you, Mr. Tamazaki, I wasn't traveling alone in the Caribbean in October of 1961, or at any other time, for that matter," the provost said. "Ever since my marriage, nineteen years ago, I have never vacationed without my wife." He couldn't quite keep the note of regret out of his voice. "Furthermore, I would never take a two-week cruise during the school year. I'd consider it a dereliction of duty, considering what some of these hellions might likely get up to in my absence." Evidently, the provost didn't know that the mother of a former student had gone missing from a cruise ship two and a half years after that student's graduation. "You must be seeking another Douglas Atherton."

Mr. Tamazaki believed the provost. It seemed entirely within Lucas Drackman's character to have fun with the alias that he used to commit murder, a puerile joke that would amuse no one but him and those of his co-conspirators who were equally immature.

Using the provost's name—which had been supported with false ID—wouldn't convict Lucas Drackman. It didn't qualify as evidence admissible in court, because as yet no link existed to prove who had booked the cruise in that name. If anything could be learned about who rented the post-office box in Charleston to which the cruise line sent the ticket, the case against Drackman might be advanced.

When Mr. Yoshioka was informed, both he and Mr. Tamazaki thought that this discovery seemed promising and that with luck justice might find its way to young Mr.

Drackman, the Cassidy twins, Aaron Kolshak, and anyone else associated with them—which might include my father. If that were to happen, they would cease to pose any threat to me or my mother or Mr. Yoshioka.

In retrospect, the argument could be made that Mr. Tamazaki's discovery marked the moment when the storm began to form that, not long thereafter, would change all our lives, and not for the better.

Fifty

TUESDAY, JULY 4, WE HAD A PICNIC DINNER IN THE park. Fireworks at first dark, the sky painted with cascading colors.

Mother and Grandpa Teddy set off together Wednesday morning. Woolworth's had offered her a longer shift than she had been getting, and although she was frustrated not to be able to find a singing gig, she needed those extra hours. Grandpa still performed five nights a week at the hotel, but he had taken on two more afternoons at the department store. Until school started in the autumn, I would be on my own every weekday.

That morning, I sat on the porch steps, hoping Malcolm would see me and take it as an invitation to come over and rock the living room again. I had neglected to find out which of the houses across the street was the Pomerantz residence. If he came over, I couldn't pour out to him everything that I'd been hiding from my mother. In fact, I didn't dare tell him any of it. But neither *The Star Beast* nor any other book would fade my worry back to mere concern. Neither would practicing the piano alone. At least with Malcolm, as well as he played and as smart as he talked, I'd be too distracted to continue imagining one death scenario after another.

When the woman strode along the public sidewalk from my left, through a dappling of sunlight and tree shadows, I didn't initially pay much attention to her, preoccupied as I was with all the dreadful events that I could imagine forthcoming. I was vaguely aware that she dressed pretty much like Grandma Anita had dressed for work in the monsignor's office: sensible black shoes with a low heel, dark-gray suit with a mid-calf skirt and hip-length jacket, white blouse. When she turned onto our front walk, I saw she also wore a black straw hat with soft crown, straight brim, and three blue feathers. I knew her.

I started to get to my feet. "Miss Pearl."

"Stay where you are, Ducks. I don't expect you to dance with me. I'll just share that step with you."

I hadn't seen her since June of the previous year, the day after my mother packed my father's belongings and locked him out of the apartment. Miss Pearl had been among the crowd in the Abigail Louise Thomas Room, listening to Mom sing while I played the piano. I'd only ever seen her twice before; I couldn't count the two times she'd been there in the dark after a dream, because once she'd been just a voice and the other time a voice and a silhouette.

Scented faintly with rose perfume, she sat down and put her large black handbag between us. She was still tall and pretty and mahogany, but not as glamorous as she had been when dressed all in flamingo-pink.

"How have you been, Ducks?"

"Not so good."

"Yes, I see you're just as glum as that day I first saw you on the stoop at your old apartment building. You looked like the king of grump that day, like you must've been sitting on nails and chewing thumbtacks. You remember what you were so down about?"

"I guess because . . . Tilton was never going to let me take lessons and be a piano man."

"And how did that work out for you?"

"Pretty good, I guess."

"You guess? Don't give me no guess. You're already a piano man before you're even a man."

"Thank you for the piano, Miss Pearl."

"You see? If you get in a mood and scowl at the world,

the world will just scowl back at you. Vicious circle. No point to it. Is this the sunniest of sunny days or isn't it?"

"What?"

"You've got eyes, child. Look around, look around!"

"Sure, it's sunny."

"Then you be sunny, too, and things will turn out better than if you aren't."

"I've got bigger trouble now than I did back then. Way bigger. Just thinking sunny isn't going to help."

She arched one eyebrow. "You mean your father with Miss Delvane, Mr. Smaller screaming like a lunatic at police, Fiona Cassidy going to Woolworth's, plus Lucas Drackman plotting with your father and the rest of them?"

I met her eyes, and as before, I saw nothing scary in them. Kindness is what people do for one another; it isn't something that you can peer into their eyes and see. Yet in *her* warm brown eyes, I saw unmistakable, inexhaustible kindness. They sparkled, too, not with morning sunlight but as if she were gazing at some glittering display of diamonds, instead of just at me. My breath caught in my throat—I don't know why—and I was filled with such wonder and such a sense of mystery that I thought I might swoon and pass out.

She put a hand on my shoulder, and that brief touch seemed to release me from a trance, so that I could breathe again. I looked away from her, at the trees along the street, which struck me as far more beautiful than they had been only a moment earlier.

When I could speak, I said, "How do you know about them and their . . . plotting?"

"Well, who was it first showed you Fiona and Lucas in dreams?"

"Yeah, and how could you do that? You're not a witch."

"That's a bull's-eye, Ducks. I don't live in a gingerbread house in a spooky old woods, and I don't have a cauldron somewhere full of boiling eye-of-newt stew."

"Then who are you, what are you?"

As calmly and sanely as I've ever heard anyone speak, she said, "Think of me this way, Jonah . . . I am the city, the soul of the city, spun up from threads raveled off the better souls of all those who have lived here and died here, also those who live here now. One thread of my soul is borrowed from yours, another is a thread from your mother's soul, another from your grandpa's soul. Millions and millions of threads. Another is from your Grandma Anita. When you memorized the Our Father, your grandmother gave you a silver dollar and told you to spend it on the day of your confirmation. In your sweet way, you asked her quite solemnly what you should buy with it, and she whispered in your ear, 'Spending doesn't mean always buying something, Jonah. Buy nothing. Give it to the poor.'"

"You can't know that," I protested.

"Is that what your grandma said or isn't it?"

"Yes. But how—"

"I've taken a special interest in you, Jonah."

She told me what I recounted to you at the beginning of this oral history. As the city, she worried that in spite of all she had to offer her citizens, she might be failing too many. The city knew its every avenue and back street, its every height and all its depths in intimate detail, but it didn't know what it felt like to be human and live in those thousands of miles of street. And so she, the soul of the city, had taken human form to walk among her people.

As I've admitted before, I had a spacious imagination as a boy; and that morning, I found plenty of room in it to accommodate Miss Pearl's claim to be the soul of the city made flesh. Lately I had spun so many lies, like one of those jugglers on the old *Ed Sullivan Show* who sets plates spinning atop bamboo sticks of various heights, racing back and forth to keep them in motion, spinning more and more plates until it appeared impossible that he could take them down one at a time before they all crashed to pieces on the stage. They say that you can't lie to a liar and deceive him. Maybe because I had become such an accomplished young liar, I recognized the pure truth of Miss Pearl's story, regardless of how fantastic it might seem.

Instead of contesting a word she'd said, I asked, "Why would you—why would the city—take a special interest in me?"

"Because of what you are, Ducks."

"I'm just a messed-up kid."

"That's not all you are."

"That's the bigger part of it."

"That's the tiniest part."

"Is it because of the piano?"

"You've got great talent, Ducks, but it's not because of that, either. It's because of *what you are*—and you won't understand what that is for a long time yet."

A covey of noisy vehicles passed in the street, and when quiet returned, I said, "You know everything that's ever happened in the city and everything that's happening now."

"I do, yes. Sometimes it amazes me how I can keep track of it all. There are a lot of unpleasant things I'd rather not know, I'd rather just sweep out of my head forever, but I'm aware of them all, anyway."

"And you know what's going to happen next?"

She shook her head. "That's a step too far, Ducks. What happens next is up to all the people who live along my streets. Your part of it is up to you."

Although I tried to be sunny, I couldn't fully cast off

glum. "I'm afraid of what might happen next, and I don't know what to do."

When she saw that I was shaking, she put an arm around me, but she offered no advice.

"Tell me what to do," I pleaded.

Fifty-one

BIRDS SANG IN THE TREES, CRICKETS CHIRRUPED in the grass, bouncy doo-wop music came from a phonograph at the house next door, three laughing children played some game on a porch across the street, and it all sounded like doomsday music to me.

"Tell me what to do," I said again.

"That's one thing I can't do, Jonah. I've already given you all the help I can. You'll have to decide yourself what to do as things happen. But you know what?"

"What?"

"You already know what to do."

"But I don't."

"You already know," Miss Pearl insisted, "and whatever

happens, good or better, bad or worse, you'll know what to do step by step."

I buried my face in my hands.

She sat silently beside me for a while. Then: "If you trust me, believe what I'm about to say, it'll help you in the darkest times."

Speaking into my hands, I said, "What is it?"

"No matter what happens, disaster piled on calamity, *no matter what,* everything will be okay in the long run."

I spread my fingers to filter my words. "You said you can't see the future."

"I'm not talking about the future, Ducks. Not the way you mean. Not tomorrow and next week and next month."

Frustrated, I said, "Then what *are* you talking about?"

She repeated, "No matter what happens, everything will be okay in the long run. If you believe that, if you trust me, nothing that might happen in the days to come can break you. On the other hand, if you won't take to heart what I've just told you, I don't expect things will turn out as well as they could."

I didn't mean to cry, not out there in public, not on the front porch steps for just anyone to see who might pass by, tears flooding from me as if I were a baby. I was past ten, going on eleven, more than halfway to being a man, or so I thought, and if I had to carry a weight, I should

be able just to shut up and carry it already, but I felt small
and weak and confused.

In the most tender voice, Miss Pearl said, "Ducks, I'm
going to do something I've rarely done before. But you are
special to me, and I'll give you this."

Despairing at my weakness, I wiped tears from my eyes
with both hands. "Give me what?"

"A peek inside my purse." She patted the black handbag
between us. She picked it up and smiled at me and set it
in my lap.

"Your purse? What could be in your stupid purse that'll
make any difference?"

"You won't know until you look. Mind me, you can't
have the purse, only a peek inside it."

"I'm a boy. I don't want a purse."

"Then take a look right now. Much as I love you, Ducks,
I can't sit here all day. I'm a city, and a city is always busy,
busy, busy."

In spite of my having heard pure truth when she had
told me what she was, you might think that I would at
some point, given sufficient provocation, reverse myself
and decide that she was a crazy lady. But I never did.

The handbag was large enough to carry a bowling ball
and bowling shoes and maybe a tenpin. I folded the braided
handles down, pressed the black clasp, opened it, and stared
in bafflement, at first unable to understand what lay within.

"Put your face right down close to it, Ducks, right down close. Then you'll see."

I did as she said, and I saw. I don't know how long the whole experience took. At the time it seemed to go *zoom,* all unfolding in a few seconds, but in retrospect, I thought it might have been an hour or more.

When I raised my head and looked around at the tree-lined street splashed with sun and shadow, I couldn't for a moment remember any words in the English language, and I said something like, "Unnn-gah-unng."

Fifty-two

MISS PEARL RETRIEVED HER PURSE AND CLOSED IT.

When I heard the clasp snap shut, I came to my feet, swayed, and steadied myself with the porch-steps handrail.

At the time, the peek into the purse stunned me, thrilled me, but also confused me.

As Miss Pearl got to her feet, I said, "What? What was *that*?"

"You know, Ducks."

"No. I don't. I'm confused. Amazed and confused and wow."

"You only think you're confused."

"I *know* that I think I'm confused. And I am."

"Your confusion is only on the surface, Ducks. Deep down, you understand, and that's what counts. In time, your confusion will go away, and your deep-down under-standing will rise to the surface."

She descended the porch steps to the front walk. She had no need of the handrail.

I didn't move, still half dizzy. "I wish you wouldn't go."

When she turned and smiled, standing there in her severe dark-gray suit and prim black hat, I thought of Mary Poppins. If she'd been carrying an umbrella instead of that huge handbag, I wouldn't have been surprised if she had opened it and caught a breeze and continued along the street at altitude.

"I can give you no more help. I've already given you more than I ever should. You have to make your own future, day by day, with no rescues by me. As I said before, what happens next is up to all the people who live along my streets. Your part of it is up to you."

"What if I make mistakes and people die?"

"People die every day. Wrong decisions are made, and they have consequences. Death is part of life. If you think about it, you were born into a world populated by the dead, because every one of them will die one day."

She followed our front walk to the public sidewalk, turned right, waved at me, and walked away.

I watched her until the street trees and the shadows and sun glare and sheer distance allowed me no further glimpse of her.

Because I knew what I'd seen in her purse but not what it meant, because that understanding came much later, I won't tell you at this point what the handbag contained. This is my life I'm talking, and I'll talk it in the way that makes most sense to me. Everything in good time.

After Miss Pearl was lost to sight, I went unsteadily into the house to lie down on the living-room sofa until my dizziness fully passed.

I assured myself that no matter what happened, if disaster piled on calamity, everything would be okay in the long run. Meanwhile, on that fifth day of July 1967, nothing serious yet.

Fifty-three

THAT SAME MORNING, BY TELEPHONE, MR. Tamazaki of the *Daily News* reached out to the Nishi Hongwanji Buddhist Temple in Los Angeles. In part of this ornate house of worship had been stored the belongings of some of those Californians sent to relocation camps during the war. A limited number of items were never reclaimed, and a curator looked after them even these years later. In addition, the curator maintained a lengthy list of the people who had been sent to the relocation camps, as well as a smaller list of those who wished for their whereabouts to be known to others who had endured the camps and who regularly updated their addresses with the temple.

Mr. Tamazaki wished to know if the temple might be aware of a former internee of any of the ten War

Relocation Authority camps now living in or around Charleston, Illinois. Within an hour, he received a confirmation call. A woman named Setsuko Nozawa had been interned at the camp in Moab, Utah, and currently resided in Charleston. She had already agreed that her address and phone number could be shared with Mr. Tamazaki.

Mrs. Nozawa proved to be quite a talker. Mr. Tamazaki learned that she was twenty when released from Moab, that she was forty-four now and, with her husband, had become a successful entrepreneur. They owned a car wash, two dry-cleaning shops, and an apartment building. Their younger daughter was a sophomore at Northwestern University in Evanston. Their older daughter was a senior at Yale. And their son had begun work on his MBA at UCLA. She loved to play bridge, taught origami to interested friends, was learning French cooking from the book by Julia Child, found the Beatles unlistenable, but was fond of the music of the Osmonds even if Utah didn't have good associations for her.

When Mr. Tamazaki finally managed to explain his situation and described the information he hoped that she would attempt to collect for him, she at once agreed. She was currently at the front desk of one of the dry-cleaning shops, but could get someone to cover for her within the hour.

Fifty-four

AFTER MISS PEARL LEFT, I WENT INSIDE TO LIE down on the sofa, and I fell asleep at once. For half an hour I remained oblivious, until the doorbell woke me, ringing incessantly. Of course the insistent visitor proved to be the twelve-year-old geek saxophonist.

At the open door, squinting and blinking blearily against a day fiercely bright by comparison to my dreamless sleep, I was reminded that the sun is a continuing nuclear holocaust, ninety-three million miles from our doorstep.

Assessing my appearance, Malcolm said, "Drinking this early in the day, you'll be dead of liver failure before you're famous."

Without being quite so mean as to indicate that his belt

line was just inches below his nipples, I said, "At least when I'm found dead, I'll be dressed with style."

"What does that mean?"

"Nothing. I was asleep on the sofa. I don't know what I'm saying. Come in."

He shuffled across the threshold, tripped on the throw rug in the foyer, and stumbled into the living room. Already, I found his lack of coordination endearing, as if it were his cross to bear just like Quasimodo's deformity in *The Hunchback of Notre-Dame,* only not so tragic and grotesque. Because he never excused himself or showed the least embarrassment when he careened through a room, you had to admire his determined pretense of grace; and considering how well he blew that sax, he would win the heart of the pretty Gypsy girl that Quasimodo had lost, assuming a pretty Gypsy found him one day.

"I hope I didn't bring my axe for nothing."

"That's like fingernails on a blackboard to me. Please don't call it an axe."

"What do you want me to call it?"

"Sax, saxophone, brass-wind instrument, reed instrument, I don't care."

"So if you don't care, I'll call it my axe. You've got to loosen up a little, man. So why were you taking a nap at ten-thirty in the morning?"

"Because I didn't sleep well," I lied, but it was a little

white lie to avoid being taken for a nut if I told him about the woman who was the city and what she had in her handbag.

"Hey, you know what'll always put you sound asleep?"

"Listening to you?"

"A glass of milk before bed. Use it to chase a Benadryl."

"I don't do drugs, and I never will."

"Benadryl isn't a drug. It's an allergy medication."

"I don't have any allergies."

"Take a walk on the wild side, Jonah."

"You want to play?"

"Did I bring my axe?"

So we played. Here it was 1967, when rock 'n' roll already had a storied history, and we liked a lot of that music, we really did, and we played some. But in truth, we were throwbacks, born too late, and our hearts were in the swing era. Since we'd learned the previous day that we both knew the songwriter and arranger Sy Oliver, we took the sax and piano parts the way we heard them on vinyl, and tried to be faithful to them, first on his arrangement of "On the Beach at Bali Bali," which he'd done for Jimmie Lunceford's band, a great band back in the day, and then we swung into "Yes, Indeed!," which Oliver worked up for Tommy Dorsey.

We had played fifteen minutes when the doorbell rang. Standing up at the piano, I could see a girl on the porch. She looked about seventeen, her blond hair in a ponytail.

Malcolm could see her, too. He said, "She's my sister, Amalia," and he went to open the door for her.

If you're ten, you can recognize pretty women when you see them, but you appreciate them only when they're at least a decade older than you—preferably more—so that you live in separate worlds. Girls any closer to your age are interlopers at best, annoyances at worst, and alien in any case, just getting in the way of what boys might want to do.

When I first laid eyes on Amalia Pomerantz, I was prepared to dislike her, and maybe I did for half an hour. She was pretty enough, but I didn't think she was beautiful, not like my mom, except I had to admit that her eyes, the exact shade of lime-flavored Life Savers candy, were extraordinary. I didn't like the way she dressed, which seemed to strain for the style that her brother would never achieve: blue-and-white vertical-stripe knitted-cotton top with short sleeves and a wide slashed neckline; white bell-bottom pants cut low on the hips, wide red-leather belt with a big buckle; white canvas shoes with blue-rubber soles and heels. It was like Gidget had been moved from the beach to a marina and updated to 1967.

I think I winced when I saw that she was carrying a clarinet, because it was my opinion, based on the makeup of all the classic swing bands, that girls had no place in the jazz world, except as singers behind a microphone.

She didn't even wait to be introduced, but said, "Hey, Jonah, if you're half as good as I hear, you're going to be playing to a sold-out house in Carnegie Hall before I find a guy I want to date more than once, if I ever do. Can't wait to hear you run those keys." She also carried a small insulated picnic chest. "Brought lunch. I'll put stuff in the fridge and be right back." She breezed to the kitchen at the back of the house.

I braced Malcolm. "You didn't tell me you had a sister."

"Isn't she great?"

"Sure, she's okay."

"She's the best. You'll see."

"She's not going to play the clarinet, is she?"

"Maybe," he said. "Depends on if she wants to join in or not."

"Why wouldn't she want to join in?"

"Music isn't her everything, isn't her future, the way it is for you and me."

"An amateur," I said with a note of disdain.

"She's good, though. She's been playing since she was nine."

"I've been playing since I was eight."

"Yeah, but you're only ten now."

I had no rejoinder except, "Jeez." I made the sign of the cross. Returning from the kitchen with just the clarinet, Amalia said, "I need some lively music, guys. I've had a boring morning. Did the laundry, half the ironing, cleaned the kitchen, washed the breakfast dishes." Directly to me, she said, "My mother has far, far too many obligations to be able to do much housework. She's committed to smoking two packs of Lucky Strikes a day, and she has to spend a couple of hours with Mrs. Janowski next door analyzing the sad marital relationships of our various neighbors, catch the afternoon soap operas on TV, the game shows later, to all of which, by the way, she has often applied to be a contestant. She's most frustrated that she can't get a spot on one of the nighttime game shows. She wanted to be on *What's My Line,* but by 'line' they mean line of work, which is *so* unfair, and she wanted to be on *I've Got a Secret,* but the only secrets she has all regard the terribly sad marital relationships of our various neighbors, many of which are too risqué for TV." She flopped onto the sofa. "Give me some music that makes me forget I'm an indentured servant."

We went Ellington on her, starting with "Satin Doll" and moving on to "Jump for Joy," trying as best we could to give the flavor and the essence of what the full band might have sounded like, though we knew that we were fools for even trying, just two of us and kids to boot. When we started "It Don't Mean a Thing If It Ain't Got That Swing," Amalia sprang off the sofa and snatched up her clarinet, and when the reed was wet, she came in not note for note, because maybe she didn't know it that well, but inventing riffs not of the song but totally in harmony with it, playing them over until she found a place to slip in and repeat a new one.

When we finished, she said, "Fabulous, you're great, that was fun. Lunchtime. If you don't want me to eat it all myself, you have to help me put it on the table, and don't give me any boys-don't-do-kitchen crap."

She'd brought three amazing submarine sandwiches, potato salad, macaroni salad with black olives, and rice pudding for dessert, all of which she had made herself, the sandwiches that morning between laundry and dishes, the rest of it the day before. All of it was first-rate food, and I don't know what impressed me the most—her ability as a cook or the way she could eat. She was about five foot five, slim as any model, but she sure could pack away the food, and she ate with great relish.

Malcolm's appetite didn't match his sister's, but his approach to food was more colorful than hers. She and I made do with a single plate each, but he would employ his plate for only his submarine sandwich. He used two small dishes for his portions of potato salad and macaroni salad, and if his primary plate had been the face of a clock, the macaroni was placed beside it precisely at ten o'clock, the potato salad exactly at two o'clock. He ate the former with a fork but preferred a tablespoon for the latter. He sliced the ends off his sandwich and set them aside, never to be eaten, then cut the submarine in three equal pieces with such calculation that I expected him to pull out a tape measure.

Because Amalia didn't remark on her brother's table habits, neither did I. As the years have gone by, however, and as he has gradually become more obsessive-compulsive, I take some comfort in knowing that I couldn't be the entire cause of his condition, that he had embarked on these rituals long before he ever knew me.

I don't mean to imply that Amalia Pomerantz dominated the table conversation, which she did but in another way didn't. She tried to draw me out, and by then she'd won me over, so I chattered a lot when I wasn't stuffing my face. I didn't want to dislike her anymore, *couldn't* dislike her. Malcolm put in his two cents from time to time, as well, but I'm not going to tell you much of what he or I said, because for one thing, none of it was interesting, and for another thing, I've forgotten nearly everything except what Amalia said. She was the first seventeen-year-old, either male or female, I'd met who cared to talk for more than a minute to a ten-year-old boy. To some degree she probably pretended to be interested in what I had to say, but she convinced me that she really, totally cared.

I wanted to know why she took up the clarinet, and she said, "To annoy my parents, to annoy them so much that they'd make me practice in the garage, where I could breathe air that smelled of automotive grease and tires and mildew instead of cigarette smoke. They're in a contest, Mom and Dad, to see who can get terminal lung cancer first. And in the garage, I didn't have to listen to their endless awkward silence."

"They say more to Tweetie," Malcolm revealed, "than they say to each other."

"Tweetie being the parakeet who lives in a cage in our living room and watches us with bitter resentment," Amalia explained, "most likely because the poor perpetually molting thing just can't stand cigarette smoke or can't tolerate my parents talking baby talk to him until he wants to scream. If you ask me, something happened between Mom and Dad long ago, and they've said all they have to say about it, but they haven't forgiven each other or themselves, so they don't want to talk to each other about *anything*. Dad's a lathe operator. In fact, he's also a foreman overseeing a shop floor of other lathe operators, and he makes good money, I guess. But judging by other lathe operators I've met, people he works with, maybe it's a trait of lathe operators that they're the strong silent type. Because he doesn't talk to me or Malcolm much, either."

"Except," Malcolm said, "to say, 'Take it to the garage.' Or, 'I'm just tryin' to watch a little TV here and forget what a shitty day I had at work, okay?'"

"But at least Dad's not a mean man," Amalia said. "He wouldn't hurt my mother or us, and that's something. He isn't mean and he isn't cold."

"He's cold," Malcolm disagreed.

"Well," Amalia said, "yes, he's cold, but maybe that's not his nature. Maybe he wasn't born that way. Maybe life has made him cold. Maybe disappointment and regret and who-knows-what has made him the way he is. Maybe he wishes he weren't that way, but he's just stuck in that mode, kind of frozen and doesn't know how to thaw."

"He was born that way," Malcolm declared, "and the last thing he wants to do is thaw." To me, he said, "Amalia's getting out. She's got a full scholarship, food and board and everything, to the state university. Leaves in September. She's going to be a writer. She's brilliant."

Her blush was lovely. "I'm not brilliant, Malcolm. I just love the language, I'm full of words, and I've got kind of a knack for putting them together. But I'm not sure I should go. Maybe I should get a job, wait a few years. The scholarship doesn't come with any spending money."

Malcolm looked pained. "You'll have spending money. Even if the old man doesn't want you going to college, he'll probably cough up a little pocket change. And I know you—you'll get a part-time job, and you'll still get top grades."

He had picked all the slices of black olives out of his

macaroni salad, but it wasn't that he didn't like them. When he finished his serving of macaroni, he then ate the olives.

I asked Amalia, "Your dad doesn't want you to go to college?"

"It's not that he doesn't want me to go to college or to become a writer, it's just maybe that he's dreading the day when Malcolm leaves, too, because then it's only the two of them and the parakeet, which would be a kind of hell."

"He resents you getting more education," Malcolm said, "because already you have more than he does. Quote, 'Pomerantzes don't need college, they never did, we don't mix with the hoity-toity.'" Malcolm turned to me, and his magnified, sad eyes were haunted by the fear that she might not take the scholarship. "She's afraid to go to the university and leave me home with them, because I'm already a social misfit."

She said, "You're not a social misfit, Malcolm. You're just awkward, and that will pass."

"I'm an awkward social misfit, and proud of it. If you don't go to college in September, it'll be my fault, all mine, and I can't live with that, so I'll blow my brains out."

"You won't blow your brains out, little brother. You faint at the sight of blood, and you don't have a gun."

"I'll get a gun, and I'll be dead before I have a chance to see the blood. You better go to college."

I tried to help out. "He won't be a social misfit when I'm done with him, Amalia. And there's Grandpa Teddy and my mom, and with them he's welcome here anytime."

After we finished the rice pudding—which Malcolm ate with a clean fork—we never did get back to making music. We talked while we cleaned up the kitchen, and then we sat at the table again and talked some more—mostly she did—and the time flew.

One thing she said about Malcolm that I'll never forget. "He thinks he's got music in him because he got it growing up with me, from me always with the clarinet as far back as he can remember, but that's not right. What music I have, I got it with iron-headed determination and grueling practice, and it's a thimble of spit compared to the ocean of natural talent in Malcolm. You heard me play, Jonah. I'd be fine for some dance band at the VFW and the Moose hall, but Malcolm's like you, he's got the real thing, and he's got it all. Mom and Dad, they're as interested in music as they are in chess tournaments, so Malcolm can't believe somehow his music came through them, but it did, just like my way with words." She turned those lime-green eyes on her brother and said, "Without me here to buck you up and keep you focused on how wonderful you are . . . what if I come home for Christmas my freshman year and you've already given up the saxophone and bought your own parakeet?"

"If you don't go to college in September," Malcolm said again, "I'll blow my brains out."

"And even if you could do that, little brother, where is a twelve-year-old going to buy a gun?"

"There's a lot of bad people in a city like this, a lot of completely wicked degenerates who'd sell a kid anything."

"And you know a great many of these wicked degenerates, do you?"

"I'm working on it," Malcolm said.

When they picked up their instruments to leave, it was nearly four o'clock, but I didn't want them to go home. Well, I didn't want Amalia to go home. I was equivocal about Malcolm going home.

I stood on the porch, watching them cross the street. When I'd first seen Amalia, I'd thought she was pretty but not beautiful. Now I had no doubt that she was major beautiful. I felt bad for having compared the way she dressed to Gidget, even though I hadn't said as much aloud, because I now saw that she had real style. In that blue-striped slashed-neck top and white slacks with a big red belt, she was cute. Sometimes a girl can be not classically beautiful but so cute that you wouldn't even notice a dozen classic beauties if they walked past naked. Amalia was really cute. And smart. And funny. And caring.

I was in love. Understand, at ten years of age, I didn't mean *romantic* love. I had not begun to save for a wedding ring and brood about ideal honeymoon locations. This felt like the same kind of love I had for my mother and for Grandpa Teddy, that I had begun to feel for Mr. Yoshioka, a noble and platonic love but so intense that I wished I owned the world so that I could give it to her.

Fifty-five

OUT THERE IN CHARLESTON, ILLINOIS, SETSUKO Nozawa proved to be as good as her word. In fact, she would become so intrigued with the investigation that she would not only report by phone to Mr. Tamazaki of the *Daily News* but would write a detailed account to mail him later, which was very useful to me in the colorful reconstruction of these events. Among her many interests, Mrs. Nozawa attended writers' conferences at the university, for she hoped one day to tell the story of her years in the internment camp, and she thought that writing the report would be useful practice.

In the company of her dog, Toshiro Mifune (named after the Japanese actor), she drove her custom-painted candy-apple-red 1967 Cadillac Eldorado to the neighboring town of Mattoon. Being a petite woman, she needed a booster pillow to see over the steering wheel, but Toshiro Mifune required no pillow, for he was a large chocolate-brown Labrador retriever.

At the military academy, she parked in a space behind the campus library and left two windows all the way down to ensure that the dog wouldn't overheat in the warm July day. Although she had heard hair-curling stories about some of the rowdier students at the school, she had no fear whatsoever that the Cadillac might be taken for a joy ride by one rich-boy ruffian or another. Toshiro Mifune had always been as gentle as others of his friendly breed, but Mrs. Nozawa had taught him to glower like a fierce samurai, growl, and bare his immense teeth when anyone put a hand on the Eldorado. She knew that this required great discipline on the dog's part, that it troubled his good heart to frighten people whom he would have preferred to lick copiously. But when she returned, she would reward him with kind words and two cookies.

Not many students—cadets, the librarian called them— were in the library when Mrs. Nozawa inquired at the main desk. In spite of her wartime experiences, she feared no one in uniform, but she found it disturbing to see boys as young as thirteen dressed like parade-ground soldiers. She told the librarian, Mr. Theodore Keckle, that one of the academy's students had done her and her husband a great favor, years earlier, and that she had always regretted not better thanking the boy. She wished to locate him now that he had graduated.

Unfortunately, though she knew the cadet had been a member of the class of '59, she could not remember his name. Even eight years later, however, she felt certain she would recognize his face. She assumed that the school library kept copies of the annual yearbook with senior photographs. Mr. Keckle—whom she would later describe to Mr. Tamazaki as "a stuck-up noodle with a mustache he shapes with pinking shears"—confirmed her assumption and directed her to a span of the history shelves that contained the volumes dealing with the five decades during which this highly esteemed institution educated, inspired, and formed young men of character.

Within a minute of opening the yearbook for the class of '59, Mrs. Nozawa found Lucas Drackman's photograph. She Xeroxed that page. On the way out of the library, she told the mustachioed noodle that she *thought* she recognized the young man but wanted to show the Xerox to her husband to see if he agreed that she'd found the right cadet.

In the front passenger seat of the Cadillac, Toshiro Mifune began to wriggle and whimper with delight when he saw Mrs. Nozawa approaching. She showered him with kind words, and he took the cookies from her fingers as gently as a rabbit nibbling grass.

After returning to Charleston, she went to the office-supply store owned by Ken and Betty Norbert. She and Betty volunteered time to a dog-rescue nonprofit and were in the same quilting club. Ken Norbert and Mr. Nozawa were tennis buddies and members of the Charleston Chamber of Commerce. If someone other than the Norberts had owned the business, Mrs. Nozawa would most likely have known them, too.

In addition to business supplies, the store offered private mailboxes for rent, which was an almost unknown business in those days, at a time when the closest competition were mail drops where you had to wait at the counter for a clerk to take your mail from a bank of pigeonholes and personally hand it to you. The boxes were in demand, because the local post offices never had enough available. It was here that a box had been rented in the name of Douglas Atherton, to which the cruise line sent the ticket for the Caribbean holiday.

In order to avoid renting to someone who might be engaged in fraudulent or otherwise dishonest business, the Norberts required two forms of identification from those who wished to secure one of their ninety-six mailboxes. In those more innocent times, however, almost any two items had been accepted, and photo ID hadn't been essential.

Ken had left for the day when Mrs. Nozawa arrived; but Betty was there with two employees and her Labrador retriever, Spencer Tracy.

The store kept a ledger of mailbox activity: the name of each renter, type of identification provided at time of rental, street address, and confirmation of payments. Concerned about liability, Ken never threw away old ledgers. Huddling over the volume for 1961, the two quilting enthusiasts found that Douglas Atherton had rented a box on the first of June, paying in cash for a full year's rental. For ID, he provided a Social Security card and a Student Activity card from Eastern Illinois University, located in Charleston.

Mrs. Nozawa copied the pertinent information and then showed the Xerox of the yearbook page to her friend. The name Douglas Atherton didn't appear under any of the cadet photos of course, and after nearly six years, Betty couldn't identify any of the eight faces on the page as that of the man who had rented the box.

When Mrs. Nozawa returned to her Cadillac and got behind the wheel, Toshiro Mifune couldn't stop trying to sniff her hands, for while in the store she had several times petted Spencer Tracy.

The dog's late-afternoon feeding time had arrived, after which he expected to be walked for half an hour. Because Mrs. Nozawa at all times had her priorities right, she wouldn't delay that feeding or cheat Toshiro out of even a portion of his walk time. Thereafter, she needed to change for dinner out with her husband and another couple.

From the office-supply store, she drove home, intending to continue in the morning with her inquiries on behalf of Mr. Yabu Tamazaki of the *Daily News*. She had promised only to get back to him no later than the close of business the following day, and he had not indicated that she needed to proceed more urgently. Between walking the dog and changing, she managed to call him to report her progress, and she was pleasantly surprised when Mr. Tamazaki praised her cleverness and efficiency, referring to her as "a real Sam Spade."

On the way to dinner, Mr. Nozawa wondered if she might be in any danger because of these inquiries. His wife replied that both of her precious parents and both of Mr. Tamazaki's were *Issei,* first-generation immigrants, and even among strangers, certain bonds were sacred obliga-- tions. He agreed. According to Mrs. Nozawa, he usually did. He encouraged her to exercise her skills at description by preparing that written report, for which I owe him.

Fifty-six

DURING THE PAST SIX WEEKS, SINCE WE'D MOVED out of the walk-up and had come to live with Grandpa, Mr. Yoshioka had called a couple of times, always during the day when I would be home alone, to ask if I was well and still practicing the piano. I told him what little had been happening in my life, and he shared what news there was of life in the apartment building we had left.

That busy Wednesday, after Malcolm and Amalia left, before Mom and Grandpa came home, at 4:15, Mr. Yoshioka called again. "Has the day been gentle with you, Jonah?"

I thought of Miss Pearl—her advice, her warning, her revelation that she was the soul of the city made flesh, her big purse and its astonishing contents—and I said, "Well,

I guess it kinda bruised me a little." I had told him every-thing except about Miss Pearl, and if I ever did tell him about her, it would have to be in a face-to-face conver-sation. Before he could ask what had happened, I said, "But I'm good, I'm great, I met these cool kids across the street."

He had called with a purpose, not just to chat. "Have you seen today's newspaper? The *Daily News*?"

"It came but I didn't look at it. The news isn't all the news there is."

"On the front page is a photo of the demonstration at City College on Monday. Among those in the photo are Mr. Smaller and Miss Delvane."

"I saw them on TV."

"As you know, I have no television, and the prospect of seeing Mr. Smaller on it does little to motivate me to make the purchase."

"I was watching . . . and I saw my father there, too."

"How very interesting. Your father is not in the news-paper photo."

"They're all up to something. They don't care about the war."

"Read the newspaper," Mr. Yoshioka said. "I think you will see what they might have been up to at City College. But first I must tell you that both Mr. Tamazaki and Mr. Otani have at last been in touch with me. There have been developments, and I will learn more tomorrow. I wish to come see you about all of this on Friday. What time would be most convenient?"

Considering that we would be talking about things of which my mother and grandfather were unaware, I said that he should come any time between eleven o'clock and four, when we could be sure that no one would know of his visit and question the reason for it.

"I will be there at two o'clock. And now I must tell you that two weeks ago, your father and Miss Delvane moved out of the place where they were living and have become impossible to trace. It is Mr. Otani's considered opinion that they have gone underground."

"What does that mean?"

"It means that they are covering their trail because they expect eventually to be sought by authorities. They may already have changed their identities. If they are, as you say, up to something, something more than what they've already done, then the something to which they are up is likely to occur this summer, perhaps sooner than later."

Miss Pearl, my apparently supernatural mentor, had visited me with her advice and warnings because the pivotal moment of my life lay in the immediate future, perhaps not mere days away but not years in the future, either. This summer, Mr. Yoshioka had said; and that felt about right.

"I will have more to tell you on Friday, Jonah. I have not meant to alarm you. I hope I have not."

"You haven't, sir. No matter what happens, everything will be all right in the long run."

"That is a very Zen recognition."

"A what?"

Rather than explain, he said, "Very wise. That is most wise. I will see you at two o'clock, the day after tomorrow. Be well, Jonah."

"I hope so. I mean, I will. I'll be well. You, too."

Fifty-seven

ON THE FRONT PAGE OF THE *DAILY NEWS*, ABOVE the fold, Miss Delvane and Mr. Smaller looked as though they had come from different worlds, heck, from different solar systems. She might have been born on the Planet of Superhot Women, while he traveled to Earth from the Planet of Unfortunate Men.

Reading, I quickly discovered what Mr. Yoshioka meant when he said the newspaper might show me what their weird little gang had been up to at City College.

Late in the demonstration, seven bombs had gone off, one after the other, at locations all across the campus. Nobody had been killed or critically injured, though six sustained minor wounds. Authorities believed that the explosives had been placed specifically to avoid killing anyone, that the purpose had been to create total chaos and distract the police and particularly the campus security forces.

Evidently, there had been plenty of chaos. As the explosions occurred at buildings to all sides of the crowd, the thousands of demonstrators hadn't known which way to run and had run every which way, crashing into one another. The bombs had been packaged with what the newspaper called "smoke accelerants," which seemed to mean that in a very short time, churning clouds of smoke spread across campus, greatly reducing visibility and causing everyone's eyes to water, their vision to blur.

Campus security men, who were not armed, left their posts and patrol routes, rushing into the melee under the impression that many seriously wounded awaited their help. The guard assigned to the Albert and Patricia Barton Gallery, adjacent to the College of Arts, locked the main entrance behind him, but the two men who looted the current exhibition blew open the door with the seventh bomb.

The security cameras caught two individuals—most likely men—dressed in black, wearing masks and gloves. They came in through the blown door and swirling masses of smoke, each carrying a cloth sack. The current show in the gallery featured seventeenth- through early nineteenth-century Chinese jade: vases, incense burners, screens, bowls, human and animal figures, scepters, snuff bottles, jewelry . . . They moved through the big room as though they knew the location of everything they wanted, ignoring the heavier items, snatching up the jewelry—necklaces, bangles, pendants, earrings—and the oldest and most exquisitely carved little snuff bottles. They were gone in five minutes.

A preliminary estimate of the loss was in excess of $400,000, an immense sum in those days. Experts suggested that the thieves surely had not stolen such items on speculation, because many were unique and all but impossible to fence. They must have had a client, a wealthy collector who wanted the pieces not for public display but for his private collection.

The assumption also had to be made that the crooks were closely tied with one or another anti-war organization. The protesters had descended on City College in a carefully coordinated surprise, but the bandits would have had to know about the event far enough ahead to scout the jade exhibition and to decide where to plant the bombs. They didn't need to be planners of the demonstration, only privy to the secret schedule.

My initial impulse was to slip the newspaper into the middle of the trash in the kitchen waste can, bag the trash, and put it in the garbage can outside. If my mother saw the photograph of Miss Delvane looking like a supermodel, it could only hurt her. If she recognized Mr. Smaller in spite of his bandana, I couldn't begin to imagine all the questions and speculations that might occur to her. Pretending to share her surprise and puzzlement, I would quickly come to a moment when she saw through my pretense, and all that I'd concealed from her might come tumbling out. The reasons for my secrecy had all seemed good and honorable at the time; but I didn't have confidence that they would seem good and honorable—or entirely defensible—now.

If I ditched the *Daily News,* Grandpa Teddy would want to know what had happened to it, and I didn't want to tell him it never came, didn't want to start lying to him, as well. My grandfather had never seen Miss Delvane and perhaps he'd seen Mr. Smaller only once or twice, briefly and at a distance; he would recognize neither. My mother didn't read the entire newspaper and often skipped stories involving violence, which depressed her.

I decided to trust my luck, let it to fate. I folded the paper, trying to make it appear untouched, and slipped it back into the thin plastic bag in which it had come when tossed into the front yard. I put it on the table beside my grandfather's armchair.

Grandpa Teddy wasn't playing in the hotel's Deco dining room that night. It would be a long evening of suspense, waiting for my mother to chance upon the photograph. I decided to go to bed early and read a book, sort of hide out. Maybe if she discovered the photo when I wasn't present, she would never mention it to me.

Anyway, the events of the day had worn me out. I would most likely fall asleep early, which was another way to hide.

Fifty-eight

LATER, AFTER DINNER, MOM AND GRANDPA TEDDY and I were clearing the dinette table when Amalia Pomerantz stopped by, sans Malcolm, with a proposal that I assumed my mother would reject after at most a half minute of consideration. Being seventeen and responsible, Amalia had for almost two years been taking the bus to other places in the city, safe places, to catch the matinee of a play, to explore a museum, to listen to a lecture, and that kind of thing. Her parents had no problem with her taking Malcolm along, and now that the geek saxophonist and I were becoming friends, she hoped that perhaps I would be allowed to join them on these expeditions.

Grandpa knew Amalia well and thought highly of her, trusted her to bring me back "unscratched and hardly tattered," and he said as much to my mother, who looked dubious. I believe that what Amalia did then was without calculation, that she was merely being her sociable self when, as she talked entertainingly about a free folk concert in Riverside Commons that she'd seen two weeks earlier, she stoppered the kitchen sink, drew hot water, squirted liquid soap into it, and started to wash our dinner dishes. Pretty soon, as Amalia rinsed and racked the plates, my mother dried them, and they were talking and laughing as if they had known each other longer than I'd been alive.

By the time I headed to my bedroom and book, the issue had been settled. The following day, I would be going with Amalia and Malcolm to some fancy art museum to look at a bunch of paintings, which just the previous day would have made me want to barf; however, if Amalia thought it would be fun, all doubts I might have had were swept away.

In my pajamas, in bed, I couldn't concentrate to read. I had a little transistor radio with an earphone, and I tried to dial in music that might elevate my mood. Couldn't find it. I took the La Florentine box out of my nightstand and looked at the Xerox of the page from the book about Manzanar, the pictures of Mr. Yoshioka's mother and sister. That made me think about the war and the riots and everybody killing everybody. The only thing that settled my mind was the haiku on the little sympathy card that had been attached to the floral arrangement at Grandma's funeral. I read it over and over again: *Dawn breaks / And blossoms open / Gates of paradise.*

The events of the day weighed me down. I slept. Toward morning, I dreamed. In the dream, my father was strangling Fiona, and for some reason I wanted to stop him, although she frightened me more than he did. Then my perspective changed, and I saw that she wasn't Fiona, that she was instead my mother, that the necktie bit cruelly into her throat. Her eyes were clouded. She was half dead. I tried to scream for help, but I literally had no tongue, and I tried to hit him, to claw at his face, but I had no hands. My arms ended at the wrists, in bracelets of coagulated and crusted blood.

I woke up, thrust up, threw back the sheet, sat on the edge of the bed in the lightless room, gasping. No residue of sleep clouded my mind. I was clearheaded, alarmed, alert. What I feared was not the nightmare, but that I might hear the voice of Miss Pearl and see her silhouette, a moving darkness in the dark, which would mean that the horror seen in sleep must be prophetic.

How greatly relieved I was when she wasn't there, but just then I glimpsed a paleness at the screened window, where the lower sash was raised to cool the room. I thought it must be the face of someone who had been watching me sleep, as Fiona Cassidy had once watched me and even photographed me slumbering unaware. If the long-awaited but unknown crisis drew nearer by the day, as Mr. Yoshioka and I both believed that it did, cowardice—even mere hesitation—might be the death of me, and so I rose and rushed to the window to confront who might be spying on me. I found no one, just a mosquito jittering against the metal mesh, such a frail visitor that it made no sound that I could hear above the pounding of my heart. If some watcher had been there, face ghostly in the waning night, she or he had fled, though perhaps it had been only a figment of my imagination.

Fifty-nine

THURSDAY MORNING, AFTER FEEDING AND walking Toshiro Mifune, Mrs. Setsuko Nozawa drove well below the speed limit on her way through Charleston, Illinois, to Eastern Illinois University. The dog was in the mood to ride with his head out the window. To drive above twenty-five miles per hour would put his eyes at risk if the wind carried in it sharp flecks of something.

Although she traveled by a roundabout route, staying mostly to quiet residential streets on which the speed limits were low, a few impatient drivers blew their horns at her. She drove with her head high, unfazed by their discontent, and she would not deign to reply in kind when crude words or gestures were flung her way. Each time a horn blew, she said, *"Namu Amida!"* which meant "Buddha have mercy." Those might have been words of forgiveness, directed toward the rude motorists, if she had not pronounced them with such an edge. The dog agreed with her, sensitive creature that he was, and matched every "*Namu Amida*" with a growl.

In the Alumni Affairs Office of the university, an attractive redhead with a constellation of freckles and an imposing bosom was most charming and helpful. Mrs. Nozawa repeated her invented story about a student who years earlier had done a great kindness for her and her husband, and the flame-haired woman explained that they were not at liberty to give out alumni addresses. Mrs. Nozawa said that she understood and appreciated their discretion, but that she only wanted to know if the Alumni Affairs Office would forward a letter from her to the kind young man if he had in fact graduated from the university. That was, of course, a courtesy that the university would be pleased to extend to her. Mrs. Nozawa was most gratified by the cordial tone of the exchange.

She doubted that Lucas Drackman had attended the university under the name Douglas T. Atherton. More likely, he had forged the Social Security card and Student Activities card with which he had qualified to rent the mailbox from Betty Norbert. Therefore, she gave the redhead the Drackman name and a likely year of graduation—1963. In minutes it was confirmed that Lucas

Drackman was indeed a graduate, and Mrs. Nozawa promised that, in a few days, she would return with her letter in a stamped and sealed envelope, which she had no intention of doing.

Mr. Tamazaki of the *Daily News* had hoped only that she would find that Drackman had been living in the area at the time Mrs. Renata Kolshak had disappeared from a ship in the Caribbean, thus establishing that he could have rented, under a false name, the mailbox to which a ticket to the same cruise had been sent to one Douglas T. Atherton. Mission accomplished.

A short while later, in her office in the dry-cleaning shop from which she oversaw the Nozawa commercial empire, she called in her report to Mr. Tamazaki, who was most grateful for her efforts. She assumed that was the end of the matter, but mere hours later, she would learn otherwise.

Sixty

I HAD BEEN IN MIDTOWN BEFORE ON OUTINGS with my mother, but never in the company of another boy with my sense of humor and never guided by a cute teenage girl who made people smile when they looked at her. When she hustled us across a street or when she hurried up a long run of stairs, her ponytail bounced and swung from side to side.

My mother had given me fifty cents, the cost of a student admission to the art museum, plus money for lunch. I felt rich and free and ready for fun . . . but a quiet paranoia plagued me.

At the bus stop from which we had departed, as we waited for our ride, I'd become obsessed with a black Chevrolet parked half a block away, in which two men sat. They were under a tree, in shadow, and I couldn't see their faces, but I became half convinced that they were Lucas Drackman and my father.

I remembered what Miss Delvane had shared with Mr. Otani when he chatted her up on New Year's Eve: that her boyfriend, recently divorced, talked constantly about one day getting his son back. If these men in the car were my father and Lucas Drackman, they might follow us. In Midtown, where I'd be far from home and vulnerable, they might try to snatch me.

When we disembarked from the bus, no black Chevrolet idled at the curb or passed by in the jostling traffic, which suggested that my fear was irrational. Nevertheless, it remained with me, a coiled tension at the back of my mind.

We had arrived at the corner of National Avenue and 52nd Street, the historical center of the city. Within two blocks in any direction stood the courthouse, the labyrinthine central library, the finest of concert halls, the cathedral, our oldest synagogue, and several ornate long-standing theaters. The architecture offered beauty at every hand, with buildings of granite and marble and limestone, even the towers, not a single hideous and inartistic glass monolith within two blocks of this core. Here was the most wonder-evoking part of the city, the beauty of order and the ordering power of beauty.

At our backs loomed the First National Bank on the

ground floor of its thirty-story Art Deco financial center. Across the street, columned like a Greek temple, stood Kalomirakis Pinakotheke, where we would see a special exhibition, *Europe in the Age of Monarchy*.

"Kal-oh-what? Pin-ah-what?" I asked.

As we climbed the front stairs, Amalia said, "Mr. Kalomirakis was an early immigrant from Greece."

"He made beaucoup bucks," Malcolm said. "I mean, the guy made Scrooge McDuck look like a pauper."

"He built this beautiful place," Amalia said, "bought just scads of great art for its permanent collection, and established a trust to ensure its continuation. *Pinakotheke* is Greek for gallery—but people here tend to call it a museum. I call it bliss."

I'd always had an ear for beauty, and maybe I'd had an eye for it as well, but until that day, I'd not recognized that the truth in great music could be found also in great art, that the heart could be lifted and the mind sharpened equally by both. By the power of her charm and the contagious nature of her enthusiasm, Amalia that day enormously expanded my world, threw open doors deep within me that otherwise might have remained closed for many years or perhaps even forever.

The paintings in the exhibition were on loan from museums as far away as the Netherlands and Paris, but also from as near as New York City. We saw work by

Rembrandt and Vermeer and van Dyck, Georges de La Tour, Jean-Marc Nattier, Caravaggio, Procaccini, and others.

Often, Malcolm would say to his sister, "Tell him the story," by which he didn't mean the story of a particular painting but of the painter's life or an arresting portion of his life. Some were amusing, some terribly sad, and each drew me into the work of the artist more than I, at that rough age, could have imagined.

I most clearly recall what she said about Johannes Vermeer, as we stood before his enchanting *Girl with the Red Hat.* That story has haunted me for almost half a century. *Why* it haunts me I won't say just yet, but soon. When Vermeer's story comes to mind on nights that sleep eludes me, I feel acutely the fragility of life, the ephemeral nature of everything we seek and create in this world.

The girl in *Girl with the Red Hat* stared at us from that small canvas, the sensuous details and the illusion of light creating a vision as liquid as reality, mesmerizingly dimensional, and Amalia said, "Vermeer may be the most masterful painter who ever lived. He was a perfectionist who worked hard but painted slowly. Maybe sixty pieces. Thirty-six have survived. Twenty-nine are masterpieces. His life was hard. He was poor, though he worked other jobs in addition to painting, desperate to feed his family. Fifteen children. Can you imagine me and fifteen Malcolms?

I'd be insane. But wait, no, it's not amusing. In those days, the sixteen hundreds, many died in childhood, and Vermeer grieved over four of his own. He, too, died young at forty-three, admired by other Dutch painters, but penniless and in his own mind a failure. His widow and eleven children, whom he'd loved as much as life, were left destitute. For two hundred years, his work was forgotten . . . *two hundred years*. But tastes change. To generations of the willfully blind, true beauty can remain unseen in plain sight, but beauty sooner or later asserts itself—always, always, always—and is at last recognized, because there's so damn little of it. He died a broken man, but now till the end of civilization, his name will be spoken with respect by many and even with awe by some."

Kids—and perhaps not just kids—are suckers for stories about underdogs who triumph in the end, even if they have to die first, and Vermeer became a hero of mine that day. By the time we were halfway through the exhibition, my paranoid expectation of being kidnapped was forgotten, and thereafter—for a while—I felt safe in the city.

Sixty-one

MEANWHILE, IN CHARLESTON, ILLINOIS, MRS. Setsuko Nozawa sat in her small office at the back of the dry-cleaning shop, balancing the business checkbook, while Toshiro Mifune slept at her feet. One of her employees appeared at the open door and interrupted to say that a professor from the university, Dr. Jubal Mace-Maskil, had come to speak with her about an urgent matter.

At the front counter stood a tall, lean man with a bird's nest of prematurely white hair. His gaunt and hard-lined face was softened only by bushy white eyebrows, and his gray eyes, flecked with green, seemed wild to Mrs. Nozawa, like the eyes of something that ought to be kept in a securely locked cage.

She disliked him on sight, partly because of how he was

dressed. In her opinion, a college professor—and a doctor yet—should not be seen in public wearing badly wrinkled khakis, a T-shirt bearing the letters MYOB—whatever that meant—and a thin, baggy khaki jacket with several patch pockets bulging with, if you asked her, all manner of things that would probably interest the police. The jacket had been torn and crudely patched in places, but of course it had come from the store that way, because distressed clothing was chic these days. She knew he wasn't unique. There were other rebels at the university, rebels everywhere these days, eager to forge a shining future by rejecting the past and all its evils. But *she* much valued tradition. The past was a trove of hard-won wisdom. Anyway, the human heart being what it was, those who erased the past would in fact purge only the wisdom and preserve the evils.

No sooner had Mrs. Nozawa introduced herself than Dr. Mace-Maskil launched into a tribute to Lucas Drackman, a former student of his, to whom he'd been mentor, a student of exceptional brilliance and integrity, majoring in political science, a young man of the most tender sensitivity and keen intellect and boundless energy. Did she know that Lucas had come to the university less than a year after his parents had been murdered in their sleep by some savage intruder? Did she know that in spite of his crushing grief and bitter loss, Lucas applied himself to his studies as few others, carrying his terrible burdens, could have done? Did she know? Did she? His future could not be brighter, for he possessed both honor and charisma, humility and noble ambition.

At first puzzled by these torrents of words, which spewed from the professor like water gushing from a fire hose, Mrs. Nozawa in time realized that those extravagant plaudits were a *defense*. Dr. Mace-Maskil apparently operated under the incorrect assumption that she had gone to the university and inquired about Drackman because she had some accusation to level against him.

When she was finally able to interrupt the professor, she repeated her story about the young man having done a great kindness for her and her husband, a kindness for which they never adequately thanked him. She only wished to express to Mr. Drackman the gratitude that he so richly deserved.

The professor listened at first intently, then impatiently, and soon revealed his disbelief by launching once more into unqualified praise for his former student. The more adulatory his words became, the more emotional he became, as well—and increasingly incoherent. His face reddened, and spittle sparkled around each word launched from his lips. If his eyes had previously looked like those of some creature in need of caging, they now suggested that he might soon need to be shot down as rabid.

Mrs. Nozawa became convinced that Dr. Mace-Maskil

had been high on some illegal substance when first he'd heard about her inquiry at Alumni Affairs, that he had misinterpreted what he'd been told, and that between then and now he had ingested more of that drug or maybe also others with contraindications. Either her astonished expression or her hand reaching for the telephone on the counter alerted him to the fact that he was by then making little or no sense, for his eyes widened, and he clamped one hand over his mouth to silence himself.

Having heard enough to be no less astonished than his mistress, Toshiro Mifune abruptly stood with forepaws on the counter and raised his big head. He regarded Dr. Mace-Maskil with limpid golden eyes, did not bark, did not growl, but expressed his opinion with a loud protracted snort.

The professor fled. No other word could adequately describe his sudden departure. Legs so long they seemed to have two knees each, arms flailing the air as if it must be more resistant than water, his rumpled and patched designer khaki ensemble rustling like a sack full of frantic rats, he careened to the left and then to the right as he sought escape. He made thin sounds of distress, as if he had wandered into the Little Dry-Cleaning Shop of Horrors and expected never to be allowed to leave. Meeting the glass door with his shoulder, he bulled through it, stumbled into sunshine, squinting as if it seared him, hurried west along the strip-mall sidewalk and out of sight, only to reappear a moment later, this time hell-bent toward the east.

Mrs. Nozawa came out from behind the counter and went to the door and stepped outside to watch the eminent educator make his way to his car. A gray Volvo. He seemed to have some difficulty figuring out how to start it. She imagined that he might be trying to insert the key into the cigarette lighter. Pulling out of his parking space, piloting the sedan toward an exit from the mall lot, Dr. Mace-Maskil blew his horn at every motorist and pedestrian he encountered, as though to warn them unequivocally that they were driving or walking recklessly. Even after the Volvo reached the street and disappeared, Mrs. Nozawa waited, listening for what seemed to be the inevitable shattering crash of a high-speed collision.

Being a shrewd businesswoman who could read people accurately, Setsuko Nozawa thought the strangest thing about the encounter was how the man had reacted to her story about Lucas Drackman having done a great kindness for her and her husband some years earlier. Although he had no reason to doubt a word she'd said, he hadn't believed her for a moment. In spite of the extravagant praise he had heaped upon his former student, perhaps Dr. Mace-Maskil found it impossible to imagine that Lucas Drackman was capable of a kind act.

Sixty-two

AS AMALIA AND MALCOLM AND I MOVED ON FROM *Girl with the Red Hat*, proceeding deeper into Kalomirakis Pinakotheke, I asked if she could not just tell me about the artist but if she could explain also what each painting meant, why its maker made it, what he wished to say.

Rapping my head with the rolled-up brochure each of us had been given when we paid at the entrance, Malcolm said, "That's a pretty stupid thing for a prodigy to ask. Tell him why it's stupid, Amalia."

"If I recall correctly," she said, "when I brought *you* here for the first time, you asked me the same thing."

"That's not the way I remember it," Malcolm said.

"How do you remember it, dear brother?"

"You were in a stormy mood that day."

She raised her eyebrows. "Stormy?"

"And you were drinking."

"Oh? What was I drinking?"

"Just everything. Brandy, beer, vodka, wine."

"Did you have to carry me over your shoulder?"

"Not at all. I said you were brain-damaged at birth, and they gave us a courtesy wheelchair."

"You're terrible."

"I don't believe you were drunk," I told Amalia.

"Thank you, Jonah."

To me, Malcolm said, "You are painfully naïve, child. Anyway, as I wheeled her from painting to painting—she would point at each one and in an embarrassing drunken way, she'd demand to know what the picture *meant*. Sis, do you remember what I told you that day? Jonah needs to hear it."

"Why don't you tell him, Malcolm?"

"I'm not sure I remember it word for word." To me, he added, "The dear girl will have committed it to memory. Even drunk, she hangs on my every utterance."

"Utterance?" Amalia said.

"I heard a really cool British actor say it in a movie. Sounds sophisticated. From now on, I'm not going to say anything, I'm going to utter."

"Utter all you want, you still won't make sense."

"Right there is a hint of her stormy mood," he told me. "She must have a flask she's been nipping from."

"What *I* said to *Malcolm* that day, Jonah, is that there's a lot to learn about art. You need to train your eye. But when it comes to what it means, no stuffy expert in the world has a right to tell you what you should think about a painting. Art is subjective. Whatever comfort or delight you get from a painting is your business. What it says, it says to you. Too many experts make art political, 'cause they believe great artists have always held the same convictions as they themselves do. But the last thing art should be is political. Yuck. Double yuck. Keep your mind free. Trust your eye and heart."

Malcolm said, "That's what I told her, word for word. Amazing she could memorize it, considering how pickled she was that day."

In his ungainly manner, he went to the velvet restraining rope that looped through the gallery from stanchion to stanchion, and he stood before a painting titled *Wheatfields* by Jacob van Ruisdael. Amalia and I joined him.

Sky filled two-thirds of the big canvas, some blue but most of it covered in masses of dark-gray clouds. The bottom third offered a vast landscape, deep shadows in the foreground, dark woods in the background, and in the middle a sunny patch of meadow through which a dirt road curved. A lone man and a woman with child walked the road. Beyond the trees, all but invisible, a shepherd herded sheep.

I said, "It makes me feel sad and happy at the same time. The people are so tiny and the world's so big."

"The people in Ruisdael's landscapes are always tiny," Amalia said. "Why do you think you feel both sad and happy?"

"Well, I don't know. It's like . . . they're so tiny, they could be crushed like bugs. By lightning, you know, or anything. That's sad."

"Unless they're bastards," Malcolm said, "then good riddance."

"My lovely brother, shut up," Amalia said sweetly.

I continued, "But then all around them, it's so beautiful, see, the sky and the woods and the meadow and everything. I feel happy for them being in such a beautiful place." I looked up at Amalia, and she smiled, and I said, "Did that sound stupid?"

"Not at all, Jonah. We both know who's king of stupid today."

Malcolm said, "I will utter something in a minute or two, and it'll be so clever, you'll be devastated."

We came next to a painting almost as beautiful as *Girl with the Red Hat,* but as I studied it, disquiet crept into me and soon evolved into fear that made me tremble.

Sixty-three

WHEN DR. JUBAL MACE-MASKIL APPARENTLY escaped into the day without broadsiding another vehicle, Mrs. Nozawa returned to her office at the back of the dry-cleaning shop. After considering the friends to whom she might go for information, she put in a call to Irinka Vavilov. Irinka and her husband, Andrei, had been musicians with the Moscow symphony when, in late 1939, they had defected while on tour in Norway and within a year had made their way to the United States. Andrei had died a year earlier, but Irinka, now fifty-five, still taught music history at the university.

Irinka had learned origami from Setsuko Nozawa and was always happy to hear from her. She knew Jubal Mace-Maskil, and she thought he was a swine. When she had first come to the university, he had made bold passes at her at faculty parties, even when Andrei was in the same room, even when Jubal's wife, Noreen, stood mere feet away.

He'd become more aggressive after his wife died in 1962, and then in just the last two years, he had taken on a whole new persona, fancying himself the Che Guevara of Charleston, Illinois, obviously indulging in recreational drugs that would eventually get him fired or, more likely, forced into early retirement. Some people said he'd started to come apart after Noreen died, haunted by the cruel nature of her death, but Irinka didn't believe Jubal had a capacity for deep empathy, not even regarding his wife.

How did Noreen die? Quite horribly. She'd gone to Arizona to visit her brother and his family. One evening, after everyone else had gone to bed, she sat outside alone by the pool, enjoying the warm desert evening. The next morning, she couldn't be found. Her rental car no longer stood in the driveway. Police located it in a shopping-center parking lot and discovered Noreen's body in the trunk. She'd been tied hand and foot and then been beaten to death with a hammer. No one was ever charged with the crime.

Did Jubal have an ironclad alibi? What an odd question. Most people thought of him as an intellectual faker and a hopeless pig, but no one would ever think him capable of murder. He was too much of a wimp, utterly gutless. As it happened, the week Noreen went to Arizona, Jubal had been chairing a three-day conference titled "The Cold War: Necessity or Contrivance?" There were ninety-two attendees from universities in sixteen states. He had put the whole thing together; and he was present throughout. Even his late-night hours were no doubt accounted for, considering that there were many women at the conference, all familiar with Jubal's carefully crafted image, but none familiar with his reality. In fact, Noreen was killed on the final night of the event, which concluded with a party that lasted until after one in the morning—by which time she had been snatched and dispatched in faraway Scottsdale.

By Mrs. Nozawa's calculation, Lucas Drackman, he of exceptional integrity and brilliance, had been a member of the junior class when Dr. Mace-Maskil had become a widower. It would be interesting to know if Noreen's life had been covered by a large insurance policy or if she had possessed substantial assets, separate from her husband's, that had passed to him through her will.

Mrs. Nozawa hoped Mr. Tamazaki of the *Daily News* would not ask her to investigate those two intriguing questions. Although she had enjoyed this little adventure, she harbored no desire to give up her entrepreneurial endeavors to become a gumshoe, which could be a most depressing occupation.

When Mrs. Nozawa said good-bye to Irinka and hung up the phone, Toshiro Mifune put his enormous head in her lap, and she stroked behind his ears. She told him that he was a good boy, the best boy ever, and that the world would be an immeasurably better place if people were more like dogs. As Labrador retrievers went, Toshiro was on the large size, but when properly motivated, he could purr.

Sixty-four

THE PAINTING THAT CHILLED ME TO THE marrow was beautiful, and all these years later I regard it as a masterpiece. The artist, Carel Fabritius, a Dutchman, might have been a pupil of Rembrandt's. At thirty-two, he was blown to bits, along with all but a few of his paintings, when the gunpowder plant at Delft exploded in 1654 and leveled a third of the city.

This painting, quite small, was called *The Goldfinch*. It is said to be the greatest painting of an avian subject in that entire century. The backdrop is a sunlit wall, and on the wall hangs a feeding box, perhaps ten inches by six, on which the little bird perches. The finch is restricted to the box by a fine-link chain attached to one of its feet, a chain at most two feet in length, allowing it to test its wings and fly only to change its position on the box, condemning it to a markedly more limited and miserable existence than that of a parakeet in a large cage.

The cruelty of the finch's captivity, its keeper's thoughtless denial of its winged nature, tortures your heart if you have a heart capable of being tortured. But the bird's circumstances were only one reason that the painting chilled me. The attitude of the bird—alert, its head raised and turned toward the viewer (in the world of the painting, toward its keeper), something in its posture that said it could be restrained but never broken by restraint—suggested stoic suffering that, if I dwelt on it too long, would reduce me to tears.

The bird's circumstances and attitude were still not entirely what so affected me. What started me trembling was its right eye. In the painting, the left eye was shaded, but in the right glimmered a liquid drop of light, a simple bit of mastery that convinced me that this painted bird could indeed see. Its stare was direct but more than merely direct. There was a depth to the eye, as if not only the bird looked through that eye at its keeper, but as if *all of nature* looked and saw and knew the extreme cruelty of this imprisonment.

No, not just that.

Suddenly I knew what the painting meant to me, and I thought I knew what it had meant to the painter. Many who believe in God also believe that He is not merely the creator of all nature but is *in* all of nature, that He is everywhere with us, in some way beyond our easy comprehension, that He is acutely aware and caring. In the right eye of the goldfinch, I saw the bird gazing at his keeper, all of nature gazing, too, but also through that moist and feeling eye, the Maker of the keeper watched. Watched and saw and loved the keeper for his potential, but mourned his cruelty. Love and sorrow informed that eye, and it regarded me as surely as it regarded the keeper of the bird, saw me and knew the good and bad of me, knew my courage but also my cowardice, knew the lies I had told. I might not have been able to put all this into words then, as a confused boy of ten, but I understood: Like the bird, I was chained, and the links in the chain were my lies, so that I was both bird and keeper, chained and endangered by my own actions.

Amalia realized that I was trembling violently. "Jonah, what's wrong?"

"Nothing. I don't know. Nothing. I'm okay."

"You're shaking like a leaf."

Earlier I had realized that we'd been so enthralled by the show that we hadn't gone to lunch. Now I looked at my watch and said, "We didn't eat. It's two o'clock. I'm starving, I guess. That's what it is. I'm way hungry. Let's go find a street vendor. I need a hot dog."

"What does the painting mean to you?" Malcolm asked as I turned away from *The Goldfinch*.

"I don't know yet. I'll have to see it again. Figure it out when I'm not starving like this. Aren't you guys starving?"

Room after room of white marble floors, down wide white marble steps, across more glossy floors . . . I didn't think we'd come this far, and I wondered if Amalia truly remembered the way out or whether we were in a maze, going around and around in some episode of *The Twilight Zone*. But then we came to the cashier windows, where we'd bought our tickets, and the doors were beyond.

I was sweating before we left the air-conditioned Pinakotheke, and though the day was warm, it wasn't blazing hot enough to explain the perspiration on my face.

As we walked in search of food vendors with street carts, Amalia said, "Are you sure it's just hunger, Jonah? I'm not sure it is."

"No, it is. It really is. I just need to eat."

Malcolm said, "Our tickets are date-stamped. We can go back in after we've grabbed some lunch."

I'd had enough art for the day, but I didn't say as much.

We found a hot-dog vendor and got two each, and Pepsi. By then we were close to the courthouse, beside which lay a pocket park. We sat side by side on a bench in the park and ate lunch. Hoping for dropped crumbs, pigeons strutted back and forth, eyeing us with less intensity than the goldfinch had studied me.

My shakes and sweats went away, as if hunger really

had been the only cause of them, and that made Amalia happy.

I pretended to be fascinated by the courthouse and asked if it was like those on TV. She said it was huge and worth seeing for its splendid architecture. By the time we explored all the public spaces, we had to run to catch the 3:20 bus at the corner of National Avenue and 52nd Street.

All the way home, I worried and wondered when the axe would fall, by which I didn't mean Malcolm's saxophone.

Sixty-five

MRS. NOZAWA CALLED MR. YABU TAMAZAKI AT the *Daily News* morgue, but he had gone for the day. She didn't leave a message, because he had suggested that his investigation was sensitive. He'd said that when she called, if she got someone other than him, she should leave no message. She called him at his apartment, letting it ring and ring, but he didn't pick up and evidently had no answering machine there.

Just then she received a call about a boiler failure at the apartment house that she and her husband owned, and when she phoned Mr. Nozawa at the car wash, she discovered he was already dealing with a major problem involving the drain in Bay 2. The boiler would have to be her baby.

Mr. Nozawa got home at 9:10, bringing with him a

medium-size pepperoni-and-cheese and a family-size salad pack from a pizza joint. When Mrs. Nozawa arrived twenty minutes later, she first gave the most patient dog his late dinner and took him into the backyard to toilet. By the time she had wiped Toshiro Mifune's paws with a wet cloth before letting him back in the house, she felt it had gotten too late to ring Mr. Tamazaki. Besides, she desperately wanted some pizza—and good red wine.

As they ate at the kitchen table, they told each other about their day. Mr. Nozawa agreed with his wife when she said that the following evening she would telephone their younger daughter at Northwestern, their older daughter at Yale, and their son at UCLA to insist that if they had professors who wore rumpled khakis with patch-pocket jackets and T-shirts emblazoned with inscrutable groups of letters, they should drop those classes and find alternatives.

Sixty-six

SINCE WE HAD MOVED IN WITH GRANDPA TEDDY, I had kept the Lucite heart, with its captive feather, in the La Florentine box instead of carrying it everywhere in a pants pocket. I suppose for a while I had felt safer in my grandfather's house than in the apartment. I'd had the same experience before: When all threats seemed to recede at least somewhat, I tended to regard the pendant as merely a curiosity, jewelry that a boy would never wear and that cluttered my pocket, but when I felt myself in great jeopardy, the pendant appeared magical once more, offering ultimate protection against the many kinds of darkness that can overcome us in this world.

That Thursday night, with the experience of the Pinakotheke so fresh in mind, and considering all that

had happened since the anti-war demonstration and bomb-
ings at City College on Monday, including the visit by
Miss Pearl and her warning to me on Wednesday, I thought
of Albert Solomon Gluck, the taxi driver and would-be
comedian, and of the pendant that he had given to my
mother, that she had given to me. I got the La Florentine
box from my nightstand, opened it, and fished the pendant
from among the other items.

As I dangled it by the silver chain, I thought my eyes
deceived me. The tiny white feather had turned golden
brown, the very shade of the bird in the painting that had
so powerfully affected me. Holding the Lucite heart in the
palm of my hand, I thrust it under the shade of the bedside
lamp, but the greater light revealed a feather of an even
brighter gold than it had first appeared. Indeed, when I
took it out of the direct light and held it before my eyes,
it retained the more intense color that it had acquired under
the lamp, and it even seemed to glow.

Wondering, I put the chain around my neck, whether it
might be girl's jewelry or not. The heart hung low on my
chest, heavy but not uncomfortable. I tucked it under
my pajama top, half expecting a faint golden light to pene-
trate the fabric, though none did.

I didn't know what to make of this development, but I
knew that it must be of enormous significance.

I never gave more than a passing thought to the

possibility that the glue cementing the two halves of Lucite into a single heart had darkened with age. For one thing, if that had been the case, not only the feather but the entire plane between the two half hearts would have yellowed; but it had not. Furthermore, the vanes of the feather, fanning out from both sides of the shaft, were as soft-looking as before, as though they had not ever been glued there but existed in a shallow void at the center of the heart, where the glue hadn't been applied.

The taxi driver's gift had seemed magical on the day that I received it, also on certain occasions since, including in the moment when I first saw that the white feather had been transformed to gold. Now, however, but two minutes later, listening to my heart beating under the still and clearer heart on the chain, I sensed that the word *magical,* although it evoked myriad thoughts of things wondrous and mysterious, might be inadequate or even wrong. I felt that this pendant must be something more than magical, though what else it might be, I couldn't say. I was quick for a boy of ten, agile of mind, but some things eluded me. The jewelry, Miss Pearl, so much that had happened during the past two years, the experience of *The Goldfinch* that very day, and even to a lesser extent Vermeer's *Girl with the Red Hat* and Jacob van Ruisdael's *Wheatfields,* all of it had something akin to magic in it, but something immeasurably deeper and stranger than magic: even the mundane moments like breakfast with Mom at The Royal and a game of cards with her at the kitchen table, the immense room of busy tailors at Metropolitan Suits, Mr. Yoshioka and the security chain that in memory shone like gold instead of brass, the ivory carving of the court lady in her nineteen-layer ceremonial kimono, Grandpa Teddy with the pack of Juicy Fruit gum as the crows danced on the sidewalk . . .

Although I felt safer with the pendant around my neck, though I knew in my bones that it wasn't just useless juju, I didn't feel entirely secure. I couldn't help but think that the transformation of the feather from white to gold signified the approach of a moment, an event, a crisis toward which I had been moving since the day I'd been given eight names—not including Kirk—that I could never live up to even if I grew as old as Methuselah.

Although the warm room wanted ventilation on that July evening, though the pale face I'd thought I'd seen at the window the previous night had most likely been imaginary, I got out of bed and pulled shut the lower sash. Locked it. Drew shut the draperies.

Sixty-seven

SHORTLY BEFORE TWO O'CLOCK THE FOLLOWING afternoon, when Mr. Yoshioka arrived on foot from the bus stop three blocks away, dressed in a three-piece pin-striped summer-weight suit, he brought two paper plates taped together to form a container. He presented it to me when I rose from the chair on the front porch, where I had been waiting for him.

"I wish to give you six coconut cookies with chocolate chips, which I have made myself and which I hope you will find edible."

"You're baking now?" I asked.

"I have been inspired by your mother's creations, and I find the process of baking to be quite relaxing."

"Should we have one now?"

"I would make no objection."

I put the container on a little table between the chairs and said, "What can I bring you to drink? I still can't make good tea."

He smiled and nodded to indicate that the lack of tea didn't disappoint him. "I have as well acquired an appreciation for Coca-Cola, if you should have any."

I brought two bottles of Coke, two glasses of ice, and a few paper napkins on a tray, and we sat side by side, the table between us. When I broke the Scotch tape and opened the lid of the makeshift container, the aroma of the cookies made my mouth water. "These smell amazing."

"I found the instructions in a magazine that I have been told is well regarded. After baking two batches that were inadequate, I made some changes to the recipe."

The cookies tasted even better than they smelled. "These are so great. You should open a cookie store or something."

"I am only a tailor, though I have considered writing to the magazine and sending them my corrected recipe. I am afraid, however, that they will not receive it with appreciation. It is good to see you again, Jonah."

"It's good to see you, too. It really is."

"This is a nice house and a pretty street with all the trees. I wish very much that you are happy here."

"I am," I said and didn't burden him with my concerns. In truth, I couldn't share my latest worries unless I revealed the final secret that I'd been keeping from him—Miss Pearl. I continued to feel that I wasn't meant to speak of her to anyone, that her visitations with me were in some way hallowed.

We spoke of everyday things for a few minutes, and then he told me about how Mr. Tamazaki of the *Daily News* had approached the Nishi Hongwanji Buddhist Temple in Los Angeles and how, through them, he had found Setsuko Nozawa in Charleston, Illinois. The previous day, Thursday, Mr. Tamazaki had given a detailed report of Mrs. Nozawa's discoveries to Mr. Yoshioka and then had set out with enthusiasm on a three-day holiday to Asbury Park, New Jersey.

Mr. Yoshioka confided that he found Asbury Park an unlikely vacation site for Mr. Tamazaki, who was shy, neither a swimmer nor a sunbather, and had no interest in the usually frivolous pursuits offered by seaside resort communities. Because Mr. Tamazaki had gone all the way to Asbury Park five times in the past year, however, and regardless of the weather, perhaps it was reasonable to surmise that what attracted him was not the town but romance.

"At mid-life," Mr. Yoshioka said, "I believe he has developed a great affection for a woman who, unfortunately for both of them, resides at a distance from him. But that inconvenience is a small matter if he has found love in a world with so little of it."

Mr. Yoshioka shared with me all that Setsuko Nozawa had learned. Of course, he didn't know that she had tried to reach Yabu Tamazaki one more time, that she had phoned repeatedly during the past twenty-four hours, after the curator of the morgue had set out for Asbury Park. She hadn't been able to pass along the news about Dr. Mace-Maskil's colorful visit to her shop or the circumstantial evidence suggesting that he'd conspired with Lucas Drackman to have Mrs. Mace-Maskil murdered. All of that we would learn only in time, because we didn't then live in an age of cell phones and text messaging.

"I have passed all this along to Mr. Nakama Otani, who is once more involved. He will coordinate the facts from Mrs. Nozawa with other information that he has recently found and is still finding, and when he believes that he has put together a convincing case, he will go to his superiors and seek to open an active file."

Half dizzy from listening to all these developments, I said, "Who are his superiors, where does he work?"

"Mr. Otani is a homicide detective."

"But you didn't want to go to the police."

After taking a sip of Coca-Cola, Mr. Yoshioka said, "I did not go to the police, Jonah. I went to Mr. Otani not in his capacity as an officer of the law, but as a fellow inmate of Manzanar."

"Oh."

"My journey through the relocation camp left me distrustful of the law. However, Mr. Otani learned a much different lesson from the experience. Because the same legal system that abused us within a few years restored to us our rights as citizens, Mr. Otani developed much respect for it and chose to become a police officer and eventually a detective. I have thought about this for quite a long time, and I must acknowledge that he is a better man than I am."

I didn't like to hear him say that. In fact, I couldn't abide hearing it. "He's not a better man than you. You just . . . well, you lost more there than he did."

He stared at me in silence for a moment and then looked out at the maples trembling and so green in the faint breeze. Finally he said, "You often surprise me, Jonah."

"Well, it's only the truth. What did I say wrong?"

"You said nothing wrong. Yes, it is the truth. Mr. Otani lost no one at the camp, thank God. But that does not excuse my failure to distinguish between an act of fate—the fire—and the acts of men. I blamed men equally for our incarceration and my loss, and that was a mistake that has shaped my life ever since."

"Mistake? No. Your mom and sister wouldn't have been there in the first place if the law hadn't sent them."

"Which is the way I thought until, so recently, I have seen that I was wrong."

"Man, you're so hard on yourself, way too hard."

He looked at me again and smiled. "If I am not hard on myself, Jonah, who will be? It is not a good thing to be soft on oneself."

I didn't know what to say. Usually that didn't prevent me from chattering away as usual, but this time I sat in silence.

Mr. Yoshioka said, "Police photographers took hundreds of photos during the course of the demonstration at City College on Monday. Mr. Otani quietly reviewed them and found Miss Delvane, your father, Mr. Smaller, Mr. Drackman, and Miss Cassidy."

"Her there, her, too?"

"Of course, it is their right to protest. Free speech."

"Then what does it mean that he found them?"

"Mr. Otani believes Lucas Drackman is living in the city under a false identity. The Drackman Family Trust, the vehicle through which the estate was passed from his murdered parents to him, still exists in Illinois. And in fact, the trust owns property here in the city. Mr. Otani is now seeking the address or addresses."

"You think that's where he lives?"

"It may be where he and Miss Cassidy live and where your father and Miss Delvane went, too, when they disappeared from their previous apartment. It may also be where Mr. Smaller now resides."

"But isn't he at the apartment building?"

"He quit his job Friday of last week, moved out, and left no forwarding address."

I pressed the cold glass of Coke to my brow. "I feel like my head is gonna explode."

"That cannot be a good feeling. Speaking of explosions, Mr. Otani has also discovered that Miss Cassidy is a graduate of one of the city's universities, where she earned a degree in chemistry."

"Wow."

"As you say, 'wow.' Mr. Otani hopes to show not just that the five of them were at the demonstration but that they also live at the same address, at least one of them under a false name and no doubt in possession of forged ID. That alone would not be enough to persuade his superiors to open a case file, but when combined with the information provided earlier by Mr. Tamazaki and recently by Mrs. Nozawa, it should be, as he put it, 'a slam dunk,' which I believe is a football reference."

"Basketball," I said.

"Ah. Then I stand corrected. Therefore, if he can get a warrant to search the premises for the stolen jade, whatever other evidence is discovered in the process might put Mr. Drackman and Miss Cassidy in prison not merely for armed robbery and terrorism but also for murder."

If that were to happen, I could at last stop worrying about all of them, about my father, too, because although Tilton hadn't killed anyone and wouldn't get a life sentence for murder, he would have a home behind bars for years.

I supposed Grandpa Teddy and perhaps even my mother would think I should regret my father's downfall and incarceration rather than celebrate it. Well, good luck with that. The best they could expect was that maybe I wouldn't gloat so much, they'd feel the need to say extraordinary prayers for my soul.

"How soon can Mr. Otani get his boss to open a case file?"

"He thinks that he will have everything he needs before noon Saturday."

"Tomorrow."

"I will keep you informed. I hope that you understand what we must do if Mr. Otani's superiors agree to proceed as he wishes."

His stare was direct and his expression one of polite concern, as minimalist as most of his expressions, but I sensed that "what we must do" would prove to be something that I might find unpleasant in the extreme.

When I couldn't infer what that might be from what he had said, he illuminated the situation for me: "When the case file is opened and the police go to court to obtain a search warrant, I must return here so that you and I may sit down with your mother and reveal to her everything that you withheld and everything that you and I have conspired to do together."

I thought this must be how men on death row felt. "Everything?"

"Yes, Jonah, there is no other choice."

"Well, maybe there is."

"No, there is not."

"You're sure?"

"I am quite certain. And so are you."

I couldn't meet his steady eyes and continue to pretend there might be another option, but when I looked away from him, even then I couldn't maintain that pretense. "All right. Okay. You're right. But . . . oh, man, this is going to be a bloodbath."

He frowned. "Surely you do not believe that your mother, the kind of good woman that she is, would resort to violence?"

"No, sir. I was just . . . exaggerating. I guess . . . fear gets my imagination running. I have a big imagination."

"If it gives you some comfort, I assure you that I will do my very best to help your mother understand that your reasons for so often deceiving her were for the most part honorable and otherwise attributable to the foolishness of youth."

I returned his frown to him. "Thanks. I guess."

"Now I should be going." He rose from the chair, adjusted his shirt cuffs, his coat, his tie, his display handkerchief, and when he looked like he belonged in a magazine ad, he smiled at me. "I must tell you, Jonah, that in spite of the anxiety and the stress that it sometimes occasioned, I did enjoy this adventure that we have been through together."

I said, "Me, too," and meant it.

He bowed to me, and I bowed to him.

He held out his hand, and I shook it.

I almost threw my arms around him and hugged him tight, but I didn't know what he would think of that, whether it might embarrass him. And so I restrained myself. One more thing eventually to regret.

"I will most likely call regardless of whether or not it is the time of the day when you are alone."

"Yeah. I know. I understand."

He went down the steps, along the walkway, and turned left on the sidewalk, making his way back to the bus stop on the main avenue.

As I had watched Miss Pearl until she moved out of sight in the opposite direction on Wednesday, so now I watched Mr. Yoshioka. As he dwindled into the summer heat, I realized that at some point in the past several months, I had stopped thinking of him as a small man, that every time I saw him, he seemed to have grown taller.

I cleaned off the porch table, washed the glasses we had used, put the four remaining cookies in a plastic bag, and concealed them in my nightstand to avoid explaining where I'd gotten them. One last deception.

Sixty-eight

WE WOULD EVENTUALLY LEARN THAT IN THE same hour as Mr. Yoshioka visited me, Setsuko Nozawa tried again to reach Mr. Tamazaki at the *Daily News*. She learned he was on holiday and would return on Monday. He had believed that her report to him had been complete, and she had thought so, too, until the crazy professor popped up like a nutty Sid Caesar character on that old *Your Show of Shows*. The new information she acquired would be of value to the reporter, but since all of this had to do with events that occurred years earlier, she imagined it would be no less valuable to him on Monday than it would be now.

We couldn't know then that the coming Monday would be the day when so many lives would be changed forever— or ended.

Elsewhere in Charleston, Illinois, at the stately Georgian home of Dr. Jubal Mace-Maskil, the professor hadn't risen from bed until past noon. Although sober, he felt queasy. He felt also as if he'd been thrashed, but his mind was clear.

Eventually we would learn in great detail everything Dr. Mace-Maskil thought and did during those days. In time, when interrogated by the police, against the advice of his attorney, the professor proved to be a talkative self-dramatizer motivated nearly as much by self-pity as by a sense of his historical importance to the utopian movements of his day.

Now sober, he considered the illegal substances that he had consumed the previous day, and upon reflection, he understood where he had gone wrong, what wicked combination of drugs had cast him into an abyss of paranoia. When he heard of Mrs. Nozawa's visit to the Alumni Affairs Office, he had leaped to the ridiculous conclusion that Lucas was about to be revealed as a murderer for hire. Actually, the boy was just a murderer, as he didn't always kill for money. In fact, he had refused to charge his beloved mentor for the elimination of the tiresome Noreen Wallis Mace-Maskil, formerly Noreen Wallis Norville, of the Grosse Pointe Norvilles. "You'll just owe me one," Lucas said when refusing payment, which had delighted Jubal until, as time passed, he'd begun to wonder what that "one" might entail.

He had thought Lucas was committed to the Cause—Jubal always capitalized the word in his mind—but in the four years since the boy graduated, he'd spent much of his time adrift, distracted by carnal pleasures. Oh, now and then, Lucas got up to something worthwhile—a train derailment, other bits of sabotage, an unsuspecting policeman executed with a point-blank round to the back of the head—but considering his sharp mind and potential, he was an underachiever.

Lately, Dr. Mace-Maskil had become concerned that Lucas might be less interested in the Cause than in taking enormous risks largely for the thrill of it. After all, he had shot the policeman outside of a Chinese restaurant, on a busy street, where there were potential witnesses, taking advantage of an unanticipated opportunity. With lightning cunning, he calculated the line-of-sight issues, determined that a blind spot existed, shot the cop, thrust the pistol into the coat pocket of a wild-haired, disoriented homeless man, shouting, "I got him, I got the bastard, help me here!" When a few men joined him in the effort to subdue the terrified bum, he used the confusion to fade out of the scene. He thought himself superior, of Nietzsche's master race, and on a regular basis, he seemed to need to prove his supreme nature by taking an outrageous risk and getting away with it.

When Lucas derailed a train or shot a cop on a public

street for the thrill of it and to prove his superior nature, instead of taking the time and care to plan a more significant operation that could be pulled off with much greater confidence that no evidence would lead to the perpetrators . . . Well, such recklessness also put the professor at risk. He'd taken some years to realize that if Lucas were arrested and convicted of just one murder, he might negotiate an adjustment in his sentence by ratting out others whom those in power would delight in persecuting. Like Dr. Jubal Mace-Maskil. The "one" that he owed his former student might prove to be his own destruction for the purpose of shaving a few years off Lucas's sentence or to buy the boy certain prison privileges that he might not otherwise receive.

Here in the light of a new day, in the cruel grip of sobriety, the professor understood, as he never quite had before, that his very freedom depended on Lucas remaining free, as well. Therefore, he felt that he should without delay phone his former student and tell him about Mrs. Nozawa's curious visit to the Alumni Affairs Office. Each time that Lucas changed phone numbers, he gave his mentor the new contact information, though he usually didn't provide an address or a mail drop. Informed of Mrs. Nozawa's interest in him, Lucas would most likely want to come to Charleston and take the woman to some quiet and private place, to discover what her true intentions were, since they were surely not related to any act of kindness for which he had not been properly thanked.

Twice, the professor picked up the phone and started to enter Lucas's latest number, but both times he hung up after pressing fewer than half the digits. Drug-free, Dr. Mace-Maskil's mind no longer spun in a tornado of paranoia, but he was shrewd enough to recognize in this situation a real danger to himself if his former student returned to Charleston to squeeze information out of the queen of dry-cleaning. Lucas might learn not only why she had an interest in him, but also about his old professor's strange visit to her shop. By that performance, Dr. Mace-Maskil had made himself a subject of interest when he previously had not been one, and it surely fed the woman's curiosity and suspicions regarding Lucas, whatever they might be. In a blink, the beloved mentor might become the intolerable burden, and following Lucas's visit to Charleston, the town's population might drop by two.

The professor decided to be prudent, to think through all of the possible ramifications, before phoning Lucas. He canceled his Friday classes to give himself time to consider his options, to ferret out the pluses and minuses of each, and to prepare defenses commensurate for the choice he ultimately made.

Although nervous and worried, Dr. Mace-Maskil denied himself any pill or powder that might calm his nerves and turn worry to serenity.

He was thirsty, but he avoided the bourbon and the brandy, and he left the wine corked.

He prepared the coffeemaker. While the brew percolated, he placed a lined legal tablet, a blue-ink pen, and a red-ink pen on the kitchen table.

Sitting there, waiting for the coffee to be done, he realized that he hadn't dressed for the day. He wore only the boxer shorts in which he'd slept. This oversight disturbed him. If his very existence were at stake, it seemed no less irresponsible to plan his strategy for survival in his underwear than it would have been to do so bareass-naked. He went to his bedroom, where he put on a sapphire-blue silk robe and supple-leather slippers, and he returned to the kitchen in a more cunning and militant frame of mind.

Sixty-nine

SATURDAY MORNING, MALCOLM AND I WERE sitting at the glass-topped wrought-iron table on the patio behind Grandpa Teddy's house, playing the game that most inspired a desire for success and independence among young boys of that time: Monopoly. We were buying properties, putting up houses and hotels, bemoaning the unfairness of fines and unearned sentences to jail, when the phone rang in the kitchen. I'd left the back door open so that I could hear the ringing through the screen door, and I sprang up at once and hurried inside, hoping for Mr. Yoshioka's voice when I plucked up the receiver. "Hello?"

He said, "Jonah, on my way to the bus stop yesterday, I realized that I had forgotten to thank you for the Coca-Cola and the cookie."

"You brought the cookies," I reminded him.

"Yes, but you shared them, and you provided the cola. Thank you for your hospitality."

"You're welcome. But . . . I hope you've got some news."

"I do have some news, yes, some hopeful and some frustrating. On his own time, Mr. Otani has identified three buildings in the city that are owned by the Drackman Family Trust. Before he can go to his superiors regarding the opening of a case file and the issuance of a warrant, he needs to discover at which of the three Lucas Drackman is currently living, if in fact he is living at any. Mr. Otani now believes that he will not get a file opened sooner than Monday afternoon."

"Well, I guess he probably knows what he's doing."

"He knows very well, yes. And he is not taking the weekend off, Jonah. He is watching those buildings, one at a time, until he sees whatever he needs to see."

"Okay, sure. It's just that I'm spooked. I mean, this whole thing is spookier than ever. I don't know why, but it is."

"Remember what you once told me."

"Huh? What?"

"'No matter what happens, everything will be all right in the long run.'"

Seventy

SATURDAY, GRANDPA PLAYED BOTH THE DEPART-
ment store and the hotel gigs. Mom didn't have to work a
lunch-counter shift; but she had made two appointments—
auditions—with booking agents, still struggling to find the
right person to get her a singing job and put her on a solid
career path; she would be out most of the day.

Under threat of having his saxophone taken away,
Malcolm was forced to accompany his mother to lunch
and a lengthy afternoon visit with her older sister, his aunt
Judith. Judith had married well and lived with her
husband, Duncan, and a pampered British white shorthair
cat named Snowball in an elegant penthouse overlooking
the city's Great Park. "My mother hopes Aunt Judy will
take pity on my exceptional geekiness and suddenly decide

to make a project of me," Malcolm explained, "in the process showering money on our entire family, which is no more likely than her roasting Snowball and serving him for lunch."

Alone, I had books to read, a piano to practice on, and a TV on which daytime movies were always light comedies or love stories, never the late-night voodoo-in-the-city monster-on-the-loose fare that would make me want to hide under my bed. I tried to settle down and get interested in one thing or another, but I kept ricocheting around the house, like a pinball, checking the windows several times to be sure that the screens were intact, rearranging the clothes in my bedroom closet and then putting them back the way they had been, examining the gleaming cutlery in the kitchen knife drawer to decide with which blade I might best be able to defend myself if a horde of barbarians—or Fiona Cassidy—burst into the house with murderous intent.

When Amalia rang the doorbell at 3:10, I was overjoyed, hoping that she had brought her clarinet, which she hadn't, hoping that maybe she had brought an art book full of Vermeers and Rembrandts, which she hadn't.

"I've got like five minutes, Jonah. I've swept the carpets, mopped the kitchen floor, dusted the furniture, changed the paper in Tweetie's cage while fending off his every vicious attempt to peck out my eyes. I'm making dinner for the family, while my nasty stepsisters dress to catch the eye of the prince at the palace ball this evening, and just to make sure *I* won't have a shot at his highness, they smashed my glass slippers. You look weird, Jonah. Are you all right?"

"Yeah, sure. I'm just, you know, kind of bored, that's all." I went to the piano and sat on the bench and lifted the fallboard to expose the keys, thinking that if I played for her, she might stay longer.

She came to the piano and stood there, but she didn't stop talking long enough for me to begin playing. "You don't know bored until you've gone to lunch at Aunt Judy's. Poor sweet Malcolm. Judy's husband, Duncan, is ages older than she is. When Dickens wrote *A Christmas Carol,* he based Scrooge on Uncle Duncan, who has nothing but deep disdain for anyone named Pomerantz, with some justification. He recently suffered congestive heart failure twice, he's not long for our world. Aunt Judy isn't able to have children, so Mom persists in the delusion that Judy will develop a great affection for her socially inept nephew, which she never did with me. Anyway, Mom hopes that when Duncan dies, Judy will turn on the money spigot to help her troubled nephew and his family. Fat chance. Aunt Judy isn't a moron. What I expect is, if Uncle Duncan hasn't gone to Heaven by the *next* time they have lunch, my mother will keep Judy distracted and expect Malcolm to find our uncle and smother him with a pillow or nudge him over the balcony railing and down forty stories to the street. Are you sure you feel all right?"

"Yeah. I'm fine. Why do you keep asking?"

"Why do you keep putting a hand to your chest?"

"What hand?"

"That hand, your hand, you just did it again, like you've got indigestion or a pain or something."

I looked down at my hand on my chest and realized that I had been unconsciously, habitually checking to be sure that the Lucite heart remained under my shirt, at the end of its chain.

"I have this little patch of stuff," I said.

"Patch of stuff? Patch of what?"

"A rash or something. It itches a little. I'm pressing on it instead of scratching it, 'cause I don't want to spread it."

I don't know why I didn't show her the pendant. Maybe I worried that she'd have lots of questions about it, and that once she got me talking, I might spill too much. What a smooth liar I had become.

"Let me see," Amalia said.

"Are you kidding? No way. I'm not letting a *girl* look at my chest rash."

"Now, don't be silly. You're still a child, and I'm not a girl, I'm me."

"I'm not a sissy, you know. I'm not going to make a big deal about a little rash."

She rolled her eyes. "Masculine pride. All right, let the skin fungus or whatever it is eat you alive."

"It's not a skin fungus. There isn't such a thing."

"Well, there is," she said. "But I didn't come over here to talk fungus. I'm thinking you and I and Malcolm ought to take the bus into Midtown on Monday, have another excursion. The poor dear deserves it after Aunt Judy, and the summer is melting away."

The following day, Sunday, both my mother and grandfather would be home, and we would probably do something fun together. On Monday, however, they would be at work again, and I would be home alone if I didn't go with Amalia and Malcolm. Mr. Yoshioka wasn't likely to hear from Mr. Otani until late Monday afternoon. If I stayed home, I'd be going a little crazier hour by hour, checking and re-checking the window screens and the cutlery drawer.

"What would we do?" I asked.

"Something cheaper. No admission fee this time. Just the bus fare and a little money for lunch. You seemed to like the courthouse tour, so I thought we could make it a day of architecture, all those fabulous old public buildings in that neighborhood. Malcolm loves architecture."

"Okay," I said. "I guess that sounds cool."

"Same time as before."

"I'll be ready."

"Cortaid."

"What?"

"For the rash," she said.

Seventy-one

BY EIGHT O'CLOCK SATURDAY EVENING, AS HE would later testify, Dr. Mace-Maskil had reached the conclusion that the wisest course would be to say nothing to Lucas Drackman about Mrs. Nozawa inquiring after him. Maybe she was telling the truth, and maybe Lucas *had* done some great kindness for her and her husband in an uncharacteristic moment of humanity, in which case he would not be high-tailing it to Illinois to kill her and perhaps the professor, too, and there would be no danger that the truth about the murder of Noreen by proxy would become known. Hell, maybe Lucas had killed someone for them. Why couldn't it be, he asked himself, that the Nozawa bitch was lying about having inadequately thanked Lucas and was instead trying to contact him because she had someone else she wanted him to blow away? She was a businesswoman, after all, queen of clean, cars and clothes, and in the professor's opinion, there were no more ruthless, bloody-minded people on the planet than business types.

Pleased by his elegant reasoning and by the calm with which he had thought his way through these dangerous shoals, Dr. Mace-Maskil mixed a pitcher of martinis.

Sunday morning, after expertly managing his hangover by taking a massive dose of vitamin B complex chased with milk of magnesia, he felt queasy, not because of the previous evening's indulgence, but because intuition insisted that he had made the wrong decision. No matter what the reason that Setsuko Nozawa wanted to contact Lucas, if she mentioned Mace-Maskil, her version of their encounter would be the first that Lucas heard, and there-after it would be more difficult to sell him a version more flattering to the professor.

After further managing his hangover with three raw eggs and a dash of Tabasco sauce blended in a glass of orange juice, Dr. Mace-Maskil spent the morning and early afternoon crafting a story of his confrontation with Setsuko Nozawa that might have occurred in an alternate universe.

Seventy-two

DURING THE WEEKEND, MR. NAKAMA OTANI HAD been able to conduct meaningful surveillance on only two of the three properties owned by the Drackman Family Trust of Chicago: a nine-story office building in the district known as the Triangle, catering to medical professionals—ophthalmologists, dermatologists, endodontists, and the like—and an eight-story upscale apartment building in Bingman Heights, with only eight through-floor units. The second had appeared more promising than the first, though at neither address did he glimpse even one of the five persons of interest or see any suspicious activity.

He took Monday as a vacation day, and by seven o'clock in the morning, he had the third property in his sights: one of the grand old houses lining the streets around Riverside Commons, a four-story Beaux Arts structure of limestone, featuring bronze windows and a flat roof with a balustrade as a parapet. Through the first half of the century, there would have been black-tie parties at this house, bejeweled women in the most stylish of gowns, horse-drawn carriages with candled lamps aglow and liveried drivers waiting, and later fine motorcars, limousines. Now perhaps the residents were thieves and thugs and mad bombers.

During the weekend, most of Mr. Otani's surveillance had been conducted from a parked car, not a comfortable post in the heat of July. But because this house faced Riverside Commons, he was able to take up a most pleasant position there. He sat just inside the park, in the deep—and masking—shade of a mature and spreading chokeberry tree. On the bench beside him were a folded newspaper, a hardcover of *In Cold Blood* by Truman Capote, a thermos of iced tea, and a canvas tote that contained packages of snack crackers, two candy bars, and his Smith & Wesson .38 Chief's Special in a holster. The tote also contained a pair of binoculars, which he would use only if absolutely necessary.

Sitting on a cushion he'd brought with him, dressed in athletic shoes without socks, Bermuda shorts, and a colorful Hawaiian shirt, Mr. Otani was the very picture of a man on his day off, settled in for a morning of nature and literature.

People passing on the paved path that wound through the park didn't give him a second look until *she* came trotting along, tanned and glowing, taking her morning exercise in white short shorts and a yellow halter top, long-legged and healthy and jiggling precisely where she should. Mr. Otani didn't forget many faces, and hers was especially memorable, even more than half a year after he had chatted her up in the nightclub on New Year's Eve, before Tilton Kirk had joined her there. And of course he had seen her photograph from the City College demonstration. Aurora Delvane.

He saw her glance at him in the shade, and he might have picked up the book and ignored her if he hadn't seen her do a double take and start to smile. The least suspicious thing that he could do was seize the initiative, so he called out to her, "Hey, hi there! Great day, huh? Remember me?"

She did remember him, in part because Mr. Otani could be quite charming but also because his physique was atypical for a Japanese American. At six foot two, weighing two hundred pounds, with hands as big as those of a pro basketball player, he couldn't make himself inconspicuous even sitting down in chokeberry shadows.

He rose to his feet as she came to the bench, and she said, "New Year's Eve. Did you ever find him?"

"No. The bitch stood me up. Pardon my French. He's history."

On that night of celebration, Mr. Otani had not approached her as if he were a guy hoping to score. He was a happily married man. Besides, any woman who looked like Aurora Delvane had been hit on so many times, there wasn't a pickup line that she wouldn't turn away from dismissively. So he had posed as a gay man whose significant other was late for dinner. He'd employed a similar ruse on other occasions. Women tended to like gay men and feel comfortable with them. Maybe it was the novelty of a male companion to whom they felt they could speak as frankly as they might with a girlfriend.

"I don't have to ask if your fella showed up," Mr. Otani said. "He'd crawl a mile on hot coals to be there for *you*."

As they talked, she kept dancing from foot to foot, perhaps to keep her heart rate up or maybe because she couldn't resist bouncing the merchandise to tease him even though he was gay. She liked to be flattered, and she was a habitual tease.

Fortunately, she didn't have a morning to kill. After a minute of talk about the weather, she returned to the path and sprinted off.

He sat on the bench and picked up his book and sat

reading, *really* reading, never once obviously staring at the house across the street. About fifteen minutes later, Aurora Delvane appeared again from his left, having made another circuit. He looked up at the sound of her feet pounding the path, and she waved, and he waved. She ran out of the park to the sidewalk, paused at the curb to look both ways, and then dashed across the street illegally, in the middle of the block. She bounded up the limestone steps and into the mansion owned by the Drackman Family Trust.

Mr. Otani consulted his wristwatch. Seven-twenty-four. He had been at his post less than half an hour.

Packing up now and going away would be a bad idea. His cover was that of a man at leisure on a summer day, settled into his favorite shaded park bench with everything he needed for the morning. If the woman had been in the least suspicious, they could watch him from the house, with binoculars if they had them. If at any moment he seemed to be something other than what he'd presented himself to be, they might bail out of that house and go to ground in another place, one that was unknown to him. In a couple of hours, he could gather up his things and wander off as though the time had come to trade the shade for a bench in the sun.

He opened the thermos and poured a cup of iced tea.

The Capote book was engrossing, and he returned to it.

Confident that he would be able to open a case file in the afternoon, he savored the possibility of obtaining a search warrant by that evening.

Seventy-three

IN SPITE OF HAVING CONCOCTED A STORY THAT he thought entirely convincing, Dr. Mace-Maskil dithered through Sunday evening without picking up the phone and calling his star pupil. He mixed a pitcher of martinis but recognized the danger, and he poured the contents down the kitchen-sink drain without taking one sip.

He slept badly, several times waking from dreams that he could not entirely remember, except that they involved bloody hammers and a decapitating machete. He abandoned his bed before dawn, pulled on the silk robe, stepped into his slippers, and shuffled to the kitchen to brew coffee.

As a true believer in the Cause, as one who was convinced that he had been a revolutionary and great fighter in a previous life, he refused to acknowledge that he feared calling his former student. But every time he moved toward the telephone, his hands began to shake and tremors worked his mouth as if he had come down with Parkinson's disease overnight.

His dread was at last overridden by shame when suddenly the professor smelled himself. Disgusting. He realized that he hadn't bathed since coming home from the confrontation in the dry-cleaning shop on Thursday afternoon. He'd been squirreled away in this house for three and a half days, and much of that time had left shockingly little residue in his memory.

Having fortified himself with half a pot of black coffee and an English muffin slathered with peanut butter and jelly, he went into the master bathroom and dared to look at himself in the full-length mirror on the back of the door. A witch's broom for hair. If he had wanted to go away for a week, he wouldn't have required suitcases; everything he needed would fit in the bags under his eyes. His teeth were stained; they not only felt furry, they *looked* furry. *And that smell.*

He brushed his teeth and then brushed them again. He took a long shower, as hot as he could tolerate. With a styling brush, he shaped his hair as he blew it dry, until it was a prematurely white, leonine mane. That hair made some women think of their fathers and fantasize transgressive sex, whereupon they became insatiable. He looked in the mirror again and saw a demigod.

After putting on clean underwear and fresh clothes, he went into his study, sat in the studded-leather chair behind the teak desk with the black granite top, swiveled toward the phone, and was gratified to see that his hand didn't tremble. He'd had touch-tone phones for three years, but he still found them odd. Somehow they didn't seem as authentic as rotary-dial phones, and Dr. Mace-Maskil was all about authenticity.

He placed the call to the number that he'd most recently been given, wondering if perhaps Lucas might be unavailable—wondering, not hoping—but the familiar voice answered: "Who's this?"

"It's Robert Donat," the professor said, referring to the actor who had played the heartwarming title role in the 1939 film *Goodbye, Mr. Chips*. Set in an English boys' school, the movie had been about a Latin teacher who starts out a bumbler but over the decades becomes a beloved school institution.

"Say hello to Greer Garson for me," Lucas said dutifully, for she had played the female lead.

If their phones were tapped, nothing was gained by using names other than their own, and they never spoke in code, but Dr. Mace-Maskil liked making contact this way. It made him feel safer than he might otherwise have felt.

He launched straight into his story about how he'd been in the Alumni Affairs Office when Setsuko Nozawa barged through the door, obviously with some kind of buzz on, drugs or liquor, hard to tell which, and demanded to know the address of one Lucas Drackman. She might have been upset about something, but she might also have been nothing more than nervous; her behavior was so peculiar that it was difficult to tell which. The secretary behind the counter, a busty redhead named Teresa Marie Hallahan, who for some time had been hot for the professor, of course informed the distressed visitor that the university guarded the privacy of alumni, whereupon this Nozawa person became belligerent. When Dr. Mace-Maskil spoke up for Miss Hallahan and university policy, the Nozawa creature turned her fury on him, became incoherent, and left in a huff.

"Who the hell is Setsuko Nozawa?" Lucas asked.

"I gather she owns a dry-cleaning shop. I thought you must know her somehow."

"I never heard of the crazy bitch."

Dr. Mace-Maskil believed him, and that was a relief. If Lucas had neither done Nozawa a great kindness nor killed someone for her, then he was far more likely to believe his mentor than a weird woman who'd thrown a fit in the Alumni Affairs Office.

"When did this happen?" Lucas asked.

"Fifteen minutes ago. I came straight from there to my office phone here at the school."

"Why does the bitch want my address?"

"She wouldn't say. But it was so strange, so very strange, I thought you should know."

"Yeah, all right. I'll think about it, look into it. My plate's kind of full right now, but I'll get to it. It's good to know you've got my back."

After they disconnected, the professor went into the bathroom, got on his knees in front of the toilet, and threw up.

Seventy-four

ACCORDING TO THE EVENTUAL TESTIMONY OF Aurora Delvane, after she returned from her run in the park that day, she showered, washed and dried her hair, and painted her toenails before she came downstairs and found Lucas with Reggie "Gorilla" Smaller, Tilton, and Fiona in the kitchen, where for one last time they'd been reviewing details of the impending operation. Aurora hadn't needed to be there, for she wasn't an active participant in the scheme; she was an observer, their chronicler, who would one day write about their exploits and the deep philosophy that motivated them.

As Aurora entered the kitchen, Lucas racked the wall phone, turned to the group, and said, "What the hell was that about?" He recounted his conversation with the professor, whom he referred to as "a total butthead I should have offed years ago."

No one knew what if anything to make of the story about the erratic dry-cleaning entrepreneur, and Aurora Delvane asked, "What is this, Jap Day or something?"

Lucas frowned. "What'd you say?"

Fiona came around the table, eyes narrowing with each step. "Yeah, what'd you say?"

Aurora told them about the gay guy from New Year's Eve, who was at that moment ensconced on the bench in the park, directly across the street. "But he's a big old nobody swish. He's reading that Capote book, the one everybody's reading, been a bestseller forever, so you know it's for dunces."

Intrigued, Lucas retrieved a pair of binoculars from the study, and they all went to the front room. After Lucas watched the bench-sitter for a minute, Fiona took the binoculars and studied the man.

She hissed, "Yoshioka."

"You mean the tailor?" Aurora asked. "The nice little guy across the hall, you never see him in anything but a suit?"

"He's a sneaky, treacherous sonofabitch," said Fiona Cassidy. "Nozawa in Illinois, this guy in the park and on *that* bench of all benches, Yoshioka sniffing around on the sixth floor, him and his security chains. It's Jap Day, sure enough."

A conversation ensued, during which they argued heatedly about whether Fiona might be excessively paranoid. They all properly and wisely embraced paranoia as being essential to their survival and success; but though paranoia could be a good thing, it could also be too much of a good thing. If one of them, for instance, began to suspect that among them lurked a Bilderberger, the other four had to conduct a friendly intervention and get him back on a rational track. In this case, the five reached a relatively quick consensus: Fiona wasn't off the rails; there must be some connection between Yoshioka, Nozawa, and this big guy in the chokeberry shadows.

Tilton said they never should have used Apartment 6-C for bomb-making, that Fiona should have cooked the pudding and packed the pots right here in the house. That ticked off Lucas, who reminded Tilton that the house was a two-million-dollar asset, not a place where you made bombs or tested flamethrowers. If Fiona blew herself to bits, that would be sad, even a tragedy, but blowing up the mansion would be something else altogether; blowing up the mansion would be a serious loss of capital. Besides, if the house was damaged by a bomb blast, the FBI would be all over the Drackman Family Trust and all over Lucas himself; even dumb bears knew not to crap in their dens.

Basically, they had two options. One, cancel the operation planned for that morning and hope to reschedule it, snatch Yoshioka instead, and torture the truth out of him. Two, proceed as planned, rather than running for the tall grass like a bunch of cowards, and *then* extract the facts from Yoshioka afterward.

Even if the guy in the park was conducting surveillance, they could leave the house by the back, walk a couple of blocks along the alleyway before coming out to a main street, flag down a taxi, and take that to the rented Quonset, once an auto-repair garage in an industrial district, from which they were staging the operation.

"Look," Lucas said, "it's weird, all these Japanese, but who are these people really? I mean, we have a tailor, a dry cleaner, and some squish, we don't know what he does, if anything. We're not dealing with Elliot Ness here. I say we go forward as planned, make this a day to remember, and later we squeeze Yoshioka until we pop the little rotten tomato."

Lucas nearly always got what he wanted, certainly not because of metaphors like the rotten tomato and not merely because he knew how to manipulate and motivate people, but also because he was a spooky dude who seemed to be perpetually on the edge of violence. His four compatriots agreed with him: the operation was on.

Seventy-five

A COUPLE OF HOURS LATER, AT 10:10 A.M. THAT Monday, Amalia and Malcolm and I disembarked from the city bus at the corner of National Avenue and 52nd Street, as we had done the previous Thursday. Across the avenue stood Kalomirakis Pinakotheke, where *Europe in the Age of Monarchy* had finished its run on Sunday. First National Bank and its thirty-story financial center towered behind us, and for a couple of blocks in every direction stood imposing and richly detailed historic buildings.

On the ride in from our neighborhood, I'd discovered that Amalia knew almost as much about architecture as she did about art, and she had stories to tell about the buildings and the people who designed them. She never acted like a know-it-all, never made me feel clueless by comparison. Instead, knowledge flowed from that girl like cool air from an electric fan. The longer you listened, the more you wanted to hear, because the things she knew and the words she used to convey them made the world around you clearer, brighter.

"Where do we start?" I asked.

Malcolm said, "Right here, the bank, it's so radical. You'll love it."

I had never been inside a bank before, and I thought they must be kidding me. "But we don't have any money to put in or take out."

"The lobby is a public space," Amalia explained. "And one of the most beautiful. Anyone can go inside. Anyone. There was a time, not so long ago, when architecture was as much about beauty as function. This place opened in 1931. It's brilliant Deco. It always gives me goose bumps."

The facade of the bank, before the tower began above it, was perhaps forty feet high and at least four times that wide. A vast rectangular frieze spanned the front of the limestone structure, a pattern of geometric shapes—mostly circles and triangles—arranged in an arresting pattern. At the top of the steps were eight pairs of bronze-and-beveled-glass doors, and we entered at the north end.

I know Amalia had much to say about the immense, spectacular lobby, but I don't remember any of that. It is lost to me as a consequence of what happened next. The last words of hers I remember that day were spoken as I passed through the heavy door behind her and looked up in wonder at the massive columns supporting the barrel-vaulted ceiling. Perhaps forty feet overhead, suspended from the apex of the vault and racing its length were stylized horses, studies in the liquidity of equine grace, cast from stainless steel.

"Isn't it glorious, Jonah?" When I turned my attention from the ceiling to her lovely face, she looked so happy when she said, "Isn't it glorious what people can do, what wonderful things they can create when they're free and when they believe everything is important, everything has meaning, when they think even a bank lobby has to please the eye and lift the heart?"

A few dozen people were doing their banking. There were maybe twenty tellers. Behind a stainless-steel balustrade, bank officers of rank unknown to me were stationed at a fleet of desks, working on documents or manning their phones, or serving customers who sat with them. Considering its grand dimensions and hard surfaces of stone and metal, the lobby should have been noisy, voices ricocheting from vault to floor, to pillar, to post. Due to the amazing finesse of the architects, however, the enormous chamber was hushed, as though everyone must be whispering to one another when in fact they weren't.

Although I can't remember what Amalia said to me and

Malcolm, I recall wandering through the lobby almost as if through a joyous, exhilarating fantasy film. Each time that I thought I had seen the best of the layered Deco details, I noticed another more enchanting than anything before.

Each teller's window flanked by shimmering stainless-steel fluting and surmounted by a semicircular pediment of steel in which had been cast the head of the Statue of Liberty, the rays of her crown each pointing to a stylized star . . .

The pale-gold granite floor inlaid with intricate medallions of black, blue, and green marble, surrounded by a border of the same . . .

Four evenly spaced enormous chandeliers of stainless steel, each with many bulbs and six branches, a bronze sculpture of what seemed to be the robed Miss Liberty seated at the end of each branch . . .

Spaced along the center of the lobby were tall tables of carved green marble, at which people stood to prepare deposit slips and to endorse checks before going to the tellers' windows. As I was passing one of these, a small golden feather floated down before my face, in every way identical to the one that had turned from white to gold in the pendant that I wore under my shirt.

I halted, startled, and the feather floated in a fixed position less than an arm's length in front of my face, as though the draft that had brought it to me now held it motionless for my inspection.

If the architecture and exquisite decoration of the bank lobby had drawn me into a state of quiet rapture, the feather added to that the quality of a dream, specifically the singularity of movement in some dreams, when the dreamer and everything he experiences progress in slow motion.

I reached to my throat and pinched the silver chain and pulled the pendant from beneath my shirt.

The Lucite heart, transparent in the chandelier light, remained intact, but it contained no feather.

As the pendant slipped from my fingers and dangled at chain's end, the airborne feather began to move south through the lobby.

The voices in the hushed chamber faded to silence, and though people moved in slow motion around me, not one foot struck a sound from the stone floor.

I could hear only my heart, which beat as slow as a drum in a funeral cortege, surely too slow to sustain me.

Like a deep-sea diver walking against a resisting mass of water, I followed the feather farther toward the southern end of the lobby.

Although I didn't understand what was happening, I knew I moved now toward the moment that I'd been anticipating for so long.

I seemed to float, to drift, my feet not quite touching the floor.

A sensation that should have been exhilarating instead became a source of fear, as though I might slip the bonds of gravity and never come down again.

I passed two of the tall marble tables, and the feather stopped at a third.

As it had drifted down into my line of sight, so now it settled farther, until I saw beneath the table a brown-leather briefcase.

Still the only sound, my heartbeat accelerated.

The feather rose before my eyes, and I almost reached for it, but I intuited that to seize it would be wrong.

Looking past the feather, I saw her as she'd never presented herself before: in high heels, a businesslike skirt and blouse and jacket, eyeglasses, ink-black hair pinned up in a chignon.

Fiona Cassidy.

She moved toward one pair of bronze and beveled-glass doors. As she walked, she looked not back at me, but north.

Turning my head, following her stare, I saw him as he had never presented himself before: in black wing tips, a dark-gray business suit, white shirt and tie, a hat with a pinched crown and black band and snap brim.

Tilton.

My father.

He moved toward a different exit from the one Fiona approached. He had shaved off his beard.

He reached the door.

She opened her door and stepped outside. I looked down at the briefcase.

Over the thundering of my heart, I heard myself say, "Bomb."

Seventy-six

IN ILLINOIS, MRS. NOZAWA'S MONDAY HAD NOT begun well. After his breakfast and his walk, Toshiro Mifune didn't want to go back into the house. He was agitated, panting, and as she tried to settle him, he vomited copiously in the grass.

On occasion, Mr. Nozawa complained that his wife treated the dog better than she did him, to which she replied, with affection, that he wasn't as dependent or innocent as their sweet Labrador retriever. Now she coaxed Toshiro Mifune into the backseat of her Cadillac, not in the least concerned that he might make a mess there. A car was just a car, but the dog was her fourth *child*.

Never previously an imprudent person, Mrs. Nozawa

disobeyed all the speed limits, as if the car were an ambulance. She arrived at the veterinarian's office with a squeal of brakes.

Dr. Donovan examined the dog and performed an array of tests while Mrs. Nozawa sat in the waiting area, on the edge of her seat, her hands fisted in her lap, as if she were the mother of a wrongly condemned man, waiting outside of the prison's execution chamber, waiting either for word of the governor's stay or for the crackle of the electric chair.

As it turned out, Toshiro Mifune had a fever and an infection, nothing mortal. He would be all right after a course of antibiotics and rest.

Mrs. Nozawa drove home at a sedate pace, continuously talking in a soothing tone to the dog in the backseat. She called the drycleaning shop to say that she would be out all day.

The Labrador's favorite place in the house was on the padded window seat in the living room, where he could watch activity in the street. Once he was lying on those cushions, nose to the glass, she sat in a nearby armchair with a copy of Julia Child's cookbook, reading recipes.

Now that Mr. Tamazaki of the *Daily News* had returned from his holiday, Mrs. Nozawa needed to tell him about Dr. Mace-Maskil, the murder of his wife Noreen, and the plausible assumption that Lucas Drackman had killed the woman for the professor. She had meant to call by nine o'clock his time, but already it was after ten o'clock there. As soon as Toshiro Mifune went to sleep, she would reach out to Mr. Tamazaki. No hurry.

Seventy-seven

AS I SAID, "BOMB," I TURNED TOWARD THE NORTH
end of the lobby and saw that I had put some distance
between myself and Amalia, who stood perhaps forty feet
away with Malcolm, both of them studying the ornate
ceiling, the procession of stainless-steel horses in perpetual
gallop. No one moved in slow motion anymore, and sound
returned, and I realized that I had said, "Bomb," so softly
that no one had heard me.

I broke the paralyzing grip of dread and shouted it this
time—*"Bomb! Bomb!"*—and started toward Amalia. *"Get
out! Go! There's a bomb!"*

She appeared startled, confused, and Malcolm looked
at me in disbelief, as if he thought I must be pulling some
stupid stunt.

By then I wasn't just shouting, I was screaming—*"Oh, God, oh, God, oh, God!"*—and my fright must have been convincing. Suddenly electrified, the crowd cried out in many voices and rushed toward the exits.

Even in the thrall of terror, I thought there would be time for everyone to get out, that Fiona Cassidy wouldn't have set the bombs to detonate so soon after she and my father departed, that she would not have taken such a risk with their lives.

As we would eventually learn, the bank wasn't their primary target. It was but a distraction, a misdirection, a blood-drenched tactic, and the success of their operation depended on the bombs going off just as she and my father reached the bottom of the exterior steps.

I was twenty feet from Amalia and Malcolm when the briefcase placed by my father detonated. I don't know what shrapnel took her, whether it might have been part of the bomb, bolts and nails included to increase its deadliness, or whether it might have been slivers and chunks of the room's elaborate architectural details. I don't know why some nights I lie awake thinking about that. Whichever it was, it changes nothing, doesn't diminish the monstrousness of the deed or reduce to any degree my father's guilt.

In the days immediately after, I hoped that he had never seen me there in the bank. I found it too terrible to think that he saw me and went ahead with the plan anyway.

That was a possibility so dark, if true, it might make me wish that I had never been born.

Amalia looked surprised—eyes wide, mouth an O—as the blast wave lifted her off her feet and flung her forward, and I do not believe she lived long enough to feel a moment of pain. That is a thing I *must* believe.

Poor devastated Malcolm, standing no more than two feet from her, driven to his knees by the blast, glasses knocked off, hair disarranged, but suffering only minor lacerations, while she lies slain before him, between him and me. One moment she is beautiful, vibrant, in love with life. An instant later she is a tumbled heap, clothes torn and bloody, dazzling green eyes wide and sightless.

They say five seconds elapsed between the first blast and the second. All I know is that it was time enough for Malcolm to look up from her body and meet my eyes, his face a wretched portrait of disbelief, horror, and piercing grief.

I have no memory of the second blast. Malcolm says it threw me harder and farther than the first one threw Amalia, that I came to the floor very near to her, my left arm outstretched, three fingers atop her right hand, as if I were imploring her to take me with her.

Because of her green stare and the breathless O of her mouth, he could have no doubt that his beloved sister was dead. But my eyes were closed, and he thought he saw plaster dust stir on the floor in front of my mouth, as if moved by my breath. He scrambled past Amalia and came to me and took my wrist and found my pulse. When he saw my back, he knew that he dared not move me—and that I would never walk again.

Seventy-eight

AS THE POLICE LATER PIECED IT TOGETHER, Fiona and Tilton waited to enter the bank until Mr. Smaller, stationed a block away, told them by walkie-talkie that the armored car had turned the corner onto National Avenue. Past observation had shown them that it would arrive in front of the bank in no less than three minutes and no more than five. Traffic that Monday suggested to Mr. Smaller that the armored car—actually a truck of the Colt-Thompson Security fleet—would be there in four.

Tilton was sitting on a bus-stop bench near the corner of 52nd Street and National Avenue when he received that message. Fiona stood under a tree toward the south end of the bank, with a walkie-talkie of her own. Each briefcase featured a four-tumbler combination lock, which she had converted into a timer for the detonator. They had only to click each tumbler to zero, and with the fourth, the clock in the briefcase began the countdown.

They entered opposite ends of the busy bank. She put her briefcase on the floor beside her and under one of the tall marble tables. He did the same. They picked up blank deposit slips from the supply each table provided and pretended to fill them out, but after two minutes or less, they left First National without approaching a teller's window.

The armored truck stood at the curb when they came out of the bank. Because the nation had recently been plagued with race riots and violent street demonstrations, Colt-Thompson Security's revised protocols required three—rather than the usual two—men per vehicle on certain routes in selected cities: two up front, the third in back with the money, bonds, and other valuables.

As Tilton and Fiona came down the steps from the bank, the street-side door of the truck opened, and the driver was the first out of the vehicle, which was standard procedure. The door locked automatically when he closed it, and the ignition key was in his pants pocket, on a long chain fixed to a metal ring on his belt buckle.

Lucas Drackman, in hospital whites, carrying a white first-aid kit with a red cross on it, as if he were a medical technician on an errand, turned the corner from 52nd

Street onto National Avenue as the driver got out of the truck.

As soon as the driver exited and the truck wasn't at risk of being hijacked through a curbside assault, that door opened, and the second guard got out.

In the bank, the first bomb went off, glass shattered in a flash of light, the muntins in a pair of bronze doors distorted as if they were made of plastic, one door tore loose of its hinges, clanged and clattered halfway down the steps, and the sidewalk vibrated underfoot as if, deep in the earth, something massive and Jurassic were waking from a hundred million years of sleep.

Everyone on the street pivoted toward the bank, except those who had known what was coming.

Lucas Drackman reached under his loose white shirt, drew a pistol from a cloth holster sewn to the inside of his waistband, turned to the shocked and distracted guard, shot him twice in the chest, and tucked the weapon under his shirt once more as the dead man dropped.

As Drackman was drawing the gun, the driver reached the back of the truck. Fiona came off the bank steps as the first bomb exploded, angling toward him, her right hand under her suit jacket, where she carried a pistol in a shoulder rig.

Just then, Mr. Smaller pulled to the curb behind the Colt-Thompson vehicle in a gray paneled van on the sides of which were emblazoned the name and logo of the armored-car service. Wearing a counterfeit Colt-Thompson uniform, he got out and headed toward the driver of the truck.

Fiona reached the driver first, and when he glanced at her, she came in close, doing her best to look terrified, saying, "Please, can you help me?" The second blast occurred, and the driver flinched, looked away from her. She shoved the muzzle in his gut and shot him dead, and Mr. Smaller arrived just in time to help her manage the body to the pavement, as if they were assisting a fellow worker who had suddenly been taken ill.

Pandemonium. People screaming, running, not sure what might happen next, oblivious to the heist in progress.

Lucas Drackman knelt next to the fallen guard on the sidewalk, by the open door of the armored truck, and popped the lid of his first-aid kit as if the man weren't dead but merely in need of medical assistance.

At the back of the truck, Mr. Smaller dropped to both knees beside the dead driver. He used a small bolt cutter to sever the chain that connected a ringbolt on the man's belt to the ignition key in his pocket.

After taking the key from Smaller, Fiona went to Drackman and tossed it to him. She quickly followed him into the truck as he clambered into the driver's seat, and she pulled the door shut behind her. For security reasons, the windows were heavily tinted.

Mr. Smaller got up from the dead driver and once more got behind the wheel of the paneled van.

For use in an emergency, the Colt-Thompson truck had an array of flashing blue lights and an oscillating siren different from that of any police- or fire-department vehicles. Drackman switched them on and drove away from the curb just as the passing traffic began to jam up because of motorists gawking at the smoke now billowing from the shattered doors of the bank.

Mr. Smaller followed close behind in the paneled van. They turned right onto 52nd Street, where traffic was lighter.

When the remaining guard, closeted in the cargo hold, couldn't get a response on the in-vehicle intercom, he made the mistake of assuming that twenty years of drama-free experience in his job must be predictive of twenty more. Curious but not sufficiently alarmed, he violated standard procedures and slid aside the steel plate that covered a two-inch-by-six-inch slot in the heavily armored wall between his redoubt and the forward compartment, calling out to the driver, "Hey, Mike?"

Prepared for this possibility, Fiona Cassidy thrust the muzzle of her pistol through the gap and emptied the magazine into the cargo hold. Following the roar of gunfire and the shriek of ricochets in the enclosed space, there was only silence from the third guard.

One block east of the bank, Drackman switched off the flashers and the siren, and at the end of the second block, as the truck and the van stopped for a red traffic light, my father got up from the bus-stop bench to which he had walked from the bank, and he joined Mr. Smaller in the second vehicle.

Seventy-nine

WHEN MRS. NOZAWA FINISHED RECOUNTING HER confrontation with Dr. Mace-Maskil and laying out her suspicion that Lucas Drackman had killed the professor's wife, Mr. Tamazaki, in good spirits after his holiday, knew that he had enough circumstantial evidence to ensure that Mr. Otani could open his case file and obtain a warrant.

He worried, however, that if Mace-Maskil had warned Drackman about the woman's interest, both she and Mr. Yoshioka, and perhaps others, might be in danger.

"Another good reason for my *written* report," she said, "and now a good reason to have it notarized so it will serve as evidence if anything happens to me, though nothing will. I'm a tough cookie."

After commiserating with Mrs. Nozawa about Toshiro

Mifune's poor health, he called Mr. Otani at the homicide division of the central police command, only to be told that the detective had taken the day off. When he tried Mr. Otani's home number, no one answered.

Mr. Tamazaki shivered with a presentiment of tragedy.

Eighty

UNCONSCIOUS ALL THE WAY IN THE AMBULANCE to Saint Christopher's Children's Hospital, I have no memory of being taken into surgery. I have one hazy recollection of the recovery room, when I came out of general anesthesia, although I was then, by way of intravenous drip, immediately on painkillers that fogged my mind. I remember only my mother beside the gurney, looking down at me, so very beautiful. She appeared to be terribly aggrieved, as I'd never seen her before. My thinking was so muddled, I worried that something awful must have happened to her. I tried to speak but lacked the wit and energy. I remember also turning my head toward her, whereupon I could see she was holding my left hand in both of hers, and I thought how odd it was that I could not *feel* her hands pressed around mine. But then, when I wished to feel them, I could. Her warm fingers. Although she clasped my hand tightly, I detected her tremors, and I saw that she was shaking badly, not just her hands but her entire body. She said something, her voice far away, like voices in dreams that sometimes call to us from some far shore, and I couldn't understand what she was trying to tell me, and so I slept.

Eighty-one

I WAS IN THE ICU FOR THE FIRST FORTY-EIGHT hours, until they could be certain that all my vital signs were stable, but I remained in a painkiller haze—I don't know what—maybe a morphine derivative. I slept more than not, and though my every dream should have been a nightmare, they were with one exception pleasant, although I barely recalled them when I woke. Nurses attended me from time to time, as did a man in a white smock with a stethoscope around his neck.

Although friends and family were usually restricted to short visits in the ICU, someone I knew seemed always to be there in a bedside chair when I rose from the slough of forgetfulness that was as real as the mattress on which I lay. I always knew who I was, of course, and approximately where I must be, and I knew these visitors and loved them, but the *why* of being there eluded me, or I eluded it, choosing amnesia over the intolerable truth. I think that I could have spoken there in the ICU, that my silence was not a consequence of either my injuries or the drugs. Perhaps I feared to speak because words mattered in our family—in the beginning was the Word—and when I spoke, thereafter would come conversation and with conversation the reality, the *why*. Mom was there, watching, sometimes putting cold wet compresses on my brow, sometimes giving me a sliver of ice with the admonition to let it melt in my mouth. In her absence, Grandpa Teddy appeared, and although I'd never previously seen him with a rosary— Grandma Anita, but not him—he always clung to one now, his fingers traveling from bead to bead, his lips moving and the words whispered. I should not have been surprised to see Donata Lorenzo, once our neighbor, my sitter, who in her widowhood had been counseled by my mother, heavier now than when I'd last seen her, wiping at her eyes with a cotton handkerchief prettily embroidered at the corners or twisting it into knots around her fingers. When I opened my eyes and saw Mr. Yoshioka in the chair, I thought of the photos of his mother and sister in the book about Manzanar, and I spoke for the first time since the bomb: "I'm so sorry." He couldn't know to what those words referred, but he came to the bed and took one of my hands and held it as my mother had held it. He said softly, "'The summer storm / Hid in the bamboo grove / And quieted away.'" I thought I must be getting the hang of this haiku thing, because I understood that he was saying the worst had passed, that all would be better from now on. Something serious had happened to me, but nothing mortal yet.

Sometime in those hours after surgery, I came to realize that I couldn't move my legs or feel them. I would have been afraid if my arms had also been unresponsive, if my hands refused to obey me. But I thought of what Mr. Yoshioka had lost in his life, of what Mrs. Lorenzo had lost, of Grandpa without his Anita, and I flexed my hands and played imaginary chords and melodies on the bedsheet, and I knew, no matter what, I'd be all right, though there was still the matter of the damper, sostenuto, and una corda pedals. *Don't think about that, not now, not yet.* Even then, I held at bay the *why* of being in the hospital, held tenaciously to forgetfulness.

The one nightmare came, so they tell me, at nine o'clock the second night. In sleep, my mind approached what it couldn't admit when I was awake: *I am in the bank, under the airborne stampede of steel horses, following the golden feather to the briefcase. Fiona moves toward an exit. My father in business attire makes his escape. I turn to see Amalia and Malcolm. "Oh, God, oh, God, oh, God." The blast. The sweet girl seems almost to take flight, angel that she is. But does not rise on white wings. Does not rise. Collapses and does not rise, a girl no more, a broken bird, a tangle of ragged clothes and torn flesh and lifeless bones.*

I woke screaming and couldn't stop, and the nurses rushed to my cubicle, and soon they brought my mother. "Amalia's dead!" I told her as she sat on the bed and took me in her arms. "Amalia's dead, oh, God, she's dead, Mama." Of course they knew that she had perished—and not she alone. The only revelation I had for them was what I said next: "I killed her! It's me, I did it, I killed Amalia!" My mother held me and assured me that I had killed no one, but I refused to accept absolution so easily. "You don't know, you don't. I should have told you, you don't know everything I should have told you." She said that Mr. Yoshioka had explained everything to her, that nothing I'd done had been sinful or even wrong, that I'd done what any child my age might have done under those circumstances, that perhaps if I'd done anything differently, Fiona Cassidy might have killed me long ago. What happened at the bank was something else altogether, one of those terrible things that seemed to be happening more every year.

I couldn't rely upon the excuse that I'd done what any child my age would have done, for as I had once said to Mr. Yoshioka, I was not my age, an assertion to which he had agreed.

"But you don't understand," I insisted. "Maybe even Mr. Yoshioka doesn't. They didn't just steal all that jade stuff at City College. They did worse. It was *them* at the bank. Fiona . . . and Tilton. I saw them. They had brief-cases. They put down the briefcases and left."

She stiffened with shock, and I believed that she must realize what had become clear to me: that if she had never become pregnant with me, if my father hadn't married her but instead had followed some other path in life, Amalia would be alive, Amalia and however many others had died at the bank. Because I was born, Amalia died.

From where I sit nearly half a century later, I understand the fallacy of that reasoning. But in the aftermath of the bank, in my grief, I believed that it must be inarguably true.

After a while, when I couldn't be adequately calmed, a nurse injected a sedative into the IV port, and I fell into an unwanted sleep in my mother's arms. I did not dream again that night.

In the morning, when Mom visited, I asked her if anyone knew what had happened to the Lucite pendant that I'd been wearing.

To my surprise, she said, "It was still around your neck when the paramedics found you, sweetie. They took it off you in the ambulance."

She produced it from her purse and gave it to me. Within the shapen heart, the feather lay soft and white.

Eighty-two

WEDNESDAY, WITH ALL MY VITAL SIGNS STABLE, they moved me from the ICU into a private room. I didn't need traction, or an orthopedic corset. Mine wasn't what they called an "unstable injury" that needed time to heal. It was plenty stable, all right. My spinal cord had been severely impacted, and that was the end of the story. No surgeon in the world, then or now, could repair the damaged nerve tracts.

During the few days that I remained in the hospital, receiving treatment for my lesser wounds and undergoing tests to determine the extent of my disabilities, the nurses could do little more for me than turn me regularly in bed to prevent sores from forming as a result of my immobility and lack of sensation in my legs.

Physical therapy began on Thursday. The therapist worked my legs for me, flexing my ankles and my knees, which someone would have to do for me daily from now on, to prevent my joints from locking and my muscles from contracting as the result of paralysis.

I didn't mourn the loss of mobility, didn't lie abed in anguish over having become a cripple, which was a word used casually then, not one considered less sensitive than "disabled." I felt that I had received what I'd earned and that enduring my condition without complaint might be my sole hope of redemption.

Fewer painkillers were now prescribed, and I could no longer retreat into a haze of medication. Neither did I continue to wrap myself in calculated silence. I spoke to everyone, although not in my former garrulous way. I felt that nothing I said could be worth anyone listening, not after the suffering that my presence in the world had caused; for the most part, I limited myself to responses, initiating few exchanges. I remained aware that my grief and acute sense of blame distressed my mother and Grandfather Teddy. But to pretend to feel other than I truly felt would have filled me with self-disgust.

As when I'd been in the ICU, someone was always with me, often more than one person. Mr. Yoshioka visited so frequently, two and three times a day, that I felt obliged to tell him that he would lose his job. He only smiled and said that he had taken no vacations or sick leave for years and had accumulated a considerable number of earned days off.

He came once with Detective Otani, who questioned me about what I'd seen at First National and recorded my testimony regarding Fiona and Tilton. Aurora Delvane had been arrested but professed ignorance of her comrades' darker intentions. "We were just this sort of little commune; free love, that's all I ever saw." She promised cooperation, but she hadn't yet made bail. The others were on the run.

On Thursday, when covering for Mother and Grandpa Teddy while they went to lunch together, Mr. Yoshioka sat by my bed, his arms resting on the arms of the chair, in one of his characteristic serene postures. "Jonah, do you remember a great long time ago when you were not yet ten, when you were merely nine, and you told me that you dreamed about Miss Cassidy and Mr. Drackman even before you ever met them?"

"Sure. I brought you chocolate-chip cookies."

"Most delicious cookies. That day I told you of a prophetic dream of my own, in which my mother and sister perished in a fire."

"I found their pictures," I said.

He raised his eyebrows. "Did you indeed?"

"In a library book about Manzanar. I Xeroxed the page to keep."

For a while he stared at his right hand, where it rested

on the chair arm, as if he preferred not to look at me, and I wondered if I had in some way invaded his privacy, his sense of what was sacred, by finding and keeping photos of his mother and sister.

When he looked at me once more, he said, "I told you back then that I believe we who have suffered greatly may from time to time be given the grace of foretelling, so that we may spare ourselves from further torment. In those days, I was a bitter young man, so very angry about our internment in Manzanar. My anger was hot, Jonah, so white-hot that for a while it burned away my faith, faith in this country, faith in my father, whose docile acceptance infuriated me, and even faith that life has meaning. And so although I dreamed of the fire seven days before it occurred, I could not believe that it was more than an ordinary nightmare. In my anger, I could not accept there might be such a thing as grace, that I had been given the dream so that I might be spared the loss of my precious mother and sister. I valued my anger too much to let go of it, too much to believe."

I said, "You couldn't know it was prophetic."

"Yes, I could have. If I had not been consumed by anger. If I had allowed myself to receive the transitions and vicissitudes of life with more wisdom and with a more generous heart. Manzanar was wrong. However, the internment camps were created in a time of fear, and the fear was rational. But fear can lead people to do things they would never contemplate in placid times. Fear can blind us, but so can anger."

I almost said something, almost issued another assurance that he had no blame for the kitchen fire. But judging by the directness with which he regarded me, by his air of anticipation, I thought that he must be waiting for me to consider what he'd said, to sift from his words some essential insight.

After a silence, he continued: "Surrendering to fear destroys many lives. Indulgence in stubborn anger destroys even more. But guilt, Jonah, is no less a destroyer of lives. I speak to you as an expert on all three. Fear can be overcome. You may let go of anger. And guilt can be forgiven."

Turning my head away from him, I said, "Forgiving yourself doesn't mean you're really forgiven. That's too easy."

"But you can and must, especially when the guilt is so little earned. The way is simple. You must remember the love you had for the one you lost. Your mother tells me that you adored Amalia. It seems that everyone did. Remember that adoration. Do not let your feelings of guilt turn her out of your heart. Open your heart to her, and bring her back into it, so that she will always be with you. Guilt forbids her entrance. Sorrow instead would be a gift to her, a way forward that allows the hope of happiness. Believe me, Jonah, I am as well an expert in the matter of sorrow and its value."

Eighty-three

LATER THAT DAY, I WOKE FROM A NAP AND HEARD
my mother's voice and another that I needed a moment
to identify. Mrs. Mary O'Toole. She had given me piano
lessons at the community center. Something in the tone of
their conversation encouraged me to close my eyes and
pretend sleep.

"He would sometimes come to the back door of the
center in the late afternoon," Mrs. O'Toole said. "He'd step
into the hallway and wait to hear the piano. The piano
room is just across from my office. If there was music, he
could always tell at once whether it was Jonah or someone
else."

"He doesn't play an instrument himself," my mother
said.

"But I swear, Sylvia, he's got an ear. At least he has an ear for that boy. If Jonah was playing, he'd go into the file room next to my office and sit behind the half-open door to listen."

"And Jonah never knew he was there?"

"No. That's how he wanted it. He either left before Jonah was done for the day or left only after Jonah had been gone five minutes. To tell you the truth, I thought at first it was a little creepy, but I didn't feel that way for long."

Faking sleep, I realized they must be talking about Tilton, that my father had secretly come to hear me play. I didn't know what to make of that, desperately didn't want to make anything of it.

Mary O'Toole said, "On only his second or maybe third visit, he stepped into my office afterward and said, 'Do you feel as I do—that when he plays, God enters the room?' I guess I misunderstood, because I said Jonah was a great kid but not a saint. So he said, 'No, I mean to say God enters the room at the sound of Jonah's playing. That's how I feel.' Then he said it was an honor to listen, and he left."

"I never knew," Mother said.

"There was a day last winter, I looked in on him in the file room, and he was sitting there so primly, still in his heavy topcoat, holding his hat in both hands, tears just streaming down his face. He apologized to me for his tears, of all things, and said that he'd made of his life an isolation. Those were his exact words. He never speaks so personally, he's reserved. But he said he'd made of his life an isolation, it was too late for him to be a father to a child of his own. He said, 'The world is full of beauty, isn't it? There's grace everywhere if we'll just see it.' He's such a nice little man."

Of course, she had not been talking about my father. Mr. Yoshioka had come to the center now and then to listen to me play, and I had never known.

The particular day to which Mary O'Toole referred must have been the snowy afternoon when I came out of the community center close behind him, when he had looked so dashing in his topcoat, neck scarf, and fedora. I had delighted him that day when he discovered that I'd memorized a haiku by Naitō Jōsō.

Now, in the hospital room, I acted as if I just then came awake, and for a while I strove to be more my former self with Mrs. O'Toole. But as I pretended a lighter mood than the one in which I was still submerged, a worry grew in me: that Mr. Yoshioka might be in danger. Lucas Drackman, Fiona Cassidy, Mr. Smaller, and my father were still free, on the run or gone to ground. If they saw a police press conference on TV or read the newspapers, they might become aware that Mr. Yoshioka and the Manzanar posse had been instrumental in fingering them for the authorities. Most likely, my father would choose to run, to hide, to slip into another life, but I could too easily imagine the other three being driven by a thirst for revenge.

Eighty-four

FRIDAY BEGAN WITH NEWS THAT I HADN'T realized Mom and Grandpa were hoping to receive. My doctors determined that incontinence would not be a condition of my disability. Although my legs were paralyzed, I should be able to pee and move my bowels unassisted. As a first test of this conclusion, a nurse removed my urinary catheter and the collection bottle attached to it, and I was encouraged for the next couple of hours to drink a goodly amount of water.

Finally I felt the urge. To spare me the embarrassment of being attended in this matter by a stranger, Grandpa Teddy carried me into the adjoining bathroom and put me on the toilet.

"Just us guys," he said when my mother tried to follow, and he closed the door.

After sitting there for a moment, I said, "What now?"

"Now you give it a try."

"A try?"

"Like always. You've been doing it more than ten years, haven't you?"

"Yeah, I guess."

"You guess? I don't think you've been faking it all this time."

I strained a little but then stopped. "Well . . ."

He couldn't conceal his worry. "Well what?"

"I don't know."

"What don't you know, son?"

"It doesn't feel right."

"How does it feel?"

"Funny," I said.

He stared down at me for a long moment, so tall and imposing, a bullfrog to my tadpole. Then his eyes went wide and he made them bug out a little, and he said, "Do you mean funny weird or funny ha-ha?"

I started to giggle, as I suppose he knew I might.

"I'm only asking for a definition," Grandpa said. "Funny weird, like maybe a flock of birds might come flying out your whizzer? Or funny ha-ha because I look so silly standing here like a pee-pee coach?"

The giggles wouldn't stop, but the pee started.

Afterward, he held me up at the sink. I washed my hands and pulled a paper towel from a dispenser and dried them. Then he gently lifted me into both of his arms, cradling me, and kissed my forehead. "As long as a man can pee, Jonah, he can take on anything the world throws at him." He carried me back to my bed, beside which my mother stood smiling even as she cried.

Eighty-five

TUESDAY, EIGHT DAYS AFTER THE EVENTS AT THE bank, the doctors and therapist decided that I could go home on Thursday, which was a great way to begin the morning. The nurses and orderlies and everyone had been very kind to me, but I was nonetheless sick of the hospital. None of the gang that took down the Colt-Thompson armored transport had been apprehended, nor had the stolen truck or the third guard been found, but I reasoned that if a bank wasn't safe, neither was a hospital.

Later that afternoon, I was staring at some stupid afternoon movie on TV, with the sound off, worrying about Mr. Yoshioka, when Mom came in from the hall. "Jonah, there's someone very special here to see you. You might not want to visit, but you should, even if it's hard." I asked who, and she said, "It's every bit as much about him, sweetie, as it is about you."

"Malcolm?" I asked.

She nodded. "You can be strong for him, can't you?"

"I'm scared."

"No reason to be. He's worried about you. Aren't you worried about him?"

I closed my eyes and took a deep breath and let it out and opened my eyes. I knew what my mother expected of me, and why she expected it, and even why she *should* expect it. I switched off the silent TV. "Okay."

As ungainly as always, pants hoisted high, four inches of white socks showing between cuffs and shoes, he came into the room, and my mother closed the door as she stepped into the corridor, leaving us alone. He didn't so much as glance at me but went to a window and stood gazing out at the summer day, which was as bright and warm as if no tragedy had ever occurred in the city.

When he didn't say anything, I wondered if I should speak first and what I should say, but then he found his voice.

"I came by myself. I know buses. It's not so hard. One transfer that was a little tricky, that's all." After a pause, he continued. "I don't cry, see. I haven't for a long time, and I'm not going to start now. You cry in our house, man, it's like you let them win. I figured that out a thousand years ago. Even when they say 'Take it to the garage,' you can't go out there and get weepy, because they'll know. I don't know how they know, but they do. Amalia said sometimes she thought they fed on our tears because they couldn't make any more of their own. But then she always backed off and said it wasn't their fault, something had happened to them to make them that way. I'm not so generous."

I realized that nothing I could say mattered at that moment. Malcolm needed to talk, and he needed me to listen, no matter how difficult listening might be.

"That morning," he continued, and I knew the morning he must mean, "she got up really early. She had a lot to do before she could take us for some fun without getting a lot of crap from them. She has to make them breakfast every morning, two different ones at two different times because they hardly ever eat together and they never want the same thing. I emptied the last night's ashtrays for her, those two never think to do it, and changed the birdcage paper, did some other things. When the old man had breakfast and left for work and our old lady had her breakfast tray in her armchair in front of the TV, Amalia still had to do a bunch of stuff, so that when we got home from Midtown late afternoon, she'd be able to put dinner on the table and on the TV tray by the time he came back home bitching about everyone at work. You'd think he had to teach every idiot on the shop floor how to use a lathe every day, as if the whole crew of them can't remember their job overnight. So Amalia, that morning, she's peeling carrots and putting them in a bowl of water, and I'm peeling potatoes and putting them in another bowl of water, and we're getting things done until she comes to the mushrooms. The lord and lady, they like their mushrooms. I mean, if there's meat in the meal, there's got to be gravy, and the gravy's got to be chock full of sliced damn mushrooms. Or if there's not gravy and it's lasagna, that damn lasagna better be so thick with mushrooms you could choke to death on them. So Amalia, she's got pounds of mushrooms, I don't know how many, and she has to get them cleaned and peeled the way *they* like them, all before the three of us can catch that bus. But she won't let me help, she says I'm too rough with mushrooms. Even if the damn mushrooms are in the damn lasagna or covered in gravy, the master of the lathe and his beloved can tell if they've been roughly handled, and you better steel yourself for the whining and the scolding and the general all-around pissiness."

He paused to take a few deep breaths and steady himself. Still he faced the day rather than face me.

"So Amalia, she's hurrying to get all those mushrooms done, trying to hurry without being rough, God forbid, and I'm watching her hands shake. I mean, she's so nervous about those freakin' mushrooms, about doing them right and getting all of them done on time, as if the fate of the world depends on it. I look up at her face, and she's focused on those mushrooms, man, totally focused, biting her lip to help her concentrate. She's this brilliant person, *brilliant* person, she knows art and architecture, she knows music and books, and she can write, oh man, she can write, she's going to be the most famous writer in the world or something, she's got this *full scholarship* for four years, and they don't see it or don't care, all they want to do is bust her ass if she doesn't prepare enough damn stupid mushrooms or doesn't do them to the highest standards of the Pomerantz house."

He didn't speak for a long time, breathing hard and fast at first, almost gasping, but in time he grew calm.

"They make noises since it happened. The kind of noises they know they're supposed to make at a time like this. How awful it is. How unfair it is. How much they miss her. How empty the house seems now. But it's all just noise. There's not a tear between them. They get takeout for dinner from this restaurant, from that one, and they complain about it. They try TV dinners, and they complain about them. They watch the boob tube like before. I swear, they talk at the walls instead of to each other. I take it to the garage without being told to take it. The only thing that's really changed about them, besides what they have to eat, is how much they smoke. They're two factory stacks, worse than ever, like they're trying to fill the house with smoke so they won't notice . . . she's gone."

At last he turned from the window and came to the bed and stared at my useless legs.

"She was so damn close to a clean getaway, you know."

I dared to speak. "I know."

"Full scholarship, the university in September. She could have been anything. Which is another reason I won't cry. Hell if I will. She had it all. She was pretty and brilliant and funny and graceful and kind. She was so kind to everyone. She understood more about life, about the world, than I ever, ever, ever will. She lived so intensely, man, just so intensely. She lived more in seventeen years than most people would in a hundred, and that's nothing to cry about. That's nothing to cry about, is it?"

I said, "No."

At last he met my eyes.

I said, "I loved her, too."

Fortunately, earlier I had been taken off the IV drip as well as off the catheter. After Malcolm put down the safety railing, he climbed into bed with me, no less clumsy than ever. He put his head upon my chest, as if he were smaller than me, younger than me.

One of the many wonders of this world is that, if we allow it to happen, anyone newly met can all but overnight become a central figure in our lives, hardly less essential to us than air and water. Although we've made it a world of hatred and envy and violence, the preponderance of evidence proves to me that it is a world created to inspire friendship and love and kindness.

He said, "Don't hate yourself, Jonah. You're not your father and you never could be. You've got to be yourself, you and me still the way we've always been with each other. You're all I have now, Jonah. Just you. Just you."

His pledge never to cry lasted only until then.

Eighty-six

SO MANY PEOPLE CAME TO VISIT ME AT THE
hospital, but the one I most expected—Miss Pearl—never
appeared. She had said that she'd given me more help
than she ever should, what happened next would be up to
all the people who lived along her streets, and my part of
what happened next was up to me. I still hoped to see her
again.

Until we were on our way home in Grandpa's twenty-
one-year-old Cadillac, I hadn't given a thought to the cost
of the medical care. I knew we had an inexpensive form
of insurance, and suddenly I realized that the care I'd been
given must have been the best.

Riding beside me in the backseat, Mom said, "The
hospital refuses to bill us, sweetie. And all the doctors, too.

We don't want charity. We made our case to be allowed to pay over time, but none of them will take a dime. I don't know, it is a Catholic hospital, and maybe all those years your grandma worked for the monsignor is why."

I said, "There sure are good people in the world, aren't there?"

"There sure are," she agreed.

From behind the wheel, Grandpa Teddy said, "And I'm proud to be a chauffeur today for two of the best of the good. What say we stop at Baskin-Robbins and relieve them of three hand-packed quarts of ice cream for dessert, each of us with the right to pick one flavor?"

Mom said, "You don't have to ask me twice."

"You didn't have to ask *me* the first time," I declared.

"Just so you know, there are still rules in this family, and we're not cool with gluttony. We're not eating it all tonight."

When we arrived home, I discovered that the front porch steps had been replaced with a long, sturdy ramp. The first-floor doorways, exterior and interior, had been cut wider and reframed to accommodate a wheelchair, and new doors had been hung throughout. The wheelchair stood in the living room, and Grandpa put me down in it, warning that speed limits indoors would be strictly enforced. All the area carpets in the lower four rooms had been rolled up and put away, completely baring the hardwood floors—linoleum in the kitchen—and furniture had been rearranged, so that I could move about freely. The dining-room furniture had been put in storage, and my bedroom furniture had been brought downstairs in its place.

The most impressive change proved to be a ground-floor bathroom where my grandfather's little study had once been. A low pedestal sink allowed me to roll right up to it. Sturdy railings framed the toilet, so that I could maneuver myself out of the wheelchair onto the throne and back again, with little danger of falling. The bathtub also had safety grips.

Amazed, I said, "How could you do all this in only eleven days? And holy-moley, what did it cost?"

"Same answer to both," Grandpa said. "A lot of good tradesmen go to our church or they live in the neighborhood. This was all volunteer labor. We didn't even ask, they came to us. Plus I'm a wizard with a paintbrush, even if I do say so myself. We paid only for materials, and we could handle that easy enough."

I could see that the kindness of our neighbors moved him.

What I didn't know then, didn't know for years, because they kept it from me, was that initially one of the city's newspapers had tried to make something of the fact that I happened to be in the bank at the same time my father put down the briefcase. And how could I know, they asked, that it contained a bomb. This was back in a time before the media worked in concert and chewed people up and spit them out largely for the fun of it; therefore, the assault wasn't unanimous.

When journalists at the other two major newspapers sought more details from police, they learned that my father had abandoned us and divorced my mother, that for a long while, our family and a friend of the family had been suspicious of his activities and of the people with whom he consorted. Among police officials participating in a press conference, Detective Nakama Otani declared that without the help of the Bledsoe family—my mother had reverted to her maiden name—they would at this point have not a clue to the identity of those who had perpetrated the First National horror. He also said that if I hadn't been there, if I hadn't glimpsed my father, those in the bank would have had no chance to flee or to take shelter, resulting in a much higher death count. "The boy could have run and saved himself, but he tried to save others," Detective Otani said. "And for his bravery, he will never walk again." After that, even the offending newspaper joined with the others to declare me a hero.

My mother and grandfather had impressed upon everyone from the nurses to all of our friends that were I to learn I'd been declared a villain and then a hero, the knowledge would do me no good and might cause emotional and psychological harm. We were but a family of musicians, entertainers, and we wanted applause not for doing the right thing in a moment of stress, which anyone might have done, but for hitting the right notes in the right order and with a dash of style.

Mom and Grandpa Teddy were so wise. Considering my guilt and sorrow, I might have taken refuge in the label HERO, and worse than refuge—satisfaction. I know myself well enough to realize that such a choice was within my character to make. Such high self-regard at an early age would have warped my life perhaps no less than did paraplegia.

That Thursday when I came home, the piano remained in the front room, though a new bench had been constructed. The seat of it matched the dimensions of the previous bench; however, a padded back had been added. As I eventually discovered, I would need years to be a hundred percent confident of my balance when sitting forward on an armless chair, let alone on a bench without either a back or arms. Happily, having grown in the past two years, I didn't need to resort to my butt-slide technique to increase my keyboard reach, because that would no longer be a trick I could perform.

My grandfather had modified his beloved Steinway to an extent that uglified it a little, which made my heart sink. With admirable cleverness, he had devised a way for me to use the damper, una corda, and sostenuto pedals even now that my feet were useless to me. He had taken off the fallboard, leaving the keys permanently exposed, and he had drilled into the casing behind it to install three controls similar to the draw knobs—or stops—on an organ. Each one controlled a wire strung tautly through two pulleys behind the lyre and down to the pedal, which he had extended through the back of the lyre base. Pulling on a knob engaged the pedal function; pushing it released the pedal. Not elegant, not ideal, but workable, he assured me. Even if I wanted to play something as formal as Mozart, I would have to do so with some degree of improvisation, to allow a free hand to quickly push or pull the draw knob when needed.

Or otherwise, perhaps I could use the extensions to the knobs, which he had put to one side until then. With some nervousness, his voice as solemn as his face, he showed them to me. The extensions brought the grab knobs over the keyboard and about ten inches above it. They were sheathed in rubber, so that by craning my neck just a little as I played, I could pull a knob with my teeth, push it in with my chin.

"It works, it really does," Grandpa said with sober conviction. "Oh, sure, you'll need to get the hang of it, you'll be frustrated for a while. But I've practiced with them, developed a technique. I think I can teach it to you pretty quickly. It's not elegant, it's not ideal—"

When I chimed in, "—but it's workable," he looked uncertain for a moment, saw that I was not despairing, and smiled broadly.

How it must have grieved him to devise for his prodigy grandson such a contraption as the pedal control. He played, as I have said, with good taste and distinction, with the best left hand you'll ever hear, with superior style. In two years, I had progressed so far that I could match him, and he took pride in my talent, looked forward eagerly to the moment when I would surpass him, which he had not long before insisted was mere days away. He had to know that now I would never surpass him and that it would be a miracle if, with the grab knobs, I ever again played as well as he did. Yet he believed that I might, and he wanted me to believe. I had always loved him so very much, but at that moment I loved him as never before.

My mother and grandfather didn't suggest that I play, although I knew they expected that I might try. I'd been away from a keyboard for eleven days. Ordinarily I would have been eager to get at it. But I didn't ask them to help me shift from the wheelchair to the bench. I pled extreme weariness, a plausible excuse in the circumstances.

The physicians had declared that I possessed full upper-body function and strength. After the first waking moment in the recovery room following surgery, when for a disturbing moment I couldn't feel my mother's hands pressing around one of mine, I'd had no reason to suspect that I suffered from even the slightest loss of sensitivity or coordination in my hands. But on that first day home, with the additional challenge of the grab knobs, I was afraid to test the doctors' declaration.

In the morning, I found my courage. Man, would I need it.

Eighty-seven

THE FIRST NIGHT IN MY NEW BEDROOM, I HAD
lain in the dark, repeating softly in sets of ten a motivating
mantra that I devised myself: "I am not like Tilton Kirk,
I am not like Tilton Kirk. . . ."

In the second set, I emphasized the first word: "*I* am
not like Tilton Kirk, *I* am not like Tilton Kirk. . . ."

Then I stressed the third word: "I am *not* like Tilton
Kirk. . . ."

For the fourth set, I emphasized the name in a tone of
contempt: "I am not like *Tilton Kirk*. . . ."

I don't know how many hundreds of repetitions I whispered, but I fell asleep with those words on my tongue.

No doubt my mother would have been dismayed at me.
Or maybe not. In the morning, I was the first out of bed.

By the time Mom came downstairs, I had drawn a tub of hot water, bathed, and dressed, with a lot of fumbling. She found me at the grand piano, trying to play and work the grab knobs with my hands.

"Would you put on the extensions for me?" I asked.

She didn't remark on my application to the challenge before me, though later I heard her singing in the kitchen as she prepared breakfast.

When Grandpa Teddy came downstairs, we three ate at the dinette table, and then he sat with me to show me some of his grab-knob-extension technique.

He was still on leave from his department-store gig that Friday, and I suspect he would have sat with me all morning if he hadn't needed to collect Mrs. Lorenzo and her belongings. She had agreed to accept a position as my caregiver, manipulating my legs through the exercises that the therapist prescribed and otherwise looking after me. The position came with my former bedroom upstairs, a salary that might not have been much to start, and board.

After Grandpa left, I continued to practice with considerable frustration until by chance I looked up and, through a front window, saw Malcolm crossing the street. I swung off the piano bench, into the wheelchair, and opened the door when he rang the bell.

"Where's your axe?" I asked.

Shifting awkwardly from foot to foot, looking down at me, he said, "I'd rather call it my saxophone."

"Like hell you would."

"Well, I would."

Maybe he was aware of what Grandpa had done to the Steinway, but if he didn't know, I wanted to prevent him from seeing the changes for a while. "Let's sit on the porch."

That July day was so hot and humid that birds wouldn't fly and bees wouldn't buzz. You could almost hear the street sizzling.

"How're you doing?" I asked.

"I've been better."

"What about your folks?"

"My *folks*? Makes me sound like Beaver Cleaver."

"I'm just asking."

"The old man is talking all the time about getting a promotion. Where do you go from lathe-shop foreman? Is there a lathe-shop king?"

"What about her?"

"She's taken to smoking in bed. I expect to be immolated in my sleep. Which wouldn't bother me."

"Don't talk like that."

"Well, it wouldn't."

"If you're gonna talk like that, I don't want you here."

"Throw me off the property, why don't you?"

"Maybe I will."

After a silence, he said, "You see that van parked down there by the Jaruzelski place? You know what it is?"

"A Ford."

"Didn't your mom and grandpa tell you what it is?"

"I don't need them to tell me it's a Ford."

"It's a police stakeout."

"What're they staking out?"

"Your place. In case your old man shows up or any of those crazy people he threw in with."

"Where'd you get this?"

"That day I came to the hospital, before your mom saw me in the hallway there, she was talking to this cop, and I overheard what he was saying. The van's been here ever since."

The windshield was tinted. I couldn't tell if anyone was in the van.

"Why didn't they tell me?" I wondered.

"Probably they didn't want to scare you. I don't care about scaring you."

"I don't scare that easy anymore."

"That's why I don't care about scaring you."

Maybe Mom intuited that I didn't want Malcolm to see the piano just yet. She brought us a small cooler with four Cokes on ice and a plate of cookies.

We sat for a while, watching, and no one got in or out of the van.

Eventually Malcolm said, "They can't have a toilet in there."

"Maybe they're catheterized like I was in the hospital."

"Cops aren't *that* dedicated."

"They might be if they came from Manzanar."

"What's Manzanar?"

I told him everything I knew about it from what I'd read in the library.

He said, "Sometimes I think it's good to be white."

"Sometimes?"

"Most of the time, I'd rather be Samoan. You know, from Samoa."

"Why?"

"Those guys are like six-four, weigh like three hundred pounds, but they have such smooth moves, you'd think they were dancers in another life. I'd like to be huge and strong, but graceful."

"Maybe you'll be a Clydesdale in your next life. Anyway, Samoans look white to me."

"Everybody looks white to you. What do you think those cops in the van are saying about us?"

"'What a couple of geeks.'"

"I do believe you're psychic."

We remained on the porch for quite a while, and when Malcolm got up to go home, I said, "Don't come back till Monday, and then bring your axe."

"Why not till Monday?"

"I'm spending all weekend at the keyboard getting back into shape."

"Bring my saxophone, huh?"

"Bring your axe."

"You say potato, I say po-tah-to."

"Get out of here."

He descended the ramp, stopped on the sidewalk, and turned to me. "Man, I'm glad you're back."

"I'm not back yet," I said, "but I will be."

I sat on the porch by myself for a while. On the hour, a paneled van turned the corner at the west end of the block and parked behind the tan Ford in front of the Jaruzelski place. The two vehicles were identical. After a minute or two, the first van left. Shift change.

Eighty-eight

MAYBE THERE'S A LAW OF NATURE THAT YOUR LIFE can only go down so far before there's a rebound. I could make a case that when I didn't die in the bomb blast, when I only lost the use of my legs, that was my personal-best down, and that things started turning around for me—and for my family—when I learned that I would still be able to pee in the same fashion that I had peed all my life, except always from a sitting position henceforth. That Friday, we began to catch some good breaks.

Mom got a call from a booking agent who hadn't wanted to handle her but now offered her an audition at a place called Diamond Dust, at 4:30 the next afternoon. It was the swankiest nightclub in the city, and she assumed they might want her for two low-traffic nights, maybe Mondays and Tuesdays. The agent said, no, this was for lead singer, five nights a week, working with a fourteen-piece band. The club had changed hands, and they were looking for an even classier image than what they already had.

The agent said, "The way they want to run it is kind of unusual, but I'm sure you can cope. They want to hear 'Embraceable You,' 'A Tisket, A Tasket,' and 'Boogie-Woogie Bugle Boy.'"

That evening at the dinner table, a grim possibility occurred to Mom. She put down her fork and said, "Oh, no. What if this is because of Tilton?"

Grandpa looked up from the delicious chicken lasagna that Mrs. Lorenzo had brought with her in the move. "How could it have anything to do with Tilton?"

Shaking her head, frowning, Mrs. Lorenzo said, "That man."

"The bombing was a nationwide story," my mother said. "He's a fugitive. Maybe I'm worth the job only because I'm the fugitive's ex-wife. Maybe they expect I'll bring in a lot of curious idiots who think I'm Bonnie to his Clyde."

"I hate that movie," Mrs. Lorenzo said, "except Gene Hackman. He's going to be somebody."

"Diamond Dust," Grandpa said firmly, "isn't a place that pulls publicity stunts. They're serious about their music. Anyway, if that was it, then they'd want you only for the low-traffic nights."

"I guess maybe," she said, but she sounded doubtful. "How would a place like that even know about me?"

Grandpa threw up his hands as if in exasperation. "They saw you at Slinky's or somewhere else and realized you far out-classed the venue. Don't second-guess your guardian angel, girl."

Saturday she went to the audition, expecting a piano player, but they gave her the entire band, which had come in early. The manager, Johnson Oliver, obviously hands-on in the *right* way, presented her with arrangements for the three songs they wanted her to sing and gave her plenty of time to look them over in a quiet corner. "Just get the sense of how we approach the music. The boys will adjust to the way you sing."

She sang, and they adjusted, and she thought she had never been better. By the time she got to "Boogie-Woogie Bugle Boy," at least a dozen guys on the kitchen staff came out to listen, and they cheered her when she wound it up, and even the members of the band applauded.

The agent hadn't mentioned that he would be there, but he was, and after he conferred with Johnson Oliver, he astonished my mother by bringing her an offer, right then, more than she'd ever imagined they would pay.

Her only remaining concern was that the owner might have ideas like those of others whom she'd had to fend off. She asked when she might meet the big boss, and

Johnson Oliver, with whom she felt comfortable, said, "Young lady, I'm the new owner *and* manager—and with you on board, this place is going to be a great investment."

Saturday night at dinner, Mom regaled us with the story, and I swear we could have put out the four candles on the table and just dined by her glow.

With so many rotten things recently behind us, I was happy for her, happier than I can put into words. If when I went to bed that Saturday night you had told me that I'd be walking in the morning, I might have believed you.

Eighty-nine

SUNDAY NIGHT, TWENTY-FOUR HOURS AFTER returning to the city, Fiona Cassidy sat on the edge of her motel bed, picked up the phone on the nightstand, and placed an out-of-state call.

With her long hair cut short and styled funky and dyed blond, with her peaches-and-cream complexion now bronze from hours under a sun lamp and then under the sun itself, she was confident that no one would recognize her as the bomb-maker in the photo that the police had released to the media. Using one of the three sets of false ID that Lucas had given her a month earlier, she'd rented a car and taken a room in a nondescript motel.

When Lucas picked up his phone three hundred miles away, she said, "They're watching, sure enough."

"How's it work?"

She told him about the Ford vans.

Ninety

MONDAY MORNING, GRANDPA TEDDY DROVE MY
mother to Woolworth's to turn in her uniforms. She didn't
need that job anymore.

Shortly after Mrs. Lorenzo put me through my daily
exercises, Malcolm arrived with his axe. If he knew about
the modifications to the Steinway, he convincingly pretended
to be surprised by them.

I wanted him to listen to a few numbers and watch me.
I started with Fats Domino's "Walking to New Orleans,"
which moves easy, and then did Fats's "Whole Lotta
Loving," which truly, righteously rocks. Neither of them
called for that much pedal work, but then I finished with
a swing piece, "Easy Does It."

When I wrapped it, I didn't look at him when I said,

"Now let's do a couple numbers together." He named a piece, and we rode through it well, and I named a piece, and that one went all right, too.

After the last chords faded in the heart of the Steinway, I dared to look at him. "So how did I do?"

"You did great, fantastic."

"Don't blow smoke up my butt, Malcolm Pomerantz."

"No, you were really good. I mean, you've been through hell and away from the keyboard, so it's going to take time. I wouldn't think you'd be this good, this soon, especially with those grab knobs to pull and poke."

I nodded. "You want to go in the kitchen, grab us a couple of Cokes, and meet me on the porch?"

He shook his head. "Let's do some more here."

"We will. We'll do more together. But right now, meet me on the porch with those Cokes."

I wheeled myself through the front door. The Ford van wasn't parked to the west near the Jaruzelski place, but to the east, near the Rakowskis' house.

Malcolm brought two ice-cold Cokes, almost dropped one, snared it before it hit the floor, gave me the other one, sat down, and said, "I think my old man hit her."

"Who—your mom?"

"She has this bruise along her jaw. But then I think she hit him back or first, or whatever, 'cause he has a black eye."

"When did this happen?"

"Sunday, when I was in the garage. I'm always in the garage. I'd be there all the time if they'd just move the car out and give me more space."

"This ever happen before?"

"Not that I know about. But things change, things are always changing, and not for the better."

The day was a repeat of Friday, so hot that the birds stayed in the trees or walked around in the yard in the shade of the big maple, pecking at things in the grass as if they didn't really want to eat but felt they had to go through the motions.

"I can still play," I said, "and I'll get better, but I'm never going to perform in public."

"Sure you will. That's what it's all about."

"It better not be what it's all about, because if it is, then I'm through."

"What're you saying? I don't know what you're saying."

"Those grab knobs don't cut it when I use a hand. Can't get the right performance that way. What's it look like when I use my teeth?"

"What does it look like? What do you mean?"

"Suddenly you don't understand English?"

"It looks okay," he said. "It looks fine. It's interesting."

"As interesting as a monkey juggling?"

He glowered at me. "What the hell kind of thing is that to say?"

"I don't want to be a novelty pianist. 'Playing tonight, Jonah the Crippled Prodigy Bravely Soldiering Forward.'"

He hissed through his teeth. "Man, I really don't like you when you put yourself down."

"Well, you know, somebody's got to do it. If I'm not hard on myself, Malcolm, who will be? It isn't a good thing to be soft on yourself."

"Who told you that?"

"Somebody smarter than both of us."

"That could be almost anybody."

"Exactly."

In silence, we drank what remained of our Cokes, and then I said, "It's not a bad thing, Malcolm."

"The hell it isn't."

"I've been thinking about Vermeer."

"What about Vermeer?"

"How he was totally forgotten for two hundred years, and now everybody thinks he's the greatest ever."

"So you're ditching the piano for a paintbrush?"

"If Vermeer had been a piano man, a performer, he'd never have been rediscovered two centuries after he died."

"Man, you're losing me."

"He was rediscovered *because he created something.* You see? They didn't dig him up two hundred years after they buried him, and he's been walking around ever since. His *paintings* were rediscovered."

"Believe it or not, I realized that."

"If I can't be a performer, on a stage in front of people, maybe that's good, because maybe what I can do is write music. Create."

"You mean write songs?"

"At least the melodies. I don't know about the words."

"You're ten."

"I'm going on eleven. And I don't expect to have a hit tomorrow. It'll take years and years to learn."

"What kind of songs?"

"Rock 'n' roll, I guess."

"That's what sells. No market for new swing."

"Rock 'n' roll is a place to start."

"Maybe ballads, love songs," he suggested. "Maybe blues."

"Sure. Why not?"

"Country and western?"

I shrugged. "I don't have anything against it."

"Broadway show tunes?"

"Could be interesting."

"Symphonies?"

"Well, maybe not symphonies."

"Not until you're twelve, anyway."

"I'm no Mozart," I said.

"I wondered when you'd start being hard on yourself."

"Maybe I'm not anyone, not Mozart, not Cole Porter or

Doc Pomus or anyone who can write good music. But I've got to try, don't I?"

"You've got to try," he agreed. "And you are someone."

We went on like that for a while, and as he was about to go home, I said, "You have a penlight?"

"What do you want with a penlight?"

"I'll tell you sometime. I just need one."

"I can get you one."

"That would be swell. Maybe tomorrow?"

"Yeah. I'll get you one tomorrow."

Ninety-one

THE FOLLOWING DAY, HAVING THE SUTURES taken out of my back hurt, though not as much as getting blown off my feet by a bomb. The doctor declared himself pleased with my progress, and I said that I was happy with it, too, though in fact I didn't think I'd made any progress and didn't expect that I ever would, at least not as far as walking was concerned.

With my father loose in the world, Grandpa didn't want my mother taking the bus to work or walking alone any distance, and he didn't trust the reliability of taxicabs. That same day, he fronted her the down payment for a used car, a 1961 Buick station wagon the precise soft brown of a chocolate Necco wafer. For a wagon, that car had cool body styling; and because my wheelchair was collapsible,

Mom would be able to stow it in the back of the wagon and take me places with her.

Having been invited the week before, Mr. Yoshioka came to dinner that evening, bearing an immense bouquet of roses that must have been difficult to manage on the bus. He admired the Buick, which was in tip-top condition even though it had sixty thousand miles on it. Over dinner, when I suggested that he should buy a car for himself, he replied that he'd never had the time to take driving lessons.

"Besides," he said, "I would miss walking to work. I have taken the same route for so many years that every building and every crack in the sidewalk and each of the many details along the way is like an old friend."

"But when it rains, you wouldn't have to get wet," I said.

"Ah, but the rain is a special friend, Jonah. It has such a soft voice, and if you talk to the rain, it always agrees with anything you say." He hissed like falling rain does, but he made a word of it: "*Yesss, yesss, yesss, yesss.* It cannot make the sound of *no.* The rain is a most agreeable companion."

Mrs. Lorenzo clapped her plump hands quietly, quickly, as might a delighted little girl. "That's such a lovely thought."

Mr. Yoshioka was excited to hear about my mother's new job, and he said that he would like to see her opening-night performance.

"You best wait a week," Mother told him. "My rehearsal with the band is tomorrow. The first week, we'll be on a kind of shakedown cruise, finding our best sound together."

After dinner, Mr. Yoshioka hoped that I might play the piano, but I pretended that the discomfort of having the sutures removed would prevent me from being my best.

The pedals worked as well by foot as they always had, and Grandpa Teddy played three of his favorite Jimmy McHugh tunes, while Mom stood by him to sing them: "On the Sunny Side of the Street" and "I Feel a Song Coming On" and finally "I'm in the Mood for Love," all with lyrics by Dorothy Fields.

Mrs. Lorenzo and Mr. Yoshioka sat on the sofa during that little performance, and the tailor's dark eyes shone with enchantment.

After the third number, he said to Grandpa, "If I cannot see your daughter tomorrow night, then I must come to see you."

"I'd love to have you as my guest," Grandpa said. "But next week or the week after. This week, there's a big convention, the hotel's very busy through Sunday. Already a month ago, the restaurant where I play had booked every reservation available."

Later, after I had gotten into my pajamas and then into bed, my mother came to say good-night. "That was a lovely evening. I've become quite a fan of your friend, Jonah."

"He's a good guy."

"And you're a brave one. I'm sorry the sutures hurt."

"Well, they're out now. Just a little tender. I'll be okay."

"You will be okay," she agreed. "You always will be."

"Your first day off, can we go somewhere in the station wagon?"

"That would be Monday. Where do you want to go?"

"Somewhere really cool."

She smiled. "It'll be so cool, your breath will fog up." She leaned down and kissed my forehead. "Sweet dreams."

After she left, I switched off the lamp. Lying in the dark, I took the penlight from under my pillow.

Malcolm had found it at a five-and-dime. He'd not been willing to tell me how much it cost. "Maybe I shoplifted it. How do you know? If you're going to switch it on after your mom says lights out and then write symphonies when you should be sleeping, don't tell her where you got it."

Maybe the dream about being trapped somewhere with a dead woman would come true, and maybe it wouldn't. But if I woke up in pitch blackness with rushing-water sounds all around, I would not want to be without a source of light.

When I tried the penlight, the narrow beam didn't travel far, but farther than I had expected. It painted a pale ring of light on the ceiling, the center darker than the periphery. Kind of like an eye staring down at me.

Ninety-two

JOE TORTELLI SPENT A WEEK IN VEGAS, LIVING IN a complimentary suite at a major hotel, where he was a valued "whale," a high-roller. It happened to be the week of the First National bombing. After Las Vegas, he took a showgirl to San Francisco and later south to a resort in Newport Beach, a honeymoon without benefit of marriage. During this period, he had no interest in the news.

He returned to our city, sans showgirl, on the afternoon of the day that I had my sutures removed. His trusted right-hand man, Tony Urqell, had known better than to disturb Tortelli when he was engaged in such a romantic adventure. But upon his boss's return, Urqell

informed him that a manager of various Tortelli properties believed he might have rented a building to one of
the men wanted for the bank bombing and the Colt-
Thompson heist.

Joe Tortelli owned a great deal of real estate in our city:
apartment buildings, office buildings, parking garages, and
more. Among the things he owned were several large,
rusting, and mostly unrented Quonset huts in an old manu-
facturing district slated for redevelopment. One of these
Quonsets was the building in question, which had been
rented out for six months, supposedly to supply the lessee
with much-needed temporary storage.

Urqell had not acted on the manager's suspicion because
it was Joe Tortelli's policy to regard the police as an enemy
and to avoid giving them a reason to become suspicious
of any of his enterprises, even though most of them were,
these days, legit. With Tortelli back on home base, Urqell
informed him of the manager's report and wanted to know
what he should do.

"Go have a look," Tortelli said. "Take some guys with
you. If these bomb-throwin' cowboys used the place, they
won't be there now, but we've got to get out in front of the
story."

Urqell and the three guys who went with him found the
armored truck, the van painted to look like a Colt-Thompson

support vehicle, and the very ripe body of the third guard, missing for fifteen days.

By Wednesday morning, the bombing-heist saga, which had faded somewhat from the news, was once more the top story.

Ninety-three

THREE HUNDRED MILES FROM THE CITY, IN A neighboring state, Lucas Drackman, Smaller, and Tilton were holed up in a comfortable house on a 210-acre farm, long fallow, that he had bought years previously in case he ever needed it for this purpose.

If their original plan had unfolded as intended, they would never have left the city. The authorities would have had no clue as to the identities of the perpetrators. As soon as Smaller had opened the armored door with a cutting torch and they had gotten their hands on the 1.6 million in cash, they could have gone directly back to the house overlooking Riverside Commons.

The Japanese swish on the park bench should have suggested to Drackman that their scheme might not unfold precisely as designed. But by then, they were on the cusp of action, and he believed that victory never favored the hesitant.

After the heist, in the Quonset hut, they had a police-band radio, an ordinary radio, and a TV to monitor the breaking news. Smaller hadn't quite breached the thick door when Fiona called their attention to the TV. A reporter stood outside First National, talking to a disheveled woman with bits of debris in her hair, a bank teller who had been at work when the bombs went off.

"A little boy, a little Negro boy," she said. "He shouted there was a bomb, we should get out. I thought it was a prank, then I knew it wasn't. He saved my life. I dropped to the floor behind my window, the teller's window, so I was protected."

"A boy?" the reporter pressed. "Is he here now, do you see him now, this boy?"

She shook her head, and her voice quaked with emotion. "No. He was hurt bad. I thought he was dead. Like the girl. The girl . . . she was dead, it was horrible. This other boy was kneeling beside him. I tried to take him out of there with me, the white boy, I mean, but he said his friend was still alive, he couldn't leave him."

"His friend?" the reporter asked.

"The little Negro boy. Jonah. The other boy, he said, 'Jonah's still alive, I can't leave him.'"

Drackman might have killed Tilton at that moment, right there in the Quonset. But when he had looked at my father, he'd seen genuine shock. He'd decided against a hasty execution.

Standing beside Drackman, Fiona had said ominously, "*Juju.*"

The occult interested Lucas Drackman. "Juju? Voodoo? What're you talking about?"

"Jonah. Jonah Kirk. I should have smashed his monkey face that first day. He's a weird little freak. He believes in juju. He has a metal box full of *wangas.*" When she saw that Drackman didn't know the word, she described my collection of interesting junk as I would not have thought to define it: "*Wangas.* Charms. And fetishes—objects that are supposed to possess supernatural power."

Now, Wednesday morning, sixteen days later, Drackman, Smaller, and my father were sitting around the kitchen table in the farmhouse, talking about the coming revolution, when the TV news reported that the Colt-Thompson truck and the missing—and murdered—guard had been found, though of course the 1.6 million in cash was long gone.

For days, Tilton had argued against ever going back to the city. Drackman had remained adamant: "We have a score to settle. Unless you don't have the guts. No one's immune if they're in the way of the Cause, brother." Smaller vacillated on the issue, but he had so long been steeped in paranoia that he tended to side with Drackman most of the time. Finally Tilton accepted the inevitability of the venture.

Although they had planned to go back on Friday, Drackman felt that the discovery of the armored truck required an adjustment in their timetable. He was a great believer in bold action and in the predictive power of Tarot cards. He was also a great believer in Hitler and Stalin, but they were dead and could give him no advice. Following the counsel of the Tarot, he had already sent the new-look Fiona Cassidy back to spy on us. Now he opened the deck again and shuffled the seventy-eight cards and laid five of them on the kitchen table in the form of a cross. After revealing them one at a time, he brooded a while before saying, "What it's telling me is not to pull back, not to delay, to move ahead even faster."

As Drackman would later tell the police, the best thing about having a big pile of cash and not giving a damn about the law is that you can get anything you want, and you can get it fast. As a man of means, he hadn't needed what he and his crew stole from Colt-Thompson. But if you were going to be a player in the Cause, if you were on the revolutionary road, you should bring down the corrupt system with the system's money, not with your own. After Fiona called him on Saturday to report that our house remained under surveillance, Drackman had made contact with like-minded individuals of long acquaintance, in a city other than ours. For a price, they agreed to supply a Ford van of the same year, model, and color as the stakeout vans on our street, credible license plates, and a registration card in the name of one of his false identities. The supplier intended to deliver it Thursday afternoon.

Drackman's intention had been to meet with Fiona on Friday, compare notes, and go into the Bledsoe place that night. But trusting his intuition and the Tarot cards, he said, "We drive back tomorrow instead, and we go into that house tomorrow night."

When the weather map on the TV news at that moment predicted heavy rains throughout the region beginning Thursday afternoon, Drackman knew that he must be right to move more quickly. A rainy night would provide perfect cover for the job.

Ninety-four

WHEN MY MOTHER CAME DOWNSTAIRS SHORTLY
after eleven o'clock Thursday morning, I was parked in
my wheelchair at the kitchen table, reading one of my
grandpa's books, a memoir of Tin Pan Alley, which was
a nickname for a neighborhood in New York City, a
stretch of 28th Street between Broadway and Sixth
Avenue, where music publishers and songwriters had
flourished from 1886 until rock 'n' roll changed that world
in the late 1950s. I figured that a first step in becoming
a songwriter should be to read about successful ones, the
guys who made Tin Pan Alley famous: W. C. Handy,
Harry Warren, Irving Berlin, Cole Porter, Jimmy Van
Heusen, Lerner and Loewe . . .

Mrs. Lorenzo worked at the cutting board, near the

sink, slicing potatoes thin for home fries to accompany the omelets that would be Mom's breakfast and my lunch.

When my mother entered the room, I thought she was fast becoming like Grandpa Teddy, like Grandma Anita had been: a Presence. You just *had* to look at her, not merely because she was beautiful, but also because something about the way she carried herself, something about her quiet confidence and dazzling smile and sparkling eyes made you say to yourself, *Now hold on a minute here, this isn't just passing scenery, this is SOMEBODY.*

Her first night at Diamond Dust had gone exceptionally well, which surprised her, though it surely didn't surprise me. She liked everyone she worked with, and they seemed to like her. Some of the patrons talked through the instrumental numbers, of course, but few talked when she sang, and in general the customers came there because they loved swing music and jazz and the blues; therefore, they had respect for musicians. If some of them were gawkers drawn by the fact that her ex-husband was wanted for a sensational crime, she couldn't tell them apart from those who came for the music, food, and booze.

By the time that lunch was on the table and the three of us had finished eating, the storm began with a flash of lightning and a long crash of thunder. To keep out the rain, Mom and Mrs. Lorenzo hurried around, closing the windows that had been opened for ventilation.

Wearing a voluminous yellow slicker that he shed on the porch, Malcolm visited in the afternoon, just after Mrs. Lorenzo finished flexing my leg joints. He was having a butter-side-down day, unable to get his mind off Amalia. I knew how he felt, as I had bad patches of my own, days of melancholy, also hours of more piercing despair, especially when I woke at night and thought of her and couldn't get back to sleep.

He didn't want to talk. He said he just needed to be somewhere that didn't reek of cigarette smoke and wasn't a garage. We sat in the living room, and I read aloud to him about Tin Pan Alley, about how Harry Warren and Al Dubin, a lyricist, came to write "Lullaby of Broadway" and also all those great songs in the movie *42nd Street*. At one point, for a while, he turned his back to me, and I pretended I didn't hear the small, sad, stifled sounds he made.

Ninety-five

TILTON RODE UP FRONT WITH LUCAS DRACKMAN, while Mr. Smaller stretched out on a pile of blankets in the back of the van. He slept through the larger part of the drive.

The scourge of Bilderbergers was a little less hairy than usual. He had changed his appearance by shaving his head, though he had also grown a mustache, which had sprouted into a thick brush in no time. Although he had never before been able to lose weight, he'd dropped ten pounds in sixteen days, which he attributed to the fact that for the first time in his life he was "doing something that mattered." Blowing up a bank, making off with a fortune, and thereby sticking it to the establishment gave him greater self-esteem than he'd ever had before, and he wanted to look better.

Drackman had dyed his blond hair black and had started growing a beard, which he also had to color. Although it was necessary, he regretted the dye job, because he'd always been immensely pleased with his looks just the way they were.

Like Mr. Smaller, Tilton had shaved his head and had started to cultivate a mustache. He didn't think he had changed his appearance enough to be out in public when the police, the FBI, and every Dick and Jane were looking for him. He didn't want to return to the city. He didn't want any part of what Lucas intended to do. But the man terrified him, and he was in deep now, and he knew he couldn't split, couldn't survive and stay free on his own.

He missed Aurora. She knew how to soothe a man's nerves. She'd gotten him into this, just as she'd drawn Smaller into it. Playing at revolution excited the woman; it was a real-life romance novel to her, spiced with violence. She had an edge to her that he hadn't been aware of at first, and for some reason guys wanted to cut themselves on that edge. He had thought she was a brainiac before he'd spent a lot of time with her; now he suspected that nothing complex happened in her head.

The windshield wipers thumped, thumped, thumped like a hammer rhythmically striking something soft, and from time to time the rubber blades stroked a thin sound from the glass, reminiscent of the whimper of a beaten animal.

Ninety-six

MALCOLM STAYED FOR DINNER WITH GRANDPA, Mrs. Lorenzo, and me. Mom was already off to Diamond Dust. We dined on chopped salad, slow-cooked Swiss steak, baked corn custard, carrots with tarragon, and green beans with minced onions.

Grandpa said he felt too full to have a slice of the peach pie right then, but maybe he would enjoy it later, when he got home from his gig at the hotel restaurant. Because of the bad weather, he left early, making sure that Mrs. Lorenzo locked both deadbolts on the front door.

Malcolm's mood had improved somewhat through dinner. He scooped the vanilla ice cream while Mrs. Lorenzo plated three pieces of pie.

When he put my dessert on the table in front of me, he said, "You okay?"

"Huh? Sure. I'm great."

"You have indigestion or something?"

"Indigestion?"

"The way you keep touching your chest."

The pendant. I was repeatedly feeling for the Lucite heart, as if some sneak thief might have slipped it from the chain and made off with it.

Ninety-seven

THE THREE ARRIVED IN THE CITY AS THE daylight steadily washed out of the turbulent sky. The storm had no more lightning in its quiver, but rain still fell in torrents, flooding some intersections.

Judging by the few cars in the parking lot, the motel had many vacancies. A two-star enterprise in a one-star part of town.

Lucas Drackman took a parking slot close to Room 14. There was no one in sight when he rapped on the door. After Fiona ushered them inside, she looked left and right along the covered promenade that served the rooms, saw no one.

She'd gotten sandwiches and bags of potato chips from a deli. They plucked bottles of beer from the bathroom sink, which was filled with ice.

Two of them had chairs, and the other two sat on the bed. In recognition of the thin walls between units, they spoke softly, but for the most part, they ate in silence.

Drackman could tell that Fiona was wired, strung tight. She'd drunk a Mountain Dew instead of beer, but it wasn't the caffeineladen soft drink that had drawn her so taut. Whatever she had taken, if anything, her condition probably had less to do with drugs than with anticipation of the pending operation. She was excited, ready. Fiona loved action. And she had a particular appetite for action against the Bledsoe family.

To remind them that they were part of something cool, he said, "Man, all these riots, huh? New York, Toledo, Grand Rapids. I mean, how radical is that—riots in *Grand Rapids*?"

"Detroit's half burned down," Tilton said.

"Carl Sandburg's dying," Fiona said.

Smaller frowned. "Who the hell is he?"

"A poet."

"Ah, that's all phony shit, all them rhymes and stuff."

"Sandburg's poems don't rhyme," she said.

"That ain't right. So how's he a poet?"

"Because he says he is."

"Then I'm a damn poet," Smaller declared.

"We're all poets," Drackman said.

"We're all something," said Tilton.

Fiona drilled him with her purple gaze. "You up for this?"

"I'm here, aren't I?"

"You better be up for this," she said.

"I'm here, okay? I'm here."

They weren't going into the Bledsoe house until eleven o'clock. Drackman glanced at his watch. Going to be a long evening.

Ninety-eight

AFTER MALCOLM WENT HOME, MRS. LORENZO wanted to talk over a cup of coffee at the kitchen table, so I had a cup, too. She was happy to be living with us, and she didn't get teary every time she mentioned her husband, so I thought she must be healing from that loss. But she had been alone for a year during which she'd had a lot of time to think. I suppose there were thoughts she'd had when all by herself that she wanted to share with someone.

Over coffee, she told me that the four things she loved most, loved with all her heart and soul, were her father, her husband, God, and food. Her father died young. So did her husband. She still loved God, she said, in spite of His habit of taking from her the people she loved with all her heart. The problem was that no matter how much she loved God, He remained invisible, and the only way she knew how much He loved her was to read scripture, which could be hard going. Meanwhile, the love that she brought to her cooking was returned to her daily by the flavor of what she put on her plate.

She was well aware that gluttony was a deadly sin, but there were three reasons why she didn't worry about that. First, the formal definition of gluttony was eating and drinking to excess, but Mrs. Lorenzo didn't drink. Second, before eating her meals all by herself back in the apartment, she always said grace, thanking the Lord for His bounty. Therefore it seemed to her that if the Lord disapproved of the size of the portions she ate, He would make her even poorer, so that she couldn't afford so much food. Or He would reclaim from her the culinary genius that was her gift, so that what she cooked didn't taste worth eating. Third, she kept a list of what she ate, soberly considered what might be excessive, and at the end of the week read every item during her confession and received absolution. "Whatever weight I put on, Jonah, is sanctified fat."

"I sure wish I could get some sanctified fat," I said. "I'm still a stick."

"If I cook long enough for you, child, you'll be a regular Godfrey Cambridge."

He was a terrific comedian and actor back then, a bit

on the hefty side. I might have given up music to be as funny as Godfrey Cambridge.

Anyway, after a while, Mrs. Lorenzo decided to go upstairs and read in bed, either scripture or recipes, she couldn't decide which. She checked the locks on all the doors and windows before leaving me alone on the first floor.

After I brushed my teeth and completed my other bathroom business, I put on my pajama top and wrestled my uncooperative legs into pajama pants. I sat up in bed for a while, reading about Tin Pan Alley: the legendary Fats Waller and Jelly Roll Morton; Jerome Kern; George Gershwin, who started out by writing a song for Sophie Tucker to sing and went on to become the greatest composer of the century.

All of it was interesting and inspiring, but I couldn't see myself in anyone I read about. Nevertheless, I intended to keep reading a thousand such books, if I had to, until I figured out how they did what they did.

At ten o'clock, I took the penlight from the nightstand drawer and switched off the lamp. Lying in the dark, I listened to the storm for a while, and it bothered me that the drumming of the rain masked all other sounds.

Eventually I clicked the penlight and swept the room with the narrow beam. I discovered no zombies or emotionless seed-pod people from outer space, no monsters of any kind. I decided to leave the penlight on for a few minutes.

Ninety-nine

EARLIER IN THE DAY, USING HER SECOND SET OF false ID, Fiona had rented another car, a Chevrolet, and parked it at the motel. Before leaving Room 14, at Lucas's direction, she gave the keys to Mr. Smaller and said, "Don't make it too easy for the sneaky bastard. We're in this soup because of him."

"You sure maybe they ain't watchin' him, too?"

"If they are, they're invisible."

Mr. Smaller departed in the Chevy. Drackman and Tilton drove away in the paneled van, and Fiona followed in the Dodge that she had rented when she'd first returned from their farmhouse hideaway.

The metropolis glistened in the storm, all silver and black, headlamp beams wriggling like bright snakes across the streaming streets, every bulb and tube of light reflected in one or more wet surfaces, and yet Drackman thought the city appeared darker than usual, cloaked and riddled with mystery. Perhaps because the oily blacktop contrasted so starkly with the reflected lights, it looked blacker than on other nights, blacker than black. There were vistas, scenes, moments when the buildings and bridges, all of it, seemed like an illusion projected on the screen of rain, nothing really there except the rain-captured light and a fearsome void beyond it, an abyss below. It spoke to him, this trembling city of ephemeral light and the darkness underlying it, and he felt at home.

When Drackman turned the corner onto the Bledsoes' street, the surveillance van, identical to the one he drove, stood at the curb where he had been told it would be. Police stakeouts often involved three shifts, eight hours each, but just as often, as in this case, they ran it in two twelve-hour shifts, maybe because it allowed the cops to pile up overtime hours at double their usual pay, maybe because at the moment the department was understaffed. Twelve-hour shifts, day after day, were a big mistake. The detectives grew bored, tired, less than fully observant, slow to react, and if they returned for duty every twelve hours, the effects were cumulative.

Fiona had observed that the shift changes came at four o'clock in the morning and four in the afternoon. When

Drackman pulled to a stop behind the first van, almost five hours early, the detectives on duty had to be thinking either that some dink at HQ had altered the shift-change time without telling them or that a clueless dispatcher had sent these newcomers to the wrong stakeout . . . or that bad actors had entered the picture.

That last possibility, if the cops jumped to it quickly enough, could mean trouble for Drackman. Boldness was the hallmark of his style, however, and now he pulled up the hood of his jacket, got out of the van, and hurried forward through the driving rain, intent on giving them little time to think.

No traffic on the street just now. Everyone preferring home and hearth in the storm. Perfect.

He didn't know if the new-shift guys had a way of talking to the old-shift guys, van to van, by radio or walkie-talkie. He didn't have a radio or a walkie-talkie, and he didn't want to talk to them, anyway, because his cover would be blown the moment he said the wrong thing or didn't say the right thing.

He had a badge, a shield, a real one, a heavy chunk of gold-plated bronze that he'd taken off a detective he'd killed eighteen months earlier. When he reached the driver's door of the stakeout van, he bent down and, with his left hand, held the shield to the window. The tinted glass offered a clear view from inside but not much from outside.

He could see a shape, a paleness of face, the guy in there checking out the shield, seeing it was real, but it could go badly wrong at any moment.

The driver began to crank down the window, a good sign, and now the big question was, *Both guys in front or one in front and one in the back?* They were running a two-man stakeout for maybe a couple of weeks, and nothing to show for it. So one guy might be napping in back, although it was a violation of department policy, or maybe he was back there taking a leak in a bottle, whatever. The window came down far enough that Drackman saw two in front, the ideal situation, because in his right hand he had a pistol fitted with a state-of-the-art sound suppressor. As the cop lowering the window started to say something, raising his voice above the incessant rain, Lucas Drackman pumped six rounds into the interior of the van, aiming down to spare the windows. A shattered window would be as revealing as a scream to anyone who might drive by.

He knew the driver was dead, but he couldn't be certain of the cop in the farther seat. He opened the door, and the ceiling light came on, and the moment he saw the passenger's broken face, he knew he'd gotten them both.

After rolling up the window, he closed the door and waved at the van he'd been driving. The hood of his jacket raised, reminiscent of a monk in a movie Drackman had once seen, Tilton came toward him, carrying the little kit that contained the glass-cutter, the suction cup to keep the cut piece from falling into the house, and several other burglary tools that they might need.

Fiona turned the corner behind them, drove past them in the rental Dodge, and parked two houses beyond the Bledsoe place. They would abandon the van and leave in her car when they had concluded their business.

Two vehicles passed in the street, but neither of them slowed. As far as he could tell, no one thought he and Tilton were sinister.

They could have skulked through backyards, dodging from tree to tree, over fence after fence, but in Drackman's view, that was riskier than walking straight to the front door. Even at that hour, you never knew who might be looking out a window. If they saw you lurking about and trying to blend with the shadows, they *knew* you were up to no good. A bold approach appeared less suspicious.

According to Fiona, telephone service in the neighborhood came above ground at the front right corner of each residence. When she got out of her car, not having bothered with a jacket, as wild as the storm itself, she walked directly to the Bledsoe place, lashed by rain and buffeted by a sudden wind that seemed to spring up just to welcome her. At the house, she squatted to find and cut the phone-service line. As Drackman and Tilton climbed the porch steps,

Fiona rose, her task completed, and rounded the porch to join them.

As hard as the rain had fallen, it fell now harder still, in thick tropical skeins, and Drackman thanked whatever unknown mystic had devised the Tarot deck as far back as at least the thirteenth century. The Tarot, juju, countless disciplines of magic, fate, the stars, the weight of history, and the power of progress—all were behind his crew this night, and there would be no stopping them.

One Hundred

MR. SMALLER, WHO ACTUALLY WAS TEN POUNDS smaller than when he had walked out of the superintendent's job forever, drove past the apartment building, scanning for stakeout vehicles, pretty sure he would recognize one, keenly suspicious, not to say paranoid, but he didn't see anything that alarmed him.

He turned left at the corner, left again at the alleyway, and cruised behind the place. Nothing there got his hackles up, either. After parking on a side street a block from the building, he returned to the alley on foot, shoulders hunched, head held low, grumbling to himself about the intensity of the storm that pummeled him and the wind that dashed rain under his hood and into his face.

Before leaving his position as building superintendent,

he had made a copy of the passkey that operated every lock in the building, and he had no doubt that it still worked. The swine who owned this empire of tenements and the black-hearted company men who licked their boots and did their vile work for them would have rather slit their wrists than hire a smith to reconfigure every lock in that moldering pile of masonry.

At the rear of the building, at the door to the back stairs, as the key turned smoothly and as he felt the deadbolt retracting from the striker plate in the jamb, Mr. Smaller grinned and said, "Cheap bastards."

Inside, he closed the door quietly. He stood there dripping and listening. He heard a TV in the distance. Faint. Water racing through the old pipes as someone took a late shower.

The trick now was to get up to the fifth floor unseen, do the deed, waste the sneaky little creep, pull a little Pearl Harbor on him, and then get out without encountering anyone. After the bank and the heist, he was already wanted for murder; it hardly mattered if they hung one more capital charge around his neck. If he was seen by a tenant, however, they would surely recognize him in spite of his shaved head and mustache and weight loss, and then he would have to kill again, just to ensure that he would have time to get out of the city before the police knew he'd been there.

He started up the stairs.

One hundred and one

IN THE STORAGE SHED AT THE BACK OF GRANDPA
Teddy's property, he sat on a stool in the gloom, holding
the door open a few inches, watching the dark house. Sears
had done a good job when they erected the shed, and
it had served him without problem for years. But right
now he would have cursed it if he had been a cursing man,
because the rain pounding on the metal roof deafened him,
as if he were standing in a giant snare drum inside an even
more giant kettle drum.

He'd been on leave from his night gig for a week, ever
since Jonah came home, which is why he had told George
Yoshioka the fib about every restaurant reservation being
sold out, so that the tailor wouldn't come to see him play
and discover he wasn't there. Grandpa Teddy had begun

to think that he might be a fool. Well, every man was a fool—how could it be otherwise in a fallen world?—but Teddy Bledsoe thought he might be an even bigger fool than he had ever previously imagined. He trusted the police, he really did. To a point. To an extent. With some reservations. You didn't live more than half a century as a black man in this world and be completely trusting of authority. This was his house, his family; and if the police made a mistake, he would suffer the loss. There had been enough losses lately. He didn't believe he could live through another one and still face the days ahead with his usual enthusiasm. But on this eighth night of his vigil, he thought perhaps the police were wrong when they predicted this Drackman character, given what was now known about his worthless life, would come busting in sooner than later. They had done some psychological profile and swore on it as Grandpa Teddy would have sworn on the Bible in a courtroom. But a profile was a guess—a bunch of guesses, really. It seemed now that every one of those guesses had been wrong.

Well, if after this night he called it quits, at least no one would know that he'd been playing detective or security guard, or whatever it might be that he thought he was doing. He'd left home every evening in his show tux. He'd driven to a service station and changed into clothes more suitable for a storage shed and for the rough-and-tumble encounter he anticipated. He'd returned by the weedy vacant lot that backed up to his property, scaled the fence as if he weren't but a decade away from Social Security, and ducked into the shed to stand guard until it was time for him to change back into his tux and pretend to come home from a session on the bandstand.

Maybe something had gone wrong with his mind. A man could take only so much. When you lost your angel of a wife, when a grandson who should have had the world at his feet suddenly can't walk on the feet that he has, when all those most precious to you in the world seemed to have their necks through the lunette of a guillotine, a man could be excused for going a little crazy, secretly changing clothes like Clark Kent becoming Superman, sneaking among the trash and trees in a weedy lot, hiding in a shed with a weapon he was loath to use.

He sighed and said softly, "Old man, you're a musician, you aren't muscle."

One hundred and two

BOY. I WOKE FROM A DREAM, BUT IT SEEMED TO me that the word had not been spoken in the world of sleep, that someone had whispered it in my ear.

I realized that I had left the penlight shining when I'd gone to sleep. The pale beam passed across the bedclothes . . . just to the right of an object I couldn't identify, a shadowy roundness at the edge of the light.

Pushing with my left arm, I eased up from the pillow, reaching with my right hand for whatever lay there. I plucked the object off the sheet and knew at once what it was, even before I brought it into the light: the stuffed-toy eye.

"Snoop and liar," Fiona Cassidy said.

I tried to cry out but couldn't. My throat was like an

organ pipe in which a grab knob had been engaged, cutting off the flow of air and sound.

Looming out of the dark, she switched on my bedside lamp and smiled at me. Neither kindness nor humor informed that smile.

She had cut her hair and dyed it and gotten a deep tan, but I would have recognized her if she'd made twice as many changes to her appearance. The steel edge of the switchblade gleamed in the light.

"Get in your wheelchair, crip."

When I didn't at once obey, she slashed the air in front of my face, and I flinched away from the flashing blade.

With contempt, she said, "There's no juju in you, boy, and there never was. No juju in the fetishes you keep in that candy box."

I almost reached to touch the Lucite heart that I wore under my pajamas, but I stopped myself, for I knew that she would understand and find the pendant and take it from me.

"Get in your chair, crip!"

One hundred and three

MR. SMALLER REACHED THE FIFTH FLOOR without encountering anyone. At Apartment 5-C, the passkey smoothly opened the deadbolts of the double locks.

His remaining concern was that the security chain would be engaged. Using his fingers, he should be able to reach through the gap and, with enough time and patience, finesse the slide bolt out of the doorplate, but it was likely to be a noisy effort. He smiled to find the chain hanging loose from the retainer. How careless. He eased the door open.

He knew that Yoshioka left early for work, even before sunrise in winter, and that by now he must be sleeping. Expecting darkness, Smaller came with a flashlight, but in the living room, the ivory carving of the court lady in her elaborate kimono was brightened by a light from above.

The ivory babe was probably some sacred thing that had to be kept lit around the clock, according to whatever alien religion the weird little tailor embraced.

A faint light came from the kitchen, too, but no sound issued from there, no suggestion that Yoshioka might be preparing a latenight snack.

Silencer-equipped pistol in his right hand, flashlight in his left, softening the beam with two fingers over the lens, Smaller crossed the living room to the hall. He'd been here several times to deal with plumbing problems, a stuck window . . . Yoshioka's bedroom was behind the first door on the right, which stood open.

A small lamp about ten inches tall, with an amber glass shade, stood on an altar table against one wall, another 24/7 deal to keep lit the photos of a middle-aged Japanese man and woman, another of a teenage girl. When he'd seen them before, Smaller had assumed they were relatives, but he hadn't cared enough to ask.

The tailor lay sleeping.

One hundred and four

"HERE COMES THE HERO," FIONA CASSIDY SAID AS she wheeled me fast out of the bedroom that had been a dining room. "Savior of bankers and other low types." She pushed me into the living room, where the shades had been drawn at the windows. A single lamp burned low, next to Grandpa's armchair, its light glimmering in puddles of rainwater on the hardwood floor.

I was relieved to see Mrs. Lorenzo alive, sitting on the sofa in a kind of muumuu that she evidently wore to bed. She looked terrified but also embarrassed.

Standing near to her, Lucas Drackman was recognizable in spite of his jet-black hair. And standing beside the piano, my father.

"You're a troublesome boy," Drackman said to me. "How

can such a skinny-minnie twerp like you be so much trouble?"

I could breathe again, but I still couldn't speak. I suspected that silence was the best response, anyway.

"Your Jap friend will be dead by now, skinny minnie. What do you think about that?"

I felt sick and weak and defeated, but I bit my tongue to keep from crying. I wouldn't give him tears.

To my father, Drackman said, "I think you should do it," and indicated the pistol that Tilton held at his side, muzzle toward the floor.

No matter what he was or what he had become, no matter how often he'd abandoned my mother and me, even if he could love only himself, I thought he would shoot Drackman then. I *knew* he would.

Instead, avoiding my eyes, Tilton said, "Do we have to do this? Why do we have to do this?"

"We're known now," Drackman replied. "Because of this skinny minnie. We're known, and we're hunted, and we have nothing to lose. The one advantage still available to us is terror. Everybody needs to be scared shitless of us, afraid to speak against us, because we'll do anything. Keep them so scared that when they come looking for us, they'll be nervous, not fully in control of themselves, so maybe they don't really search for us as hard as they could. Terror, man. It's our friend. You made this skinny minnie, you erase him."

My father shook his head. I thought again he would shoot Lucas Drackman. He shook his head once more.

Drackman said, "You wanted to get rid of him before he was born. She wouldn't do it, your Sylvia, but you wanted to. If you wanted to have the little bastard scrubbed away before he was born, what's so hard about doing him now?"

My father would not look at me, would not, and I knew then that he would never shoot me—nor would he shoot Drackman. In spite of all his talk about owning a chain of restaurants and being boss over an army of employees one day, there was no such capacity in him. He was not a leader, which was in the end the reason his dreams were always beyond his reach. He was a follower, and he would follow whoever made him feel useful and knew how to manipulate him.

When Tilton put his pistol on the lid of the piano and sat on the bench, his posture wasn't that of defeat, only that of a weary man who wanted this moment to be over so that he could get on to something better.

Lucas Drackman stepped close and let me peer down the elongated barrel of the silencer-equipped pistol.

Mrs. Lorenzo sobbed and pleaded with them and prayed all at the same time. As scared as I was, I also thought how terrible it would be for her to see me shot in the face.

I wanted to close my eyes, but I didn't. He would just call me skinny minnie again or something worse.

He walked behind the wheelchair, and I wondered what he was doing, and then he put the muzzle of the gun against the back of my head.

When I looked at Fiona Cassidy, what I saw so terrified me that I had to look away. In her leering, twisted countenance, I glimpsed something other than the woman herself, something that had for a long time lived within her and that now rose like some beast out of deep dark water.

To taunt me further, Drackman took the gun away from my head, grabbed the wheelchair, and spun me, and I wished that I had the pistol that my father had put aside on the piano.

The gun roared, and I was kicked sideways in my chair, and a pain of great intensity rocked me. A blackness came upon me, and I fell away, as off a cliff, accelerating by the second, breathless and plummeting, until someone seemed to catch me, and a voice said, "Not yet, Ducks. It's not your destiny to be tossed dead into a car trunk with that woman." As I was lifted higher, higher, light formed around us. She materialized at my side. She wore an amazing white dress more layered than the kimono of the court lady in Mr. Yoshioka's living room. And the dress flowed out in all directions, to every horizon, where there had been only darkness, and the dress was light. I met her eyes and felt a chill. She blew upon my face. Her breath smelled of roses, a sweet breath that had weight and closed my eyes. When I opened them again, I was in the wheelchair, without pain, and apparently Drackman had not yet fired the shot that killed me. Make of all that what you will, though I do have more to say about it later.

Reflexively, my right hand had gone to the Lucite heart. I don't know why I fished it out of my pajama top, whether perhaps I thought there might be magic in it just when magic was most needed. But that would have been asking too much after my resurrection, too much.

Never in my life until then had I heard my grandfather raise his voice in rage, but when he charged into the room, swinging a baseball bat as if Babe Ruth had nothing on him, he bellowed like an angry bull, a raging bear. Drackman turned and fired and missed. Grandpa Teddy broke the creep's right arm, and the pistol that had seemed to be my fate clattered across the floor, rattling to a stop against the left wheel of my chair. Howling in pain, Drackman slipped on the wet floor and fell, and in spite of his arm, he scrambled toward the weapon.

A paraplegic in a wheelchair can't reach objects on the floor to pick them up, which is why a lot of us acquire assistance dogs, not only for companionship but also to retrieve objects we've dropped and to call elevators for us, open doors. The pistol was beyond my grasp, but I let go of the Lucite heart and with both hands spun my chair

180 degrees, getting the gun *behind* the right wheel and under the chair as Drackman reached for it, trying to move it with me and keep it away from him.

Grandpa swung at the good hand with which Drackman sought the pistol, missed when the killer snatched his hand back, and struck the floor a blow that must have resonated through the bat and for a moment numbed his hands, weakened his grip.

Switchblade sprung, Fiona rushed at Grandpa in his one weak moment. I grabbed the heart pendant again, jerked it hard enough to snap the fine silver chain around my neck, and threw it at her face. It was the only thing I had to throw, nothing more than a chunk of Lucite, weighing a few ounces, but it hit her in the eye, and as she reeled past my grandfather, missing him with the blade, she squealed perhaps more in surprise than pain.

Grandpa swung the bat again, fractured Drackman's other arm, and turned to Fiona. I think it might have been a close thing as she slashed at Grandpa again, but her blade missed and his bat connected. Suddenly she had a handful of shattered and bleeding fingers, the pain apparently so bad that she staggered toward the front door, fell to her knees, and vomited.

For a moment, my grandfather's face was such a mask of wrath that I thought he might continue to swing the bat until he broke down Fiona and Lucas so completely that they would never walk again or have the power in their hands to hold a gun. Instead, he put the bat in his armchair. He picked up the knife, folded the blade into the handle, and dropped it in a pants pocket. He took Tilton's gun from the piano and tucked it in his waistband, scooped Drackman's pistol off the floor and held it.

"You okay, son?" he asked.

I let out my breath in a whoosh, and I nodded.

"Mrs. Lorenzo," he said, "our phone lines have been cut. Will you go next door and wake the Velakovskis and use their phone to call the police?"

Curled in the fetal position, Fiona sobbed and begged someone to help, her hand a basket of exposed and splintered bones that probably could never be put back together properly. Lucas Drackman was another portrait in misery, both arms useless.

Looking bewildered, shaking violently, Mrs. Lorenzo rose from the sofa and stood there as if uncertain what she'd been asked to do.

Grandpa said, "Are you able to do that for me, Donata? Go next door? I'd be most grateful if you could."

"Absolutely," she said, "I'll do it right away."

"Better put on your raincoat," he said. "It's nasty out there."

She carefully stepped over the puddle of vomit, retrieved

her raincoat from the closet by the front door, and went out into the storm.

Tilton got up from the piano bench. "Mr. Bledsoe, I'm no threat to you or to anyone. Let me go. You'll never see me again, I swear. You know you never will. You know."

After regarding Tilton in silence for a long moment, Grandpa said, "Sit down," and Tilton sat.

One hundred and five

WHEN MR. SMALLER STEPPED CLOSE TO THE BED and shot Mr. Yoshioka, something about the reaction of the body wasn't right. He threw back the light blanket— and found only more blankets shaped into a human form.

I never knew that in addition to tailoring and Asian art and haiku, Mr. Yoshioka was interested in martial arts. Neither did Mr. Smaller. Later, my friend explained it to me: "I introduced Mr. Smaller to my apartment. I introduced him to one wall and then to another. I showed him the door and then another door and then the floor. We took a tour, and though he knew the apartment from his years as the building superintendent, he seemed to be repeatedly surprised by what he encountered."

One hundred and six

NEXT DOOR AT OUR NEIGHBOR'S HOUSE, AFTER Mrs. Lorenzo called the police, she was sufficiently self-possessed to ring Diamond Dust and have my mother brought to the telephone immediately at the end of the number that she was performing. By the time Mom could make her way home through the storm-washed city, police cars cluttered our street, their emergency beacons flashing red and blue, so that the falling raindrops almost looked like showers of sequins. Drackman had been loaded into an ambulance and taken away. Policemen had succeeded in subduing Fiona, who became dangerous again when she saw them arrive; though in great pain and bleeding from her shattered hand, she nonetheless shrieked and kicked and bit with all the ferocity of a wildcat. As my mother hurried up the walkway, the paramedics were conveying a bound and bitter Fiona to the second ambulance.

In the living room, two plainclothes detectives had sorted out things with Tilton, who remained as docile as Fiona Cassidy had been obstinate. They cuffed him, and a uniformed officer escorted him toward the front door. Just then my mother entered, a vision if ever there was one, her hair diamonded with rain, as lovely as a princess in a fairy tale, raincoat flaring like a royal's cape. Tilton looked up, met her eyes, and seemed to be surprised, not only that they should encounter each other at this last possible moment, but as if he both knew her and did not know her, as if he might be seeing the real and complete Sylvia Bledsoe for the first time, because among the other emotions kaleidoscopic in his face, the most striking was a look of wonder. In her face, by contrast, there was neither anger nor pity, nor contempt; she would not give him the satisfaction of an emotional response, but regarded him as she might have any piece of furniture, and after a moment she stepped aside, out of the way, so that he might be moved elsewhere.

She came to me and dropped to her knees on the rain-slick floor and took my face in both of her hands and kissed my forehead. For the longest moment then, we stared into each other's eyes, neither of us capable of speech even if there had been anything we needed to say. Grandpa stood over us, smiling and, I think, a little bit bewildered by what he'd been called upon to do and by what he'd done. Finally she said, "You know you're up *way* past bedtime," and I said, "Yes, ma'am, but it won't happen again." She said, "It better not," and I knew then that we were at last safe.

One hundred and seven

WE HAD SOME FINE YEARS AFTER THAT. OH, IN the wider world, there were wars and more wars, riots upon riots, murder and mayhem and much hatred and the threat of nuclear annihilation. But in the gentler and more contained world of the Bledsoe family, we had much for which to be thankful. Mr. Yoshioka bought a car, a 1956 Packard Executive, yellow-and-white and in good repair, and Grandpa Teddy taught him to drive it, whereafter he could come more often for dinner. Mrs. Lorenzo remained with us, and although she didn't get her weight under control, it was all sanctified fat. My mother packed them in at Diamond Dust, and she got some offers to sing backup on records by recording artists whose names just about everybody knows. I kept at the songwriting thing, and when

I was fifteen, my mother liked one of them so much—I called it "One Sweet Forever"—that she had an arrangement of it done for the Diamond Dust band, and they played it regularly. One night, this executive from a record company had dinner there with friends, and he went wild for the song. I wish he would have signed up my mother, but he didn't. If you don't follow pop music enough to know, I'll just say he signed me, and he placed the song with a pretty big star, and it topped out on the *Billboard* chart at number four. That released something in me, and what had been difficult before became easy. Like they say, the hits just kept on coming. Eventually we could buy a better house, but we didn't want to leave the neighborhood, which no one would mistake for Beverly Hills but which suited us just fine. When the house next door came up for sale, we purchased it, remodeled it to accommodate one wheelchair and one clumsy saxophonist. When Malcolm turned eighteen and went to work in the Diamond Dust band, he moved across the street with me and never had to take it to the garage again. Amalia always haunted him, but he let despair lead him wrong only that once, when he was twenty-two and left the city and saved himself with banish-the-devil music. I won't read this sentence to him, in case he really doesn't know the reason for some of his obsessive-compulsive behavior, in case to understand would rob him of the power of these rituals to soothe his sorrow, but here's what is clear to me: He hates mushrooms, will go to any length to avoid the sight of one, because the morning that Amalia died, he watched her anxiously cleaning a large pile of them, reduced to a scullery maid by their parents; he will neither buy nor borrow a newspaper on Tuesday because she died on Monday, and the news was in print the next day; the night of the day she died, there was a full moon, and so he goes to a church the first night of every full moon to light seventeen candles, one for every year she lived. I love you, Malcolm. So now to Lucas Drackman. His arms in casts, he had chattered nonstop to the police, recounting his every act and thought and feeling, as if he believed that he had triumphed and that they were disciples transported by his tale of glory; he and my father and Fiona and Smaller were convicted of their many crimes and sent away for life. Aurora Delvane? She turned state's evidence and got a two-year sentence. In prison she wrote a novel. It never sold. At the start of this, I said my first and last names were Jonah Kirk, with seven others in between. But if you know my music, you know that my legal name, since I was eleven, is Jonah Bledsoe, with eight other names in between. I kept Kirk in there because he was my father, even if he never wanted to be, even though he had no use for me; my mother loved him once, after all, even if she was young and naïve at the time, and were it not for that love, I would not exist.

After nine years of good times, we had a bad patch. Life doesn't run smooth your whole life, and no one ever promised that it would. One day, Mr. Yoshioka didn't feel right, and the problem turned out to be cancer, a particularly quick-moving one. The last two months, when he was weakest and the hospital could do nothing more for him, we moved him in with Grandpa Teddy, so all of us could be close to visit with him and care for him. The night he died, I sat bedside, reading haiku to him, and sometimes he would recite them back to me in Japanese. Near the end, he asked me to put the book of poetry aside and listen closely to something he needed to say. He told me that he liked my pop songs, which he had told me before, but he believed that I had a greater destiny than that. He told me what he had once told Mary O'Toole, that in the days when I could play the piano at my full strength, God walked into the room every time He heard my music. Mr. Yoshioka said that I was earning a good living at such a young age but there was more to life than earning a living. In his gentle way, he insisted I should, as soon as possible, devote myself to writing grander things, so that when other people played my music in the years to come, God would walk into the room again. I was holding his hand when he died, and for the longest time I could not let it go. We were surprised how many came to his funeral, surely everybody at Metropolitan

Suits but a great many others besides, and when I insisted that I must go not just to the church but also to the grave, across cemetery grounds that a wheelchair could not navigate, Grandpa and Malcolm took turns carrying me, and I am pleased to say that I didn't give my grandfather a heart attack and that Malcolm did not drop me.

Two days after the funeral, when Omi Kobayashi, Mr. Yoshioka's attorney, visited us, I discovered that in my friend's will, he left everything to me. The pair of tiger screens were reproductions of those by the Meiji master Takeuchi Seiho. Because he could not have afforded the real thing, he commissioned the copies as a gift to his father, who had once owned the originals before Manzanar. His father had lived seven years with those reproductions before he passed. I was given, as well, the ivory carving of the court lady, which was dated 1898 and signed by the Meiji master Asahi Gyokusan and which Mr. Kobayashi said was of great value. Mr. Yoshioka's father had owned that piece, too, before Manzanar; when his son could eventually track it down and could afford to purchase it years after Manzanar, the father had been overjoyed. But then the father died and Mr. Yoshioka no longer felt motivated to seek other items the family had once owned. To my surprise, I also inherited Diamond Dust. Johnson Oliver, the manager, only claimed to be the owner at the direction of his boss, Mr. Yoshioka. I inherited, too, Metropolitan

Suits, where Mr. Yoshioka punched a time clock, just like all of his employees.

In our lives, we come to moments of great significance that we fail to recognize, the meaning of which does not occur to us for many years. Each of us has his agenda and focuses on it, and therefore we are often blind to what is before our eyes. That day so long ago, when Mr. Yoshioka opened his door and found me waiting with a plate of cookies, all I saw was a neighbor, a shy man, who even at home was dressed in a suit and tie.

And so at the tender age of twenty, I no longer had to work for a living. I could devote myself to the creation that he had asked me to pursue. His request seemed now to be a sacred obligation. As time passed, there were years when I thought he overestimated me and that I would disappoint him in the end. But then came the movie scores, the Oscar, and then another Oscar and a third. Broadway and the Tony Award. Broadway again and again. They say a Pulitzer this year for the lyrics and libretto of the current play, but I don't think so. A bridge too far, perhaps. Funny thing is, the awards are no more what it's about than is the money. Though I'll keep both, thank you.

What it's about is the music itself, that moment when I'm hearing it in my head for the first time, as I'm trying to get it down on paper, and it's like hearing something from another, better world. It's about the music and the people, and it's about the street where we live even now that my beloved Grandpa Teddy is long gone, a street on which we've bought and remodeled every house on both sides of that special block, that sacred piece of earth where Amalia walked and where Anita lived, where my mother, now seventy-five, still lives three doors down from me, and Mrs. Lorenzo in her own place with her second husband, and so many others. Not least of all, this is the street where my wife, Jasmine, lives with me and our three children. The ability to pee presumes the ability to perform otherwise.

One hundred and eight

MISS PEARL, WHO SAID SHE WAS THE CITY, THE soul of the city, gave me a piano when I desperately needed one, and she gave me warnings and advice that proved of great value. She gave me back my life, too, after Lucas Drackman took it, after he shot me that night and I fell into death. Otherwise, something would have gone much differently than it did, and Fiona would have been killed as well, perhaps by Drackman, and my body and hers would have been put in the trunk of her car, to be driven away in the rain and perhaps left in some parking lot to be found as the body of Dr. Mace-Maskil's wife had been found. The dream I was given was not predictive; it was only the way things might have gone, a warning. That's what I think, anyway. Miss Pearl said we have free will, that what happens next is up to all the people who live along her streets, that my part of it is up to me. The next to the last time I saw her, she said that she had already done more for me than she should, that I was on my own thereafter, and yet she caught me in that long dark fall and brought me back into the world, from death to life. As you might imagine, I have thought about that a lot over the years, and about her claim to be the city.

When I was twenty-one, I sought out Albert Solomon Gluck, the taxi driver who had given the Lucite heart to my mother when I was eight years old. He never became a famous comedian. He still drove a taxi when I found him, and shortly thereafter he moved into a house in our neighborhood and became my driver. Back in the day, he had assured us that a woman, a passenger, had given him the pendant six months earlier and had told him that she wanted him to pass it along to someone. When he asked who, she said he would know who when that person crossed his path. The second time that I saw Albert, thirteen years after our first encounter, he told me more about that woman. He remembered her vividly. She was tall and beautiful and moved with the grace of a dancer. The outfit she wore was not like anything Miss Pearl had worn, but it *did* include a feathered hat. She favored a light rose-scented perfume. She called him Ducks. But here's the thing: Her skin was not mahogany, not any shade of black or brown. She was a Jewish lady, no one he knew and yet so reminiscent of some of the women in his family that he felt akin to her the moment she got into his cab.

If you recall, when I was in that dying fall and lifted by her, just before she breathed upon my face and brought me back to life, I met her eyes, felt a chill. The character of that chill was like unto what I felt in the Kalomirakis Pinakotheke, when I stood before the painting by Fabritius, *The Goldfinch,* and looked into the masterfully illumined right eye of the little bird and understood what the artist might have meant, understood that not only one cruelly treated bird watched me through that eye, but also all of nature watched, and not only all of nature. When I looked into Miss Pearl's eyes just before I woke from death to life, I saw a rush of images, more than I could count, passing in mere seconds, a few of which were: my dear mother kissing my fingers, one at a time, as she had done that night soon after we moved in with Grandpa Teddy; Grandpa sitting bedside in the hospital, his fingers moving bead to bead as he kept watch over me; Grandma Anita giving me a silver dollar to spend only on the day that I was confirmed; the faces of Mr. Yoshioka's mother and sister, not the internment-camp photos from the book, but those framed in silver, which he had kept always lighted, which he also had left to me, and which he had asked me to keep lighted as well; and the eternity of candles, the small flickering lights, that were part of what I'd seen in that big black purse . . . And there as I rose with Miss Pearl out of death, just as I passed back to life, I knew that she was not the soul of the city made flesh, or at least that she was not only the city, that she was not just black, as she appeared to me, that she was of all races and continents and times, that she wore no rose perfume but was herself the embodiment of the rose, that she was the mother of the ancient story, that I had known her not just since I was eight, but always.

The purse. *Put your face right down close to it, Ducks, right down close. Then you'll see.*

At first I had seen a confusing agglomeration of angled shapes thrusting toward me, but then they resolved into the skyscrapers of a city in miniature, and I was gazing down through those buildings into a maze of busy streets. Gazing down and then falling down, not with fear but with exhilaration, swooping between those glittering towers, flying as sometimes I had flown in good dreams. The city was no longer a miniature; it was real and vast, borderless, reaching to infinity, filled with gorgeous and mysterious light. I flew low, near street level, along avenue after avenue alive with busy people, and I began to realize that the mysterious light came from them, that it came from me, too, that we were the people of the city *and* the light of the city, flickering like endless tiers of candles in endless cups. And suddenly I saw the city in time, backward to its origins and forward through centuries, as it had been and as it would be, all existing now; and in every age, those ancient and those of the future, the lovely light did shine, our light.

What a purse.

I've thought often about what she showed me there on the porch steps of my grandfather's house. Now that I've lived long enough, I understand the essence of it, but I don't understand it entirely. No sweat. What matters is the day at hand and what we do with it, one day at a time, some butter-side-down days, some butter-side-up. And what *should* we do with the day? What direction is the one to take, which choice wrong? When I'm confused, I recall what she said that day, and I can hear her voice, remembered as clearly as I remember any music I've ever heard. *No matter what happens, disaster piled on calamity,* no matter what, *everything will be okay in the long run.*

KILLER READS

DISCOVER THE BEST IN CRIME AND THRILLER.

SIGN UP TO OUR NEWSLETTER FOR YOUR CHANCE TO WIN A FREE BOOK EVERY MONTH.

FIND OUT MORE AT WWW.KILLERREADS.COM/NEWSLETTER

Want more? Get to know the team behind the books, hear from our authors, find out about new crime and thriller books and lots more by following us on social media:

 /KillerReads   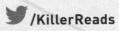 /KillerReads